Hugh stumped toward Jamie. "Och, lad, thank God ye're here. I feared ye'd be off up the Kennebec."

"Is it Elizabeth?"

"Nay, lad. Yer bairn's fine. 'Tis Mistress Cameron."

Jamie stopped short. Even here on the Isles he couldn't escape her! Every night she haunted his dreams; every day she floated before him, eyes green and hazy as the water swirling around the rocky shore. He clenched his jaw, trying to eradicate the memory of her exquisite flesh, half-clad in the silvery moonlight. Och, he could almost see her, so slim yet so lusciously curved. He could almost taste the intoxicating sweetness of her lips, open beneath his. Desire shuddered through him, hot and raw.

No, he would not torture himself with such hopeless longing. He had made a vow, to himself and to Rebekah's memory. No matter how he longed for that beguiling, emerald-eyed enchantress, he was sealed in a tomb of his own making.

"What's she done this time?" he inquired, quirking a sardonic eyebrow.

"Wipe that look off your face, Jamie Maclean. Ye may be laird and me sworn to serve ye, but I'll no' suffer yer teasin' ways this time."

Jamie's brows shot up in alarm. "Is something wrong?"

"Aye. They've arrested Mistress Cameron as a witch."

Dear Romance Reader,

In July, we launched the Ballad line with four new series, and each month we'll present both new and continuing stories set everywhere from medieval England to the American West—the kind of passionate, romantic stories you love best, written by the most gifted authors. At the back of each book, we'll tell you when you can find subsequent books in the series that have captured your heart.

This month dazzling new author Lynne Hayworth begins *The Clan Maclean* series, the passionate and dramatic stories of three brothers torn apart in the aftermath of Culloden. In **Summer's End,** one of these proud Scottish men must choose between fulfilling a debt of honor . . . and losing the woman he has come to cherish. Next, talented Cynthia Sterling completes the *Titled Texans* trilogy with **Runaway Ranch.** What happens when a reformed rogue and brand-new vicar finds himself at a shotgun wedding—where *he* is the groom?

New favorite Sylvia McDaniel continues the funny, sexy saga of *The Burnett Brides* when a man haunted by the Battle of Atlanta rescues a woman from stagecoach bandits. Soon enough, **The Outlaw Takes a Wife!** Last, rising star Gabriella Anderson offers the second book in the charming *Destiny Coin* series, in which taking a headstrong American girl's hand in marriage becomes **A Matter of Pride** for one rakish British bachelor. Enjoy!

Kate Duffy
Editorial Director

The Clan Maclean

SUMMER'S END

Lynne Hayworth

ZEBRA BOOKS
KENSINGTON PUBLISHING CORP.

http://www.zebrabooks.com

ZEBRA BOOKS are published by

Kensington Publishing Corp.
850 Third Avenue
New York, NY 10022

All Kensington titles, imprints and distributed lines are available at special quantity discounts for bulk purchases for sales
promotion, premiums, fund raising, educational or institutional
use.

Special book excerpts or customized printings can also be cre-
ated to fit specific needs. For details, write or phone the office of
the Kensington Special Sales Manager: Kensington Publishing
Corp., 850 Third Avenue, New York, NY, 10022. Attn. Special
Sales Department. Phone: 1-800-221-2647.

Zebra and the Z logo Reg. U.S. Pat. & TM Off.
Ballad Books are a trademark of the Kensington Publishing
Corp.

First Printing: January, 2001
10 9 8 7 6 5 4 3 2 1

Printed in the United States of America

Chapter One

Kittery, Province of Maine, 1763

Holy Mother, where on earth was Robert?

Clemency Cameron tapped her foot and scanned the docks for what seemed like the twentieth time that morning. All around her was chaos. Fishermen heaved barrels of salt cod from a graceful Georges Banks schooner, trappers smoked and cursed while haggling the best price for their beaver pelts, and the sounds of shipbuilding rang through the shimmering air. But Robert was nowhere to be seen.

A forest of masts bobbed in the tide, and Clemency pulled a handkerchief from the pocket in the fold of her skirt. With a quick glance around, she lifted her coil of long black hair and wiped perspiration from the back of her neck. It was June twenty-first—Midsummer's Day—and the noon sun poured down on her like hot molasses. She wrinkled her nose and suppressed a smile. If Robert didn't collect her soon, she likely *would* have hot molasses poured over her, for she sat smack in the way of a group of sweating stevedores who were unloading great casks of syrup from the brig *Neptune.*

Clemency fanned herself with restless little flicks of the wrist, then stepped away from her trunk and paced around the bustling docks. Beside the *Neptune,* with its cargo of sugar, molasses and rum from Barbados, sat a British naval vessel and the *Golden Eagle,* which had brought her across the Atlantic from her home in England, and she wouldn't miss its dank, pitching confines one whit.

With a little pang of homesickness, she breathed in the dizzying scents of brackish water, rotting barnacles and tarred rope baking in the heat. Why, America smelled just like the wharves back in Bristol. But something different laced the diamond air—spruce trees, perhaps? Robert had written to her about Maine's evergreens, his letters brimming with tales about the dark forests that stretched ever westward, far beyond anyone's imagining. Her pulse accelerated. What would it be like to live in such a wilderness?

The scent of frying pork drifted from a dockside ordinary, and her stomach growled in a most unladylike fashion. To distract herself from the fantasy of a crusty beef pie, she turned and studied the familiar figurehead thrusting from the prow of the *Golden Eagle.* Squat and bearded, its somber clothing ticked out in glossy black paint, the carved wooden image bore an excellent resemblance to the ship's captain, Abiel Reed.

Captain Reed had been kind to Clemency on the long voyage from Bristol. Over a game of loo he had explained that Maine—claimed by both France and Great Britain during the recently ended French and Indian War—was now governed by Massachusetts Colony. "And the locals ain't too happy about it, neither, I can promise ye that," Reed had grumbled as he slapped his leather playing cards on the table. "But what with King George taxin' the bejesus out of 'em, they got other nits to pick."

When Clemency had disembarked, Captain Reed had promised to keep an eye on her until Robert arrived, but his cargo of English manufactured goods had quickly claimed his attention. Now, from her position under the *Golden Eagle's* bowsprit, Clemency could hear him bellow as his crew swung a bale of cloth over the side: "Mind the capstan, ye filthy curs! Careful now, careful! 'Twould be a crime to lose such fine goods, and none but louts and lackwits to blame."

With a wry smile, she wiped her damp palms on her skirt and fervently hoped she still looked presentable. Early this morning, eager to make a favorable first impression, she had donned her best traveling gown, then laced her stays as tight as they would go. Now her blue-and-white sprigged muslin skirts lay limp with dust, and perspiration darkened the underarms of her shift. Doubtless Robert would regret his proposal, if he ever arrived. Anxiety gnawed at her empty stomach, and she fidgeted with her fan. He should have been here hours ago.

"Your pardon, madam."

Clemency whirled, almost tripping over the British naval officer who lounged behind her. He swept off his black tricorne hat and bowed elegantly, his avid eyes fixed on the curve of her breasts.

"I have observed you waiting here for hours, madam. The sun is deuced hot, is it not?" The man's lips parted in a lazy smile, and his eyes never left the trickle of sweat disappearing into her bodice. "May I prevail on your good graces and offer you a light refreshment? There's a fine ordinary just a few steps beyond the quay."

Clemency raised her chin and tried to look haughty. Unfortunately, her new straw hat—the London milliner had declared its wide brim and low crown the latest fashion—flapped in a sudden breeze and slipped over her left eye. "I'm sorry, er . . ." She clawed at the hat, then settled it back in place.

"Captain Jeffries. Your servant, madam."

Clemency fought an impulse to kick the smug officer in the shins. Jeffries captained the HMS *Dash*, which was being loaded with gigantic pine logs claimed as masts for Royal Navy warships. Several times during the morning, Clemency had shifted her position on the docks to avoid the bold stares of the seamen under his command. Jeffries himself had accosted her earlier, retreating only when Captain Reed had hawked a great glob of chewing tobacco within inches of the officer's silver-buckled shoes.

She stepped back and tied her hat's blue silk ribbons with a firm yank. "I'm sorry, Captain, but as I told you earlier, I'm waiting for my fiancé."

Jeffries grabbed her elbow and pulled her close. He reeked of sour sweat, bay rum cologne and clove oil—a sure sign of rotten teeth. Although he was not much taller than her own middle height, muscles strained under his scarlet uniform, and his fingers dug into her flesh. With a nonchalant smile, he propelled her toward the tavern, his mushroom-pale eyes never leaving hers.

"Come now, my dear. Any man fortunate enough to be your fiancé would never leave such a beauty alone on a quay riddled with sailors. Why, most of these rogues haven't seen a woman in months."

"I'm sorry, sir, but I cannot go with you." Clemency wrenched her elbow free.

Jeffries snaked his arm around her waist and lunged under her hat brim, fumes from his ale-soaked breath blasting her cheek. Swiftly, five British seamen closed in around her, blocking her from view. Jeffries' face broke into a triumphant leer as he shoved her into a gap between two towering stacks of fresh lumber. Her heart raced under her stays, and a bolt of raw fear shot through her, swift and devastating as lightning. Holy Mother—she knew what he wanted. But this couldn't be happening—not here, not now. She tried to dart around the nearest sailor. Should she scream? Would anyone help if she did?

Suddenly her gaze locked on to a tall man striding toward her. The man's mouth froze into a grim line, and he gave her one sharp nod, eyes riveted on hers. Jeffries yanked her close, and her hat slipped over her eyes.

"Mistress Cameron!" The man's deep voice rang out, and she heard the British sailors shuffling back. "Is this any way to greet your intended husband?" The voice held a warm Scottish burr laced with bantering humor. From under the brim of her blasted hat, Clemency saw a large hand clamp down on Jeffries' shoulder. Jeffries flinched, and his lips glanced off her cheek. "Och, I canna say I blame ye. Such a lovely lassie's enough to make any man lose his head." The hand jerked Jeffries back, then lifted the hat brim from her eyes. "But since she's mine, I'm sure ye'll no' begrudge me the first kiss."

Clemency caught a fleeting impression of wide-set blue eyes and sun-streaked auburn hair before the tall man bent and kissed her. The lips pressed against hers were warm and firm, and they quirked into a smile as she squirmed against him. His strong arms tightened around her waist, and she heard a riff of laughter from the British seamen as he tilted her back. Suddenly she lost her balance and gripped his powerful shoulder. He lifted his mouth from hers, and for a shocked split second she realized she wanted this delicious kiss to continue. A hot blush shimmered across her skin, and the man's eyes darkened from blue to indigo. Then, with a devilish wink, he planted his muscular legs securely around her and lowered his mouth to hers once more.

This brought a roar of approval from the sailors. "I always heard them bloody 'ighlanders were given to rapine," one man snickered.

Jeffries' clipped tone knifed through the general hilarity.

"Well, sir. Your claim appears better established than mine."

The tall man released her so quickly she almost stumbled. "That it is, gentlemen. And I'll thank ye to remember it." His voice was velvet-smooth, belying the twitching muscle in his lean cheek. He tucked her behind him and gave her arm a reassuring squeeze. "Now, if ye will excuse us." He dipped his burnished head in a formal bow, then took her arm and escorted her through the knot of sweaty sailors.

They strode away, and Clemency gasped for breath. Why must she always lace her stays so tightly? She darted a quick glance at her fiancé. She had never met Robert MacKinnon, who was her dead mother's cousin. When Clemency was sixteen, her mother had renewed a long-broken acquaintance with her kin in the Colonies, and soon Cousin Robert had begun writing to Clemency. His letters had demonstrated keen intelligence and unusual sensitivity, and when her mother had died, Clemency had been honored—and desperately relieved—to accept his proposal of marriage. Now she regretted her impulsive decision.

With the nonchalant grace of the very tall, Robert steered her around a crate of squawking chickens, leaving a small flurry of interest in his wake. No doubt the drab colonists were as stunned as she by his appearance, for Robert was the height of untamed masculinity. His fiery hair flowed in thick waves below his shoulders, and two tiny braids bound with leather thongs swung against his wide cheekbones. He wore a kilt of subtle blue-and-green tartan belted around his narrow hips, and with each long stride a sporran of exotic fur swung against his thighs.

Clemency's palms grew clammy. Robert looked like a lusty and brazen Highland savage, not a sensitive and learned man. A shiver shot down her spine, and she resisted the urge to lick her lips. She could still feel the tingling heat of his kiss, a kiss no gentleman would force on a lady to whom he had not been properly introduced. Holy Mother—perhaps

Robert *was* a Highland savage. What on earth had she gotten herself into?

Robert's pace slowed, and she stole an anxious glance at his aristocratic profile. His nose was long and severely straight, and the muscle still twitched in his tanned cheek. As if sensing her scrutiny, he shot her a dark blue glare. She blinked, startled by the fierceness in his eyes. He stopped and looked down his nose in a distinctly aloof manner.

"I hope I was correct in my assumption that ye didna fancy yon British captain's depredations." His Scottish burr was thicker now, the *r*s rolling like summer thunder, and his shoulders were as tense as a crouched wildcat's.

Clemency inhaled sharply and drew herself up to her full height. This placed her almost at eye level with Robert's collarbone—not the best position from which to be outraged. Because of the heat, he wore no waistcoat or cravat, and his shirt lay open at the throat. She opened her mouth, momentarily distracted by the auburn curls nestled on his broad chest, then closed it with a little click. She glanced up and found he was watching her with an annoying air of amusement.

"Of course I didn't fancy that scoundrel!" she snapped. "What on earth do you take me for, some dockside light o' love?"

"Now, dinna be losin' your temper with me, lass. I'm the one who rescued ye, as ye'll recall." One side of his mouth curled into a smile, and his wide-set eyes crinkled at the corners. "So the captain's a scoundrel, eh? And light o' love, yet! I didna know gently reared lasses kent the purpose of a light o' love." He cocked a rakish brow and gave a low, teasing whistle. Clemency entertained the idea of kicking *him* in the shins.

Suddenly his amused look vanished, and he gazed out over the harbor. "Weel, I must say I agree with ye—Jeffries is a scoundrel. I have no love for the English, myself."

Clemency knotted her fingers in the folds of her skirt.

What on earth should she say to that? Robert's entire family—indeed most of the Clan MacKinnon—had fought against the English during the Jacobite Rising of 1745. Loyalist and Catholic, the MacKinnons had supported young Charles Edward Stuart in his crusade to regain the throne of Great Britain from King George II. They couldn't possibly have foreseen the devastation their loyalty would bring.

From his letters, Clemency knew that Robert had paid bitterly for his involvement in the Rising. His father had perished in the awful Battle of Culloden, and Robert had suffered grievous wounds. He and his brother Samuel had been captured and imprisoned by the British, then banished to the Colonies as bond servants. Strangely, this had been an unforeseen stroke of good luck, for after his victory at Culloden, the Duke of Cumberland had laid waste to the Highlands. He burned crops, confiscated estates and killed any man suspected of Jacobite sympathies.

It had been sixteen years since the British had crushed the Jacobites; sixteen years since Cumberland had destroyed the Highland clans. Sixteen years should have been time enough to heal the wounds of grief and recrimination, but Clemency knew from harsh experience that some things could never be forgotten.

She bit her lip. It was clear that Robert hated the English. And she was English.

Suddenly Robert turned, his kilt swinging gracefully around his knees. His brows shot up at the size of her trunk, which rested below the *Neptune*'s bow. "Is that your baggage, lass? Thank St. Columba I brought Hugh and the wagon with me. Perhaps I should have brought the team of oxen as well, aye?" With a wink, he bent and hefted the trunk, then grimaced theatrically.

A sudden surge of warmth rippled through Clemency's veins. Savage Highlander or not, Robert was her intended husband, and she was grateful for the kindness and merriment in his eyes. With a tentative smile, she held out her hand. "Robert, I want to thank you—"

"Och, lassie, in all the excitement, I forgot to tell ye." A startled look flashed across the Highlander's handsome face, and he dropped the corner of the trunk. "I'm no' Robert."

Chapter Two

Clemency's jaw dropped.

"Ye best close your mouth, lass, or the flies will get in," the man said with a wink.

"You're not Robert? Then who the devil are you?"

He had the decency to look chagrined, although a smile still danced in his eyes. With a sweep of his arm, he made a leg and bowed—an action of unusual grace for such a tall man. "James Ian Alasdair Maclean. Your servant, madam."

"James Maclean?" She pressed a hand to her burning cheek. "Oh, you're *Jamie* Maclean. Robert mentioned you in his letters. But why are you here? And how on earth did you recognize me?"

Jamie reached into his sporran and drew out a small framed miniature, which he gently pressed into her hand. It had been painted six months ago, when Clemency had turned sixteen. The artist, a rising star named Cosway, had done a fine job portraying her startled green eyes, her ridiculously high cheekbones and her too-full lips. She wrinkled her nose. Cosway darn well should have done a fine job—he had been paid well enough.

She thrust the miniature at Jamie. "I never cared for the likeness."

"Aye? Weel, it doesna do ye justice." Jamie's dazzling grin displayed an even row of gleaming white teeth. "Ye're much bonnier in the flesh."

"I didn't mean that," Clemency retorted. This towering Scot was beginning to vex her. "If you're not Robert, then why on earth did you ... um ..."

"Why did I kiss ye? Weel, as ye may have noticed, there were six of them and only one of me. And while I'd have dearly loved to thrash *tha musach cuilean,* those odds called for wits, no' fists." A devilish smile played at the corners of his mouth, undermining his look of wide-eyed innocence. "Will ye forgive me?"

"Well, I suppose so, under the circumstances." She couldn't help returning his impish grin. Then his unwavering gaze dropped to her lips, and his eyes darkened. She caught her breath. "What's *tha musach cuilean?*" In a rush to divert his attention, she stumbled over the unfamiliar pronunciation.

"It means 'the filthy dogs.' " Jamie shot her a strange look. "Do ye no' understand Gaelic, then?"

Clemency swallowed at her near slip. "Er ... no. My mother never spoke it."

"So, Jamie, is this our Mistress Cameron?"

Clemency spun at the sound of a rough Scottish voice. A short man stood a few feet away, his face striped by the rippling shade of the *Neptune*'s masts. Ragged gray hair crept down his shoulders, and he wore his ancient kilt and plaid like a king in coronation robes. Their eyes met, and a pained expression fled across his wrinkled face.

"Och," he whispered, bowing low. "Ye could be none

other than Margaret MacKinnon's daughter.'' His dark blue eyes devoured her as if starved for a lost memory.

Jamie stepped forward. ''Mistress Cameron, please allow me to introduce Hugh Rankin. Hugh was my uncle's *gille ruith*—his aide and runner—back in Scotland. Hugh and I were imprisoned together after Culloden, and he came to America with me.''

''As if I had any choice.'' Despite his grumbling tone, laugh lines radiated out from the corners of Hugh's sunken eyes.

Clemency felt a tiny stab of envy at the affectionate glance that passed between the two men. She had never known the blessing of close kin, had never experienced the comforting web of allegiance, protection and blood ties that had characterized the old Highland clan system. But all that would change when she became Robert's wife.

''How do you do, Mr. Rankin?'' she said, curtsying politely. She turned and glanced around the docks. ''Didn't Robert come with you?''

All merriment fled from Jamie's face, and he gently touched her shoulder. ''I'm verra sorry to tell ye this, Mistress Cameron. Perhaps we'd best go to the ordinary and get ye something to eat first.''

Clemency's stomach did an odd little somersault. ''What is it?''

''I'm sorry, *mo druidh*. Robert's verra sick. He may be dying. He asked me to come fetch ye in his place.''

Jamie's husky voice grew distant and blurred, as if filtered through thick wool batting. Clemency clutched one hand to her lurching stomach and blindly reached out with the other. Jamie caught it and drew her to his side.

''Sit down, *mo druidh*,'' he murmured, settling her on top of her trunk. ''Ye've had a wicked shock.''

Holy Mother, this couldn't be happening. Robert couldn't be dying. Slivers of ice shot through her veins. If Robert died, what would happen to her? She didn't have a shilling, and she couldn't go back to England—not after the night-mare she had left behind.

Stop it, girlie! Clemency gasped aloud as her dead granny's voice rang through her mind. *Didn't I raise you to be a healer? Now get a hold of yourself. Robert needs your skill, and there's work to do—so do it!*

With trembling fingers, Clemency tucked an errant curl behind her ear. Then she straightened her shoulders and struggled to her feet. "Thank you for telling me, Mr. Maclean." She took a deep breath and raised her chin. "Please, take me to him."

"Aye." Jamie studied her face, then cocked a practiced eye at the sun. "We'll be hard pressed to make it home by dark as it is."

Hugh fetched a gray Percheron hitched to a rough wagon while Jamie purchased meat pasties and small beer for their noonday meal. A giggling barmaid followed him onto the tavern's porch, casting admiring glances at his broad shoulders and long legs, flaunting her ample curves. Jamie flashed the wench a rakish smile but kept walking toward Clemency. Drawing abreast of her, he winked. "Do ye think me such easy prey, lass? It takes more than a bonny face to turn my head, ye ken."

Jamie and Hugh swiftly loaded her trunk in the back of the wagon. As she waited to be handed up, Clemency eyed a pile of scaly reddish bark which lay in the wagon bed.

"Since we had to fetch ye anyway, we brought a few pine logs down to the sawmill," Jamie said, noticing her inquiring look. He lifted her onto the wagon's seat as if she weighed no more than a sparrow.

"How practical," she murmured. He climbed aboard, and with a soft *gee up!* they lurched off.

Soon the prosperous shops and Georgian homes of Kittery fell away, and they turned northwest onto a rutted mud track that barely deserved to be called a road. As they jolted along in the blistering sun, Clemency took a deep breath and gathered her courage. "Mr. Maclean, what exactly is wrong with Robert?"

"Please, call me Jamie." He flicked a rein to shoo a fly off the horse's rump. "None of the MacKinnons call me Mr. Maclean." A warm flush rose on Clemency's cheeks, and she lowered her gaze, oddly pleased that he considered her a part of the MacKinnon family.

" 'Tis the smallpox," he continued. "Robert never caught it as a child, ye ken. About three weeks ago he traveled to York—that's the shire town—on business. We think he picked it up there. Our settlement at Sturgeon's Creek is verra small, and no one's been sick all summer."

Clemency's heart plummeted. "Holy Mother—smallpox is ruthless. There's no cure." She closed her eyes and recalled her granny's instructions: *Six out of every ten who contract the disease die a horrible death. The few who survive often suffer blindness or scarring from the pox's rotting pustules. You can only make the patient comfortable as he awaits death or recovery.*

"What are his symptoms?" She tried to keep her voice calm.

Jamie shot her a glance, one brow cocked. "Ye ken something about illness, aye?"

"Yes. My grandmother on my . . . um . . . father's side was a healer. People called her a wise woman and midwife, but in truth, she was a doctor. When she was a girl, she decided to enter a convent in Calais. She thought she had the calling to become a sister, you see." Clemency's lips curved in a sad little smile. "At the convent she came to the attention of an Italian physician. He was impressed by her skill with the sick and trained her in the medical arts. Eventually she returned to England. She always said one could minister to the spirit through the body."

"Your family was Catholic, then?" Jamie looked mildly surprised. "That must have been hard in England. They're none too fond of Catholics."

"Well, we weren't very devout." Clemency swiped demurely at a muddy splatter on her skirt. "My grandmother—her name was Amais—taught me what she could. She died six months ago."

"I'm verra sorry for your loss." Jamie's voice was low and kind, and Clemency acknowledged his condolence with a nod. "Ye've had the pox, Mistress Cameron?"

"In a manner of speaking, yes. My granny inoculated me when I was a child. I caught a mild case and now I'm immune."

"Inoculation?" Jamie's brows shot up. "I've heard they tried that after the epidemic in Boston."

"And a terrible riot it caused," Hugh interjected with relish. "Illness is the Lord's way o' teachin' humility. Man has no business meddlin' wi' His ways."

Clemency bit back a tart retort. How many times had she and Granny Amais fought this battle? She cast the old gillie a wide-eyed gaze. "Mr. Rankin, I'm living proof that inoculation works and is safe. Would you rather see me in my grave?"

Hugh gave another *hummph* and subsided. She heard a soft chuckle and glanced up just as Jamie rearranged his face into bland politeness.

"Have ye performed inoculation yourself?" He might have been asking her if she took sugar in her tea.

She bit back a spurt of irritation and met his level gaze. "Not by myself, but I know how 'tis done."

"I'm glad ye're skilled. We'll have need of it if the pox spreads. An epidemic could destroy Sturgeon's Creek in a matter of days."

Clemency's brows contracted, and she stared down at her clenched hands. Holy Mother—not an epidemic. She wasn't prepared; she didn't know enough. Oh, if only Granny Amais were alive to guide her, to tell her what to do. . . .

She bit her lip and scanned the countryside. Clumps of brown mud splotched the grass at the road's edge, and tiny yellow butterflies flitted about, lighting on rank weeds that bore no resemblance to the heather on Devon's moors. The trees seemed like an endless green prison, and she felt the spears of homesickness and depression slash at her heart. This place was too wild, too rough, too different. Everywhere she looked there was nothing but silent, towering forest, savage and strange.

Suddenly she missed England's gentle fields and neat hedgerows. She missed the ancient stone cottage where she had spent her childhood. Most of all, she missed her granny's level head and brave heart. What on earth was she doing in this stifling heat, on this rickety wagon headed toward disease and death, jostling back and forth between two barbarous Highlanders?

She gulped and peeked through lowered lashes at the men's legs. On her left, Hugh's scrawny pins huddled under the wool folds of his plaid. On her right, Jamie's rumpled kilt revealed a healthy expanse of muscled calf and sturdy knee. Faint freckles and tiny copper hairs flecked his golden brown skin.

"Mistress Cameron." Jamie's apple-sweet breath brushed her cheek. She blinked back tears and glanced up as he gently touched her elbow and gestured with the reins.

A short distance down the rutted track a doe and two fawns hovered in the dense shade. Clemency gasped and flashed Jamie a quick, delighted smile. He reined the horse to a stop, and she gazed at the lovely creatures, marveling at their melting dark eyes and comically long lashes. Their velvety ears stood alert, trained toward the wagon, but they didn't so much as quiver.

Jamie leaned under her hat brim and whispered in her ear, "They're verra bonny, aye?" His warm breath caressed her skin and sent an intoxicating ripple down to her toes.

From the corner of her eye she saw Hugh reach into the wagon bed and draw a rifle from beneath a pile of canvas. Opening her mouth to protest, she jerked toward Jamie, and her hair brushed his cheek. They froze, lips a mere whisper apart. Flecks of gold floated in the unfathomable blue of his irises, and his dark lashes cast crescent shadows on his high cheekbones. A flustered expression flashed across his handsome face, and he pulled back, inhaling sharply.

"Don't let him shoot," she whispered, grasping his arm. "Please, show mercy."

Jamie studied her for a moment, his face still and unreadable. Then he reached across her and laid a restraining hand on the rifle. "We'll let the wee beasties go, Hugh."

"Hummph." Hugh's snort told her exactly what he thought of silly English lasses who let sentiment stand in the way of supper, but he put the gun down. Jamie clucked to the horse, and they jerked forward. The deer vanished into the woods with one fluid leap.

"Thank you, Jamie, and Hugh." Clemency slanted them a dimpled smile. "I know you must need the food, but deer are so beautiful. I can't bear the thought of shooting anything so lovely."

"Aye, weel. Yon betrothed husband could ha' gathered a lot o' strength from a Scotch broth made wi' that venison." With brows lowered over a hooked nose, Hugh resembled a disgruntled hawk.

Her momentary happiness vanished. She glanced at Jamie, eyes wide. "Do you truly think Robert may die?"

"That's in God's hands. But Robert's had a wicked headache and fever, and the rash broke out on him days ago. There's little doubt 'tis the pox . . ." Jamie's voice trailed off, and Clemency completed his thought: a severe case of pox at age forty-three in the middle of a wilderness was a likely death sentence.

She batted at a persistent horsefly. "Who's nursing Robert while you're fetching me?"

"Lydia MacKinnon." Jamie's Scottish burr vanished, and his voice sounded oddly hollow. "Robert's brother Samuel married her about a year after I married her sister Rebekah."

Clemency suddenly felt cold. She stared at the horse's flicking ears and took a deep breath. So, Jamie had a wife. Well.

" 'Tis kind of Mistress MacKinnon to help." She kept her tone neutral. "I look forward to meeting her, and your wife, too, of course."

The wagon jolted through a deep puddle, and she lurched against Jamie's powerful shoulder. He stiffened and pulled back, his face hardening into a grim mask.

"I'm afraid that willna be possible. My wife died four years ago."

Chapter Three

They rode in silence for several hours, and Clemency's backside passed from ache to agony to final blessed numbness. She sighed and rolled her shoulders. Holy Mother, if she ever made it off this blasted wagon, she would never sit down again.

They followed on the heels of the setting sun, heading west away from the coast into a wilderness of low hills where haze rose from the land like a gentle exhalation. It caressed Clemency's skin and hushed the jingling creak of wagon and harness until she fancied they were no longer jolting through air but swimming through water. Pearly clouds piled up and fled before them, and the sun's dying glow stretched like a soft orange ribbon above the dark hills. Clemency wriggled her toes and breathed in the damp air. Wilderness it certainly was, but she had to admit it was beautiful.

They started down a steep slope, and she heard the sound

of rushing water as the churned-up mud deepened. With gentle clucks and Gaelic words, Jamie drove the horse around the road's loose rocks and ruts. They rounded a bend, and the rushing sound increased. Then a river appeared through the trees, its swift tan water riffled with white.

Clemency's lips went dry. Surely Jamie didn't intend to cross *that*. Before she could speak, he called, "Whoa," wrapped the reins around the wooden shaft used as a brake, then jumped down, followed closely by Hugh. A tree branch hurtled past on the muddy current. The horse gave an uneasy snort.

She brushed a strand of hair from her eyes. "Jamie—"

"Can ye drive, *mo druidh?*" Jamie met Hugh's gaze over the horse's tossing head.

"Well, yes, but surely—"

"There was a wicked rain last night, and the water's higher than when we crossed yesterday. Hugh and I will have to lead Gray through."

Clemency's pulse began to pound. She opened her mouth to protest, but Hugh beat her to it.

"Ye're takin' an awful risk, Jamie. The lass doesna look a hand wi' a horse, and the wagon's no' loaded heavy. It could be swept away."

"Aye, but we must get to Robert. Ye agree, don't ye, Mistress Cameron?" Jamie ran his large hand along Gray's sweaty hide and raised questioning blue eyes to hers. The horse calmed under his touch.

Clemency stared at the churning water and thought of Robert, then of the box of herbs and medicines tucked in her trunk. "Well . . . if you think we can make it."

Jamie gave her a reassuring nod. "Do ye have a shawl, *mo druidh?*"

It took only moments to unpack a wool shawl from her trunk. Jamie bound it over the horse's eyes; then he and Hugh grabbed the Percheron's bridle. They led him forward, and Clemency clutched the reins as if they were lifelines.

She couldn't show fear or Gray would sense it. She commanded her heart to slow, took a deep breath, then relaxed
her wrists. The animal stepped into the swirling water.

With a rush, the current slammed into the men and splashed up in a shower of crystal drops. The water's force thrust
Jamie into Gray's shoulder, and the horse whickered shrilly.
Jamie's low voice whispered a soothing mix of endearments,
silliness and encouragement to the frightened beast as he
urged him on. The wagon's front wheels entered the flood,
and the thin wooden spokes creaked and shuddered under
the strain. Clemency's stomach roiled. For a horrible
moment, she thought the muddy river bottom would suck
the wagon down. Then the crunch of solid gravel vibrated
through the vehicle's frame.

"We must go faster!" Jamie yelled. "We'll be swept
away if we dinna. On my count, slap the reins, Mistress
Cameron. Hugh, get ready to run for all ye're worth. Ready
now? One, two, three—"

"Hyaaah!" Clemency lashed the reins across Gray's
rump. Hugh and Jamie lunged against the roaring wall of
water. With a frightened squeal, Gray sank back on his
haunches, then plunged forward, dragging Hugh and Jamie
in his wake. The wagon surged into the middle of the river.
The rear wheels rose and floated sideways. Clemency's heart
froze.

A wave crashed over Hugh's head, and he clung to Gray's
bridle. Jamie heaved his body from side to side and struggled
to make headway against the implacable flood. Gray gave
another heroic plunge, and Clemency almost fainted with
sheer relief as the water suddenly grew shallower. The
wagon still veered dangerously sideways, but the bank was
so close. . . .

Gray scrabbled for footing on the rocky bottom, then
leaped forward as if chased by shrieking demons. A sudden
underwater crack juddered through the vehicle straight into
Clemency's bones. All forward movement stopped, the wagon

slewed wildly and Gray reared, squealing and kicking spray in all directions. Hugh lost his grip on the bridle, and the river dashed him toward the wagon. With a gargling cry his head slipped underwater. Clemency heard a sickening thunk.

"Hugh!" she cried, standing and yanking on the reins. The rear wagon wheel struck a rock, and she staggered. Suddenly Jamie was there, his long auburn hair gleaming like wet satin in the fading light. With swift, sure hands, he unharnessed the terrorized horse. Gray clambered onto the rocky bank.

"Stay there," Jamie bellowed at Clemency. "The wagon's stuck fast. Ye're safe." He vaulted over the traces, then scanned the rushing water, frantically searching for Hugh.

"Here, mon." Hugh dragged his head and shoulders out of the pounding current and clung to the back of the wagon. A rock had gashed his forehead and scalp. Blood pulsed into his eyes, and a piece of skin flapped away from his skull as he struggled to pull himself into the wagon bed.

"Hold still, ye old bugger." Jamie's voice was hoarse. He positioned one broad shoulder under Hugh's lower body, then lifted him out of the water. In a moment, the old man was safe on the bank. Jamie stripped off Hugh's plaid, then wadded it up and pressed the soaking wool against his friend's forehead.

"Jamie—" Clemency called.

"No' now."

"But—"

"Hush, woman. I must stop the bleeding. Ye're safe where ye are."

"James Ian Alasdair Maclean, listen to me this instant!" Furious, Clemency gathered up her shirts and jumped. The icy current hit her like a stampeding bull and knocked her breathless. Muddy water tasting of algae and dead fish slapped her face and splashed into her mouth. She spluttered wildly and took a giant step toward the men. Her heavy muslin skirts caught the current and dragged her back.

"Blast!" she snarled

"Ye wee idiot! What are ye doing?" Jamie scooped her into his arms and lifted her onto the bank, his fingers biting into her flesh. His indigo eyes blazed, and for one dizzying moment he pressed her against his chest. Then he shook her, hard.

"Let go of me! The only way to stop that bleeding is to stitch it closed, and I'd like to see those big hands of yours do *that.*" Clemency thrust her face inches from his, daring him to defy her. "Now, get my trunk. There's a wooden box near the top with all my medical equipment. Bring it to me."

She whirled and slogged toward Hugh. Jamie growled something—a Gaelic curse, no doubt—and splashed into the river toward the wagon.

She squatted beside the old Highlander and deftly examined the wound as his blood pumped over her fingers. Thankfully the gash didn't extend far into the scalp, and the flap of flesh lay neatly back in place. Keeping her face calm, she noted the frayed edges of skin and the fine bits of scum the current had pounded into the cut.

"Will I live, lassie?" Hugh hazarded a weak smile.

"Yes, you old devil." She gave him her warmest, dimpled grin and patted his leathery cheek. It was rough with stubble and unnaturally cold.

Jamie set her box of medicines beside her. She opened the cedar lid, and as always, a warm surge of contentment washed through her. Her life in England might be over, her future as uncertain as Robert's chances of survival, but this would always be with her. This—the herbs, the gold instruments, the receipts and secrets of healing—*this* would always give her the security she craved.

Jamie watched her lay out her instruments, and she caught his eye. "Do you have any clean water?"

He nodded and handed her a waxed leather flask. "I fetched it from the wagon. I figured ye'd have need of it." He held up a second flask. "And whisky."

She held the flap of skin away from Hugh's scalp and poured water over the wound. Bit by bit, the river dirt flushed away. She uncorked the second flask with her teeth, then held it to Hugh's lips.

"One good swig," she ordered.

"Surely more than a wee nip," he protested. She pinned him with a stern eye, and he swallowed obediently.

"Jamie, you might want to hold his hand. This will sting." She upended the whisky over the wound. Hugh winced but didn't make a sound.

As Jamie's solemn eyes watched steadily, she threaded a curved gold needle, then held the flayed edges of skin together and began to stitch. Stark white slashes bracketed the tall Highlander's generous mouth, but he held tight to Hugh and murmured encouraging words in Gaelic. She knotted the last stitch, then cut the thread with a tiny pair of scissors. Both men sighed with relief.

The twilight sky had faded to bruised lilac, and she could barely see as she examined Hugh's head one last time. "You'll probably have a scar, but it won't impair your beauty," she said. She leaned over and brushed her lips an inch above the stitches.

Hugh flinched. "What's that for?"

She winked. "Hasn't anyone ever given you a kiss to make it better?"

An hour later it was full dark, with no moon to light their predicament. After a heated argument among the three of them, Jamie decided to leave Hugh to rest and keep an eye on the stranded wagon. Jamie and Clemency would ride on to Sturgeon's Creek, taking with them the few medicines that might help Robert.

"But we can't leave a wounded man alone in the woods," Clemency declared, hands on hips.

"Fah!" Hugh spat. "I'm no' a babe. Robert has greater need o' ye and yer potions than I. Jamie will git ye safe to him and come back for me tomorra'."

Jamie settled Hugh with the rifle and a blazing fire, then propped the flask of whisky beside him. "Now, dinna drink it all at once," he said, winking. "Ye dinna want to ruin your aim if a bear drops by." His Scottish accent had thickened, and Clemency noted his look of concern as he gently patted his old friend's shoulder.

She turned away. Oh, how she longed for someone to treat her with such tenderness. She had counted on Robert to fill her empty heart, but now. . . .

She selected several herbs and tinctures from her box, then wrapped them in her shawl. "I'm ready."

"Can ye ride astride?" Jamie dubiously eyed her wide, flounced skirt.

"Of course." With an air of exasperation, she gathered up her damp petticoats. Her white cotton stockings, gartered above the knee with blue silk ribbon, peeped into view, and a faint blush rose on Jamie's lean cheeks.

He mounted, then reached down to help her. She grasped his arm, then with a heave and a most unladylike squirm, flung her leg over Gray's broad back.

"Good night, Hugh," Jamie called. He clucked to the horse, and they jogged off.

Clemency immediately lost her balance and grabbed at Jamie's shirt. She wriggled back into place and rolled her eyes. What else was going to happen on this godforsaken trip?

After two more near slips, Jamie snorted. "Ye better catch a hold of me, *mo druidh,* unless ye want to land in the puckerbrush. I'll no' bite, ye ken."

She blushed and laid a tentative hand on his narrow hip. "Come now, dinna be shy." He chuckled devilishly.

"Surely a lass who can stitch a man's wounds isna afraid to grab him about the waist."

She suppressed a smile and slipped her arm around him, silently admiring the taut strength of his muscles. What else was going to happen on this trip, indeed?

They rode in silence, and soon Clemency found herself struggling to stay awake. The black woods rustled with soothing sounds: a light breeze sighing through the giant white pines, a small creature scurrying through the thick undergrowth, a million tree frogs cheeping a night song. Gray's hide was warm and sweaty beneath her bare thighs, and each time she shifted her weight, the scratch of the horse's hair tickled her skin. She swayed forward, fighting the urge to lean against Jamie's strong back.

Sleepily, she said, "Jamie—why did you name your horse Gray?"

A chuckle rumbled deep in his chest. "Weel, that's his color, aye?"

"How practical," she murmured. With a sigh, she leaned forward and rested her cheek in the warm hollow between his shoulder blades. Surely he wouldn't mind. She tightened her arm around his narrow waist, and for an instant, his hard stomach muscles jumped and quivered under her touch. His linen shirt had dried in the cool air, and she inhaled the rich scent of clean masculine sweat mingled with evergreen and some sort of spice. Cinnamon, perhaps? She wriggled her toes. Mmmmm . . . absolutely delicious, and utterly intoxicating.

When he spoke again, his deep voice was unnaturally loud in the stillness. "Besides, I didna pick the name. My daughter Elizabeth chose it."

Clemency felt herself being dragged down into the silky depths of sleep. So, Jamie had a daughter. Well, well.

"Do you think Robert will live?" she murmured.

For a long moment the clop of Gray's hooves was the only sound. "Aye. If anyone can save him, ye can."

Muddled happiness lapped at the edges of her mind, and she snuggled closer. Tiredness seeped through her arms and legs. Sleep was definitely winning this battle.

"Jamie—what does *mo druidh* mean?"

His warm hand closed over hers and pulled her arm tight around his waist. He gave her fingers a reassuring squeeze, and for the first time in her life she felt completely secure. As velvet waves of sleep closed over her head, she heard his voice, soft and deep in the silence.

"*Mo druidh?* It means 'my magic one.' "

Chapter Four

"Mistress Cameron? Mistress Cameron, we're here."

Someone was gently shaking her arm. With a weary groan, she opened her eyes and found herself astride a horse, her cheek pressed against a man's back. The shirt under her skin was wrinkled and prickly with perspiration, although the night air was cool.

What on earth? She struggled into an upright position. Then it all came rushing back.

"Considering what we've been through, perhaps you ought to call me Clemency," she said dryly. To cover her sudden embarrassment, she slid off the horse, hitting the ground with a little *unnh*. "Please accept my apologies, sir. I didn't mean to fall asleep."

" 'Twas my pleasure," Jamie said, rolling his *r*s extravagantly—a mannerism she was beginning to recognize as mild teasing. He swung down beside her. The scratchy wool of his kilt brushed her hand, and she jerked away as if bitten.

"Are we here?" She peered around the clearing where they stood. On either side dark pines rose like sentinels into the night sky, and she could hear the soft splash of waves lapping against a shoreline. She strained her eyes toward the sound and caught the reflection of water shining through a canopy of black branches.

Jamie took her by the shoulder and turned her around. She could just make out the bulk of a cabin huddled against the forbidding woods.

She swallowed. "But where's the town?"

"We passed it. This is Robert's cabin—'tis about a mile through the woods from the settlement. Ye canna truly call Sturgeon's Creek a town. My wee house is a bit farther along." He took her elbow, and his teeth gleamed as he flashed a reassuring smile. "Shall we go in?"

Suddenly the cabin door swung open, and a woman darted out, backlit by guttering candlelight. She brushed past Clemency without a glance. "Oh, Jamie, thank God you're home!" she cried. "I was so worried."

Jamie's grasp tightened on Clemency's elbow, and he inclined his head in a slight bow. "Lydia, please allow me to introduce Robert's betrothed, Mistress Cameron. Mistress Cameron, this is my sister-in-law."

Clemency curtsied, then impulsively held out her hand. "How do you do, Mistress MacKinnon."

Lydia dragged her gaze from Jamie's face, then ran it down Clemency's figure as if she were appraising a barrel of rancid salt pork. "Very well, I'm sure," she drawled, ignoring Clemency's hand. Her nasal voice sounded pained, as if one of her whalebone stays had jabbed her in the ribs. Clemency dropped her hand and nervously smoothed her wrinkled skirt.

"Oh, Jamie, I thought you'd never arrive," Lydia said, slipping her hand through Jamie's arm.

Lydia was tall and full breasted, although her waist was thicker than the latest London fashion dictated. Her spotless gray muslin gown was cut in the latest style, and her white-blond hair clung to her neck in fashionable ringlets. Although there was no denying her attractiveness, a petulant air marred her features, and she kept her thin lips closed when she smiled—perhaps because her teeth were rotten?

Clemency couldn't resist a bit of cattiness; then she gave herself a mental shake. No doubt Lydia was upset by Robert's illness. She could hardly be expected to welcome a stranger at such a time.

Lydia continued to simper up at Jamie, and Clemency grew impatient. She snatched up her herb-filled shawl and strode into the cabin.

Inside, the heat was suffocating, and a single candle cast grotesque, writhing shadows on the log walls. A bedstead of rough-hewn pine projected out into the room, its ropes strung so loosely that the man lying on it seemed to hover mere inches above the plank floor. She picked up the candle and leaned over him, then stifled a gasp.

Shilling-sized sores riddled Robert's face and neck. Most were scabbed over, but several still oozed yellowish pus. The same putrid discharge seeped from the corners of his closed eyes, and Clemency knew without looking that the rash had spread inside his lids. The fetid-sweet odor of rotting invaded her nostrils. She gulped and battled a sudden urge to weep. It didn't matter how many times she had seen this; it always affected her the same way. The merciless cruelty of smallpox left her stunned.

She raised a trembling hand and stroked the man's cheek, feeling the crusty ooze of his sores under her fingers. His skin was still warm, and for a moment she fancied he would open his eyes, smile and say it was all a prank.

"Robert?" she whispered.

A dark figure hurtled around the corner of the bed. It grunted, lunged and grabbed her hand, then yanked it away from Robert's cheek. Clemency recoiled and stared into the eyes of a savage. Two black braids, glossy as a raven's wings, framed the Indian woman's gaunt face and glittering eyes. The guttering candle cast demonic shadows on her mahogany skin, distorting her flattened nose and broad cheekbones. Clemency bit back a scream and tried to snatch her hand away.

The Indian grunted again, more softly this time, and her eyes slowly filled with tears. Although the room was hot, the hair rose on the back of Clemency's neck. Without breaking eye contact, she set the candle on the bedside table. The Indian still held her wrist in a painful grip, and Clemency lightly touched her hand.

"I know," she whispered. "But we must let him go in peace."

A hand grasped Clemency's shoulder, and she jumped like a scalded cat. She and the Indian sprang apart.

"Mo druidh . . ." Jamie's voice trailed off.

At his words, the Indian gasped and searched Clemency's face, her tragic eyes startled. Clemency's brows drew together. Did the woman understand Gaelic?

Jamie knelt beside the bed. His long hair glowed like polished mahogany in the flickering candlelight, and the tender curve of his lower lip moved in silent prayer. Clemency reached out to comfort him, then pulled back. She was a stranger here; it wasn't proper for her to intrude on his grief.

Suddenly he groaned and smashed his fist into the bedstead. In an instant she was on her knees beside him, all thoughts of propriety flown.

"Shhhhhh," she whispered, touching his shoulder, stroking his hair. It slipped through her fingers like cool, liquid fire. "I know you loved him—"

He turned and grasped her shoulders, his handsome face twisted with grief. "He was my dearest friend! What shall I do without him?"

A single tear trickled down his lean cheek. Without thinking, Clemency raised a finger and traced the teardrop's path until the salty diamond disappeared. His eyes held hers for what seemed like eternity, and she caught her reflection there, swimming in twin pools of gold and indigo.

"May I ask what you are doing?" Lydia's nasal voice knifed through the stillness. "I must say, Mistress Cameron, I hardly expected to find you in my brother-in-law's arms when your betrothed husband is lying dead before you."

Clemency struggled to her feet and fought for breath. Blast her miserable stays. "I beg your pardon? I was not in Jamie's . . . Mr. Maclean's arms."

"Faith." Lydia sniffed and made a little sound that in a less imperious woman would have sounded like *huh*. "Whatever you say, Mistress Cameron."

She swept around the bed like a square-rigger under full sail and cornered the Indian woman. "Mollyocket, fetch some water from the lake. We best prepare Robert for burial. He won't last long in this heat." Mollyocket shot Lydia a look of pure venom and slipped out.

Clemency lifted the candle and leaned over Robert's body. If one ignored the ravages of the pox, it was plain that he had been an attractive man. Silver streaked his wavy black hair, and his elegantly straight nose reminded her of Jamie's.

"Were you blood relatives?" She arched an eyebrow at the tall Highlander, then continued to examine Robert's face.

"Nay." Jamie hovered near her in the candle's meager light, and she could feel the heat radiating from his body. "Clan MacKinnon followed Clan Maclean in battle and allied with us in disputes. Our families intermarried as weel, but Robert and I were no' relatives—just friends and soul brothers." His Scottish accent thickened, and she realized he barely held his emotions in check.

She lifted the blanket off Robert's body. Lydia snatched it from her hand. "Faith, Mistress Cameron, what *are* you doing?"

"Leave her be," Jamie said. "Mistress Cameron's a verra experienced healer."

Clemency shot him a grateful look, then flinched as her eyes fell on the stump that had once been Robert's right leg.

"He lost it at Culloden," Jamie murmured, following her gaze. "Did he no' tell ye in his letters?"

"No."

She looked back at Robert's face. Generous laugh lines bracketed his eyes, and even in death his expression showed that he had been kind. Dear Robert—he *had* been sensitive and educated, as well as a courageous warrior. Oh, Holy Mother, if only she had been with him for this last battle. She leaned forward and brushed a kiss over his black hair. "He didn't tell me, but it wouldn't have mattered."

Mollyocket appeared in the doorway, carrying a wooden bucket of water. She set it at Clemency's elbow and melted into the shadows. Clemency fixed Lydia with a steady gaze. "Mr. Maclean tells me you nursed Robert?"

"Yes, for all the good it did. But Robert always was the weak one."

"May I ask why his sores haven't been washed?" Clemency kept her voice neutral, but her fists clenched in the folds of her skirt.

"Excuse me?"

"His sores haven't been washed in days. It probably wouldn't have saved him, but at least he would have been comfortable—"

"How dare you speak to me like this! Who are you, anyway? Some little English upstart who claimed to be kin and lured Robert into marriage—"

"That's enough." Jamie's deep voice cracked like musket fire. "Lydia, get on with the laying out. I'll take Mistress Cameron to your house. I'm sure she's exhausted from the trip."

"But I'd like to help," Clemency protested.

"Nay, lass. 'Tis no' proper for a maiden to"—Jamie actually blushed—"to see a man unclothed."

"But—"

"No buts, madam. Are ye coming or no'?" He strode to the door, kilt swinging gracefully about his knees. In a flash she decided a man in a kilt wasn't such a strange sight after all. In truth, it was rather pleasant.

"Yes, sirrah!" she retorted. She turned back to Lydia. "When you're finished, strip the bed, his clothes, your clothes, everything. They'll have to be burned"—she held up a hand to stop Lydia's complaint—"or they'll spread the disease. Has anyone been near Robert who hasn't already had smallpox? Your husband or any of the villagers?"

"No. Samuel's had it, and he took Jamie's daughter and our three sons to stay with Goody Mitchell the moment we realized Robert had the pox." Lydia began stripping the bedclothes from beneath Robert's body, pouting and rolling her ice blue eyes.

"Good. Let's pray it hasn't spread. 'Tis unusual to see a smallpox epidemic in the summer, but one never knows." Clemency nodded to Lydia and the dark corner into which Mollyocket had disappeared, then gathered up her shawl and herbs and followed Jamie outside.

Halfway across the clearing she sensed someone behind her. She whirled and bumped into Mollyocket, who hustled back several paces, face wary. They stared at each other for a long moment. Then Clemency squatted down, unwrapped her shawl and drew out a crumpled sprig of dried white heather. She handed it to the Indian.

"This is white heather—from Exmoor in Devon, not Scotland, I'm afraid. My mother told me it was the MacKinnon clan badge. It distinguished the proudest, strongest MacKinnon warriors in battle. Perhaps you could wrap it in his shroud."

Mollyocket's bottomless black eyes studied Clemency's face; then she nodded and took the heather. She glided into the cabin and soundlessly shut the door.

Jamie lifted Clemency onto Gray's back; then they rode

through the woods in silence, her hand touching his hip just enough to keep her balance. His voice was as soft as the sighing pines when he finally spoke: "That was a verra kind thing ye just did, *mo druidh.* Ye have a braw heart."

They clopped along, and Clemency realized she was no longer sleepy. Being scared witless by a savage, arguing with the icy Lydia and examining the body of her dead fiancé had left her wide-eyed and twitchy. Her nerves thrummed like catgut violin strings, and she felt a sudden foolish urge to leap off the horse and run screaming through the woods. Just as she began measuring the distance from Gray's back to the ground, they broke out of the forest into a tiny settlement.

Clemency glanced around in the dark and decided Jamie had been right: one could hardly call Sturgeon's Creek a town. Her eyes adjusted to the weak moonlight, and she saw a dozen houses huddled around a flat open space that vaguely resembled the village greens back in England. Ghostly sheep blobs stood motionless on the square's grass. A larger building with a squat steeple anchored the north end of the green—the church, she supposed. Or had Robert written that they were called meetinghouses in New England? Her exhausted mind couldn't recall.

Jamie reined Gray to a halt before a sizeable house covered with hand-riven siding. The weathered wood was bare, and the top floor overhung the bottom by a good foot's length, giving the structure the appearance of a tiny garrison. Clemency glanced over her shoulder. Did this architectural design protect the colonists during Indian raids? No, there were no raids in Maine now. Robert had written that most of the Indians had died or gone west decades ago.

Jamie ushered her into the darkened house, then fumbled with the embers on the hearth, trying to light a splinter of fat pine. The stick flared up, and she saw they stood in a spacious keeping room with a low-beamed ceiling and whitewashed walls. Shiny copper pots surrounded the enormous fireplace, and a narrow, wooden table board perched on two trestles down the center of the room, its matching benches drawn up on either side. Polished pewter plates and tankards filled several shelves, and braids of onions and bunches of drying herbs hung from the ceiling, perfuming the air with their tangy scent. The hearth was swept clean, and a spinning wheel sat in one corner, a full basket of spun wool skeins resting beneath.

Clemency strolled to the hearth. Whatever her faults, Lydia was a fine housekeeper. Suddenly, she recalled another of Robert's letters. She glanced around the room, which was cheery now that Jamie had lit a second candle. Yes, there it was. Resting in the place of honor on an oak sideboard was Lydia's pride and joy: an English sterling silver chafing dish. Robert had written how he and Jamie, drunk from too much rum at a barn raising, had stolen the dish. They had given the frantic Lydia a series of bawdy clues until she finally discovered it down a neighbor's privy. Of course, Jamie—being taller than Robert—had to venture down after it.

Clemency imagined the imperious Scot squirming down the privy hole, Robert clutching his long legs and shouting directions. She began to giggle.

Jamie shot her a strange look. "May I ask what's so funny?"

She pointed to the chafing dish. "Robert wrote me about the privy." She sailed into a fit of hysterical laughter and wished for the hundredth time today that she hadn't laced her stays so tightly. What did a tiny waist matter, anyway? Robert hadn't gotten to admire it. Tears blurred her vision, and she collapsed on the settle. Oh, poor Robert. . . .

"Och, *mo druidh*. Dinna cry. 'Tis been a nightmare for ye, I ken . . ." Jamie sat and pulled her to his broad chest. She dissolved against him as he folded her in his strong

arms. Murmuring in Gaelic, he tenderly rocked her back
and forth and stroked her disheveled hair.

"Oh, Jamie, what am I going to do?" She sobbed and
burrowed in her pocket for her handkerchief. "Now that
Robert's dead, there's no reason for me to stay. And I can't
go back."

Jamie stood and fished a coarse linen napkin from the
drawer in Lydia's oak sideboard. He bent and wiped her
tears, then gently held the cloth to her nose.

"Here. Blow." She sniffed daintily. The corners of his
mouth twitched, and he shot her a stern, blue-eyed glare.
"Dinna trifle with me, lass. I said blow."

Clemency rolled her eyes over the folds of cloth and gave
a great honk.

Jamie chuckled, warm and deep, and her heart catapulted
from despair to joy. "Ye remind me of my wee Elizabeth
when ye do that," he said, tossing the napkin onto Lydia's
pristine table. "Now, dinna let me hear ye fash again. Your
place is here, aye?"

"But I—"

"No buts—"

The front door flew open and crashed into the kitchen
wall. She gasped, and Jamie leaped to his feet, hand flying
to the dirk in his belt. A thin, sandy-haired man staggered
over the threshold, his pale eyes wide. Clutched against his
shoulder was a small child wrapped in a quilt.

"Samuel—" Jamie began.

"Thank God you're back!" Samuel MacKinnon gasped.
"Elizabeth's taken the pox."

Chapter Five

The color drained from Jamie's lean face. Shoulders rigid with tension, he gently lifted Elizabeth from Samuel's arms and laid his lips against her flushed forehead. The little girl's long, red curls mingled with his and gleamed in the candlelight. Clemency's heart turned over.

"All is well, *m'annsachd,*" Jamie murmured. "Your *athair* is here." He slumped on the settle and cradled Elizabeth against his chest. "She's burning with fever." He looked up at Clemency, eyes stricken. "Can ye tell if 'tis the pox?"

She knelt and laid her hand against Elizabeth's cheek. The little girl stirred and gave a soft whimper. Her skin burned under Clemency's touch.

"There's no sign yet of the smallpox rash. When did you notice the fever?" Clemency asked Samuel. She slid her fingers to the base of Elizabeth's jaw. The child's pulse raced like a trapped bird's.

"Right after Jamie left yesterday morning. She began complaining about a bad headache, then started puking. The fever got worse all day. I didn't know what to do."

"What about your sons?" Clemency undid the lacing on the child's shift. No rash on the neck, chest or extremities. With God's help, Elizabeth might have only a remittent fever.

"As soon as Elizabeth started puking I took her to Goody Barton's." Samuel stared down at his muddy boots. "She's a widow with no children. The boys stayed with Goody Mitchell. They seem well so far."

Clemency sat back on her heels and stared up at Jamie. He tucked Elizabeth's shiny copper head under his chin, hugged her to his chest, then rocked her back and forth. His indigo eyes were raw with misery.

"What's wrong with her?" he whispered to Clemency, as if speaking aloud would loose the demons of death and disease on his daughter.

" 'Tis too soon to tell, but with a fever this high 'tis likely the pox. I'm so sorry, Jamie. But she's young—about four?" He nodded. "And she's strong. With God's help, she'll fight it off."

She stood and gathered up her shawl, the role of no-nonsense healer settling over her like a cloak. "We must get the fever down. I have a few herbs with me, but they'll only last a day." She sketched a curtsy to Samuel. "Mr. MacKinnon, we had an accident with the wagon on our way here, and Mr. Rankin was injured and remained behind. My medical box was left behind, as well. Do you think you could fetch them?"

Samuel's eyebrows shot up, and he glanced at Jamie, who nodded. Clemency stirred up the fire and adjusted the iron bar holding the tea kettle over the coals. "I'll brew catnip tea and make a clister. That should bring the fever down." She laid a hand on Jamie's broad shoulder. "Take her up to bed. All will be well, I promise." Now it was her turn to give him a reassuring smile. "Oh, and gentlemen? We must keep people away from the house—and away from us—until the disease is contained. If it is the pox, we can't risk an epidemic."

Four days later, Clemency collapsed on a stool in one of the cramped upstairs bedchambers in the MacKinnon house. Numbly, she ground and pounded a smooth maple pestle into the mortar, working the mass of yellow dock root into a powder suitable for a poultice. The late afternoon sun had waned, and lavender shadows crept across the pine floor. A light breeze drifted in the open window, cooling her cheeks.

She leaned back and wiped her hand across her forehead. Thank heaven the stifling heat was gone, banished by the terrible thunderstorm that had battered Sturgeon's Creek two nights ago. She had never seen such a tempest. Like the wrath of God, grape-sized hail had pounded the settlement and shattered precious panes of window glass in the meeting-house.

All during the storm, Elizabeth's fever had raged. Clemency's best efforts with catnip tea and clister hadn't eased the child's torment, and she slipped into a deathlike stupor. As hailstones pelted the roof and wind gusted against the eaves, Jamie had snapped.

"Do something!" he had bellowed, frenzied with worry and lack of sleep. He had grabbed Clemency's shoulders and shaken her. "Ye must save my daughter."

Clemency had closed her eyes and said a silent prayer, first to God, then to the Holy Mother, then to her dead granny. At once inspiration had hit, and she had ordered Jamie and Samuel out into the storm to fill trenchers with hard, white hailstones. Then she had poured clean water into the enormous iron kettle used for soap making. She had tried to cool Elizabeth's body with wet cloths several times during the day, but the water had never been cold enough to lower the child's temperature. Now God had sent ice, and Elizabeth's fever broke at last.

A lazy fly darted in the bedchamber window and swooped past Clemency's nose. Its dull drone added to her lassitude. Elizabeth slumbered under the sedative effects of skullcap and valerian, her breath coming in light, even snores, and the house lay as silent as a chapel during prayer. Out in the cornfields Samuel and Hugh hoed weeds, and Jamie slept in the next chamber, driven there by exhaustion and Clemency's reassurance that she could nurse his daughter alone.

She batted at the fly and wrinkled her nose. It was a wonder she had been allowed to care for the child at all. The moment Lydia had heard of Elizabeth's illness, she had abandoned Robert's laying out and rushed home. She had flounced into the bedchamber just as Clemency eased a clister—a suppository of catnip suspended in purified fat—between Elizabeth's bare buttocks. A heated argument had broken out, and Jamie had been forced to decide who should care for his daughter. He had chosen Clemency.

She sat on the edge of the bed and picked up a wooden bowl. With a tired sigh, she dipped a soft muslin cloth in the eyebright infusion, then gently swabbed the little girl's eyes. So far the smallpox rash hadn't crept under Elizabeth's lids, and she didn't intend to let it.

Elizabeth stirred, and a tiny smile flitted across her face. Clemency caught her breath. The child was exceptionally beautiful and the image of Jamie: the same fiery hair, the same generous mouth and the same wide-set, indigo eyes. She leaned forward and brushed a kiss on Elizabeth's delicate lips—lips so like Jamie's—then sat back. She would sacrifice anything to keep those beautiful eyes from losing their sight.

Footsteps trudged up the stairs, which wrapped behind the house's giant central chimney; then Lydia strode into the bedchamber. After minutely appraising her niece's condition, she flounced down on the stool. Clemency sighed.

"Faith, I'm pleased to see that Jamie is sleeping at last," Lydia said. "The poor dear was worn out with worry." She leaned over and sniffed at the concoction of wet cornmeal in the pewter basin by Elizabeth's bed. "What's that in there with the Guinea wheat?"

" 'Tis a poultice," Clemency said. "Goldenseal and ground yellow dock. It will prevent the rash from itching and turning putrid."

Lydia's eyes took on a speculative gleam, and she smoothed her full black skirts. "Of course, 'tis natural that Jamie is so upset. I've never known a man to love a child the way he loves Elizabeth. He's besotted with her, although that shouldn't surprise me, considering how he felt about Rebekah."

A sharp pain jabbed beneath Clemency's left breast, no doubt from lack of sleep. She yawned and daubed the poultice on Elizabeth's bare arms. "Rebekah was his wife?"

"Yes. She was my older sister. Our father is a prominent merchant in Kittery. Patrick Stevenson—perhaps you've heard of him? No? Well, he was born in Scotland. Of course, he was never involved in any rebellion against King George."

"How loyal," Clemency murmured. She dropped the soggy cloth into the basin. Why on earth was Lydia hanging about? She certainly hadn't come to help, not without Jamie here to see her devotion.

"Rebekah was reckoned a great beauty in Kittery," Lydia said in a silky tone. "In the entire colony, for that matter. We were practically twins, you know." Lydia fixed Clemency with raptor's eyes, as if trying to judge the effect of her words. "Rebekah could have had any man in the colony, but from the moment she saw Jamie, she would have none but him, even if he was a bond servant."

"Jamie was a bond servant?" Clemency asked. "I knew Robert and Samuel had been, but—"

"Oh, yes," Lydia interrupted. "Jamie was sixteen when

he was banished with naught but the clothes on his back and a price on his head if he ever set foot back in Britain.'' She scowled at Clemency's startled expression. ''There's no disgrace in banishment,'' she snapped. ''Samuel and Robert both worked hard, but Jamie worked hardest of all. He bought out all their indentures before their seven years were up.''

She sighed and looked at Elizabeth's sleeping form. ''Jamie decided to wed when he was twenty-eight. It was the happiest day of Rebekah's life. She was twenty-three then, and had waited for Jamie for years.''

Clemency laid a clean muslin cloth over Elizabeth's poultice, then wrapped it with a length of faded calico. She was exhausted and her back ached, but she wasn't about to show weakness in front of Lydia. That would be like running from a bear.

''Jamie was the most devoted husband you ever saw.'' Lydia gave an airy flick of her hand. ''He did everything for Rebekah, worked like a slave—surveying, fishing, trapping and trading with the savages—all so he could buy land and build her a house.''

She pursed her thin lips. ''Buying land was a bit of problem, and my father was most vexed about it, let me tell you. Jamie was Catholic, you know. Most of the Jacobites who came here were, although most converted and joined the Congregationalist church. They had to if they wanted to buy land.'' She shook her head. ''But not Jamie. Oh, he wasn't devout, but he clung to his religion like it was his last tie to Scotland. All a heap of Highland stubbornness, I say.''

She paused, hand clutched to her chest. ''But when he reached thirty—the age when he could buy land—tragedy struck.''

''What happened?'' Clemency asked.

''Rebekah got with child after they'd been wed a year. Jamie was so proud, thrilled to have a child with his darling wife. But it was a hard confinement. Rebekah had never been strong, and when her time came ... well, the poor lamb never had a prayer.''

She gave a dramatic sniff. ''We don't have a midwife in town, and her travail came on so fast there wasn't time to ride for the doctor in York. I was newly married and didn't know what to do, but several of the neighbors came to help. Somehow we managed to deliver the babe, but we couldn't stop the bleeding. Dear Jamie fought like a tiger to save her, but she was beyond hope. He had to sit and watch his beloved die.''

Lydia wiped a nonexistent tear from her eye. ''When poor Rebekah breathed her last, he went mad with grief. When I tried to place his daughter in his arms, he thundered, 'That creature killed my *wife!*' He cursed me and stormed out of the house.

''Hours later he came back, drunk as a lord, eyes red with tears. He growled and turned away when he saw the baby, but I finally got him to look at her. That was all it took.'' Lydia's cold face softened, and uneasiness prickled along Clemency's skin. ''No one in the colony has a heart bigger than Jamie's, and he fell in love with Elizabeth at first sight, just as he'd done with her mother.''

Clemency's heart hammered under her stays. She must have laced the blasted things too tight again. If Lydia would leave, she could loosen them. She walked to the window so Lydia couldn't see her flushed face, then leaned out for a breath of air.

''Jamie mourns Rebekah to this day.'' Lydia's nasal voice followed her. ''Her death snuffed his spirit like a candle. He gave up his Catholic faith, converted and bought land beside Robert's. He wanted to leave Elizabeth an inheritance like the one he had lost back in Scotland, I suppose.''

She stood, eyes trained heavenward, hands clasped to her bosom. ''Faith, he even commissioned a headstone for Rebekah's grave, and wrote the epitaph himself.'' She recited:

In this dark, silent Mansion of the Dead,
A lovely Mother, a sweet Wife, is laid.
Of ev'ry Virtue of her Sex possest,
She charm'd the World, and made a Husband Blest.
Of such a Wife, O righteous Heaven, bereft,
What joy for me, what joy on Earth is left?
Still from my inmost Soul, the Groans arise,
Still flow the Sorrows, ceaseless from my Eyes.
But why these Sorrows, so profusely shed?
They may mourn but ne'er can raise the Dead.

Lydia's voice grew hard. "Since then, every lass in the colony has tried to win him, but they may as well be flies, for all the attention he pays. He just ignores them and goes on his way." Suddenly she strode toward Clemency, black silk skirt rustling ominously. "So don't be fancying he'll take to you, Mistress Cameron."

"I beg your pardon?"

Lydia waved a bony finger under Clemency's nose. "Don't play innocent with me. I saw you watching him when he was fretting and praying that Elizabeth would survive. There was no mistaking the fawning look on your face. Just remember, he's spurned better than you a thousand times."

With a parting glare, Lydia gathered up her skirts and swept out.

It was twilight, Clemency's favorite time of day. Outside Elizabeth's bedchamber window, barn swallows swooped and darted through the soft lilac sky, and the muffled clang of cow bells drifted through the hushed, hazy air. It was so peaceful here, almost like England—if she overlooked the dark, impenetrable forest beyond the cornfield.

Yesterday Reverend Rogers, the Congregationalist minister, had laid Robert to rest in that forest, in a tiny plot at the edge of the lake. Clemency and Jamie hadn't attended the brief graveside service; they had been too busy nursing Elizabeth, and Clemency had feared their presence might spread the pox. A tiny spurt of triumph rippled through her, and she clasped her hands. Praise be to God, as yet no one else in Sturgeon's Creek had taken ill.

She heard a sound and turned as Jamie stooped to avoid the low doorway and entered the chamber. He was clad in an old muslin sark and snug breeches; he hadn't worn his kilt since the day Elizabeth had fallen ill. His hair was tousled from sleep, and here and there red-gold waves stood on end. Clemency grinned. He looked like a naughty little boy caught rolling in the hay.

He bent over the bed and kissed his daughter's cool cheek. With a delighted smile, he glanced up. "She's getting better, aye?"

"Yes. The rash hasn't spread, and the sores are healing. If we can keep her calm and not let her scratch, she should be better in a week's time—hopefully with no scars."

"Och, thank God." He caressed Elizabeth's limp curls, and Clemency's heart contracted. What must it feel like to be touched with such love?

"Jamie, may I ask you something?" she blurted, anxious to turn her thoughts.

"Aye?"

"When the scabs fall off, may I collect a few of them?" His eyebrows arched, and she rushed to explain. "Elizabeth has the best type of pox—relatively mild, despite the high fever. By grinding up the scabs from her sores, I'll have the material to inoculate others in town—Lydia's three boys, for example. Inoculation is safe, and I've done it before." Excitement thrilled through her. "Just think, Jamie, we could save lives!"

He studied her face for a long moment, then nodded. "Aye, then. Collect your wee scabs, *dotair*—doctor," he added, seeing her puzzled expression. "But dinna be sur-

prised if everyone in town thinks ye're loony, or worse."
He winked and slanted her an elfin grin. "I must say, ye're
the strangest woman I've ever had the rare good fortune to
meet. Next ye'll be collecting fleas off the dogs."

He chuckled and sat on the floor, back against the bedstead, knees drawn up to his chin, then stretched his arms
over his head in a movement as sensual as a cat's. "Ye
look melancholy, *mo druidh.* Is it the time of day or have
I worn ye out with nursing?"

Clemency tried to muster a smile. "Twilight is so beautiful, but I always find it terribly sad somehow."

"Aye, I ken. Loneliness hits the hardest when other folk
are settling in for the evening and ye've no one."

He gave her a smile of utter sweetness, and sudden tears
choked her throat. Holy Mother, why did he have to be so
kind? She could be cool and strong when he was blustering
and bellowing and ordering her about in that gruff Scottish
accent. But his tenderness disarmed her completely.

"Oh, Jamie, are you lonely too?"

The question popped out before she could stop it.
Appalled, she clapped a hand over her mouth. Of course he
was lonely. He had lost his Scottish birthright, his Catholic
faith and his beloved wife, and he had spent the last four
years alone—alone like she had always been. Their eyes
met, and suddenly she longed to cradle his bright head on
her bosom. Then she recalled Lydia's words: Jamie's heart
was in the grave, and he wasn't about to let Clemency
resurrect it.

"I'm sorry," she said. "Forget I ever said that. Oh, blast!"
Hot tears blurred her vision, and she swiped at her eyes.
How could she break down like this? Jamie must think her
a spineless ninny. "I . . . I must be tired out. I'm not usually
so emotional."

Jamie took her hand, pulled her down beside him and
encircled her with his arms. "Lean on me, *mo druidh.*"

She rested her head on his shoulder. His muslin sark was

soft under her skin, and she reveled in the strength of his arm around her waist. He murmured something in Gaelic, and his warm breath fanned her neck. Then he pulled his shirt cuff over his hand and wiped the tears from her cheeks. Giddiness raced through her veins. He leaned over her until his lips were a mere whisper away, then clasped her chin in one big hand and fixed her with an unwavering blue gaze. Her heart slowed to a languid, intoxicating beat.

"I must thank ye, *mo druidh,*" he murmured. "For I owe ye my life. By saving *m'annsachd*—my darling child—ye saved the one thing on this earth that I love."

Clemency's head whirled. His musky male scent, his indigo eyes, his apple-sweet breath—they were enthralling her, making her forget reason, forget propriety, forget his sick daughter asleep on the bed above them. Her lips parted, and she swayed forward.

Then the import of his words sank in: *Ye saved the one thing on this earth that I love.* Her hands curled into fists. Holy Mother, Lydia was right—and she was a fool.

Jamie leaned back, flashed her a beguiling smile, then tapped his long finger on the tip of her nose. " 'Tis your turn to sleep now, *mo druidh.* I'll watch over Elizabeth." He stood and held out a strong hand to help her to her feet.

Clemency sighed and rolled onto her back. Blast this lumpy cornhusk mattress; every time she moved it rustled. Not that a comfortable, *quiet* bed mattered, anyway. She couldn't sleep. She had tried her granny's old remedy of counting sheep, she had tried reciting the Catechism, she had even tried humming old Devon lullabies. It was hopeless. Lydia's story and Jamie's words chased through her mind like a fox after chickens.

She flounced onto her side and buried her face in the goose-down pillow—the same pillow Jamie had slept on all afternoon. She inhaled deeply and detected his scent: a delicious, masculine combination of clean perspiration, wood smoke and cinnamon blended with the warm musk of sleep. It conjured Jamie as surely as if he were lying beside her.

Jamie beside her. *Oh, my.* She dimpled and wriggled her toes, then brought herself up sharply.

Now that Elizabeth was on the mend, Clemency had to make a decision. There was no possibility of returning to England. She had slammed and locked the door on the misery and shame of her past, and now that she had met Jamie, she couldn't turn back even if she wanted to. But could she go forward?

She closed her eyes and conjured Jamie's handsome face. She was entranced by his elegant profile, the beguiling curve of his lip, the dancing gold flecks in the deep indigo pools of his eyes. She knew the gentleness of his hands—hands that had so lovingly nursed his sick child—and she longed to feel them on her skin, to know the wild, abandoned glory of his touch, surging with mystery and heat and life.

Oh, Jamie. . . . She dug her nails into the soft flesh of her arms. What could she do? What did she want? She felt helpless, adrift, as if her mind and will were scattered to the winds like a thousand crushed leaves whirling in an autumn gale. And yet. . . .

And yet she knew. She wanted Jamie. She craved the tenderness he showered on his little girl, she yearned for the adamant devotion he still gave his dead wife, she longed for him to wrap her in his arms and call her his magic one, his beloved, his heart. And she ached for the hot pressure of his mouth on hers, for demanding kisses full of joy and passion—and love.

With a tiny despairing wail, she flung an arm over her eyes. Why did she torture herself with hopeless dreams? Skilled she might be, but no healer could salvage that which did not wish to be saved.

Buck up, child. Her granny's voice swept through her

mind, and once more her thoughts scattered like chaff. *Faint heart never won the field.* Clemency's lips softened into a smile. That had always been her granny's favorite saying.

For a long time she lay staring at the darkness. Then she prodded the pillow and snuggled down onto the lumpy mattress. "All right, James Ian Alasdair Maclean," she whispered, closing her eyes. "Your heart might be in the grave, but you've never dealt with me. I own no faint heart."

Chapter Six

Giles Bryant closed his eyes and bit down on a stick of kindling. Clemency made one quick slice with her razor-sharp surgeon's blade, and pus burst from the swollen carbuncle on Giles's callused thumb. He winced.

"Hold tight, Mr. Bryant." Clemency smiled, then rested her tongue lightly between her front teeth. She doused the cut with boiled water, then swabbed it with distilled alcohol and tincture of goldenseal. "Now that I can see, we'll have your splinter out in a trice."

As Hugh Rankin clucked and hovered over her shoulder, she extracted the splinter, then bandaged Giles's hand with clean muslin strips. She fished through her medical box, then handed the young farmer a small glass bottle.

"Change the bandage twice a day and soak your hand in hot water with three drops of this before you go to bed," she directed. "You'll need to keep the wound as clean as the parson's heart or it will fester again. If you'll ask your good mother to stop by, I'll give her a receipt so she can brew more if you run out. The main herb is slippery elm. I'm not sure if 'tis available around here, but several other herbs work as well.''

"Thankee, miss, you've relieved me already.'' Giles touched his cap, and his prominent Adam's apple bobbed. " 'Tis glad we all are to have a healer among us. I've never taken to that doctor in York—stuck up, he is, and not half as pretty as you.'' Blushing furiously at his awkward compliment, Giles clutched his bottle of medicine and ambled away.

When he was out of earshot, Clemency wagged a finger at Hugh. "What are you grinning at, Mr. Rankin?''

"Och, no' a thing. I've just noticed that the lads in this town are comin' doon wi' a mess o' cuts and bruises since word got 'round aboot the bonny new healer.''

"As long as Mr. Bryant confines his wounds to his appendages and not to his heart, all will be well,'' she retorted.

Hugh chuckled as she whipped off her apron and slid her medical box beneath Lydia's sideboard. It was a glorious July afternoon, and she was itching to be out-of-doors. She was sick to death of being Lydia's scullion, saddled with an endless drudgery of chores: mucking out the chicken coop, scrubbing the floors with sand, stirring the bubbling cauldron of lye soap over a blazing fire in the midday sun.

She jerked up her chin and tied her straw hat's blue ribbons. No, it wasn't the chores she hated. She had always worked hard, and she loved looking after Lydia's three mischievous sons. She just couldn't take any more of Lydia's catty complaints and pointed reminders that Clemency would be homeless if she and Samuel hadn't decided to do their Christian duty and take her in.

At the thought of Samuel, Clemency wrinkled her nose and suppressed a tiny shudder. In the two weeks since Jamie had taken Elizabeth home to his cabin, Samuel had degenerated from a shy, well-mannered kinsman to an alarming pest. When he drank too much, which was almost every night, she had to step lively to stay out of his way. Only last evening he had caught her in the barn as she milked the cow. Before she could scoot out of his reach, he snaked his arm around her waist and lunged in for a kiss. Thankfully his sudden movement had startled Old Buttercup, who bellowed and smacked him in the cheek with her dung-caked tail. Clemency giggled at the thought.

"And what are *ye* grinnin' at, lassie?" Hugh offered her his arm and escorted her out the door.

For a moment she debated whether to tell him about Samuel's advances. Her palms began to sweat, and a chill shot down her spine as she remembered what could happen if a man's interest got out of hand. But no, Hugh and Jamie were Samuel's oldest friends. They had fought side by side during the Jacobite Rebellion, and she couldn't make trouble between them.

"I'm happy to be out with such a fine gentleman on such a lovely day," she said, flashing him a dimpled smile. "And I'm happy to be visiting Elizabeth."

"The wee lassie misses ye sorely. She's aboot her old self again, always draggin' home wee creatures and up to devilry."

They strolled up the forest path that led from the settlement to Jamie's cabin, and Clemency stifled an impulse to skip. At last she could see Jamie without Lydia hanging about.

Jamie had dropped by the MacKinnon house now and then over the past weeks, but Clemency never had the chance to speak with him alone. Lydia always clung to his side. As the days had flown, Clemency had watched Lydia giggle and twitch her tail at Jamie like a mare in heat. Slowly, an awful suspicion had begun to grow in her mind: Lydia was in love with Jamie.

Oh, no matter that she was married with three children, and that Jamie was her brother-in-law; there was no mistaking her bold flirtation. Whenever Jamie visited, Lydia found a pretense to whisk past him and brush her wide skirts against his breeches. When he ate supper with them, Lydia insisted on sitting beside him, and her hand touched his a fraction too long when she passed him his trencher of stew. Again and again Clemency had caught Lydia gazing longingly at his elegant profile when no one else was looking.

Clemency gritted her teeth. Lydia acted like a lovesick maiden trying to lure her beau into . . . into what?

The thought that Jamie might return Lydia's affections tortured Clemency. Her stomach lurched each time she heard his light step coming up the walk, and jealousy gnawed at her heart like a plague-ridden rat. Her only consolation was that Jamie avoided Lydia as much as politeness allowed, and he adroitly declined all opportunities to be alone with her. Clemency found this odd, as Lydia was said to be the image of Jamie's dead wife. Wouldn't it be natural for him to bear at least *some* affection for Rebekah's sister?

She slanted a glance at Hugh. His craggy face was impassive, and the muted hunting tartan of his kilt blended with the greens and grays of the trees. For a moment she fancied he was one of the wee folk grown tall, or more likely a savage. He had taken to stopping by in the evening to bring her medicinal roots and herbs trusted by the Indians, or a bunch of wildflowers that he thought might please her. A man of deep stillness, he docilely helped her card wool while she wove tales, carefully edited, of her life back in Devon. Now and again he spoke of Scotland, and she listened with deep sympathy to the longing in his voice. Only once had he asked about her mother, and she had told him what little she could with Lydia in earshot. He could be trusted.

"Hugh?" She kept her voice nonchalant. "Was Jamie's wife Rebekah very like Lydia?"

"Rebekah like Lydia? Nay, lass. Och, they were near doubles to look at—tall and fair, ye ken. But Rebekah was a joy—a kinder, softer-hearted creature ye'd never hope to meet. She reminded me o' yer mother Margaret that way.

Always lookin' after sick creatures an' wee bairns. Nay, she and Lydia couldna ha' been more different.''

Clemency squeezed his arm. "Why, Hugh, I think that's the most I've heard you say since we met."

The old Highlander chuckled. "I talk when I ha' somethin' to say, no' like some I ken."

"You don't mean me, I hope?" she said, dimpling. Hugh snorted. "Well, since you're so talkative this afternoon, tell me why Jamie was wearing his kilt the day he fetched me in Kittery. He hasn't worn it since."

Hugh shook his head. "Jamie Maclean is the soul o' stubbornness. He kent there'd be Sassenachs—Englishmen—on the docks that day, an' there's nothin' he loves more in this world than badgerin' the Sassenachs."

"Does he truly hate the English?"

"Och, lass. Hate's a strong word. But Jamie would ha' been a powerful laird back in Scotland if the English hadna beaten the Jacobites. His family owned a verra great estate, ye ken. Jamie was raised as a gentleman, wi' a fine European education. He was close kin to the Maclean chieftain, Sir Hector Maclean, and his uncle—" Hugh fell silent, a scowl deepening the sharp lines between his brows. After a long pause and several throat clearings, he resumed.

"The honor o' the Macleans is bred deep in Jamie's bones, lass. I dinna think he hates the English, but he hasna forgotten, nor will he ever forgive. And avengin' a slight against a man's honor is a verra old custom in the Highlands."

They turned off the main path and walked through a cool patch of shade. Clemency shivered. Moments ago the forest had embraced her, a sun-dappled haven of supple branches and tender leaves. Now it seemed cold and hostile.

"I'm English," she murmured.

Hugh patted her arm. "Nay, lass. Ye're of Scottish blood, that's what counts. And Jamie certainly doesna hate ye. Far from it."

Clemency blushed and grinned like an idiot. Could Hugh tell how she felt about Jamie? She met his sharp blue eyes, and he winked.

The trees thinned as they neared Jamie's cabin. She screwed up her courage. "Hugh, I know how much Jamie loved his wife, and how much he's grieved for her. Lydia told me all about it. Do . . . do you think he'll ever get over Rebekah?"

Hugh folded a gnarled hand over hers. "Jamie's suffered and grieved hard, lass, but I dinna think his is a case o' undyin' love so much as mule stubbornness. He's grieved so long 'tis become a habit, ye ken. No one's ever stood up to him, nor shaken him up so he'd have a reason to change."

They were almost to the clearing. *Faint heart never won the field.* Clemency bit her lip. "Not even Lydia?"

"Hummph. Ye watch yourself wi' Mistress MacKinnon. Nothin' but trouble e'r came from that one."

They stepped out of the woods, and Clemency gasped with pleasure. A wide meadow of tall grass swept down to the rocky shore of a lake, where the water danced and glimmered in the afternoon sun. A light breeze billowed through the field, carrying the scent of fresh-cut hay. From the clearing where they stood, a trampled path led uphill to Jamie's cabin, which faced west toward the lake and a ring of distant blue hills. As they started up the path, a bright blue bird with a red belly shot across the field, its song cascading through the diamond air.

"Mistress Cam'ron! Did you see him?" Elizabeth raced from behind a tree, red curls flying out behind her, white cheeks flushed with excitement. "My bluebird! Did you see him? Da says he's good luck." She barreled into Clemency's skirts and flung her arms around her knees.

"Ooof, Elizabeth, you're as strong as a bear." Clemency bent and kissed the child's sweaty head, right on the delicious white part which divided her curls into burnished auburn curtains. She inhaled, then dimpled. Elizabeth even smelled like Jamie—all cinnamon and evergreen. "How are you, pumpkin pie?"

"I'm not a pumpkin pie!"

"Yes you are. Your hair's as red as a pumpkin, and you're as sweet as pie."

Elizabeth stuck out her tongue and yanked on Hugh's kilt. "Carry me, Uncle Hugh."

The gillie rolled his eyes. "Carry a strappin' big *each* like ye? I think not."

"I'm not a horse, I'm a selkie!" She grabbed Clemency's hand and tugged her up the path. "Da says we can go swimming when he's done the hay. Can you swim?"

"Yes, but are you well enough to swim?" Clemency asked.

"Uh-huh. Molly says I'm all better."

They rounded the corner of the cabin, and Clemency saw Mollyocket standing on the stone slab that served as Jamie's doorstep. She hadn't encountered the Indian woman since the night Robert had died, and her black eyes and jutting cheekbones startled Clemency anew. Although Mollyocket wore a patched homespun skirt and pinner over her linen shift, she still looked like a savage.

The Indian curtsied with liquid grace, then gestured toward an enormous silver maple that shaded the north edge of the cabin. Several chairs and a table board on trestles perched beneath the tree. On the table, a sweating earthen jug and a brace of tankards promised something cold to drink.

Clemency offered a smile. "Mollyocket, this looks delightful."

The Indian glided toward the table, and Clemency discreetly studied her through lowered lashes. Tiny strands of silver threaded Mollyocket's braids, and fine lines webbed her eyes. Pockmarks—testimony to a battle won against smallpox—scarred her face, but she was still a handsome woman. Clemency felt a small pang. Did Jamie find his daughter's nursemaid attractive?

Elizabeth scampered ahead and grabbed for the damp jug. " 'Tis special cider," she said. "Molly puts herbs in it." The jug was out of reach, so she snatched a corn cake from its pewter platter.

"Elizabeth!" Clemency admonished. Mollyocket lightly smacked the little girl's hand and pinned her with a dark stare. Elizabeth had the grace to blush and drop the cake.

Hugh leaned back in his chair, yanked up a stalk of grass and chewed on the end. "More spoiled ever' day, I say. Ye're supposed to wait for yer *athair,* me lass."

Elizabeth jumped from one foot to another. "Let's go get Da, Mistress Cam'ron."

"Nay, ye brazen toe-rag," Hugh said. "Sit wi' me and learn some manners. Mistress Cameron will fetch your da." He poured cider into a tankard and handed it to Clemency, then cast her a meaningful look. "Go 'round the cabin and follow the path through the trees. Jamie's in Robert's field."

Clemency sauntered off, her placid expression masking the excitement that raced through her veins. She wanted to jump up and down like Elizabeth!

The path headed uphill to a fringe of graceful birches bisected by a rough stone wall. Careful not to spill the cider, Clemency hoisted her skirts and clambered over the rocks. She hurried through the arched alley of birches, then halted at the edge of Robert's land.

A field rolled away before her, down to the palisade of dark balsams which encircled Robert's cabin and the lakeshore. Jamie stood in profile halfway across the field, rhythmically scything the waist-high grass. The scythe's long, curved blade flashed in the sun, and Jamie's auburn hair, pulled back and bound with a leather thong, glowed like broken embers. He was shirtless, and his muscular arms tightened and relaxed, tightened and relaxed with each swing of the scythe. Sweat trickled in little rivulets from his broad chest to his narrow waist and had soaked the top of his snug breeches.

She was about to call his name when he turned away. Afternoon sun gilded his skin, highlighting his rippling muscles and the sleek indentation of his spine. She flinched, aghast, and her fingers convulsed with the urge to touch, to heal.

Jamie's back was brindled with the jagged scar tissue of a brutal whipping.

She pressed a hand to her stomach. Oh, darling Jamie. Who could have tortured him so?

Still unaware of her presence, Jamie dropped the scythe. He tucked his hands to the small of his back, arched his spine, and twisted side to side. Then he wiped a hand across his brow and gazed out over the lake. A light breeze kissed the sun-dazzled water and whispered through the meadow, and an expression of deep serenity flickered across his face.

Turning, he stretched his hands out at his sides, palms down, then brushed them lightly over the tasseled tops of the grass. She held her breath as he drifted toward her through the rippling gold, his eyes fixed on the swaying stalks. His hands glided back and forth, trailing slowly, slowly, as if charming and caressing a great unseen presence.

He entered the birches' shade, looked up and saw her. He stopped short, his face half in shadow, his hands still resting on the waving grass. His eyes darkened, blue as heart-flame. A slow pulse began to pound at the base of her jaw. She struggled to speak, to escape from the spell of his gaze before it consumed her. Just as she thought her fluttering heart would burst, he held out his hand, as if inviting her into his daydream.

She stepped forward, and promptly tripped over a tree branch. The tankard flew from her hand. Cider sloshed down her shift and trickled between her breasts. "Blast!" she snapped. She grabbed for the tankard, bit back another oath, then staggered upright. Jamie's rapt expression dissolved into amusement.

"Clemency, *mo druidh,* how kind of ye to *drop* by." He grinned, white teeth glinting. He picked up the tankard with one hand and reached out to help her with the other. She batted it away.

"James Maclean, don't you dare tease me."

He arched his brows, widened his eyes and tried to look innocent. "Tease ye? After ye made the *trip* all the way out here to see me?" A naughty grin twitched the corners of his mouth.

She raised her chin and tried to sound haughty. "Sir, the pun is the lowest form of humor, and yours aren't even funny."

"Aye, weel—I'm funnier in Gaelic," he said abstractedly, peering into the half-empty tankard. His expression was so woebegone she burst out laughing.

"I'm sorry I spilled it. There's more back at the cabin."

"In the meantime I willna let this go to waste." He tilted his head and lifted the tankard to his lips.

Clemency stopped mere inches from his bare chest. She inhaled, savoring the musky, masculine scent of his body mingled with the tang of fresh-cut hay. She ran her eyes down his throat, visually caressing the powerful width of his shoulders and the shadowed hollow beneath his collarbone. The skin on the underside of his massive tanned biceps was pale and tender, and fresh perspiration clung to the red-gold curls on his chest. She bit her lip and wriggled her toes, entranced by the way his sculpted stomach muscles moved up and down as he breathed. He was so utterly, perfectly male. . . .

She heard a low chuckle and looked up. Jamie's slanted blue eyes sparkled with devilry. "Ye're staring, *mo druidh.* Have ye never seen a man without his sark?" He rolled his *r*s like loaded dice. Then he winked and flashed her a captivating grin. A blush singed across her cheeks. She wanted to reprimand him for his impudence, but his elfin charm disarmed her.

"I've seen lots of men without their shirts," she retorted. "You're just the first one who's been healthy."

He threw back his head and laughed, then took her elbow. "Come then, *dotair*. We best go find my sark before ye're overcome."

They collected Jamie's shirt from the front porch of Robert's cabin, then raced down to the lakeshore. The sun reclined on the hills to the west, and the water shimmered like sapphires set in gold. Tiny wavelets lapped against the rocks, making a rhythmic glugging sound, and the birch leaves fluttered like silver coins in the breeze.

Clemency could feel Jamie standing close behind her, but she fixed her attention on a sleek black bird that had just popped out of the water. The bird's head glistened like jet, his bill was long and pointed, and his ebony-and-white body gleamed. Moments later, a second bird bobbed up in the center of the lake, then dove back under the water. Clemency held her breath. How long could it stay down? Just as she was about to jump out of her skin with worry, the second bird surfaced inches from the first, a tiny silver fish clasped in his bill. He offered the fish to his mate, who ate it in one greedy gulp. She and Jamie watched in silence, and it seemed to Clemency that a strange new emotion shimmered between them. The sun lowered, the breeze died, and the birds touched bills and floated on the peaceful water.

"They're loons." Jamie's voice was husky. "Ye should hear them at night. They have a wild, cackling cry that'll raise the hair on your neck. If a man's out of his mind, folk around here call him 'loony,' after the bird." His eyes sought hers, and he disarmed her with a deep blue gaze. "Loons mate for life, ye ken."

Clemency's pulse began a slow, languid pound. Now, what did he mean by that?

No. She wasn't going to waste this moment worrying about what was going on in that enigmatic Scottish mind. The afternoon was too perfect. She stepped away from him, stretched out her arms and twirled in a circle, skirts flaring around her ankles.

"Oh, Jamie, 'tis so peaceful here, so beautiful. 'Tis like a dream come true. This is what I've always wanted—a place of my own where I can be safe and happy, and loved."

Jamie's handsome face took on a queer expression. He bent down and unlaced his worn leather brogues, then stripped off his gray woolen stockings. "I'm verra sorry ye lost Robert. He would have made ye a fine husband." He stepped around the slick, mossy stones and waded out into the lake.

"Robert loved this farm verra much," he continued, his voice suspiciously neutral. "It pleased him to think of ye living here. He never made a will, ye ken, and of course the property is Samuel's now, but I think Robert would have wanted ye to have it."

He splashed about, and Clemency stared at his muscular buttocks, which his tight homespun breeches revealed to perfection. What was he trying to tell her? Oh, how could she think with his alluring backside distracting her? She closed her eyes.

"Jamie? Do . . . do you think I could live here anyway? 'Tis bad for a building to sit empty, and I could work the fields for Samuel. I don't want anything but what I'd need to live on, and some space for an herb garden."

Jamie swung around to face her, and she rushed on. "I lived alone after Granny Amais died. I'm very self-sufficient; I could support myself. Already half the townfolk have asked me to physic them. I delivered Rachel Hammond of a son two nights ago when the doctor couldn't get here from York. Mr. Hammond gave me six eggs and a pound of sugar as a fee. That's more than most male doctors made back in Devon.''

He slowly waded toward her, back-lit by the golden sun, radiant as a Viking god. His indigo eyes did not look amused.

"Please, Jamie!'' Oh, it hurt to plead with any man, least of all this imperious Highlander. ''I hate it at Samuel's. Lydia's a vindictive old cat and—''

''That's enough, Clemency. Ye mustna say such things about your kin.'' He towered over her, then lifted his strong chin so he could glare more sternly down that long nose of his.

''But—''

''No buts. They were verra kind to take ye in after Robert died.'' His expression softened, but his voice was still iron-firm. ''I should never have put ideas in your head about living here. Robert may have wanted ye to have the farm, but it belongs to Samuel now.''

''Jamie, listen—''

''Ye're not even seventeen, and a maiden to boot. 'Tis no' proper for ye to live alone. I know Lydia can be harsh, but ye must abide.'' He patted her on the shoulder as though she were a petulant child. ''As bonny as ye are, ye'll have another man asking to wed ye soon enough.'' Hope bounded through her, and she caught her breath. Could he possibly mean himself? ''Giles Bryant, for instance. Hugh told me—''

''James Maclean, you stop right there. You are not my kinsman and you have nothing to say about my life.''

Oh, how could she have hoped? Fool. She should have known better. She itched to wipe that self-satisfied smile off Jamie's aristocratic face. Stubborn, smug Scottish. . . . ''Giles Bryant, indeed! And why are you and that rickety gillie gossiping about who may or may not want to marry me? You're as bad as two old fishwives.''

She glared up at Jamie's kind, pitying face. An awful thought flashed through her mind, and she flinched. *Pity.*

That was all he felt for her. When he spoke of her marrying, he clearly didn't consider himself a candidate. Tears choked her throat, and she bit her lip. She would not cry.

She took a deep breath and drew herself up to her full height. *Faint heart never won the field.* "I'll never marry," she spat. "Men bring nothing but grief and heartache and trouble!" Hadn't her mother always said so?

And didn't you learn that lesson the hard way? This time it wasn't her granny's voice, but her own memory that spoke.

Jamie chose this inopportune moment to laugh. "Ye say so now, *mo druidh,* but wait and see. Ye'll be hankerin' to wed by summer's end." He chuckled and bent down to retrieve his brogues.

"Jamie Maclean—"

"Aye?" He blandly arched a brow.

"Just . . . just leave me alone!"

She whirled and raced up the hill as fast as three petticoats and imprisoning stays would allow. She couldn't bear going back to his cabin and sitting through refreshments and polite conversation. She couldn't bear looking at his devilishly handsome, blithely taunting face for another moment! Hoisting her skirts to her knees, she plunged into the woods, ignoring the sound of Jamie's feet pounding after her.

Chapter Seven

Clemency cupped the burning splinter of fat pine and bent to light the strips of birch bark under the dye pot. The dry oak kindling caught with a *whoosh;* then she fanned the fire until it blazed. Although it was only six o'clock in the morning, sweat crawled down the back of her neck and dampened her petticoats until they clung to her legs. She kicked peevishly at a piece of kindling. Leave it to Lydia to dye wool during a heat wave.

She wiped beads of perspiration from her forehead and glanced at the path leading into the woods. It had been two days since her embarrassing little argument with Jamie. Her cheeks burned as she recalled her childish behavior. No wonder Jamie didn't take her seriously. A proper healer never lost her temper—but then most healers weren't provoked by stubborn, smug, *infuriating* Highlanders.

She pouted and lit the second fire. Jamie must be taking her at her word, for neither he nor Hugh had sauntered down the path since her little tantrum. The only person who had appeared out of the forest was Mollyocket. At dawn this morning she had arrived to help with the household chores so Lydia and Clemency could dye wool.

Clemency strode across the yard toward the kitchen just as Lydia shot out the back door and vomited into the holly-hocks.

"Are you all right?" Clemency lightly touched the older woman's elbow.

A greenish tinge leached from Lydia's cheeks, and she nodded. "Fine. 'Twas bad meat at supper last night, I reckon." She hurried inside before Clemency could ask more questions.

All morning the two women steeped the roots, plants and bark which made up the dyes: madder for red, sassafras for yellow, maple bark for brown, and sorrel for black. Mollyocket scrubbed the floor and pounded corn for samp, and it quickly became clear that she didn't relish working for Lydia. She broke one of Lydia's prized green glass bottles and emptied the chamber pots outside the back door instead of down the privy.

After the noon meal, Clemency picked burdocks and dung from the sheared wool while Lydia greased the fluffy fleece and tossed it into crocheted dye bags. Mollyocket slipped outside with Lydia's three sons. Within moments screeches and laughter exploded from the backyard.

"What on earth?" Clemency said, bounding up. She and Lydia rushed outside.

Two barn cats writhed in the dusty kitchen yard, cater-wauling and scratching like frenzied demons. A leather thong bound the poor creatures together by their tails. Mollyocket and the three boys giggled and looked smug.

"Oh, the poor things!" Clemency leaned down and cap-tured the two cats, then untied the thong. "For shame." She pinned Lydia's sons with an angry glare. "How could you be so cruel? Ow!" The orange tabby tomcat slashed her hand.

"Mollyocket, take the boys swimming," Lydia ordered. She scowled and shooed the terrorized cats. The Indian and her charges slipped away toward the lake.

"Aren't you going to reprimand the boys?" Clemency asked.

"Faith, 'twas Mollyocket put them up to it. She should be punished, not them."

Clemency opened her mouth to protest, but Lydia had already returned to the stifling kitchen. Clemency trailed after her and sank down in front of the seemingly endless pile of wool. Curiosity got the better of her. "Does Mollyocket work for Jamie?"

Lydia appraised her with cold eyes as her fingers greased the wool. "No more than she works for the rest of us, if you can call what she does working."

"Where did she come from?"

Lydia sighed as if the very thought of Mollyocket was unbearably irksome. "As far as we know, she's an Abenaki. They were all over Maine seventy or eighty years ago, but most died of smallpox. A few, like Mollyocket, still hang about, begging or selling roots and herbs. She has skill in that area. You two should get along." Her upper lip curled in a faint sneer. Clemency ignored it.

"Doesn't she have a family?"

"Robert told me she's a widow. Her husband—if indeed they were married—was a French-Canadian trapper. He drowned when his canoe overturned in the spring runoff on the Androscoggin." Lydia snatched up a fresh handful of wool, and her face took on an expression of perverse triumph. "She can't talk, you know."

"She doesn't speak English?"

"No, she understands English well enough. I mean she can't talk. She had her tongue cut out when she was a girl."

Open mouthed, Clemency dropped a handful of fleece and leaned forward. "Are you jesting?"

"Not at all. Ask her to show you some time." Lydia's tone was unconcerned, and Clemency itched to shake her.

"That's horrible! 'Tis a wonder she didn't bleed to death, or starve." Clemency paused, trying to comprehend such barbarity. "How did it happen?"

"No one knows for sure, but Mr. MacIntosh, the peddler, told me she was charged with witchcraft in Massachusetts. That must have been . . ." Lydia tapped a decayed front tooth with a bony long finger. "Oh, twenty-five years ago, at least. There wasn't much evidence, so the magistrate let her go, but not before ordering her tongue cut out."

Clemency gnawed the inside of her lip. While on board the *Golden Eagle,* Captain Reed had regaled her with tales of the Salem witch trials. But that had been decades ago. Surely no one was accused of witchcraft these days. Her stomach shifted. Many of the Salem accused had been midwives and healers.

She straightened her spine and snatched up another handful of fleece. "That's the most appalling thing I ever heard."

Lydia arched an eyebrow. "Faith, 'tis a lot better than hanging. That's still the punishment for witchcraft, you know."

A burdock pricked Clemency's thumb. She pulled it out with her teeth, then sucked at the bright spot of blood. "How did Mollyocket come to live here?"

"Blame Robert for that. After her husband died, she and her baby roamed around until she showed up on my doorstep, filthy and reeking of bear grease. Her baby was sick. I feared my sons would catch the disease, so I turned her out. She wandered up to Robert's cabin and stayed. She's been around ever since, doing this and that, sleeping wherever she can find a spot. Mostly she stayed with Robert, though. He was so taken with her he even taught her to read and write."

Lydia's tone was insinuating, and Clemency felt a twinge

of uneasiness. Had Robert been involved in some way with the Indian? She stirred the madder root dye, then set her jaw. She wouldn't give Lydia's cattiness an opening.

"What happened to Mollyocket's baby?" she asked.

Lydia stood, briskly brushing wool from her skirt. "It died."

The evening sky gleamed like polished pewter as Clemency wearily climbed the stairs to her attic bedchamber. Behind her Samuel and Lydia slouched at the kitchen table, a jug of rum between them. Samuel's disheveled shirt lay open at the throat, and the skin on his scrawny neck was flushed.

"Come back and have a drink, Clem'cy!" he called.

"Hush, you id'jut." Lydia's voice slurred.

Clemency sped up the stairs. She had never seen Lydia drunk, and she didn't intend to start now.

She checked on the sleeping boys, then slipped into her chamber. She stopped dead. Mollyocket lay curled in Clemency's bed, clad only in her shift. The Indian's eyes were tightly closed, but her erratic breathing signaled that she wasn't asleep. Clemency hesitated a long moment, then undid the drawstring on her skirt. No doubt this was what Lydia meant about Mollyocket sleeping wherever she found a spot.

She wriggled out of her skirt and petticoats, unlaced her bodice and stays, then heaved a sigh of relief as her lungs expanded for the first time all day. Unlike most women, she refused to sleep with whalebone pinching her skin. She unpinned her hair, then ran her fingers through the long black waves, sighing as her headache eased. Now, if Samuel would stop his blasted drunken singing, she could get some sleep at last.

She perched on the edge of the bed and eyed Mollyocket.

"Are you awake?" she whispered. The Indian's eyelids twitched but didn't open. "I . . . I wanted to tell you I'm sorry about what happened to you. I mean, about your baby dying." She took a deep breath, then lay down.

Clemency's eyes flew open. Mollyocket's arm jerked against hers, muscles tensed and trembling. A grotesque shadow leaped and writhed on the wall opposite the doorway; then Lydia staggered into the room. She clutched a candle and Samuel's riding crop.

"I said *get up,* you filthy redskin savage!" Lydia lurched forward and slammed the candle on the bedside table, then swiped a pale hank of hair from her eyes. The neckline of her shift sagged off her shoulder, and one melonlike breast popped free. Clemency scrambled up. "Get out of my way!" Lydia snarled.

"What on earth are you doing?" Clemency cried. Lydia shoved her aside, and she gasped as the stench of rum and decayed teeth hit her.

"Tha' savage stole my silver chafin' dish, maybe with your help, you English huzzy." Lydia's blue-marble eyes bulged. She grabbed Mollyocket's ankle and dragged her off the bed. The Indian clawed at the bedclothes and gave a guttural moan.

"Stop it, Lydia! You're drunk. Mollyocket didn't steal anything." Clemency tugged at Lydia's arm, trying to free the Indian's leg. Lydia lashed out and slapped Clemency with all her strength.

"Ohhh!" Clemency staggered back and pressed her hand to her face.

Lydia grabbed the back of Mollyocket's shift and yanked. The fabric tore with a *rrrrp!* Clemency gasped. Horrible weals crisscrossed the Indian's back. Lydia twisted Mollyocket's arm and forced her to her knees, then pushed her forward until she sprawled over the bed. She raised the riding crop and slashed down. Mollyocket groaned.

Clemency whirled and raced downstairs, taking the steps two at a time.

Samuel lolled on the settle, snoring softly. She grabbed his arm and shook it. "Samuel! Wake up!"

His eyes rolled. "Wha'?"

She snatched the jug of rum and sloshed it in his face. He staggered up like a crazed bear. "What'd ye do that for! Wastin' good rum—"

Another screech knifed down the stairs, and the boys wailed, "Mama? Mama!"

Clemency reached up, grasped Samuel's ear and twisted. His hazel eyes popped wide. "Listen to me," she snapped. "Lydia's drunk. She's beating Mollyocket and scaring your sons half to death. You get up those stairs and call her off or so help me I'll tell your wife and every soul in town about your wandering hands."

Samuel jerked away and rubbed his ear. "Aw right, aw right. No harm meant. Lydia beats that Injun ever' chance she gets." He turned and shuffled up the stairs, Clemency on his heels.

He staggered into the bedchamber and caught Lydia's arm on the upswing. "That's enough. Ye're scarin' the boys."

Lydia cursed and clawed at his face. "Get off me, you drunk sot!"

Samuel crushed his wife's arms to her sides and dragged her into the hall. Her oaths and shrieks rang down the stairwell.

Clemency snatched up the candle and swiftly examined Mollyocket's back. Several of the old weals had burst open, and blood oozed down the Indian's dark skin.

"Oh, you poor thing." She helped Mollyocket into a sitting position. "Can you walk?"

Mollyocket nodded. Clemency pulled up the Indian's torn shift and swiftly tied the lacing. Mollyocket winced.

"I'm sorry to hurt you, but we've got to get out of here." Clemency stood and grabbed their skirts and bodices. "Here, I'll help you get dressed."

Minutes later, they slipped out the kitchen door, then scurried up the path to Robert's cabin. Clemency set her jaw and dragged Mollyocket behind her. Roots and rocks tripped her, whiplike branches scratched her arms and an enormous spider web raked her cheek. She gasped with disgust and clawed at the sticky silk. Thank God and the Holy Mother there was a moon, or they would likely stagger into a bear trap.

They hurried on, starting and glancing back at every strange sound. Clemency's eyes adjusted to the darkness, and she saw the fork in the path ahead. The left fork would take them to Jamie's cabin, the right to Robert's. Unsure what to do, she stopped. Mollyocket plowed into her. Clemency shot her a questioning look and nodded to the left fork. Mollyocket grunted, shook her head and pulled Clemency in the other direction.

"Good decision," Clemency whispered. "Jamie would just pat us on the head and send us back to Lydia."

After what seemed like an eternity, they stumbled into the clearing in front of Robert's empty cabin. Moonlight streamed across the hayfield, limning the spruces with silver and reflecting off the black surface of the lake. Without a sound, Mollyocket turned and crept into the cabin.

Clemency followed the Indian inside and watched her curl up on Robert's bare mattress. The cabin was unbearably stuffy, and after a moment Clemency longed to sink into the lake's cool, mirrored waters. She touched the Indian's arm. "Mollyocket? Don't you want me to wash your back?"

Mollyocket grunted and waved her away.

"Are you sure?" She hovered until Molly angrily shook

her head. "All right, I'm going for a swim, then. There's no way I can sleep now."

She slipped into the silver night and ran down to the water. Dizzying excitement pumped through her veins. She raised her arms, let out a cry of joy and twirled in a circle. Free at last! And no one—not Samuel, not Lydia, and most certainly not Jamie Maclean—was going to tie her down again.

Jamie couldn't sleep. It was a lifelong problem, born from the duty and burdens of being the laird's brother, worsened by the bitter betrayal he had suffered at Culloden, and strengthened by the passing years. Whenever he had a problem, his mind gave him no peace until he found a way to fix things.

He closed his eyes against the silvery moonlight and took another sip of whisky—real Scots whisky imported by his friend, Sir Andrew Pepperrell. The rich, peaty aroma seduced his nose, and he inhaled slowly, luxuriating in the smoky vapors. He leaned back on his elbows, crossed his long legs and stared out over the moonlit field. This spot—at the top of the hill between his land and Robert's—was his favorite place to hide when he needed to sort things out. Sighing, he lay back in the dewy grass and stared up at the starry sky. Clemency would love it here.

The thought startled him so badly he almost spilled his drink. Then he shook his head and chuckled. Why should he be surprised to think of Clemency? She—green-eyed enchantress that she was—was the reason he had lain awake the last two nights. He frowned and shifted his shoulders, trying to find a comfortable position on the hard ground. He never should have mentioned Robert the other day, never should have brought up the farm. But how was he to know she would want to live there? And alone, no less.

His mouth twitched, and he pinched the bridge of his nose

with thumb and forefinger. Och, why was he surprised? He should have known such a headstrong lass would stir up trouble. He sat up and took another sip of whisky. The question was, what had she stirred up in him?

A call echoed off the lake, and he froze. Someone was at Robert's.

His hand instinctively closed around the dirk in his belt, and he considered collecting his gun from his cabin. But there were only twenty families in the area; he knew them all. The worst he was likely to find was some young buck out to show his lass the moon—and a few other things. With a soft chuckle, he stood and took a swig of whisky, then sauntered off down the field, dew-spangled grass whipping his thighs.

He had almost reached the cabin when a movement in the lake caught his eye. Someone was out for a moonlight swim. He could see the person's head, sleek and dark, gliding through the water a short distance from shore. He was about to call out when his gaze fell on a stunted spruce at the lake's rocky edge. A lady's petticoats and shift—and a familiar blue-and-white sprigged skirt—hung from its branches.

He stared down at his brogues and rubbed two fingers between his brows. Laughter rumbled in his chest. Och, this was too rich—and a sore moral dilemma. As a gentleman, he knew he should turn right around and go home. But by St. Columba, the temptation to tease that saucy, headstrong Sassenach was more than a body could bear. He heard a splash from the lake and glanced up. The decision was made. She had seen him—and he was entranced.

Clemency's long black hair lay sleek against her shoulders, and her skin glowed like pale fire in the moonlight. He stood close enough to see her full lips part in surprise, but her eyes—those green, magic, witch's eyes—lay in shadow. Silvery black water covered her nipples, framing the lush curves of her breasts and the delicious dark cleft between them.

A shaft of desire shot through him, and an urgent heat began to throb in his loins. What had he gotten himself into? He should leave—*now*. The temptation to tease had been vanquished by a temptation of quite another sort.

At last she moved, ducking down until the black water rose to her chin. "Ja . . . Jamie?" she whispered. Her teeth chattered, and he recalled how cold the lake was, even on the hottest days. He was about to reassure her and walk away with his dignity intact when she spoke again.

"James Maclean, I took you for a gentleman. Ha! Some gentleman—spying on a lady while she's . . . while she's—"

"Swimming naked in the middle of the night?" He ran a shaky hand over his mouth and tried to wipe away his grin. Truly, he shouldn't provoke her.

"How dare you sneak up and watch me? You're nothing but a"—she opened and closed her luscious mouth, obviously trying to think up a word bad enough for him—"a mangy moose!"

He threw his head back and roared with laughter. "A moose, am I? I see ye've finally learned a few of our local creatures." He deliberately rolled his *r*s, knowing it provoked her.

He sauntered to the spruce and snatched up her bodice, then dangled it tauntingly over the water. He slanted her his most devilish grin. "Weel, now. Would ye care to explain why ye're cavortin' naked in the lake when all good lassies are home in bed?" In bed. His manhood gave a longing throb. St. Columba, he had better get that thought right out of his mind.

She huffed and opened her mouth, no doubt to make another retort. He pretended to drop the bodice in the water. "Oh, Jamie, please don't," she gasped. She took a deep breath, then flashed her dimpled smile, the one she used when she wanted to charm people. "I'm sorry I called you a moose—although with those long legs, you do rather resemble one. Please go away and let me get out of this water. I'm freezing."

He chuckled softly. She was so like Elizabeth: willful and spoiled, yet irresistible, even when he knew she was charming him just to get her own way.

"Why didna ye say so sooner, *mo maise?* I'm not a monster, ye ken." He draped the bodice on the branch, suddenly noticing how small it was, how smooth the fine muslin. His fingers twitched and his erection surged. Och, he must contain himself. "But I'm no' leaving 'til ye tell me what ye're doing here in the middle of the night. I'll go up to the cabin and close the door. When ye're dressed, we'll talk, aye?"

"But, Jamie—"

"No buts, woman." He turned on his heel and strolled to the cabin, discreetly rearranging the unwieldy bulge in his breeks. He shook his head and grinned ruefully. He was only flesh and blood, after all. He had almost reached the door when he heard a splash and cry of pain. Whirling, he saw Clemency crumple onto the slippery bank.

He reached her in an instant. She had already donned her shift, and the thin linen clung to her skin, revealing more than it concealed. He lowered his gaze to her breasts. They were full and ripe, tipped with nipples as dusky and enticing as wild grapes. Her long black hair clung around them, and he had a sudden vision of holding her down by that hair, holding her down and. . . . Sweet weakness washed over him, and he dared not look any lower. Och, it had been so long, so long since he had lain with a woman.

"What happened?" he demanded, more sharply than he intended.

"I slipped putting on my petticoat." Her voice was almost meek, and her brows drew together in obvious pain.

"Are ye hurt?" He stroked her shoulder, unsure what to do.

"I think I twisted my ankle." She struggled up, then swayed toward him. "Ow! I definitely twisted my ankle."

His hands steadied her while his eyes devoured her body. Her shift hugged every enticing curve. As if mimicking the moonlight, the damp linen clung to her tiny waist and flaring hips, barely concealing the dark V at the juncture of her thighs. His heart thundered and his manhood tightened. He bit his lip, held his breath and took her elbow as she tried to hop up the bank. On the second hop she fell against him.

"Och, this is ridiculous," he murmured. He bent down and snatched her up with one swoop. She squeaked in surprise; then her arms encircled his neck. Her sweet breath warmed his ear, and he felt the cold wetness of her shift seep through his sark, cooling his burning skin. He turned his head a fraction, and her damp hair pressed against his cheek. She smelled of lake water and fresh hay and raw woman.

She drew a ragged little sigh and rested against him like a child, docile and trusting. He brushed his lips against her cool forehead. "What's wrong, *mo cridhe?*"

" 'Tis Lydia and Samuel. Oh, Jamie . . ." She trembled in his arms, and he grew worried.

"Tell me."

"They were drunk. Samuel gets drunk most nights, but this time Lydia did, too. She . . . she beat Mollyocket. She whipped her, Jamie, and she's done it before—there are weals all over Molly's back."

His arms tightened around her, and he felt the muscle in his cheek begin to jump. Clemency lifted her head from his shoulder and tried to look in his eyes. "Jamie, I saw your back. You of all people should know what 'tis like—"

"Aye, I ken," he snapped. Oh, he knew, all right. Whipping had seared his soul with a helplessness and degradation worse than any pain. But he would have his revenge. One day, the vile Sassenach who had whipped him—who had destroyed his clan and stolen his heritage—one day, that man would know the shame of whipping.

He could feel her heartbeat against his chest. "I'm sorry, Jamie," she whispered, "but you must understand that Molly and I can't go back, no matter what. I can't let another person be so abused."

Her breast pressed against his arm, and the remnants of his reason vanished. He carried her to the cabin, then set her down on the rough log bench on Robert's porch. Scowling fiercely, he knelt before her and ran his hands down her bare leg, checking for injury. Her skin felt like living satin, and he clenched his jaw, fighting the thrill that threatened to engulf him. He manipulated her swelling ankle. She gasped; then her eyes burned into his. They were the smoky green of Loch Linnhe on a rainy afternoon.

With a ragged sigh, he reached up and stroked the velvet curve of her cheek. "Ye willna have to go back, *mo cridhe*. I promise."

She caught his hand and cupped it to her cheek. "Thank you, Jamie. Once again you've rescued me." Her voice caught, and his heart turned over. Och, he wanted her. He had wanted her from that first moment on the docks when her lips had parted under his. But he could never allow passion to ensnare him again. He tugged his hand away.

Her brows contracted. Then she tossed him that dimpled, spoiled-little-girl smile. "What does *mo maise* mean?"

He sat back on his heels and tried to look stern. "It means 'my beauty,' ye wee imp."

She giggled—a delicious sound that made him long to turn her over his knee and tickle her until she squealed. Then he wanted to strip that flimsy shift from her body, bury his face in the musky sweetness between her thighs, thrust his hardness into her again and again—

Her voice jerked him back to reality. "What does *mo cridhe* mean?"

His smile vanished. After an agonizing moment he stood, hands clenched into fists. He couldn't do this to Clemency. It was wrong, unfair, *unfaithful*. "Never mind," he whispered hoarsely. Then he turned and strode into the night.

Chapter Eight

Something was tickling her leg.

Clemency opened one eye and gazed muzzily at the scaly log walls. The ticking mattress on which she lay smelled of moldering corn husks, and strong, late-morning sunlight lanced through one bare window. What time was it? And why on earth was she sleeping in her skirt and bodice?

The tickle came again, and a hairy brown wolf spider, big as a field mouse, scuttled up her bare calf. She shrieked, batted it away and leaped up, landing on her sore ankle. The spider hit the wall with a solid splat, her ankle buckled and pain scorched through her. She scrambled back onto the bed, oblivious to her ankle's throbbing ache, and frantically scanned the room for a weapon. Holy Mary, Mother of God, she hated spiders!

"Here now, lassie. What's all the grumplin'?" Hugh opened the cabin door a crack and peered in nervously, as if afraid he might catch her undressed.

"Oh, Hugh, thank God. There's a cow-sized spider in here. Please come kill it."

Chuckling, the burly Highlander stomped over the threshold. "Let me at the wee beastie." He blithely squashed the offending arachnid under his brogue, then sketched a bow. "A pleasure to serve ye, madam."

Clemency swung her legs over the edge of the bed, then stood, gingerly testing her bad ankle. Nothing was broken, and she had wrapped it securely before going to sleep last night. It was sore, but it would be better in a day or two. She cast Hugh a chagrined smile. "I guess Jamie told you that Mollyocket and I took up residence here last night."

"He didna have the chance. Mollyocket was knockin' on the door before daybreak."

"Mollyocket? What did she want?"

Hugh reached for a bucket and a tiny iron shovel, then began cleaning ashes from the fireplace. "Weel, I guess I'll ha' to tell ye, since she isna here."

"Tell me what?"

A cloud of ash sifted through the air, and he sneezed. "As the Good Book says, ye're aboot to reap what ye've sowed." He lifted the full bucket, then carried it outside.

"Hugh Rankin, stop this instant. What are you talking about?" She hobbled after him, sorely tempted to behave like Elizabeth and tug at his kilt.

He tossed the ashes into a hollowed-out log. "Why, Robert made a will after all, lass. Seems he told Samuel and Lydia he wanted ye to ha' the farm, but he didna trust 'em wi' his deathbed wish. Since Jamie and I were off fetchin' ye, and poor Molly canna speak, he decided to write it doon. He was canny, was Rabbie."

A will. Clemency's heart began to thud. Oh saints be praised, Robert truly had meant for the farm to be hers. She could be independent at last! Then Lydia's pinched face flashed through her mind. Clemency raised her chin and folded her arms across her bosom. "Do you mean to tell me that Samuel and Lydia knew Robert wanted me to have the farm, and they lied about it?''

Hugh opened his mouth to reply, then closed it as Molly-ocket materialized at the edge of the clearing. The Indian nodded to Clemency, then turned and beckoned. Giles Bryant and Rufus Hammond stepped out of the woods, carrying Clemency's trunk between them.

"What on earth?" Clemency bobbed a shaky curtsy. *Blast this ankle!* "Mr. Bryant, Mr. Hammond. Good morrow to you." The two men dropped the trunk and bowed.

"Good morrow, Mistress Cameron," Rufus Hammond said. "Mr. Maclean came by this morning and asked if I would help Giles deliver your trunk." Rufus was as dark as Mollyocket, and painfully thin. Clemency had delivered his wife of a fine, fat son less than a week ago.

"Thank you, sir." She gave her visitors a bright smile as her mind began to whirl. Why had Jamie asked them to deliver her trunk, and where the devil was he? Off sulking no doubt. Irritation spurted through her, and her smile faded. Why on earth had he stalked off last night? It wasn't as though she had slapped him. In truth, for one wild moment she would have given him anything he had cared to take. "How fare Mistress Hammond and young Alfred?"

Rufus beamed, and Clemency warmed to the paternal love in his black eyes. "Ever so well, Mistress Cameron, thanks to you."

Giles Bryant cleared his throat. "Is there anything else I can do for you, Mistress Cameron? Fetch some wood, perhaps?" He blushed to the roots of his thick, sandy hair. "Oh, I almost forgot. Mother said she would call on you this afternoon. Yesterday was her baking day. She's bringing you some bread—"

"And I would be honored to send along some cornmeal and vegetables from my garden. 'Tis the least I can do to show my appreciation for the safe delivery of my son.''

Rufus bowed again. "Now, if you will please excuse us, we must go. I know you've much to do, settling in."

Giles edged closer, cheeks lobster red. "Perhaps . . . perhaps when you're settled, Mistress Cameron . . ." His Adam's apple bobbed. "May I call upon you?"

Hugh inserted a broad, plaid-swathed shoulder between Clemency and her stuttering suitor. "Away wi' ye, lad. Mistress Cameron's mournin' her betrothed." Giles jumped back as if bitten, cast Clemency one last, adoring look, then shuffled after Rufus Hammond.

Clemency collapsed on her trunk, skirts billowing out around her. "Now will you please tell me what's going on?"

Mollyocket glided forward and handed her a smudged, wrinkled piece of parchment. Clemency searched Molly's impassive face and caught the tiniest ghost of a smile. She opened the document, and a lump rose in her throat.

It was Robert's handwriting—the dear, copperplate script that had enticed her across the ocean and given her the strength to build a new life from the ruins of her past, and her mother's. The will was short, but clear: Robert Bruce MacKinnon had willed his land, his cabin and all his possessions to his betrothed, Clemency Alexandra Cameron.

With trembling fingers, she folded the paper and pressed it to her bosom, then stared up at Hugh and Mollyocket. "But how?"

Hugh rubbed his nose, avoiding her teary eyes and quivering chin. "Mollyocket showed the will to Jamie this morning. Rabbie had asked her to hide it, ye ken. As Robert's dear friend, she just wanted to see the cut o' yer jib before she gave it to ye." He slanted the Indian a glance, then fixed Clemency with piercing blue eyes, daring her to ask further questions.

She took the hint and turned to the Indian. "Mollyocket, I can't thank you enough. I . . . I know how kind Robert was to you, and I hope we can be friends." She felt herself blush. Blast her pale skin. Why must her feelings always show on her face? "You will consider this your home as well, won't you?" Clemency gnawed the inside of her cheek. Did she truly want to live with an Indian—a savage she barely knew, a woman who may have been Robert's lover?

Don't be foolish, child. It was Granny Amais, interfering with her thoughts as always. *Take your friends where you can find them and be grateful.*

Mollyocket nodded and disappeared into the cabin.

Hugh plucked a fragment of hay from Clemency's tangled hair. "Ye look like ye've been sleepin' in the fields, lass."

"Is it that bad?" Her hands flew to her hair, and she swiftly began braiding the errant locks. "What will Mr. Bryant and Mr. Hammond think, seeing me like this?"

"Just be glad 'tis hay in yer hair and no' spiders."

She wrinkled her nose and shuddered. "Don't even think it." She finished the braid and tossed it over one shoulder. "Hugh?"

"Aye?"

"Will Lydia and Samuel dispute the will?"

He snorted and dragged her trunk onto the porch. "Nay, lass. After readin' it, Jamie lit down there like a bear on a rampage. There's nothin' like a Scot wi' his temper riled, and wi' that red hair, Jamie's worse than most. Ye could all but see the steam comin' out o' his ears."

Clemency dimpled, envisioning Jamie growling and shuffling, claws out. Then a terrible apprehension gripped her, and her smile vanished. She imagined Samuel and Lydia swooping down and turning her out of the cabin, will or no will, angry Highlander or no angry Highlander. She couldn't bear losing the farm now that she knew it was hers.

"What did Jamie say to them?" she asked.

"I wasna there, so I canna tell ye word for word, but Jamie set 'em straight. They'll no' try to get the farm from ye. 'Tis yours." Hugh's gaze darted away, and he fiddled with the lock on her trunk. "Jamie told me to come down and break the good news to ye."

The uneasiness in her stomach increased, and her ankle throbbed anew. "Why didn't he come himself?"

Hugh sighed and gave up on the trunk. "He's gone, lass. Left for Kittery. He's taken a job surveyin' up the Kennebec River for Sir Andrew Pepperrell. He could be away for months."

Jamie leaned forward and swung his long legs from the hips in the easy, ground-covering stride the colonists called "shank's mare." It was early afternoon, and he had already walked half the distance to Kittery. At this rate he would be at Sir Andrew's Kittery Point mansion by sunset.

Sir Andrew Pepperrell was the richest man in the Province of Maine, and next to Robert, he had long been Jamie's closest friend. He had inherited his fortune and title from his father, Sir William, who had received a baronetcy for his service to England during the French and Indian War.

Sir Andrew was also an accomplished musician, and Jamie imagined they would spend the evening sitting in his elegant parlor overlooking the sea, sipping whisky and playing music to the Atlantic's applauding whitecaps.

Normally the thought of seeing his friend and sharing a bawdy, whisky-drenched song or two warmed Jamie's blood and quickened his pace. But not today. He ran a hand over his stubbly chin. Today nothing could put him in a good mood—not the dappled sun filtering through the trees, not the frosting of Queen Anne's lace gracing the roadside, not even the intoxicating scent of sun-baked pine needles.

He paused and inhaled. The warm, balsam scent of the woods reminded him of Clemency: rich and mellow and enough to make a man long to lie down and spend himself in her luxurious embrace. He swallowed. St. Columba, he had to get a hold of himself. That headstrong lass had brought him nothing but aggravation—and a stiff cock—since the moment he had laid eyes on her.

He recalled her soft lips under his the day she arrived, and his knees suddenly felt weak. If he had known then how she would arouse him, he never would have made the foolish mistake of kissing her. Of course, at the time he hadn't been able to think of another way to get her out of the clutches of that damned Sassenach, Jeffries. He shoved his hands into his pockets. No doubt Clemency had led the man on. Even without overt flirtation, her beauty alone was enough to send a man off his head.

Och, he had to stop this nonsense. He bent down, snatched up a stalk of grass and chewed the end. The succulent blade reminded him of his hayfields, half-scythed, and his corn, ripe for picking. He was a fool to go charging off this time of year. His farm was bursting with life, requiring only his time and care to deliver a plentiful harvest. But those were the two things he couldn't give. Clemency and Lydia had seen to that.

Lydia. With a sound of aggravation he spat out the frayed stalk. What a tempest he had stormed into this morning, with the three MacKinnon boys keening like banshees, and Lydia and Samuel suffering from too much cheap rum. He had slapped Robert's will on the table, startling them.

"What trick do ye think ye're playing?" he thundered. "Ye knew Robert left his farm to Mistress Cameron, but ye lied to all of us. Weel, the truth is out now, and I'll see to it Mistress Cameron gets her due."

Lydia snatched up the will, scanned it and paled. "How can you betray your family this way?" she demanded. "That English whore has bewitched you. Don't think I haven't seen how she butters you up—"

"Robert was my brother," Samuel interrupted. "Ye know the farm should go to me." He blinked his enormous gray eyes rapidly, as if he expected Jamie to strike him. "He made that will when he was crazed with fever. Lydia and I meant no harm. We were just trying to do what's right.''

Jamie's stomach turned. He had always liked Samuel despite the man's weakness. Over the years he had watched his timid, fidgety friend evaporate inch by inch, absorbed by Lydia's overpowering personality, and he had often wondered if Samuel would ever stand up to his wife. It was clear he wouldn't on this issue.

"That English bitch has tried to tear this family apart from the moment she got here," Lydia spat. "Before that, even. Didn't you ever wonder why Margaret MacKinnon surfaced after all those years—after we all thought she died in the Rising? I wouldn't put it past the pair of them to be running a confidence game—"

"That's enough!" Jamie slammed his fist on the table. The startled boys scattered like quail. " 'Tis not our place to question Margaret MacKinnon or her daughter. Robert was satisfied with her story, and that's all that matters. Can ye no' see that Robert loved Mistress Cameron?''

"Loved her? He never even met her!" Lydia snorted and rolled her ice blue eyes. The gesture had always annoyed Jamie; now annoyance turned to disgust. "And what about Mollyocket? He claimed he loved her as well. Did he intend to be a bigamist?''

Jamie felt the blood drain from his face, and the muscle twitched in his cheek. "Ye'll no' malign a dead man. Robert was my best friend. Remember to whom ye speak.''

Samuel edged forward, clawing a forelock of lank brown hair from his eyes. "Jamie, even if Robert wanted it, Mistress Cameron can't live alone in that cabin. 'Tis not proper. What will people say? We must guard her reputation. If Mistress Cameron is indeed our kinswoman—"

Jamie suppressed a snort of derision. "Guarding Mistress Cameron's reputation, is it? Is that all ye want to do with her?'' He quirked an eyebrow, and Samuel had the grace to blush. "Weel then, if that's all the objections, consider it settled. Robert's farm now belongs to Mistress Cameron. And while she lives there, she will be under my protection." Lydia made a sound of protest, and he raised an accusing finger. "By St. Columba, I'll brook no more foolishness. Is that clear?" Before they could reply, he whirled and stalked out.

Halfway up the path, Lydia caught up with him. She grabbed his arm and dragged him to a stop.

"I dinna want to hear another word," Jamie said in the iciest voice he could muster. "Ye've shamed us all, and I'll no' be a part of it."

Lydia raised a hand to her throat and scanned his face. "By the good Lord, she truly has bewitched you."

"Och, stop your blethering. My only concern with Mistress Cameron is that she no' be abused by her family." He spun on his heel and strode away. Lydia trotted along beside him.

"Jamie, don't do this," she pleaded. "You can't side with that scheming adventuress."

The grim set of his mouth eased into a smile. "If Mistress Cameron's a scheming adventuress, then I'm King George."

Lydia slipped in front of him and blocked his way. "Look at you, even when you're furious your face lights up when you speak of her. She's bewitched you and you don't even know it." She grasped his arm and pressed her ample bosom against his chest. "Please, Jamie. Don't throw away what we have—"

Fury flashed through him like lightning, and his pulse accelerated until it thundered in his ears. He wrested his arm from her grasp, snatched her elbow in an iron grip and jerked her face inches from his. "There is nothing between us. *Nothing*. Do ye hear?"

"But we—"

"Never speak of it again. 'Twas a mistake. It never happened." He pushed past her, then turned back, his Scots accent as rough and wild as any ancient Gael's. ''For God's sake, Lydia, let me be!''

Even now, hours later, his bowels clenched as he recalled the scene. Lydia's words reverberated through his head until his mind reeled with the consequences of his weakness, his folly. He clenched his fists and bellowed to the heavens: ''Och, Christ, help me!''

A flock of pigeons exploded from the trees and darkened the sky over his head. One black feather drifted down and brushed his cheek with the touch of an angel's wing. He caught the feather and tucked it in his sporran. He knew only one angel—a black-haired angel, with eyes the hazy, haunting green of Loch Linnhe on a stormy afternoon.

The afternoon light had waned, and a sudden wave of longing, of homesickness, washed over him. There was only one place he wanted to be right now, and it wasn't Sir Andrew Pepperrell's fashionable front parlor. His shoulders slumped, and he closed his eyes. It would take more than music and Scots whisky to break the snare that held him fast.

Chapter Nine

"Why, look at those stitches! Lydia, I always did say you were the best hand with a needle I ever saw. My Isobel will be plum tickled to have a wedding quilt like this." Hepzibah Bryant bent over the wooden quilting frame, her long nose inches from the expanse of pieced blocks tacked to an inner layer of wool and a backing of blue muslin.

Lydia drew a languid hand across her damp brow and forced herself to smile. Hepzibah Bryant looked like an old crow pecking for seeds. "Faith, my poor efforts are nothing special, Mistress Bryant," she said. "But if I can be neighborly and help your daughter set up housekeeping, I'm happy to oblige." She stood and glanced at her three guests, willing herself not to feel dizzy in the oppressive heat. "May I offer you some refreshment?"

The women nodded. "I declare, this is the hottest August I've ever seen." Hepzibah Bryant swatted at a bloated fly and fanned her flushed cheeks with a turkey-wing fan. "What a time for a wedding."

Rachel Hammond lifted her infant son from his basket and unbuttoned her bodice. She popped a swollen nipple in the baby's gaping mouth and smiled placidly. "Any time is good for a wedding if the couple be suited and the family in agreement."

"Well, thank the good Lord we find Isobel's young man to our approval." Mistress Bryant leaned forward and stroked the baby's satiny head. "Did you ever see such a beautiful child?"

Rachel Hammond blushed. "We are most gratified with him. I don't know what I would have done if we'd lost him." She pressed a hand on the child's single damp curl. "When my travail came so quick and the doctor couldn't get here from York, I thought I would soon meet our Maker."

"Oh, the first baby's always the hardest," Mistress Bryant said airily. "Having had seven myself, I know. But you're fortunate the English girl could attend you." She licked her lips and lowered her voice. "Although I do find it scandalous that an unmarried woman is doctoring folks and delivering babies." She turned to her hostess. "Lydia, do you approve of Mistress Cameron's activities?"

Lydia steadied her hand on the rim of her sterling silver chafing dish. The witch's name alone got her blood pounding. "Approve? 'Tis hardly my position to approve or disapprove. My husband's cousin is a headstrong young woman. She'll do what she will, whether we approve or not."

She crushed sprigs of fresh mint and fantasized that it was Clemency's pale face ground under the horn spoon. The greedy, troublemaking slut. It was all her fault that Jamie had left and stayed away this whole month.

"But Mistress Bryant, didn't she physic your son Giles to good effect?" Rachel's voice was serene as she burped her son.

"Yes, and he healed right well after she attended him,

although his hand had festered for weeks before,'' Mistress Bryant said. ''She indeed has the healing touch.''

Lydia set the chafing dish on the table board behind her guests, noting the blush that crawled across Prudence Everett's face at the mention of Giles Bryant. Lydia gave a little smirk of derision. So that's how it was—another fool in love. Too bad Prudence didn't know her Giles was mooning after the English bitch.

''Why, Lydia, isn't this lovely!'' Hepzibah Bryant stuck her needle into the quilt and waddled over to the chafing dish. ''Cider with fresh mint. And what a comely bowl. Is it English?''

Lydia raised her chin. At least someone in this backwoods settlement recognized quality. ''Yes. My father gave it to me. He's a merchant in Kittery, you know. He imported it as part of my dowry.'' She ran a protective finger around the dish's engraved side. ''I thought that Indian Mollyocket made off with it the last time she cleaned for me, but it turned out the boys had taken it to play.'' She shot the ladies a tight smile. ''You know how boys are.''

Mistress Bryant poured herself a brimming tankard of cider, then sucked down a huge mouthful. ''Mmmmm. You must give me this receipt. There's something in here besides mint, I vow.''

''Mistress Cameron told me the receipt when she lived with us.'' Lydia paused long enough to ensure she had her company's attention. ''She's most knowledgeable about herbs, you know. From what I understand, her grandmother was a wise woman—always making up potions and talismans. She cured everything from warts to straying husbands to broken hearts, or so Mistress Cameron says.'' She laced her voice with innuendo, then bit her lip to keep from smirking when her barb found its target.

Her three guests widened their eyes. Prudence Everett peered into her tankard, as if expecting a frog to hop out on her nose. Rachel Hammond hastily buttoned her bodice and hugged her child to her bosom. Hepzibah Bryant snorted.

"Lydia MacKinnon, surely you're not implying—"

"I'm not implying a thing." Lydia gazed at them, eyes wide. "But doesn't it make you wonder how such a young woman got so skilled at healing? Faith, surely no proper female would be physicking men and delivering babes when she's yet a maiden. And all this strange talk about inoculation for the pox. 'Tis against God's ways . . ." She let her voice trail off. In truth, this was too easy. All she had to do was toss the stone and her meaning rippled through them like wavelets on a pond.

Rachel wrinkled her brow. "If being pricked with a needle could save my son, I might consider it, but Rufus said the Reverend Rogers would never allow it. And Rufus does wonder what Mistress Cameron is doing, living all alone in that cabin. He said 'twas not proper." Her meek voice took on conviction. "He mentioned it to Reverend Rogers, and the reverend was most displeased that a woman should disport herself so."

"Huh." Mistress Bryant pursed her lips. "She doesn't go to meeting. That's why he's displeased." She helped herself to more cider, and Lydia caught a distinct glint in her piggy eyes.

"She's a Papist. That's why she doesn't go to meeting." Lydia sat and hitched her chair closer to her neighbors. "I've always heard the Papists are fond of their heathen rituals."

Mistress Bryant snatched up her needle. "Lydia, your own husband was a Catholic when he moved here."

"Yes, but he did the proper thing and converted. There's no one supports Reverend Rogers and the Congregationalist Church like my Samuel. Now, I'm not saying there's anything wrong with being Catholic." Jamie had been Catholic, she recalled with a bittersweet pang. Oh, Jamie. . . . "I'm just saying a proper Christian should go to church, whether they're Catholic or not." She bit off a length of thread and jabbed it through the eye of her needle. "I think living with that savage Mollyocket is going to land Mistress Cameron in trouble one fine day."

"Mollyocket sells me sassafras root now and again," Rachel said, nervously smoothing her homespun skirt. "Is there something wrong about her?"

Lydia stopped stitching and leaned forward. "My dear, didn't you know? Mollyocket was accused of witchcraft." Rachel's pale complexion grew even whiter, and Lydia almost laughed in her face. This was going to be easy. "She was charged with casting spells on several men in Massachusetts. They put aside their wives and behaved licentiously with her, or so I heard." She nodded knowingly, and the two older women nodded back. Prudence Everett blushed. "The magistrate let her go, but not before cutting her tongue out as a warning to other witches."

Rachel gasped and clutched a blue-veined hand to her throat. "Mistress MacKinnon, we must not speak of such things. Witchcraft is evil and—"

"I'm not saying that Mollyocket is a witch or that Mistress Cameron is either. I'm just relaying the facts of the case." Lydia sniffed and finished a dainty row of stitches. Rachel Hammond was a fool and too besotted with her smelly baby to see the truth. Lydia's lips curled in a syrupy smile. "I thought you'd like to know, since your husband has visited Mistress Cameron's cabin more than once in the past month."

Rachel's rabbity chin began to tremble. "He went there to get herbs for me. My . . . my milk wasn't coming in like it should." Her cheeks flamed scarlet, and she hung her head. "But if what you say is true, we'll avoid Mistress Cameron and the Indian in future."

Hepzibah Bryant snorted again but held her tongue, and they quilted in silence. Prudence Everett fidgeted for several minutes, then blurted, "Mistress MacKinnon, can . . . can a witch truly cast a spell over a man?"

Pain slashed at Lydia's heart, and she flattened her hand over her belly. *Oh, Jamie, why did you let her bewitch you?*

She inhaled sharply and tossed Prudence a derisive look. "Of course they can, you silly goose. I've seen it with my own eyes."

Prudence bit her lip and gathered up her tiny sewing basket. " 'Tis . . . 'tis so hot this afternoon. I'm feeling a bit faint. If you'll leave my section of the quilt, I'll finish it tomorrow. I . . . I must be going." She sketched a curtsy to the older ladies and fled.

Mistress Bryant chuckled, the sound rumbling up from her billows of flesh. "If Mistress Cameron *is* a witch, it looks like she just got herself another customer." She shook her head, the lappets of her muslin cap flapping like hounds' ears about her jowls. "Spells, indeed! It will take a lot more than a spell to get my son interested in Prudence Everett."

Something in the woman's tone caught Lydia's attention. "What do you mean?"

Mistress Bryant looked smug. "Giles's hand has been better for ten days, but he still goes up to Mistress Cameron's cabin every chance he gets. No love potion there—just the spell of a pretty face and a trim waist." Her dark eyes, sunk like currants in her pudding face, raked down Lydia's figure and settled on the straining seams of her bodice. She raised a pale eyebrow.

"Of course, with some men it takes more than a trim waist," Mistress Bryant continued. "That handsome devil James Maclean, for example. My lands—if I were twenty years younger! But he's never been one to chase after the ladies." She slanted Lydia a shrewd glance and smiled sweetly. "Don't you think he'd make a fine match for Mistress Cameron? After all, if 'tis improper for her to live alone, what better solution than for Mr. Maclean to marry her?"

Rachel pricked her finger. With a little exclamation, she began frantically blotting the quilt. "Oh, dear, I think I've gotten a spot—"

Lydia jumped up and grabbed a ladle of water from the wooden bucket by the hearth. She doused the tiny red spot and snapped, "Rachel Hammond, you always were a clumsy cow."

Rachel stood and snatched up her son. "I apologize, Mistress MacKinnon. I didn't mean to sully the quilt. And if you don't value my assistance, I'll take my leave." She swept out, baby slung over her shoulder like a sack of meal.

Hepzibah Bryant chuckled again. "Temper, temper, Mistress MacKinnon. They do say you catch more flies with honey . . ."

Clemency dipped her goose-quill pen in the squat earthen inkwell, then tapped the gray feather against her chin. She composed her thoughts and bent over her leather ledger.

August 20. Sultry. Attend'd Elihu Pratt's youngest Son, down with the putrid Sore Throat. Dosed with slippery elm and left him greatly eased. Rec'd one-half Bushel cornmeal and a young Cock as fee.

She reflected on this great fortune. She had started her chicken venture shortly after Jamie's departure, and now she possessed three black-and-white speckled hens and a half dozen chicks. She dimpled, thinking how pleased the hens would be to have some male companionship—as would she, if that irritating Highlander ever saw fit to come home.

She returned to her ledger and wrote, *Hoed Herb beds and assist'd Hugh Rankin picking the Corn. Mr. Rankin informs me Today is Mr. James Maclean's Birth Day. He is thirty-three years of Age.*

The quill tip frayed and splattered ink on the page. Clemency muttered under her breath and irritably blotted the black liquid before it ruined the precious sheet of paper.

Blast Hugh Rankin for a nosy old busybody, anyway. This morning she had been hoeing in the dew-spangled garden, all thoughts of Jamie banished from her mind. Then Hugh had ambled up, lamenting that his laird and friend wasn't around to be feted on his birthday. No doubt Hugh's entire lugubrious performance had been designed to provoke her feelings. Well, it wasn't going to work. Jamie had left of his own accord, and she wasn't about to waste one more minute missing him.

She snapped her ledger shut and propped it on the cabin's pine mantelpiece, then opened her trunk. Several books hid under her wool skirts. She pulled out a volume bound in black leather, with dog-eared edges and well-thumbed pages. On the flyleaf a woodcarving of a complex circular chart surmounted the title, which was set in Old English style characters: *The Compleat Charts of the Heavens as a Guide to Astrologers.*

Clemency felt a shiver lick down her spine. Granny Amais had owned several books dealing with astrology and alchemy, and Clemency could still hear her stern warnings to keep them hidden. She smiled, recalling how Amais scoffed at the superstition of her neighbors. *They use their bowels more than their brains. In truth, they fear knowledge. It challenges their silly superstitions.*

Clemency drew her chair out of the afternoon sunshine, then sat and opened the tome. Of course, Amais had read these books because she was insatiably curious, not because she had believed in alchemy. *The only folk making gold out of mercury are those who sell fake receipts to fools,* Amais had always said.

But Amais had believed in the effects of the stars and planets on her medical and surgical undertakings. The Italian physician who had trained her had been an accomplished astrologer, and the book Clemency held had originally belonged to him. Amais had taught Clemency to heal in conjunction with the influences of the heavens, and to this day Clemency cut when the moon was waning and watched for mental disturbance when the moon was full.

She flipped through the brittle pages, sneezing as dust tickled her nostrils. Ah, there it was—the chart for the year 1730, Jamie's birth year. She ran a finger down the page, then dimpled. She should have known. Jamie was a Leo with an Aquarius moon and Taurus rising—a combination guaranteed to produce a charming, charismatic man, a brilliant leader with a sensitive streak, and with the stubbornness of the worst, bellowing, hooves-dug-in, impossible-to-budge bull.

Her granny had told her something else about Leo men: they were sensual, passionate lovers. She wriggled her bare toes and suppressed a giggle. *Oh, my.*

A shadow fell across the book, and Clemency glanced up with a start. A thin young girl stood in the cabin doorway, nibbling on a grubby fingernail. "Mistress Cameron?" The girl's voice was so soft Clemency couldn't tell if she stuttered or suffered from nerves.

Clemency stood and placed the book cover-down on the table. "Yes, I'm Mistress Cameron. Won't you come in?" She gave the girl a reassuring smile and waved toward a Windsor chair.

"I . . . I be Prudence Everett."

The girl bobbed a curtsy, then perched on the chair. Her faded calico skirts revealed a bedraggled petticoat and dirty bare feet. Her brown eyes were wide and deerlike in her narrow face, and her sandy hair was scraped back in a severe bun. When she finally found the nerve to smile, Clemency noticed a distinct gap between her front teeth.

"May I offer you some refreshment, Mistress Everett?"

Clemency strode to the rough plank shelves that served as her sideboard and lifted the cloth that kept flies out of the cider pitcher. Holy Mother, Prudence better not look at that book! All Clemency needed was a superstitious neighbor asking awkward questions.

"No, thankee." Prudence gnawed on her thumbnail and gawked at Clemency's snug green muslin bodice and spotless green-and-white lawn skirts. "I came 'cause . . . well, 'cause I fancy a boy and he doesn't fancy me back." Her words gushed forth, accompanied by a mottled blush.

Clemency shook her head. Oh, dear. Another poor soul in love. Was there something in the water of Sturgeon's Creek? "What's his name?" she asked, smiling brightly.

Prudence scooted her chair closer, and Clemency caught a whiff of unwashed sweat, spoiled milk and horses. " 'Tis Giles Bryant."

Oh, dear again. Young Mr. Bryant had been making himself a pest since the day Clemency had physicked his hand. He dropped by her cabin on the weakest of pretenses, shuffling his huge feet and gawking at her as though she were Lady Godiva. She had discouraged him at every turn, but he persisted—rather like a bad case of worms.

Clemency cocked her head and appraised her visitor. Prudence's bone structure was excellent, and her big brown eyes hinted at a lively imagination. Maybe with a good scrubbing, a flattering hairstyle and a new dress she could capture Giles's affections.

"Giles is a fine, upstanding man," Clemency said. "I heartily approve your choice. But why are you telling me?"

Prudence peeked from beneath sandy lashes. "Well, I heard . . . I mean, they do say that you know about love potions and such." She ducked her head, as if expecting to be turned into a black cat. After a long moment, she glanced up with a tremulous smile.

Clemency's brows drew together. Oh dear, oh dear, *oh dear.* Astrology book or no astrology book, if rumors like that took hold, she could be in serious trouble.

She shivered, recalling the many times she and Granny Amais had been the victims of dangerous gossip. It was common for country folk to assume a female healer versed in herb lore was a witch. In truth, when her neighbors requested it, Amais had dabbled in harmless spells. A bunch of mistletoe placed in a blue drawstring bag and doused with cold water, then hung in the heart of the home as a charm against fire, for example. Or willow wands used to divine water when a farmer needed a new well.

But now and again someone's cow would go dry or their sheep would wander onto Exmoor and disappear. Then the grumbling against Amais would begin, dying down only when good fortune returned or when someone needed an herbal tincture to break a fever. Ultimately it had all been harmless, if nerve-wracking and annoying.

Clemency bit her lip. But here in the Colonies, dozens of men and women had been hung as witches, convicted on little more than a neighbor's spite. Here, minor rumors could turn deadly.

"Mistress Cameron?" Prudence joggled her wrist. "Please, mistress, can you help me? The Bryants are hosting a husking bee next week, and I so hope Giles will kiss me."

Clemency's attention snapped back to her guest. "What's a husking bee?"

Prudence sighed, and her thin face glowed under its pall of grime. " 'Tis ever so much fun. When a family has a big crop of corn to husk, they invite all the neighbors to share in the work. There's music and food and rum to ease the chore. When a man finds a red ear, he can claim a kiss from any girl he fancies." She gave Clemency a hopeful smile. "Can't you give me something so Giles will choose me?"

Clemency stood and paced the cabin's single room. She shouldn't meddle in this; it could only lead to trouble. She turned to say no and caught the starved look in the eyes of her thin, dirty visitor. Poor Prudence was so anxious to find someone to love, someone to fill her lonely nights.

Clemency knew all too well the torture of loving where one wasn't loved in return. She gnawed the inside of her cheek and suppressed a rueful smile. If she knew any genuine magic at all, she would have tried it on Jamie weeks ago, although no doubt the stubborn Scot would be impervious to any spell she cast. But this—this problem she could help. A little magic would be just the thing.

She whirled, then snatched up her medical box and lifted its carved cedar lid. Slanting Prudence a mysterious smile, she drew out a bunch of dried vervain. Amais had used the herb often in make-believe love philtres for mooning Devon girls.

"Here." Clemency tied the herbs with a red silk ribbon fished from the bottom of her trunk, then thrust the bundle at Prudence. "This is called 'Tears of Isis.' Isis was a great goddess of knowledge and love. This plant is sacred to her. Once a week and especially the day of the husking bee, crush a spoonful of it, steep it in a tubful of water and then bathe all over, with soap."

"A bath? But 'tis unhealthy."

"Nonsense. Isis will protect you. Oh, and do you have any roses at home?"

"No, but Rachel Hammond has a cinnamon rose in front of her house."

"Ask her for a few blooms. Steep them and mix them in the bathwater as well. It makes the charm more powerful."

Clemency closed Prudence's limp fingers over the vervain and fixed her with solemn eyes. Oh, she shouldn't be doing this! But already the young girl's cheeks glowed, and her brown eyes sparkled. She was rather pretty beneath all that muck.

"The day of the bee, come back here," Clemency said. "I'll put the finishing touches on the spell." She mentally selected one of her gowns to lend Prudence—a lavender dimity she could take in at the bosom to fit the girl. She would restyle Pru's hair with scented pomade, lend her an English fan and teach her to sit and walk like a lady. That should be all it would take to finish poor Giles. "Now be off with you, and promise me you won't tell a soul about this.''

"Oh, yes, Mistress Cameron, I promise. Thank you ever so much. I ... I be so happy. I *know* Giles will love me now!'' Prudence swooped down and kissed Clemency's cheek, then blushed to the tips of her ears and scuttled out.

Clemency smiled wryly and tossed the black book back into her trunk. "If love were only that easy.''

Chapter Ten

"There. Isn't she lovely?" Clemency grabbed Prudence Everett's clean, perfumed hand and twirled her around in a swirl of skirts and petticoats.

Hugh and Mollyocket, their dark skin and high cheekbones stained amber by the setting sun, stood in the cabin doorway and admired Clemency's handiwork. After several hours of primping, Prudence was fit to grace any polite gathering from Boston to London. Clemency had altered her lavender dimity gown to accentuate Pru's bosom to the best advantage. Then she had warmed a clean poker over the coals and transformed Pru's lank hair into a glorious mass of sandy ringlets held in place by clove-scented pomade and black velvet ribbons.

"Aye, lassie, ye're right bonny." Hugh waggled his bushy eyebrows and rolled his *r*s outrageously. Clemency's heart lurched. So, Jamie had learned that little trick from Hugh.

She dropped the tin of pomade on the table. Oh, if only Jamie were here, then the evening would be perfect.

She plastered a smile on her face and tucked an errant curl behind Prudence's ear. The girl blushed and ducked her head.

"Now, Pru, remember what I told you," Clemency admonished. "Back straight." She grasped the girl's thin shoulders and pulled them into position. "Chin up." She tapped two fingers under Pru's chin until it rose to the correct level. "And elongate that neck. Think, 'I am a *queen.'* "

Clemency dimpled and demonstrated queenliness by sailing like a graceful shallop around the room. She dropped a deep curtsy before Hugh, then fluttered her eyelashes and stifled a giggle.

"Och, lassie, ye're the image o' yer mither, and she the bonniest lass in all o' Scotland." Hugh reached out a callused paw and pulled Clemency up from her curtsy. His voice was thick, and she thought she detected the glimmer of tears in his eyes.

She swiftly kissed Hugh's leathery cheek. "Why, thank you."

The scent of wood smoke, whisky and spruce clung to the folds of his plaid, reminding her of Jamie. Tears blurred her vision, and for an instant she longed to lean against Hugh's strong shoulder, to lay on him the burden of her loneliness. Instead she adjusted the circular silver brooch pinning his plaid to his shirt and slanted him a wobbly smile.

"I'm the luckiest girl in the Colonies," she said, "to be escorted to the husking bee by such a gallant Highland warrior."

"Away and raffle yerself, ye wee flirt," Hugh grumbled. "I expect Jamie Maclean's the Highland warrior ye wish to have at yer side, no' the likes o' me. But his loss is my gain, aye?"

She chuckled and smoothed the wide lawn overskirt of her apple green gown. In truth, she did look pretty tonight.

With Mollyocket's help she had threaded her freshly washed hair with emerald green ribbon, then piled it on top of her head in an artful tousle. Ringlets trailed down her cheeks and neck, gold earrings swung from her ears, and she had laced her stays as tight as they would go.

She tried to draw a lungful of air. Impossible, laced this tight, and fainting was a very real possibility. Why on earth had she gone to all this trouble to look pretty when Jamie, that infuriating rogue, wasn't around to appreciate it? She pinched her cheeks to heighten their rosy color. Well, as Hugh had said, it was Jamie's loss.

"I couldn't care less about Mr. Maclean," she pronounced airily. She tucked her hand in the crook of Hugh's arm. "Prudence, let's go set the gentlemen on their ears."

Clemency sat on a bale of hay in Rufus Hammond's barn, a heap of fresh-picked corn at her feet. Blue velvet night had settled outside the tall barn doors, and the building reeked of fresh clover, sweaty bodies and hard cider. Smoky whale-oil lanterns cast fantastic shadows on the jovial faces around her, and old Mr. MacIntosh played reels on his fiddle. All evening long, her neighbors had laughed, gossiped and traded jokes while they plowed through their piles of corn.

Holding her tongue just so, Clemency separated a sticky wad of silk from its bed of pale yellow kernels. She tossed the silk next to a billowing mound of moist green corn husks, then added the bare ear to the waist-high pile beside her.

Rufus Hammond stood and called, "Dinner, everyone!"

His eagerly murmuring guests gathered around the make-shift pine-plank tables, and Clemency's jaw dropped. She had never seen such a feast! The tables bowed under the weight of towering platters of corn, acres of pigeon pie, roast turkeys the size of ponies, steaming mountains of squash and beans, and moist, sweet slabs of yellow cornbread. The company chattered, the food disappeared, and great oak barrels of rum and hard cider gushed their contents into eager mugs.

Then the serious carousing began, and Clemency realized with a shiver of unease that she shouldn't have worn such a fetching gown. Mr. MacIntosh sawed on his fiddle, the half-drunk men tore through the corn, and the women giggled in anticipation of a stolen kiss. Suddenly a yelp of triumph pierced the merriment.

"A red ear!" Samuel MacKinnon cried, flourishing his prize.

Clemency tried to melt into the shadows, but Samuel staggered toward her. With a quick prayer for deliverance, she jumped a hay bale, ducked behind a post and dashed for the barn door. Samuel caught her waist, swung her around, and planted a wet smack on her lips. Cheers and guffaws rang through the crowd.

"Atta boy, Samuel!"

"Caught ye a live one!"

"Don't let her get away!"

Clemency blushed and squirmed free as the men hooted and stamped. Lydia, who had greeted her coolly but properly earlier in the evening, sneered and turned to whisper something to Rachel Hammond. Clemency slunk back to her hay bale and prayed for a dearth of red ears. As she sat, Giles Bryant caught her eye. He grinned, then frantically pawed through the pile of corn, no doubt searching for a red ear of his own.

She raked a tumbled curl off her cheek. Holy Mother, hadn't Giles noticed Prudence at all? She scanned the shadowed barn and saw Prudence sitting alone, her gaze pinned hopefully on Giles's broad back.

Prudence's prospects didn't improve as the evening wore on. Rum flowed, music lilted, voices rose and one by one, more red ears appeared. Rufus Hammond got the second ear and demurely kissed his wife and infant son. Isobel

Bryant's fiancé found the third, and he kissed Isobel soundly to the shouted approval of all.

Then Giles brandished a red ear. "Mistress Cameron, you better start running!"

She didn't need the warning; she was already halfway toward the door. As she tripped over the thrust-out boot of one of Giles's friends, Prudence's stricken face swam before her eyes. Clemency cursed silently. Blast male caprice and her confining stays! She lowered her head, dashed forward and plowed straight into a man standing in the barn doorway.

The man gave a soft *unh!* of surprise; then Giles's ham-sized hand seized her wrist. He twirled her around, caught her shoulders and kissed her. Her nostrils burned with rum fumes, and she squealed and wriggled as the men whooped and clapped.

Inspiration struck, and she dropped straight down to her knees, breaking Giles's stranglehold. Gasping for air, she staggered backward and sprawled against the hard thighs of the man standing in the doorway. Strong hands clasped her under the arms, and warm apple-scented breath tickled her ear.

"Must I always be rescuing ye from the arms of other men, *mo druidh?*" The man's voice was laced with amusement, his Scottish accent thick and sweet as clover honey. He pulled her to her feet, and she whirled.

"Jamie?" she gasped.

Her heart jolted, and her constricted lungs expelled what little air they still contained. Jamie straightened to his full height, and she stepped back, devouring him with hungry eyes. His sun-bronzed skin was stretched taut over his wide cheekbones, and dust clung to his tousled auburn hair. Perspiration plastered his linen shirt to his broad shoulders, and the crisp red-gold curls on his chest peeped through the garment's open lacing. She gaped, speechless, and his generous mouth curved into a grin. White teeth flashed in his smudged face, and his tired eyes crinkled with laughter.

"Aye, 'tis me, and no' a moment too soon, from the looks of it." He glared in mock severity down his knife-straight nose, then winked. "Ye do seem to make the lads lose their wits, *mo druidh*. Och, mind your earbob." His warm fingers brushed her skin as he adjusted the dangling earring. Her knees weakened, and a feverish chill washed over her. She felt dizzy and breathless and foolishly happy.

"Mr. Maclean, 'tis a pleasure to see you, sir, but you've interrupted my kiss." Giles lurched forward and grabbed Jamie's arm, rum and desire fueling his courage.

"Come now, lad. Hasna your da ever told ye to leave the lassies wanting more?" Jamie's deep voice rang across the barn, and the crowd convulsed with laughter. He winked broadly, then escorted Clemency across the straw-strewn floor. He settled her on a hay bale, then bowed with elaborate grace. "Your most humble servant, madam."

His indigo eyes met hers, and for an instant she thought she read something more than rakish devilry there. Then he turned and sauntered across the barn floor, pausing to exchange hearty greetings and ribald jests with his friends and neighbors.

Clemency felt a warm rush of pride. Jamie towered above the other men, astonishingly tall and straight and elegant of carriage. As he bowed to his elders and clapped his friends on the back, she read respect and affection on every man's face—and longing on every woman's. In a flash, she recalled Hugh's words: Jamie was a laird's son, born and bred to lead and protect people like these. Her heart contracted, then grew full in her chest. What must it be like for him to have lost his home, to have lost the land where his clan had lived and loved and died? She bit her lip. Had loss scarred his soul the way whipping had scarred his body?

The corn husking resumed. Jamie gave Lydia a cool nod, then strode to the tables of food. With a surge of relief,

Clemency watched him toss back a tankard of cider and devour a roast turkey leg. Then he sat on the barn floor directly across from her. His lips curved in a secret little smile, and there was no mistaking the warmth in his eyes.

"Here, Jamie." Rufus Hammond tossed him several ears of corn. "You're behindhand."

With nonchalant grace, Jamie leaned against a hay bale and crossed his long legs in front of him. "Aye, ye're right. If I fancy the chance to chase after Mistress Cameron, I'd best get to work."

With a low growl worthy of a plundering Viking, he ripped the husk from the first ear. The kernels shone innocent yellow. A look of exaggerated disappointment crossed his handsome face, and he tossed the ear over his shoulder. The men stomped their feet and roared with laughter.

He snatched up a second ear, then slowly, tantalizingly peeled away each individual husk, as if unwrapping a precious treasure—or undressing a beautiful woman. At last the corn lay bare, a pale, virtuous yellow. Jamie rolled his eyes, fanned his damp shirt away from his chest and dramatically wiped his brow. The crowed hooted and whistled.

"Where's your luck, Maclean?"

"Someone'll be lonely tonight!"

"Don't let a pup like Giles Bryant get the best of you!"

Jamie rolled his shoulders from side to side as if limbering up for a race. Then he laced his fingers together and stretched his arms, palms out, until his knuckles cracked. He took a deep breath, grabbed the third ear, winked at the crowd and yanked.

" 'Tis red!" his neighbor hollered. A great shout shook the barn as the men started stomping and clapping in time: "Kiss! Kiss! Kiss!"

A blush flamed across Clemency's cheeks. From beneath lowered lashes she watched Jamie stand, then bow to the company. She closed her eyes and knotted her hands in her skirt. What if he didn't choose her?

The stomping and cheering grew louder, and the old lady sitting next to Clemency poked her in the ribs. She opened her eyes and saw Jamie's dusty brogues inches from the hem of her skirt. He bent and held out his hand.

"May I have the honor, *mo maise?*" His voice was so soft she barely heard him through the thundering in her ears.

She struggled to her feet, and he lifted her hand aloft, resting it lightly atop his in the courtly stance of the minuet. Catching his intent, she raised her chin and sailed with him to the center of the barn's dusty floor. Flickering light from the oil lamps highlighted the planes and hollows of his face, and his indigo eyes locked onto hers. They darkened and grew languid, as if he were offering her the most intimate of caresses. His lips parted, and she heard the soft intake of his breath. Then he broke into an elfin grin, and his expression transformed into the image of a very rakish devil—one nonchalantly aware of his devastating effect on women, and on her in particular. He clasped one hand to his heart, then bowed and gestured theatrically.

Dimpling, she fluttered her lashes and sank into a demure curtsy. The spectators roared their approval.

"Kiss her!" Rufus yelled.

Jamie clasped her around the waist and caught her to his powerful chest. She felt the burning heat of his skin and inhaled his musky masculine scent. He bent his head and she closed her eyes, melting against him, praying not to faint. His lips brushed hers with the light, delicate touch of a butterfly's wing, and she sighed and swayed closer, inhaling the cider sweetness of his breath. For a split second, she felt the hot thrust of his tongue against her lips. Then he released her and stepped back.

Instantly she felt exposed, disoriented, like a mole unearthed and cast into the sunlight. Then Jamie's strong hand closed over hers. He winked broadly. "My pardon, ladies and gentlemen, but ye must excuse us." He gave a jaunty bow, then led her out into the night. Yelps and guffaws ricocheted around the barn.

They were barely over the threshold when he grasped her elbow and whispered in her ear, "Unless ye want them after us, *run.*"

Chapter Eleven

Clemency caught up her skirts and tore after Jamie. They skidded around the corner of the barn and pelted toward the woods, and she laughed aloud as giddiness bubbled through her veins. They reached the stone wall between forest and field. Jamie halted, then grabbed her around the waist and swung her over. The woods were black as ravens' wings, and she stumbled and smacked into a pine's low boughs.

"This way." Jamie slipped his arm around her waist, and his husky voice tickled her ear. He guided her through a maze of trees until they left the noise and light of the party behind. At last they reached a clearing carpeted with silvery pine needles. Jamie stopped.

"Oh, thank God," Clemency gasped. She bent at the waist and pressed a hand to her side. "I thought . . . I'd die. I can't . . . breathe."

"Here." Before she could protest Jamie stepped behind

her. With deft fingers he began loosening the laces down the back of her bodice. Her pulse bounded.

"Jamie Maclean! What *are* . . . you doing?"

"I dinna want ye to faint, woman." He chuckled, the sound low and sultry in his throat. "Why the devil do ye lace so tight?"

Praise God, she could almost breathe again. She smacked his hand and scooted away. "Well, I certainly don't do it for your benefit, since you're never around to see it."

He quirked a roguish brow. "May I take that to mean ye missed me, then?"

She reached up to repin her straggling hair. "You certainly may not. I hardly noticed you were gone."

In a flash he stood before her. "Dinna do that," he murmured, catching her hands and imprisoning them against the sculpted hardness of his chest. "Ye look like a selkie with your hair long and wild in the moonlight."

He caressed her curls with his free hand, then one by one removed her hairpins. She hardly dared breathe. The strong, steady rhythm of his heart pounded beneath her fingers, and she raised her eyes to the pulse at the base of his throat. Entranced, she flattened her palms against his chest, spreading her fingers to stroke the warmth of his skin.

When the last pin had dropped to the moonlit carpet at their feet, he ran his fingers through the dark, tumbled waves of her hair. Goose bumps rose on her arms and throat as she inhaled the delicious cinnamon scent of his body. All at once she felt like liquid silver, shimmering, melting, and her nipples rose and ached against the thin lawn of her bodice.

He saw her reaction and his eyes grew heavy. With a low, hungry sound, he trailed a finger along the sensitive curve of her ear, then traced the shadowed column of her throat, barely grazing the soft down of her skin. "Ye're so beautiful, *mo druidh.* A dark angel haunting my dreams." His mouth curled into a slow smile, and he caught her chin, forcing her to look into his eyes. "And I ken ye missed me a wee bit, aye?"

His sigh caressed her cheek, and his warm palm pressed into the small of her back. Her nipples burned like twin coals, and he pulled her closer, rubbing his hardness against her, dragging her tingling nipples across the chiseled muscles of his chest. Desire flared, resistance vanished and she swayed against him.

"Oh, Jamie, I did miss you, every moment of—"

His lips captured hers, and he disarmed her with kisses slow and deep and searching. He moaned softly, and his arms crushed her close. She gasped, welcoming his searing invasion, matching his desire with her own dizzying need. His tongue explored her mouth, thrusting, demanding, until she melted against him like liquid silver.

She twined her fingers in his long hair and pulled his mouth hard to hers. He lifted his head, a look of surprised delight flashing through his eyes. Then he sealed his long body against hers. His muscled thigh parted her legs, and his large hand cupped the tender weight of her breast. Languorous fire licked through her veins and kindled a throbbing heat between her thighs. He bent her back and trailed tantalizing kisses down her throat. Then he nudged the hard ridge of his manhood against her belly.

Suddenly, fear fluttered like a trapped bird through her heart. She had longed for this moment, had ached for the press of his demanding thighs, hot and naked against her own. But what if he hurt her? She whimpered and twisted in his arms, ensnared by horrible memories of violence and pain. Holy Mother, she couldn't do this. What if he took his pleasure, abused her. . . .

Instantly, he stopped. He cradled her against his chest and brushed a kiss across her brow. "Shhhhh," he whispered. "I'll no' hurt ye, *mo cridhe*." His fingers stroked her spine and tenderly rubbed the back of her neck. He murmured Gaelic endearments against her hair. Slowly, her fear van-

ished. This was no vicious brute intent on violating her.
This was Jamie, courageous warrior, honorable laird, rakish
tease. He could be trusted.

A great shimmering warmth rippled through her, and she
pressed a kiss against the salty skin of his throat. "Oh,
Jamie, I love you—"

His body stiffened and his arms fell away. "Hush, Clemency, dinna say such things." He stepped back, dark eyes
veiled, expression harsh.

She blinked, swallowed, reached for him. "But—"

"Please, I shouldna have touched ye. But ye're so beautiful, so magical. I . . . I lost my head."

Ice plunged into her heart. This couldn't be happening.
That couldn't be Jamie edging away, hardening his mouth
into a grim line, holding up a hand as if to ward her off. "I
don't understand," she said. "You kissed me, you said I
was beautiful—"

"I shouldna have said it. I shouldna have brought ye here.
But I'm only flesh and blood, aye?" He attempted a smile,
but failed miserably. He grasped her elbow, and his fingers
were cold, impersonal. "Let's go back before folk start to
talk."

Clemency swallowed. Oh, Holy Mother, why had she said
she loved him? Why had she trusted him? She should have
known better! She jerked her elbow free. "Get your hands
off me! How dare you bring me out here and treat me like
some dockside whore!"

"I'm sorry. It was wrong and I ask ye to forgive me."
His voice was a hoarse whisper, and the moonlight revealed
the pain in his eyes. "I'm honored by your friendship, but
a friend is all I can be to ye." His shoulders tensed, and
his voice caught. "Ye must understand, I'm no' fit for any
lass."

"I don't believe you!"

" 'Tis true. I have no heart to give." He drew a ragged
breath and turned away. The moonlight slanted off his ele-

gant profile and silvered his wavy hair. In the cold light, surrounded by utter blackness, he resembled a remote, pagan god. "There's so much I canna tell ye."

"Like what?" she demanded.

When he spoke, his voice sounded composed, almost mechanical, as if he had rehearsed this speech a hundred times. "When my wife died, I entered a great paralysis of mind—a paralysis still with me. It would have been better if I had died and been buried along with she who caused it."

She whimpered. He glanced back at her, brow wrinkled, eyes distressed. Then he whirled, all composure fled. He spat a stream of curses and kicked at a rotten log. "Listen to me!" he cried, dragging his hands down over his face. "Ye deserve better than a man who canna love ye."

Hot tears coursed down her face. "If you don't care for me, why did you bring me here? Why did you kiss me? I thought I could trust you!"

"Ye can trust me. That's why I'm pulling away. I dinna want to hurt ye—"

"I thought you were a gentleman!"

Oh, you stupid little fool, her memory taunted. Hadn't she learned not to trust any man, especially a gentleman?

Jamie's face froze into an icy mask, and he folded his arms across his chest. At a sudden loss for words, she opened her mouth, then closed it with a click. He didn't love her. What more was there to say?

"Why . . . why did you come back?" she finished lamely.

His voice was cold and dead: "I came back to see my daughter."

A little cry tore from her lips, and she shoved past him. How could she have opened her big mouth? How could she have thrown herself at him like that? Holy Mother, she would never be able to face him again.

She stumbled toward the barn, and he strode after her, crashing through the trees, bellowing her name. Glancing back at his dark figure, she clambered over the stone wall and crashed into Lydia.

"I thought I'd find you out here," Lydia said. She grabbed Clemency's arm and hissed in her ear, "Did you get what you came for, you little slut?"

Jamie broke out of the forest as Clemency wrenched her arm free. He climbed over the wall and nodded blandly. "Lydia."

Lydia flashed him a radiant smile. "Jamie, won't you walk me home?"

This was too much. Clemency whirled and fled back to the barn.

"May I escort ye home, lass?" Hugh stumped up behind her as she loitered in the shadows by the barn door. He bowed, then peered into her face, his eyes concerned. Unable to trust her voice, Clemency nodded. At least Hugh was a gentleman.

They walked across the dewy village green, dodging sleepy sheep and softly calling good night to the other folk leaving the husking bee. The feeble orange glow from Hugh's lanthorn lit his face from below and cast gruesome shadows on his wrinkled skin, making him look like Rumpelstiltskin. Clemency squeezed his arm. She had grown fond of this kindly old gnome.

"What's fashin' ye, sweeting?" Hugh's voice was tender. "I ken the traces of tears when I see 'em, and 'tis Jamie should be seein' ye home, no' me."

She tilted her head back and stared up at the starry sky. "Hugh, have you ever wondered what would happen if the stars vanished and came out but one night a year?"

He considered a moment. "Aye, lass. Mayhap folk would marvel and be overwhelmed, instead o' takin' such beauty for granted."

"Granny Amais used to talk about that now and then.

She used to say if the birds sang only once a year, the whole world would stop to listen.''

"Yer granny sounds like a verra wise woman."

"She was, very wise and very kind." She leaned her head on Hugh's shoulder. "I miss her so much. I . . . I'm so lonely sometimes."

"Aye, I ken, lass. Losin' someone ye love's the hardest thing in the world."

They entered the forest and followed the path toward Robert's cabin—hers now, thanks to Robert's kindness. Beyond the encircling glow of Hugh's lanthorn, moonlight silvered each branch and leaf. The breeze had died, and the usual night sounds were strangely absent. The stillness moved her to confession.

"Hugh, remember what you told me about someone shaking Jamie up, giving him a reason to get over his grief?"

"Aye."

"Well, I tried." She swallowed, then raised her chin. "It didn't work. He . . . he told me he could never love me." Oh, Holy Mother, how it hurt to say it! Hot tears welled in her eyes, and she steeled herself not to cry yet again. She was like a bloody sieve, for heaven's sake.

To her surprise, Hugh chuckled. "Och, lassie, ye dinna ken much about men, aye?"

"As much as any woman, I suppose," she snapped.

"Dinna ye ken that men are like jackasses? They dig in their heels the hardest just before they jump." Hugh's eyes gleamed in the lanthorn light. "Dinna fash, lassie. Jamie's just got a load on his mind." He fell silent, and his smile faded.

Clemency studied the old gillie's face. "Hugh, what aren't you telling me? If something's wrong, I want to know it."

His grasp tightened, and he hurried her up the path. "I dinna ken meself, lass, or I'd tell ye. But 'tis no' like Jamie to go off and leave his bairn so long. Och, aye, he was a rare hand for runnin' off back when he was grievin' for

Rebekah, but never like this.'' He tugged a finger in his shirt collar, then irritably yanked open the lacing.

They entered the clearing in front of her cabin, and he caught her wrist in one callused hand. "I will tell ye this. After ye and Jamie lit out for the woods, I bided a wee, then followed. I didna want folk to talk about ye any more than they are already.''

"No one's talking—''

"Aye, they are, lass. Folk are whisperin' that ye're a witch.''

"A witch?'' Holy Mother! With a sound of irritation, she yanked the earbobs from her ears. "Don't be silly. You know I'm not a witch.'' But what if Prudence had said something about that ridiculous love potion?

"Aye, I ken, but do other folk?''

She stalked toward the cabin, skirts swirling about her ankles. "If that's all you have to say, I'm going to bed.''

He blocked her way. "Nay, that's no' all. When I reached the woods, I saw Jamie standin' with a woman. I could tell by her height 'twas Lydia.''

Cold sweat trickled down Clemency's ribs. "Yes?'' she croaked.

"Weel, I couldna hear what they said, but 'twas plain they were fightin'—fightin' somethin' fierce. Jamie's a hard man to rile, but when his temper's up, watch out.''

"Then what happened?''

Hugh looked injured. "I turned around and left, that's what happened. Ye dinna think I'm a sneakin' wee tittle-tattle, do ye?''

Clemency bit back a smile. Hugh would eavesdrop with alacrity if he knew he wouldn't get caught.

Suddenly the weird, plaintive cry of a loon ghosted across the moonlit lake. The hair rose at her nape. "Holy Mother, that gives me chills every time I hear it.'' She stared out over the black-mirror water as if searching for a lost soul.

A tiny smile curved her lips. So, Jamie had fought with

Lydia. That didn't bode well for Lydia's little flirtation. Uneasiness roiled her stomach. Jamie had fought with *her* this evening as well. With a little huff, she folded her arms and kicked her foot against a pine root. Blast Jamie Maclean, anyway. Bloody aggravating Highlander, no doubt he just liked to fight.

"What's amiss, lass?" Hugh's eyes were kind, his voice low and gruff.

"Jamie made it plain—" She stumbled to a halt. Should she tell Hugh everything? Oh, why on earth not? She had already lost her pride once this evening; losing it again wouldn't matter. "That . . . he only came back to see Elizabeth."

When Hugh spoke, it might have been her granny's voice in her ears: "Faint heart never won the field, lass."

She sighed and raked a hand through her tangled hair. "Are you asking me to chase after a man who doesn't care about me?"

"I'm no' askin' ye to chase him. Jamie's so mule stubborn he'd run the other way if ye did." Hugh chuckled and rubbed a hand over his stubbly chin. "Just stand firm and let yer heart work its magic—if ye truly love him, that is."

Clemency swallowed. Did she truly love Jamie? The loons cried once more, and gooseflesh prickled along her arms. Loons mated for life, Jamie had said. Could she match— or fight—that kind of devotion? She raised a hand and touched her bruised lips. She could still taste Jamie's kiss, could still see his blazing eyes.

"Oh, all right, you old devil," she snapped, casting Hugh a sour look. "If you think he has any feelings for me at all—besides anger and annoyance, that is—I'll do what I can to win him, even if it means another battle with Lydia."

Hugh's weathered face broke into an impish grin. "Och, aye, lass. He cares for ye. He just doesna ken it yet, the stubborn sod. He'll come around once he gets a good kick upside the head. But ye watch yerself, dealin' with Lydia. It takes a long spoon to sup with the devil.''

Just then, footsteps pounded up the path behind them. Rufus Hammond burst from the woods and skidded to a stop. He bent over, shoulders heaving, and gasped for breath. ''Mistress Cameron, come quick! Temperance Everett's in childbed. You must deliver the babe.''

Chapter Twelve

"*Please,* Temperance, I know 'tis hard, but you mustn't push," Clemency said.

Salty sweat poured down her brow, stinging her eyes and blurring her vision. Holy Mother, she would never get this baby shifted if she couldn't see. "Prudence, wipe my brow."

Prudence Everett snatched a clean rag from the pile by her sister's bed and mopped Clemency's forehead. From the corner of her eye, Clemency caught the young girl's expression: a mix of excitement, fear and resentment. She felt a quick twinge of sympathy. Poor Pru, no doubt she wished Dr. Greene was delivering her sister's first child, not the woman who had stolen Giles Bryant's heart. She tried to give Pru a quick smile, but a groan from Temperance arrested her attention.

Clemency murmured reassurance and bent between the woman's blood-smeared thighs. Moments earlier Clemency had been forced to make a small cut to widen the entrance to the birth canal, much to the vocal shock of the women assembled in Temperance's bedchamber. Not for the first time, Clemency bit her lip and quelled resentment at the custom of social childbirth. From her perspective, birthing a child was hard enough without the neighbors interfering.

And hard enough without the child coming bottom first.

Holding her tongue between her teeth, Clemency closed her eyes and eased three fingers into Temperance's body. The young woman tensed and bit back a moan.

"Dr. Greene uses an instrument to shift the child," Mistress Everett whispered.

"Nonsense!" Hepzibah Bryant held Temperance's hand and soothed her face with a damp cloth. "The forceps injure the child. I've heard of a baby's head being crushed that way."

Temperance sobbed, "Oh, dear God, just let me die. 'Tis too hard. Save the babe, but let me die." Another contraction wracked her body and forced Clemency's hand from the birth canal. Temperance groaned.

Jumping up, Clemency grabbed a bottle of oil from her medical box. "Here." She thrust the oil at Mistress Everett. "Rub this on her belly. It will soothe her."

For the tenth time since Temperance's travail had begun, Clemency debated whether Temperance's mother possessed the skill and nerve to help her shift the baby. An experienced midwife could move the child by pressure and manipulation from outside the womb, but one glance at Mistress Everett's rabbity chin and frightened eyes told Clemency she didn't have the courage.

Fear rippled through her. She couldn't do it alone.

You'll have to do it. Her granny's voice echoed in her mind. *Faint heart never won the field.*

"Mistress Bryant, get Temperance to drink more of her tisane," Clemency directed, trying to sound calm and assured. The strong blend of red raspberry and blue cohosh should slow the womb's contractions so Clemency could shift the child.

Clemency sat back between her patient's thighs. As she waited for the contraction to slacken, she glanced around the bedchamber. Although married almost a year, Temperance still lived with her parents. Fine English walnut furniture decorated the second-floor room, and a heavily carved cradle waited in the corner. Goodman Everett earned a prosperous living running the Sturgeon's Creek tavern, and his family was admired and respected in the town. At this moment, the tavern keeper waited downstairs with his son-in-law for the birth of his first grandchild. Clemency knotted her hands in her apron. She *must* deliver this child safely.

"All right, Temperance, let's try it again." Clemency moved her hand to her patient's blood-slick privates surrounded by thick brown hair. "Breathe out. Now you'll feel my fingers. Try to relax."

There. She was in. Closing her eyes and working by instinct, she inched her fingers around the baby's tiny buttocks. After twelve hours of labor, the poor mite was wedged firmly against his mother's bones. Working swiftly, Clemency pushed against the infant's right buttock and gently tugged the right leg back up into the womb. The slick flesh and frail bones moved a fraction. Relief rushed through her.

Clemency began to pray. *Holy Mary, Mother of God, be with us now and in our hour of need.* She wedged two more fingers into the birth canal, then pushed and tugged ever so gently. The baby's body began to rotate, and she felt a burst of energy.

"He's moving!" she gasped. Her three attendants exclaimed. Temperance sobbed.

At last the baby slipped into the proper position, head forward and down. Clemency smiled. "Things should move quickly now . . ." She froze, then held her breath until her heart threatened to burst. *Oh, dear God, no!* Please *don't let this happen.*

The cord was around the baby's neck.

"Mistress Bryant, Pru, help Temperance sit up," she ordered. "Temperance, when I tell you, push for all you're worth. We've got to get him out quick."

The two women grasped Temperance's shoulders and heaved her into a squatting position. Mrs. Everett hovered and prayed. Clemency guided the baby's head. "All right, Temperance, push!"

With a gush of blood and fluid the baby slithered into Clemency's waiting hands. Working frantically, she un-looped the cord, cleaned the mucus from the infant's nose, then snatched him up. The tiny gray chest didn't move.

She held the child upside down and slapped his buttocks. No cry. Oh, God, breathe, *breathe!* She clenched her eyes shut. What could she do? What would Granny Amais have done?

The answer came at once.

She leaned over and pressed her mouth to the baby's, then breathed into his lungs with a puff of air. A shocked gasp rose from the women.

"What's she doing?" Mrs. Everett whispered.

"Mother? Is he all right?" Temperance whimpered. "Why isn't he crying?"

With growing agitation, Clemency massaged the baby's chest and puffed air into his lungs at regular intervals. Breathe, *breathe!*

Hepzibah Bryant waddled around the bed. "I've seen this before. With the cord around his neck like that, he never had a chance, poor little cuss." She patted Clemency's shoulder. "You did all you could, child. No doctor or midwife could have done better."

Clemency sat back and cradled the baby in her lap, stunned by Mistress Bryant's matter-of-fact attitude. Clemency knew babies died at an alarming rate, but never one she had delivered. She blinked, then tasted the baby's coppery blood on her lips. She avoided Mistress Everett's shocked gaze and hastily wiped her mouth.

"Temperance ..." Clemency's voice quavered like a little girl's. "I'm so sorry. Your baby is dead."

Sobs wracked Temperance's thin frame. "Please, let me hold him," she gasped.

Clemency cut the cord, then tied it off with clean twine. Prudence and Mrs. Everett stared in horror while she wiped the child with a soft cloth, wrapped him in a tiny new baby quilt—pieced and stitched with joy and love and hope—then placed him in his mother's arms.

Temperance kissed her son's forehead and ran a trembling finger down his grayish cheek. Tears streaked her face, and she closed her eyes. "It be God's will."

" 'Tis not God's will!" Prudence stamped her foot and whirled on Clemency. "You did it ... I saw! You sucked his breath away!"

Clemency sighed and wiped sweat from her brow. "Pru, I know you're upset, but please listen—"

"You saw it, didn't you, Mother?" Pru's brown eyes were wild, her voice shrill. "She killed it, I tell you! She hates me, so she killed it!"

"Pru, I'm your friend—"

Prudence backed away, a trembling hand clutched to her throat. "Mother, keep her away. She's evil, can't you see it? We never should have called her!"

Mrs. Everett stared openmouthed at her youngest daughter. What little color she possessed drained from her hollow cheeks until Clemency thought the older woman might faint. She darted Clemency a frightened glance and choked, "You'd best leave."

"Mistress Everett, I'm so sorry. Please believe me. The baby was born dead. The cord—"

"He wasn't born dead. You killed him!" Prudence snatched up the pitcher at Temperance's bedside, then hurled it with all her strength. It hit the wall above Clemency's head and exploded in a shower of shards and water. "Be gone, witch!"

The bedchamber door burst open, and red-faced Matthew Everett staggered in. "What is all this?" he bellowed. With one swift glance, he took in the bloody sheets, the weeping women, the still infant. He rounded on Clemency. "Is my grandson dead?"

Clemency shrank from his rum-fumed breath. "I'm very sorry—"

"She killed him, Father! I saw her. The witch killed our baby!" Prudence stumbled to her father's side and clung to his arm, eyes wide with terror.

Confusion flashed across Matthew Everett's face, replaced by swift fury. He grabbed Clemency with one arm and her medical box with the other. "Get out of my house. I never should have trusted you. Reverend Rogers warned me against you, but I didn't heed. Now tragedy has struck—" His voice broke, and a spurt of tears burst from his eyes.

Clemency held out her hand. "Please, sir, Temperance still needs care—"

"Silence! I'm taking this up with the reverend, and if witch you be, you'd best pray for your soul." He shoved her out the door and slammed it behind her.

Clemency clutched her medical box and woodenly descended the stairs. She felt shocked, frozen, as if she were the walking dead.

Hepzibah Bryant stood in the entry hall, shaking her head. She reached out a fat hand and patted Clemency's shoulder. "I heard, missy. If it'll help, I'll tell Reverend Rogers what I saw. But I'd watch myself if I were you. Folk here fear strangers, and you being a young woman with medical skill—well, who can blame them if they think you're a witch?"

A moan of grief and pain drifted down the stairwell, and Clemency snapped from her trance. "Mistress Bryant, you must go up and attend Temperance. There's still the after-birth to deliver and—''

"I know, dearie, I've had seven myself. I'll take care of it." With a pitying glance, Hepzibah dragged her bulk up the stairs.

Clemency opened the Everett's front door and stepped out into a glorious September day of crystalline air and azure sky. Blazing red maples whispered of autumn, and she inhaled the spicy scent of wood smoke and fermenting apples. Overhead, a ragged V of Canada geese flew by, winging south before New England's legendary cold entrapped them in an icy prison. Their cacophonous honking rang in her ears long after they had passed from sight.

Clemency gazed across the village green toward the meetinghouse. Sheep—the same sheep she had dodged on her way home last night—cropped placidly at the grass, their ragged fleece daubed with a patch of red dye identifying their owner. They seemed so peaceful, so content.

She forced her gaze away from the sheep, and chill sweat trickled between her breasts. A stocks, a whipping post and a pillory loomed before the meetinghouse door. Jamie had told her they hadn't been used in years. She fervently hoped it remained that way.

Her lips began to tremble, and she hurried up the path toward home. With each step, tears choked her throat. She had never lost a patient before, had never seen a child's tiny soul vanish under her hands. She pressed a fist to her mouth. Holy Mother, maybe she had killed the baby. If she had turned him quicker, gotten him from the womb before his breathing stopped. . . .

With a sob, she threw her head back and stared up at the sky. It was so blue, so blue—blue as the baby's eyes, which would never see September's beauty. Blue as Jamie's eyes, so full of tender kindness.

Fat tears rolled down her cheeks, and she hitched up her

skirts and ran. She had to find Jamie. She could talk to him, and he would understand.

There was no answer when Clemency rapped on Jamie's cabin door. She glanced around the fields, then looked out over the lake. The sapphire water shimmered with fiery gold in the afternoon light. How could there be such beauty amid grief and death? She lifted the wooden latch and stepped inside.

Two beds covered with patchwork quilts anchored the corners of the shadowy room, and Elizabeth's small wooden pallet lay beneath one of them. Clemency imagined Jamie lying in bed watching over his sleeping child, and a smile warmed her face.

A rough pine table stood beside Jamie's bed. On it rested a small collection of books. She ran her fingers over his goose-down pillow and read the titles. There was the Bible, of course, and a weighty tome dealing with mathematics and surveying. Clemency wrinkled her nose. Typical of practical Jamie. But there were a few surprises as well. A thick leather volume of Shakespeare, both plays and poems, leaned against Jean-Jacques Rousseau's *The Social Contract*—in French, no less! Milton's *Paradise Lost* and the complete poems of John Donne lay beneath two novels by Daniel Defoe—*Robinson Crusoe* and her favorite, *Moll Flanders*. Clemency dimpled. So, her wild Highlander was an educated man, with a taste for risqué novels!

The cabin door squeaked and swung open. Clemency whirled, her heart in her mouth. Leave it to Jamie to catch her snooping among his things!

Mollyocket glided in and nodded a greeting.

"Oh, Molly, you scared me to death." Clemency collapsed on the bed, fanning her face with a trembling hand. After living with the Indian for two months, she no longer felt constrained by her friend's silence. In fact, she had grown used to one-sided conversations punctuated by nods, gestures, and grunts.

Molly crouched in front of Clemency, and her black eyes studied her face. She held out a sealed piece of paper.

"What's this?" Clemency took the paper and studied the red wax seal: the letter *M* surmounted by some type of crest. She turned it over. It was addressed to her. "Is this from Jamie?"

Molly nodded, then stood and gently brushed a strand of hair from Clemency's cheek. She padded softly to the cabin door and slipped out.

Clemency sat for a long moment. Then, through the long golden silence of afternoon, Elizabeth's squeals and laughter echoed across the hayfields. Somehow Clemency knew the child wasn't playing with her father.

With a trembling finger, she broke the seal and opened the letter. The handwriting sprawled across the page, the *J*s bold and vigorous, the painstaking copperplate script threatened by the writer's haste and agitation.

My dear Clemency,

Please forgive a foolish man who takes up his Pen in the dark Watches of the Night, requiring of that inanimate Object an Eloquence and Honesty he himself does not possess. I am humbled beyond any Imagining by that heartfelt Declaration of Feeling with which you honored me this night; now I must beg you to understand my own heartfelt Declaration.

Although I esteem you above any Woman of my Acquaintance, I must impress upon you the Impossibility of there ever being between us any of the tender Feelings so essential to a woman's Happiness.

Do not believe I write this with any Intent other than my deepest Concern for your Wellbeing. My only Desire is to protect you from the terrible Hurt which must surely arise from any intimate Association with me. I am not the man you think I am, and Honor compels me to spare you from the Darkness which haunts my Soul.

My dearest, your Youth and tender Heart make you Impetuous—a trait that although deeply treasured by me, leaves you open to Harm. I crave your Understanding that I take this Course because I would rather cut out my own Heart than suffer yours to be wounded.

I am going away until such Time as I may behold your dear Countenance unburdened by any Taint of the Past. As a man deeply in your Debt, I beg that you will continue your kind Watch over my beloved daughter Elizabeth.

Believe me, mo cridhe, *that although Impediments stand between us, they will never prevent me from remaining*

> *Your most Affectionate and Devoted Servant,*

> *James Ian Alasdair Maclean*

Clemency folded the letter and tucked it in her bodice, tight against her heart. A curious numbness crept over her. James Maclean was the most bewildering person she had ever met. Every time it appeared a door had opened, revealing a tantalizing glimpse of his soul, something made him slam it shut and lock it against her.

She would never understand him.

Chapter Thirteen

Lydia shifted her weight on the hard meetinghouse bench and swallowed the gorge choking her throat. No matter what she did these days she could barely keep down her breakfast. She clamped her lips together and glanced around the chilly meetinghouse to distract herself from her roiling stomach.

The town's women, somberly dressed in unrelieved black and gray, sat on one side of the stark room, the men on the other. In front of the bare pine pulpit, two narrow box pews separated Sturgeon's Creek's first families, the Frosts and the Shapleighs, from the lesser folk. Lydia glared at young Abigail Frost's demure gray silk bonnet and suffered her weekly pang of envy. She should have a pew of her own—and someday she would. Then the town would realize her consequence. Faith, compared to her family in Kittery, the Frosts were nothing but gussied-up trash!

Reverend Rogers opened a hymnal, and the congregation shuffled to their feet. The reverend's flat voice sang the first verse of a psalm, and his flock repeated it back to him with disheartening dissonance. Lydia winced and clutched her prayer book, suddenly remembering the winter nights when Rebekah was alive. Lydia had been so happy then. She had loved it when Jamie—hair streaked copper and gold in the dancing firelight—took up his guitar and amused them for hours with Highland jigs and reels and ballads.

She clenched her gloved hands and curled her icy toes. How could Jamie have gone off and left her? She had laid her plans so carefully. Now what would she do?

A thump and a yelp reverberated through the meeting-house. The congregation turned and gawked. Giles Bryant's cur slunk out from under his master's bench as the wriggling mass of small boys on the balcony steps convulsed with laughter. Blushing, Giles bent stiffly and groped for his prayer book, which he had dropped on his sleeping pet. The dog watch shot Giles a sharp glare and herded the dog outside, then threatened the unruly boys with his long, brass-topped stick. Reverend Rogers glowered.

Lydia seized the opportunity to scan the congregation for Clemency. As usual the English slut was not in attendance. Lydia repressed a smirk and prayed that Reverend Rogers had noticed. If he had, the witch would receive a serious reprimand, if not a fine.

Lydia also noticed that the Everetts were not in their usual location directly behind the Shapleigh pew. No doubt Temperance had been delivered of her first child. Lydia hoped that the doctor had birthed it, not the English witch.

"In the name of Christ our Lord, Amen." Reverend Rogers finished his droning prayer, and the congregation sat with an audible sigh of relief. The reverend beatifically turned his cadaverous face to the heavens and started his sermon.

Beside Lydia on the hard pew, Samuel sniffed and wiped his dripping nose. A late summer cold had deviled him for weeks, and Lydia's usual herbal remedies couldn't cure it.

If she didn't know her husband for such a weakling, she would have sworn he was hexed. Perhaps the English witch had cast a spell to halt his wandering hands!

Lydia knew all about Samuel's weakness for a pretty face, and she didn't care one whit. If anything, she was thankful for his occasional trips to Portsmouth, where she knew he frequented the better class of dockside whore. His behavior relieved her from the trial of marital duties and gave her a reason to refuse him when he tried to claim a husband's rights. She hadn't lain with Samuel for months, and she intended to keep it that way.

Samuel sniffed again, then rooted in his waistcoat for his snotty handkerchief. Lydia shivered and edged away. Poor fool. It was chilly in the meetinghouse, as always, for even the balmiest summer weather couldn't warm the dank structure. Now, with September marching on, it was cold enough to freeze the hottest religious fervor.

Samuel blew his nose, then offered her a timid smile. With a rush of shock, she suddenly detected a faint resemblance between Samuel and his cousin Clemency. Faith, how many times had she seen that exact look of sadness in the witch's moss-green eyes? Lydia scowled and crossed her arms over her heavy breasts. Perhaps Clemency and Samuel truly were related, although she doubted it. She had always believed, from the moment Margaret MacKinnon's first letter had arrived, that Robert and Samuel's long-lost relatives were running a confidence game.

Two years ago, Robert had received a letter from a woman claiming to be Margaret MacKinnon. In the letter she had explained her long silence. She wrote that after the Battle of Culloden, she had wandered Drumossie Moor and the streets of Inverness, searching for her family and fiancé. British soldiers had arrested her as a Jacobite sympathizer. Months later, starving and weakened by dysentery, she had been released from prison. A British officer then told her that her family and her fiancé—Jamie's uncle Alexander—had been killed, so in despair she gave up her search.

Margaret wrote that eventually she had married a Lowland Scot named Angus Cameron and given birth to their daughter, Clemency. Angus had remained loyal to King George, and in time the family moved to England, where Angus became river keeper on a Devon estate. Upon Angus's death, Margaret discovered that her cousins had not been killed, but had been banished to New England as indentured servants, and a simple search of British shipping records had led her to Robert and Samuel's whereabouts.

Lydia bowed her head as Reverend Rogers began his final prayer: "Make us ever mindful, Oh Lord, that Your Son commanded us to forgive others their trespasses against us, even as You forgive our trespasses."

She dug her fingernails into her piously folded hands. Forgive! She would never forgive Clemency for stealing the farm that rightfully belonged to Samuel. She would never forgive her for bewitching Jamie, then driving him away. No matter how much Clemency resembled Samuel, Lydia knew she was lying. Her story just didn't add up.

"Lead us not into temptation," the reverend intoned, "but deliver us from evil."

Evil—that was what Clemency was, and Lydia would see her punished if it was the last thing she did.

"For Thine is the kingdom, and the power, and the glory forever. Amen."

The congregation straggled up and waited like patient cattle as Reverend Rogers and his wife walked up the aisle and out the door. Lydia had barely stepped out into the cool September sunshine when Rachel Hammond caught her elbow.

"Have you heard the news?" Rachel dragged Lydia from the pious knot waiting to shake the minister's hand. Her thin cheeks glowed. "The Everetts' daughter Temperance lost her babe in childbirth yesterday, the poor lamb." Rachel lowered her voice and pulled Lydia closer. "Mistress Cameron was the midwife. Hepzibah Bryant told me the cord was wrapped around the baby's neck, but some do say—"

"Say what? Faith, Rachel, spit it out."

"Some say Mistress Cameron suffocated the child, right there in front of everyone! She picked up the babe and sucked the soul right out of it." Rachel fidgeted with her gray wool skirt and cast a glance over her shoulder. "But that's not the worst."

Lydia noted that the townspeople stood clustered on the green, muttering and staring at the shuttered Everett house. "Tell!" she hissed.

"I hardly like to repeat it, but Prudence Everett accused Mistress Cameron of being a witch!"

Lydia suddenly felt feverish all over. Rachel babbled on, but Lydia's racing pulse muffled her words. She felt as though she had been handed a gift—long-coveted, perfect and complete. Here at last was her opportunity to be rid of that English whore.

White-hot coals glowed on the hearth in Clemency's cabin, and the delicious scent of rabbit stew infused the air. Clemency positioned an iron kettle of apple duff near the coals, stepped away from the blistering heat and turned.

"Elizabeth! Be careful or he'll scratch you!" She caught the little girl's hand and pulled it away from her new tabby kitten.

"But I want to pat him." A pout puckered Elizabeth's lips.

"You may, but don't be so rough." Clemency smoothed back the child's wild red curls and kissed the top of her head. Elizabeth's hair smelled of spruce and cinnamon, just like her father's. Stifling a pang of loneliness, Clemency scooped up the kitten and sat in the hearth-side rocker. The little tabby's body vibrated with loud purrs, and he rhythmically worked his tiny white paws into the soft flesh of her thigh.

"Why's he doin' that?" Elizabeth leaned over the kitten.

"He's hungry. He thinks I'm his mother, so he's asking me for milk."

Elizabeth giggled, then tumbled to her knees and buried her head in Clemency's lap. "I'm a kitten, too," she said, pressing her soft white cheek against the tabby's brindled fur. "Be my mother."

Clemency's heart contracted, and her fingers knotted in her apron. Did Elizabeth truly want a mother, or was she just pretending? She stroked the child's golden-red curls and ran a finger along the tender, exposed skin of her neck.

She had such mixed feelings for Elizabeth. On one hand she loved her desperately. Who wouldn't? Elizabeth was the image of Jamie—an imperious, stubborn, wild Highlander in tiny female form, blessed with her father's dazzling and infuriating charm. Yet jealousy tainted Clemency's love for the child. At every turn Elizabeth reminded her of Jamie's devotion to a woman long dead, a woman enshrined forever in his memory. Elizabeth was Rebekah's child, a living reminder of Jamie and Rebekah's love. How could Clemency compete with that?

She clenched her eyes shut and tried to blot out a vivid image of Jamie tenderly making love to his precious wife. There could be no greater intimacy than to create a child in love, to bring a babe into the world as flesh-and-blood proof of a couple's bond. Oh, Holy Mother, how she longed for Jamie's love, and for his child! But a child's birth had killed Rebekah and destroyed any hope that Jamie would ever love again.

Clemency's lips thinned in a bitter smile. The good folk of Sturgeon's Creek seemed convinced that she was a witch. Well, she would be more than willing to be branded so, if only she could summon a magic strong enough to heal Jamie's heart.

Small, damp fingers stroked the furrow between Clemency's brows. She opened her eyes and found Elizabeth's concerned face inches from hers. "You look sad," Elizabeth said, pressing her smooth forehead against Clemency's. "Do you miss Da?"

Clemency put an arm around the child's thin body and drew her close. Elizabeth sighed and snuggled against her. "Yes, I do," Clemency whispered, "very much."

Mollyocket gave the stew a final stir and turned from the fireplace. Clemency met her dark eyes and smiled. The Indian had blossomed since they had moved in together. The lines of grief had smoothed from her mahogany skin, and her gaunt figure had filled out until she could wear one of Clemency's English gowns. Her black-and-silver hair still hung in long braids, and she still wore a leather pouch filled with herbs, feathers and shiny stones on a thong around her neck, but her air of frightening savagery had faded.

Often over the past weeks Clemency had found herself wondering about the exact relationship between Mollyocket and Robert. Had they been lovers? Lydia had hinted as much, but Clemency couldn't believe it was possible. Why on earth would Robert have proposed to Clemency if he was in love with Mollyocket?

She stood and nestled the kitten in his wooden box. No, it wasn't possible. No woman, least of all proud, wild Mollyocket, would stand by and watch her lover slip into the arms of another woman.

"Come on, Elizabeth. Get the table set." Clemency wiped her hands on her apron. "Your uncle Hugh will be here in a minute, grumbling like an old bear for his supper."

"Uncle Hugh *is* an old bear!" Elizabeth giggled and curled her hands into bear claws, then danced around the table. Molly gave her a playful swat on the rump, then handed her two wooden trenchers. Clemency rolled her eyes. She disliked the colonial practice of sharing another person's plate, but she had to admit it did save on dishwashing.

Hugh stumped in and unwound his worn plaid. "Evenin', lassies. Brrrrr, 'tis colder than a witch's tit out—" He stopped and winked at Clemency. "Bad choice o' words. But ye're in for a shock when winter comes, Sassenach. No mild English winters here, ye ken. Just drifts of snow as tall as Jamie and cold enough to freeze a man in his tracks." He poured water into an earthen basin, then splashed his face.

Clemency tossed Hugh a coarse linen towel. She wished the old gille wouldn't speak of Jamie so often. She knew Hugh missed his friend, but hearing Jamie's name at every turn was like sitting next to the fire when she had a fever. "Here," she said. "You're splashing like a selkie."

"A selkie, am I? I didna ken ye kent what a selkie was."

Elizabeth raced to Hugh's side and tugged on his kilt. "Tell about the selkie!" she demanded. "Mistress Cam'ron wants to hear."

Hugh cocked a questioning brow, and Clemency nodded. "All right, we've a few minutes before supper," she said. "Tell your tale." She sat in the rocker, and Elizabeth squirmed into her lap. Mollyocket sank down on the settle, and Hugh perched beside her.

"Weel now," he began. "A selkie is a magical creature— a lass who is half human and half seal. Some folk say there's no such thing, but I ken the truth, for I've seen the selkie meself." He lowered his voice and leaned forward. Elizabeth wiggled with delight.

" 'Twas a silver-mooned night back on Lock Linnhe— a sea loch, ye ken, with bottomless, peaty water that opens out to the ocean. I was walkin' along the beach when I saw the selkie swim ashore. I thought 'twas a seal at first. Then flip, flap, she stripped off her seal skin, and there stood the bonniest lass I e'er clapped eyes on. Right quick, I turned and ran, 'cause I kent the trouble a selkie can bring.

" 'Twas not long after when I heard that me friend, Connor, had fallen mad in love with the bonniest lass in the

Highlands, and she mad in love with him. I met her one night at a *ceilidh,* and sure enough, 'twas the selkie. Despite me warnin', Connor married her. She tarried awhile, as selkies are wont to do. Och, she made him a canny wife, for all selkies are fine cooks and lovin' *mathaireil*—mothers.''

Hugh's wizened face grew sad. ''But selkies are sea creatures, and always the sea beckons them home. So one silvermooned night, the selkie slipped out o' Connor's sleepin' arms and crept back to Loch Linnhe. I was walkin' the beach, and I heard her cryin'—a high, keen, heartbreaking wail—as she slipped into her seal skin and swam away. She never returned.'' Hugh's voice faltered, and the only sound was the fire's pop.

''Then what happened?'' Elizabeth asked, eyes misty.

Hugh shook his head. ''Och, lassie, poor Connor died o' a broken heart. He could ha' kept her if he'd only hidden her sealskin. Then she'd never ha' left him. But ye see, he didna ken she was a selkie. He didna ken 'til it was too late what a treasure he held.''

Clemency shifted the little girl off her knee. ''Don't listen to him, Elizabeth.'' She bent and wiped the child's tears. ''Why on earth would the selkie leave if Connor truly loved her so? He had no need for tricks. He could have just told her he loved her; then she would have stayed forever.''

They had barely started to eat when a knock thundered on the cabin door. Hugh opened the door, hand clasped on the dirk at his side, and Clemency recognized a tall man from the village. Matthew Everett and several other men skulked behind him.

The tall man bowed to Hugh. ''Good evening, Mr. Rankin. I didn't expect to find you here. Our business is with Mistress Cameron.'' The man's cold, gray eyes scanned the room, then fixed on Clemency. His gaunt face froze into a grim mask. ''Mistress Cameron, I am Jedidiah Dixon, town magistrate. A warrant has been sworn out against you, and it is my duty to arrest you in the name of Governor Hutchinson.''

Clemency gasped. "Arrest me? Why?"

"You have been accused of witchcraft."

Clemency whipped off her apron. "Witchcraft? That's ridiculous!"

Hugh grabbed Dixon's arm. "What kind o' prank is this? Mistress Cameron is no witch."

"She is! The witch killed my grandchild!" Matthew Everett loomed in the doorway, eyes wild, red face distorted. "My own daughter saw it."

Clemency held out a placating hand. "Mr. Everett, the child was born dead—"

"If it were, it were cursed by you!" Elihu Staples, the town blacksmith, jostled in behind Everett. He turned to the magistrate. "She's a witch, I tell ye! Every time she walks by the forge my fire smolders and I can't hammer a thing into shape."

Clemency's stomach clenched. "Mr. Staples, please—"

"My son says he's seen her dancing by the lake at night, under a full moon." Staples whirled and pointed a sausage finger at the kitten dozing by the fire. "Look there—the witch's familiar!"

"Hold yer wheest," Hugh snapped. "Yer daft, mon. 'Tis a wee kitty, and Mistress Cameron's just a lass."

"She's in league with the devil!" Everett shouted. "She's tried to prick half the town with her witch's needles, claiming to stop the smallpox. Disease is God's judgement on our sins. Her notions are against God's laws. 'Tis witchery, I say!"

"And no proper maiden would live alone with a savage who's a known witch." Elihu Staples leered at Mollyocket. "Arrest her before she curses us all!"

Clemency turned to Dixon. Her heart raced, and her breath came in shallow gulps. "Mr. Dixon, I beg you, this is all a misunderstanding. I was trained as a healer, to help people. I would never harm—"

Dixon averted his eyes. "Prudence Everett and Matthew

Everett have sworn a written warrant against you. Witchcraft is a felony in Massachusetts Colony. It is my duty to arrest you and hold you in gaol until your examination and trial.''

"Her trial?'' Hugh's voice wavered.

"Yes, Mr. Rakin, her trial.'' Reverend Rogers stepped magisterially into the cabin, his black cloak blocking the candle's light. His pale mushroom eyes poisoned Clemency's courage, and she sank into the rocker. '' 'Tis the legal requirement.''

Hugh kicked at the table leg. "Ye're a minister, mon. Ye're educated. Surely ye dinna believe such ravin's.''

Reverend Rogers brandished his Bible. "Thou shalt not suffer a witch to live!''

Dixon slid a clammy hand under Clemency's elbow and yanked her to her feet. "Get your cloak, madam. We must go.''

Clemency stumbled toward the door and lifted her cloak from its peg. Elizabeth was pressed back against Mollyocket's skirt, her face frozen in shock. Clemency hugged her cloak to her bosom and started toward her. Oh, Holy Mother, how could she leave Jamie's child? Dixon caught her arm and pulled her back.

Hugh's fingers closed around his dirk, but Dixon stayed his hand. "Don't be foolish, Rankin—not unless you want to see the inside of the gaol. We have the legal right, and she'll have a proper trial.''

"Where are ye takin' her? Sturgeon's Creek has no gaol.''

"She'll spend the night locked in my shed. In the morning we'll take her to the gaol in York.''

Face ashen, Hugh stepped back. "Ye willna harm her.''

Dixon unbent slightly. "Don't worry. She'll be safer in gaol than in town. Feeling is hot against her, and you won't want her in the hands of a mob.'' He snapped his fingers. "Come along, Mistress Cameron.''

In an instant Hugh was beside her, voice low and fast. "Dinna fash, lassie. I'll get ye out, never fear.''

Hot tears scalded Clemency's eyes. Before Dixon could stop her, she bent and kissed Elizabeth on the lips—lips so like Jamie's. "Don't be afraid, Pumpkin Pie. Everything will be all right." Elizabeth sobbed and clung to her leg like a limpet. Clemency pried the child's hands loose and looked into Mollyocket's shocked eyes. "Take care of her, Molly."

Hugh wrapped his tartan plaid around Clemency's shoulders. "Here, lass. 'Twill be cold in yon shed." His lower lip trembled, and she swayed toward him, catching him in an embrace.

"Get word to Jamie," she whispered against his stubbly cheek.

Chapter Fourteen

Jamie sat on a huge granite rock six miles off the coast of Maine. He gazed at the Atlantic and felt calm for the first time in days, soothed by this broad silver mirror reflecting the pearly gray sky. Behind him, a few boats slept in the island's tiny harbor: a wherry, a shallop, a dory. All was silent. The herring gulls were not yet throating their plaintive cries, and even the offshore breeze was still, muffled by wraiths of fog which trailed between him and the islands in the distance.

He pulled his legs up, clasped his arms around them and rested his chin on his knee. He loved the Isles of Shoals, although by rights and logic he shouldn't. He had come here in 1746 as a bond slave—wrenched forever from his older brother, Diarmid, shorn of dignity and sold into seven years' labor as punishment for taking up his sword against the king. He had been sixteen: a strapping lad tortured by anger, seething with rebellion, prepared to hate everything and everyone around him. But then Sir Andrew Pepperrell had bought up his contract, and the Isles had begun to work their magic.

Through seven long years as part of Sir Andrew's fishing operations on Appledore, Jamie had fished the deep, cold water around the rocky islands. It was backbreaking work, but it had drained his soul of hate. Under the blazing sun and buffeting gales he acquired the raffish daring of a pirate and easily fell in with the wild, hard-drinking Shoalers, who scorned the laws and religion of the mainland.

Jamie still did not know what had brought him to Sir Andrew's attention. Maybe it had been Jamie's accent— that of an educated man, no matter how he coarsened it with oaths. Maybe it had been his quickness with mathematics, which set him to navigating the fishing boats after only one week under sail. Or maybe it had been his voice—mellow and smoky as Scots whisky as he sang Highland ballads to pass the long days at sea.

For whatever reason, Sir Andrew had befriended him, and Jamie's fortunes had changed. His benefactor schooled him in surveying, then released him from his indenture. Colonists poured into New England, and Jamie's surveying business had prospered to the point where he was able to buy the indentures of Hugh, Robert and Samuel. Eventually he had earned enough money to take his place in the finest colonial society.

But in Jamie's mind his greatest achievement had been tracing his brother Diarmid. The second of the three Maclean brothers, Diarmid had fought alongside Jamie at Culloden. He, too, had been banished to the Colonies as a bond slave. Jamie had wept for joy when he learned that Diarmid had become overseer on a Virginia tobacco plantation.

Jamie sat up, peace slipping from his soul. As always, thoughts of Diarmid set his mind on paths of pain and darkness, paths that led to their eldest brother, Lachlan Maclean. Jamie shook his head and ran a hand down over his face. No, he wouldn't think of it. He and Diarmid had agreed. Lachlan was dead to them, even if the past wasn't.

He reined in his thoughts and shifted his gaze inland. Sir Andrew still kept a small, weathered house on Appledore, on a point of land looking east over the Atlantic. It was here that Jamie had brought Rebekah for two idyllic days after their wedding, and it was here he had retreated in an agony of grief after her death. He snatched up a mussel shell, then crushed it between his fingers. Despite all the time that had passed since that awful event, he still felt a deep coldness inside, something dark and beyond reason. When Rebekah had died, he had longed to follow her to the grave. Now sometimes it seemed as if he *were* dead, even when he wished to live.

Och, he had daydreamed too long. He stood and stretched, then rolled his shoulders from side to side. The sun had risen and burned away the mist, and the land warmed around him. His nostrils twitched with the spicy scent of scrub juniper and blueberry bushes, and he took one last glance at the blue-glass sea, then strode through orange-hipped beach roses to the house.

A short figure in a Maclean tartan kilt stood on the stone doorstep. Jamie's heart lurched. Hugh knew not to intrude on his solitude. He never would have come here unless something was dreadfully wrong. Jamie quickened his stride and shouted, "What is it?"

Hugh stumped toward him. "Och, lad, thank God ye're here. I feared ye'd be off up the Kennebec."

"Is it Elizabeth?"

"Nay, lad. The bairn's fine. 'Tis Mistress Cameron."

Jamie stopped and bit back a sudden, irrational surge of anger. Even here on the Isles he couldn't escape her! Every night she haunted his dreams; every day she floated before him, eyes green and hazy as the water swirling around the rocky shore. He clenched his jaw, trying to eradicate the memory of her exquisite flesh, half-clad in the silvery moonlight. Och, he could almost see her, so slim yet so lusciously curved. He could feel the heavy heat of her breasts cupped in his hands, could taste the intoxicating sweetness of her lips, open beneath his. Desire shuddered through him, hot and raw.

No, he would not torture himself with such hopeless longing. He had made a vow, to himself and to Rebekah's memory. No matter how he longed for that beguiling, emerald-eyed enchantress, he was sealed in a tomb of his own making.

"What's she done this time?" he inquired, quirking a sardonic eyebrow.

"Wipe that look off yer face, Jamie Maclean. Ye may be laird and me sworn to serve ye, but I'll no' suffer yer teasin' ways this time."

Jamie's brows shot up. "Is something wrong?"

"Aye. They've arrested Mistress Cameron as a witch."

For one split second Jamie almost burst out laughing. "Ye're joking."

"Nay, lad. 'Tis serious business. They took her last night. Magistrate Dixon arrested her and dragged her off to York gaol."

Jamie shook his head as if clearing water from his ears. This couldn't be happening. He had always known Clemency was bound to get into trouble—she was too headstrong, too stubborn, too outspoken. And all that business with smallpox inoculation! He recalled her passion to heal, and a tender smile curved his lips. But he had never imagined witchcraft. "Ye must be wrong, Hugh. They havena arrested a witch in these parts for decades. Pepperrell told me so."

Hugh's face flushed a deep, livid crimson. "Weel, they have now," he roared. "She delivered Temperance Everett's baby the night o' the huskin' bee. The wee bairn was born dead—cord around the neck, Mistress Cameron said. Prudence Everett claimed Mistress Cameron killed it, sucked out the poor creature's life or some daft thing."

Jamie felt a jab of pain, as he always did, at mention of

a lying-in gone wrong. His face must have whitened, for Hugh rushed on. "Temperance is fine, poor lass. She's no' the problem. 'Tis her sister and father swore out the warrant." He jabbed a finger into Jamie's chest. " 'Tis a hangin' offense, mon! Stop starin' and answer me—are ye going to help her or no'?"

Jamie realized he had been holding his breath and expelled it in a rush. St. Columba! Why had he left Clemency alone? For all her skill at healing she was just a lass, alone and adrift in the world. He should have stayed and kept watch over her as he had promised. He swallowed and closed his eyes and there she was: hair like midnight silk, that naughty, irresistible, dimpled smile—and those eyes, witch's eyes.

"Of course I'll help her," he snapped. With two long strides he entered the silent house. He snatched up his plaid, his dirk and his *sgian dhu*—the tiny concealed knife designed to take an enemy off guard. He sensed Hugh hovering behind him. "Do ye think they'll convict her?"

"Aye. The Reverend Rogers is against her. Ye ken how powerful he is."

"Aye, I ken, and no friend of ours. Perhaps we should have gone to meeting more often." A chill licked down Jamie's spine: as a Catholic, Clemency did not attend meeting at all.

In moments they were out of the house, racing down the sandy path to the harbor. They waded through icy water to Hugh's borrowed shallop, then clambered aboard and weighed anchor. Working in silence, they hoisted the sails, caught the wind and came about. They skimmed over white-capped swells, and Jamie's mind raced along with the boat. *Clemency in gaol, accused of witchcraft, faced with hanging—lost to him forever.* The salt wind stung like acid on his face. Surely that was what made his eyes water.

They could see the thicket of masts in Portsmouth Harbor when Hugh spoke again. "Jamie, I ken only one sure way to save her. Ye must marry her."

Jamie spun around. The wind hit his back, and he lost his balance. "*Marry* her? Are ye daft?"

"Nay. Listen, lad, and dinna be settin' yer jaw at me. Ye're highly respected in the colony. Even if the Reverend Rogers doesna care for ye, the rest o' the county does. Ye've powerful friends, aye? Dixon will think twice before crossin' Sir Andrew Pepperrell. Sir Andrew's verra rich, and his dead father a war hero."

Jamie clutched the tiller and opened his mouth. Hugh cut him off. "Most folk fear Mistress Cameron because she's an unmarried lass livin' with a savage—and physickin' men, to boot. If she's married, that complaint's gone."

"But I canna marry!" Jamie bellowed. "Ye ken that. Rebekah didna want me to. She didna want our bairn to have another mother."

"Dinna shout, ye great bloody sod. Who do ye think's been motherin' Elizabeth while ye've been out here wool-gatherin'? Who's coddled and loved the bairn as if she were her own?" Thrown off balance by an errant wave, Hugh lurched forward and grabbed Jamie's arm. "Ye owe it to her, lad. She saved Elizabeth's life, aye? Who better to be her *mathair?*"

Mind whirling, Jamie dug his fingers into the tiller's smooth wood. He couldn't marry Clemency. He had never promised Rebekah aloud, but in his heart after her death he had vowed to remain single. And now there was another problem, horrible and insurmountable. . . .

"Where's yer sense o' honor?" Hugh snapped.

"Honor!" Jamie spat. Wasn't that the only thing he had left? He ground his teeth and glared until the gillie moved back.

"If they convict her, she can plead her belly," Hugh persisted. "There'll be no shame in it if she's married to ye. Then likely they'll let her go."

Marry Clemency. Salt wind whipped Jamie's face, and he closed his eyes. He imagined her swimming in the lake, moonlight silvering her lush breasts. He held her in his arms, light and frail as a wee bird but with the magic to turn his blood to fire. He felt her lips beneath his, parting in sweet innocence. He felt her passion rising, meeting his, hot and eager and unafraid. A keen shaft of desire knifed through him. St. Columba, marrying Clemency would be any man's dream!

A seagull screeched overhead, and his eyes flew open. He squared his shoulders, set his jaw and decided. "Nay, Hugh, I canna."

Hugh sprang, plowing his fist into Jamie's jaw. Jamie sprawled backward, and the tiller flew from his hand. The shallop's bow plunged, the sails snapped and they heeled over. Pain shot through Jamie's jaw and stabbed at his ribs. Cracked, by God!

Over billow of canvas and rush of water, Hugh thundered, "Dinna give me yer guff, James Maclean. I whipped yer uncle Alexander and I can still take ye. There's a limit to stubbornness, even for a Scot, and this is the end o' yours." He reached down and yanked Jamie upright. "Now, will ye marry Mistress Cameron, or do I throw ye overboard for the sharks to devour?"

Jamie rubbed his throbbing jaw, then shot Hugh a wry glance, eyes crinkled with amusement. "Aye, weel . . . given such a choice, I'll take Mistress Cameron."

The sun's last rays slanted through the barred windows and traced a distorted checkerboard pattern on the dusty stone floor of Clemency's cell. She huddled in the corner on a ticking mattress stuffed with straw. Despite the grimy walls, the place wasn't so bad, for a gaol. Certainly not as bad as Magistrate Dixon's shed, where she had shivered through the previous night on a frigid dirt floor with only her cloak and Hugh's plaid to warm her.

The gaol was situated on a breezy hilltop overlooking

York Village. It had seemed almost pleasant earlier in the day. She had arrived at the barnlike building in mid-afternoon, with Dixon and Reverend Rogers as guard and a bevy of her Sturgeon's Creek accusers as audience. A fat man in a powdered wig and grease-stained waistcoat ogled her tight bodice, then introduced himself as Jeremiah Moulton, the jailer. Behind him skulked his mousy wife, a great ring of keys jangling from her waist. Moulton ushered her into a low-ceilinged, whitewashed room, handed her a dipper of water and a hunk of cornbread, then departed, locking the door behind him.

In the hours since, she had paced the cell, tried to sleep, gazed out the window, counted the dead flies in the corners, unbraided and rebraided her hair, recited the Catechism and bitten her nails to the quick.

With a snort of disgust she flung herself on her back and sneezed as a cloud of dust billowed from the mattress. Oh, why had she gotten herself into this mess? Jamie had warned her, back when she was tearing about the village trying to inoculate the children against the pox. But had she listened? Of course not. At the time she had considered her actions noble, an answer to the call to heal. Now she saw her true motives: pride and stubbornness and the desire to be independent at all costs.

Once again her granny's words drifted through her mind: *Faint heart never won the field.* She gave the wall a vicious kick. Maybe if she had been a bit more fainthearted, she wouldn't be locked in gaol.

It grew darker, and her stomach rumbled. Would that fat lecher Moulton feed her again, or was one hunk of stale bread her daily allotment? She mustered a faint smile. In truth, Moulton's poor timid wife was rather sweet. She had looked in on Clemency a few hours ago and had whispered that the trial was scheduled to begin in the morning. This had unnerved Clemency so badly she had begun to cry.

Muttering words of comfort, Mistress Moulton had thrust a frayed handkerchief into her hand, then scuttled out.

The cell filled with dark blue shadows, and Clemency reckoned it must be about seven o'clock—less than twelve hours until she must stand and face her accusers with her life in the balance. Her lips went dry. Surely they wouldn't hang her, would they?

She rolled on her stomach and buried her head in her arms, willing herself not to cry. Where on earth was Hugh? Holy Mother, he had to find Jamie. But would Jamie want to help her?

A key turned in the lock, and the door opened with a metallic *screek*. Mistress Moulton bringing her dinner, no doubt. Light steps swiftly crossed the floor, then stopped inches from her mattress. Irritation pricked at her. Did Goody Moulton enjoy watching her sob and snivel? "Oh, for pity's sake!" she snapped, voice peevish and choked with tears. "Leave the blasted food and get out."

She heard a soft chuckle. "I see gaol hasna improved your temper, *mo druidh*. Och, but I forgot. I best no' call ye 'magic one' around here, aye?"

She gasped and sat up, shocked into silence. Jamie knelt before her. His generous mouth curved into a grin, and his indigo eyes laughed into hers. "Ye've straw in your hair," he teased, catching her long black braid in his hand. He winked and drew the braid lightly across his cheek. "Ye'll let me brush it out for ye, aye?"

Intoxicating warmth emanated from his body, and she inhaled the scent of fresh, masculine perspiration on his skin. His long lashes lay like dark crescents against his lean cheeks, and her fingers curled, longing to trace them. Then he met her gaze, and all amusement fled from his expression.

She caught his hand, then cupped it to her wet cheek. Joy and fear and confusion and excitement lit all at once and exploded in her heart like fireworks on Guy Fawkes Day. "Oh, Jamie, I was so frightened you wouldn't come!" She flung her arms around his neck. Laughing, he fell back against the wall, then gathered her in his arms.

"I'm here, *mo cridhe*," he murmured, lips warm against her hair.

There was a shuffle of feet, and Hugh entered the cell, the jailer trudging behind. "Come on, lad, we dinna have all night."

Clemency blushed and jumped to her feet, sniffing and brushing tears from her cheeks. Jamie stood close beside her, but she didn't dare look up at him. Instead she rushed to Hugh. "Thank you—"

"Shhh, lass. Keep yer voice down. We shouldna be here."

Moulton set his shuttered lanthorn on the floor. "Be quick," he said, shooting Jamie a sour glare. He sidled out and closed the door behind him.

Clemency glanced from Jamie to Hugh. "What on earth?"

"I crossed Moulton's palm with silver to let us have an hour with ye." Jamie's tone was dry, and the weak orange glow from the lanthorn revealed the twitching muscle in his cheek. He gave Clemency a wintry smile, then bowed. "Your servant, madam. And your rescuer once again, it appears."

Jamie's voice had lost its bantering tone. Clemency frowned. "Have you bribed my way out of gaol, then?"

"Nothing so imaginative as that," he remarked coolly. With the hauteur of a noble Scottish chieftain, he drew himself up and glared down his knife-straight nose, watching her with the alert, avid eyes of a falcon. "I've come to propose marriage."

She snorted and flounced down on the grubby mattress. "Jamie Maclean, don't you dare joke at a time like this!"

"Joke?" One side of his mouth quirked into a smile, doing serious damage to his aloof pose. "I assure ye, *mo druidh*, a man doesna joke about marriage."

Hugh shot Jamie a quelling glance. "Dinna tease the lass, ye great lout. Can ye no' see she's upset?" He squatted and patted her knee. "He's serious, sweeting. I've puzzled it all out, and marryin' him is the only solution. Jamie's respected in the colony"—he rolled his eyes—"though why I canna say. And he's got powerful friends. They'll no' hang ye if ye're bearin' his name. At the verra worst they'll banish ye—"

"Are you both insane?" She shoved the gillie's hand away and scrambled up. "I'm not a witch. I've done nothing. You can't seriously believe they'll hang me!" She swiped a straggling curl from her cheek and paced the cell, dusty skirts swirling about her ankles. " 'Tis barbaric, 'tis . . . 'tis insane!" She stopped and scanned Jamie's face, searching for evidence of some trick. "You can't mean it. You can't be willing to marry me just . . . just to save me from . . ." Words failed, and she swallowed, hard.

Jamie arched a brow. "I did promise to watch over ye, aye? Doesna a gentleman keep his promises?" His rs were playful growls, and his eyes glinted with amusement. "Besides, yon wee gillie gave me no choice. 'Twas marry ye or be thrown to the sharks."

"Oh!" She whirled so he couldn't see her confusion. She never would understand him. One minute he toyed with her, teasing her the way he teased four-year-old Elizabeth. The next minute he looked at her with. . . . With what?

She strode to the barred window and gazed out. She knew she was beautiful—a gift that had proved to be both a blessing and a curse—and those few brief times when Jamie had let down his guard and kissed her proved he was attracted to her. But she knew Jamie. He wouldn't marry her just to bed her. In truth, he could have had that without marriage. And surely he wouldn't marry her out of some misguided sense of duty, or worse, pity.

A quick, hot anger flared through her. She jerked up her chin. Pity. That was it, and she wouldn't have it. No matter how much she loved him, she would not let him marry her out of pity, necessity or his stubborn Scottish sense of honor.

Oh, no. If Jamie Maclean ever made her his wife, it would be out of love.

She turned and met his complacent gaze. "I'm sorry, sir, but my answer is no."

Chapter Fifteen

She felt a momentary spurt of triumph as surprise flashed across his insufferably handsome face. Then his hand shot out, and he caught her arm in an iron grip. "This isna England, Clemency. Massachusetts Colony has hung dozens of people for witchcraft. Aye, and worse than hanging—pressing to death, drowning."

His voice cracked like musket fire. "Could ye stand to be stripped naked and whipped before a mob? Ye've no idea what whipping's like. The pain's the least of it—though twenty lashes can make a strong man faint, and forty lashes kill him." His indigo eyes blazed into hers. "I'd take a thousand lashes before I'd see ye so abused!"

Her mind conjured a searing vision of the weals scarring his back. She tried to break free. His grip tightened. "Jamie, please. I'm grateful, truly I am, but I can't marry you." Mounting hysteria shrilled in her voice, and she struggled for control. "You're offering out of pity, I know. That and some outdated code of Highland honor—"

He yanked her against his broad chest, and his strong hand seductively kneaded the small of her back. He lowered his head until their lips were a dizzying whisper apart. "Pity, is it? Who says 'tis pity and no' something else?" Then his lips brushed hers, soft and more intoxicating than honeyed Scots whisky. With a little gasp she swayed into the warmth and power of his embrace, and her lips parted beneath his.

Iron keys jangled in the lock, and the cell door swung open. Jamie and Clemency flew apart. "Time's up," Moulton hissed.

Jamie reached for her, and she instinctively moved into the circle of his arms. "Five more minutes," he said, flashing Moulton a roguish grin. "Surely ye'll no' deny a lover proper time to say good-bye?"

Flickering beams from the lanthorn illuminated Moulton's leer. "All right, but be quick."

Hugh touched Clemency's shoulder. "Please, sweeting, take the lad's offer. Remember what I told ye the night o' the huskin' bee?" He avoided Jamie's quick, questioning glance and winked at her. "Who are we to question God's ways, aye?"

For a long moment, Clemency stood frozen. Then she took a deep breath and gave Hugh a tiny nod. She turned and slanted Jamie a wobbly smile, then sank into a deep curtsy. "Mr. Maclean, I'm exercising a lady's right to change her mind. I would be honored to be your wife, if the offer still stands, that is."

"Aye, *mo druidh,* it stands." He smiled into her eyes, then raised her hand to his lips, turned it over and brushed a searing kiss across the palm.

"Oh, no, I forgot!" She fiddled with the end of her braid and frowned. "There's no one to marry us. That old goat Reverend Rogers is one of my accusers, and even if he wasn't, he would never consent to perform the ceremony. I'm Catholic, remember?''

''Aye, I remember. But there's still a way. It might no' be precisely legal, ye ken, but under the circumstances . . .'' Rakish, masculine dimples hovered at the corners of Jamie's generous mouth. ''Are ye familiar with the Scottish custom of handfasting?''

She shook her head. ''Handfasting? No.''

He grinned down at her. '' 'Tis one of the better Highland inventions. It allows a man and woman to declare themselves married—in front of witnesses, ye ken—for one year and one day. At the end of that time, they must be wed properly by clergy or they go their separate ways and none the worse for it.'' His eyes were positively dancing now.

''Huh!'' she snorted, fighting the impulse to giggle. ''Sounds to me like a fine way for a man to have a woman without making a true commitment.''

Jamie's ruddy brows shot up, and his eyes widened in elaborate innocence. ''And ye think me that kind of rogue?''

''If the kilt fits,'' she said tartly.

Jamie threw back his head and laughed. ''Och, *mo cridhe*, ye'll be the death of me long before a year and a day have flown.'' He lifted her chin with one warm finger and smiled down into her eyes. ''So will ye trust me with your life, at least until summer's end, a year and a day from now?''

She hushed the host of misgivings clamoring in her ears and managed a wan smile. ''Yes, but only under two conditions.''

''Aye?''

''What does *mo cridhe* mean?''

She thought he paled, but it may have been a trick of the light. His laughing eyes grew deadly serious, but they never left hers. After a long moment, he raised his hand and slowly dragged his warm thumb over her lower lip. ''It means 'my heart.' ''

Blood thundered in Clemency's ears. Oh, Holy Mother,

what kind of test was this? Here she stood, face to face with the man she loved more than life itself. All she had to do was say the words and he would be hers—at least for a year and a day. But should she? *Could* she?

Jamie recovered his composure. He cocked his head and flashed her an indigo-eyed challenge. "So then, lass. And what's condition number two?"

She twisted her hands in the limp folds of her skirt. Turning, she said, "Hugh, would you and Mr. Moulton mind stepping outside? I must speak to Jamie alone."

The door shut with somber finality, and Jamie watched her, an expression of amused affection in his eyes. She lowered her gaze. Would he still look so affectionate after he heard what she had to say?

Her stays pinched her ribs, and she couldn't catch her breath. "Jamie, before we take any vow, I . . . I must make a confession. I owe you that, at least." Oh, Holy Mother. . . . Suddenly the room grew stifling hot. She was suffocating, spinning, drowning. A shimmering dark curtain descended over her mind, and she pitched forward.

Then she was in his arms, gathered onto his hard-muscled lap on the musty mattress. His warm fingers stroked in slow, seductive circles at the back of her neck, and he murmured Gaelic endearments in her ear.

"What is it, *mo cridhe?*" he whispered. "Nothing could be bad enough to make such a brave lass faint."

"You say that now, but you've no idea!" she sobbed. "Oh, why do I always end up crying around you? I never cry!"

He chuckled, and the sound rumbled through his body into hers. "Hush now, dinna fash." He kissed the tip of her nose, then gently wiped her tears with his shirt sleeve. Clemency dissolved against him. No wonder he was such a good father. He knew just how to comfort.

At last she got herself under control. "Here's condition number two. I'll only marry you if you ask me again, after you've heard the truth." She gathered her courage and looked into his eyes. "Jamie, I'm not a virgin. I was violated two weeks before I sailed to America."

His muscles stiffened, and his mouth thinned into a grim white slash. He shifted her off his lap, then stood, looming over her in the dark cell—a towering black figure who refused to meet her pleading gaze. He strode to the barred window and gazed out, his elegant profile backlit by the rising moon. Then he clenched the bars in two big fists and dropped his head between his arms, hanging like a man about to be whipped. There was a long, chill silence.

She had lost him for good. Pain clawed at her heart, pain so intense she begged God to show mercy and let her faint once more. "I'm so sorry," she whispered.

He turned, keeping his back to the moonlight so she couldn't read his expression. "Are ye carrying?" His whisper was hoarse, strained. Even in the darkness she could see his eyes, blazing with jealousy and rage, savagery and possession.

"Carrying?" Comprehension dawned. "Oh! No . . . no, there's no baby." She pressed her back against the cold plaster wall. She would not go to him, would not beg. She had given him the truth, at least as much as she could. There was nothing else to say.

He turned away. The silvery moonlight slanted off his high cheekbones and limned his long nose. Clemency hugged her arms to her ribs. Holy Mother, she loved this man. He was so powerful, so strong—like a ruthless Gaelic warrior. But his wide shoulders and muscled arms had comforted her with exquisite tenderness, and his brave heart had offered her the protection of marriage and the honor of his name.

He gave a long, ragged sigh, and his hands clenched into fists. With a muffled sob, she sank down on the mattress.

She was soiled goods, and no man would want soiled goods, least of all a proud, honorable Highlander.

Suddenly he whirled and smashed his fist into the brick wall. The crash shuddered through the cell as he spat out a curse. She lurched to her feet. "Stop it!" she cried, racing to him. "You'll break your hand." She grabbed his bloody fingers and turned them to the moonlight. "Are you crazy? You've hurt yourself."

"Leave me, woman!" he roared, snatching his hand away. The jailer opened the door, and Jamie rounded on him. "Out! Dinna dare bother us!" The door slammed shut.

"That will be enough, James Maclean," Clemency snapped in her best no-nonsense healer's tone. All thought of tears had vanished before his wild display of Scottish temper. "Do you want the whole town to hear you? No doubt breaking into gaol is just as much a crime as breaking out."

"Aye, and cruel punishment it would be to be locked in a cell with ye the rest of me life." His tone was still furious, but he moderated his volume a bit. He scrubbed a hand through his auburn hair until it waved in all directions. "I'm beginning to think ye *are* a witch!" He shot her a blue-eyed glare of such baleful outrage she began to laugh.

"Oh, Jamie—you remind me of my tabby kitten, the time he jumped on the hot griddle." She clutched her stomach, tension and anxiety and shame evaporating into peals of hysterical laughter. "He touched down and *zing!* right back up, madder than a . . . a singed cat. That's what you look like—a great big singed ginger cat."

"Weel, I'm glad ye're finding amusement in me breaking my hand." His Scottish accent was thick as Highland heather. "Some healer ye are, laughing at your patient." He pressed his bleeding knuckles to his lips and assumed an air of deeply injured dignity.

Clemency dimpled, and his eyes crinkled with a ghost of amusement. "Oh, Jamie, please forgive me." She laid a hand on his wrist. "I didn't want to hurt you, but I couldn't marry you without telling you the truth. I'll tell you the whole story—"

"Nay. I value your honesty, but there's nothing to forgive. In truth, 'tis I who should apologize—I behaved like a jackass. Put it down to rampant Scottish pride." He cast her a beguiling smile, then closed his eyes and drew her into his arms.

She pressed her face against the softness of his shirt. "Oh, Jamie—"

"Hush, *mo cridhe.*" His lips brushed her hair; then he lightly rested his chin on top of her head. "I've met your bloody conditions. Now, will ye marry me or no'?"

Fifteen minutes later Jamie and Clemency stood before the cell's window, bathed in a checkerboard of moonlight. Hugh and the jailer stood in the shadows beside them. Despite the icy night air wafting in through the bars, sweat trickled down Clemency's ribs. Jamie attempted a smile, then crushed her trembling hand in a death grip, all amusement wiped from his face.

"Are you sure this is legal?" Moulton muttered.

"O' course, mon." Hugh twitched his plaid into a more flattering drape. " 'Tis the same as the Quaker marriage ceremony. Ye stand before witnesses, declare yer intent, and *bang!* 'tis done."

Clemency fidgeted with her bodice neckline. Bang, indeed. This had to be the oddest marriage ceremony ever performed, and it certainly wasn't the wedding of her dreams. She glanced bleakly at her calico work skirt—stained, torn and smelling of the goats in Magistrate Dixon's shed. She raised an anxious hand to her braid. "Did I get all the straw out of my hair?"

"Aye, ye're verra bonny," Jamie managed, squeezing her hand.

"And you're very gallant, to compliment such a hag."

He bowed slightly but couldn't muster a smile. Holy Mother, he was as nervous as she. Somehow this gave her a spurt of courage.

"Let's get on with it," Moulton whispered.

"What . . . what do we say?" Clemency looked into Jamie's eyes, and her knees began to wobble. Suddenly it didn't matter that this was a forced wedding taking place in a gaol in the middle of the night. Jamie's lean, handsome face was all she saw, the enthralling warmth of his touch all she felt.

"How about this?" He cleared his throat, then spoke in a strong, clear voice. "I, James Ian Alasdair Maclean, take thee, Clemency Alexandra Cameron, to be my wedded wife . . ."

Her heart slowed, and her field of vision narrowed. Gone was Hugh, in ancient Maclean tartan. Gone was the greasy, leering jailer. Gone was the fetid cell, the cry of a night bird, the rustle of leaves in the chill September wind. Jamie's eyes were all that remained. Jamie's eyes—wide and earnest, twin pools of indigo flecked with gold.

". . . to love, honor, cherish and protect . . ." His voice was unusually deep, his accent thick, but the words flowed without break or hesitation. She must have swayed, for he laced his fingers through hers and raised her hand to his lips.

Suddenly she realized he had fallen silent. Her jaw dropped, and he raised an expectant eyebrow. "Oh," she murmured, cheeks burning. "Um . . . I, Clemency Alexandra Cameron, take thee . . ." Holy Mother, was this truly happening? She heard her voice repeat the ancient vows of the marriage ceremony, but she felt oddly detached, as if she were floating above her body and watching the scene from the cell's beamed ceiling. Perhaps she was a witch after all. Couldn't a witch leave her body and fly?

Jamie gave her hand another reassuring squeeze. His eyes

never left hers, and he even managed an elfin smile when she vowed to "honor and obey." But as each word dropped from her lips her heart accelerated with dread.

Jamie was doing this out of pity—pity and his blasted sense of honor. She knew it. She closed her eyes and recalled his words the night of the husking bee: "I have no heart to give." Everyone knew Jamie still mourned his dead wife. She knew it most of all. There was nothing, nothing at all to stop him from leaving her in a year and a day.

She halted, mouth open, heart racing. She had come to the place in the vows where she was supposed to declare, " 'til death do us part." But they weren't marrying 'til death. What should she say? What on earth had Jamie said?

He must have divined her panic, for he smiled into her eyes and closed her jaw with one gentle finger. " 'Tis all right, *mo cridhe.* Ye've said the important part. Now we're husband and wife."

They stood frozen, hands still linked, until Hugh clapped Jamie on the back. "Weel, are ye goin' to kiss yer bride or no'?"

She could have sworn Jamie blushed. He slanted her a smile of such boyish shyness it nearly broke her heart. Then he leaned forward and brushed his lips against hers. No doubt he meant the kiss to be chaste and ceremonial, befitting their strained alliance. Well, she would have none of that. Granny Amais had always told her to start out the way she intended to continue.

She parted her lips and pressed against his chest. After a start of surprise, his powerful arms encircled her waist, and she felt the hard muscles of his thighs burning through her skirts. Her hand slid under the glossy waves of his hair and urged him on. With a tiny, abandoned moan, he opened his mouth and claimed her. His tongue circled hers, lazily exploring, savoring, captivating, possessing.

"St. Columba," he murmured, breaking away at last.

"Too bad you'll have to wait for your wedding night," Moulton snickered. "Now you two men get out of here."

Looking dazed, Jamie reached into his breeches pocket and drew out a folded sheet of paper. He always wore his breeches tight, but this pair was cut in the new style, with a loose front panel buttoned down both sides. Clemency flushed and hastily glanced away. Even with the bulky paper no longer in his pocket, the loose-fitting panel strained over a formidable bulge.

The document was some type of marriage contract. Moulton produced pen and ink, and they took turns signing the paper. As Jamie gracefully bent and inscribed his name, his hair gleamed like polished mahogany in the wavering lanthorn light. Clemency's lips tingled. She ached to open herself once more to his demanding mouth.

Closing her eyes, she crossed her fingers behind her back and made a second solemn vow: at summer's end this time next year, Jamie would be hers, heart and soul.

Chapter Sixteen

"Oyer, oyer, oyer! The Quarter Sessions court of the Colony of Massachusetts, Province of Maine and County of York is now in session. All be upstanding for Judge Sewall!" Sheriff Moulton thumped his truncheon on the town house floor with awe-inspiring pomp. The crowd rose like cornstalks rustling in the breeze, and Clemency seized the opportunity to scan the room.

York's town house was a grand structure, about thirty feet wide by thirty-five feet long. Plastered and whitewashed walls supported a high ceiling crisscrossed by hefty oak beams. Bright morning light poured in through the diamond-paned windows and refracted into a riot of colors on Sheriff Moulton's costume.

Costume, indeed. Clemency doubted King George himself had clothes so grand. The jailer's powdered wig was curled, puffed and piled so high a small child would have little trouble hiding in it. A scarlet cockaded hat perched on the wig, tilting precariously with Moulton's every movement. A canary brocade surtout with sparkling brass buttons strained over his big belly, and white silk breeches, clock-embroidered hose, and high-heeled shoes completed the ensemble. Clemency sighed and glanced down at her bedraggled calico skirts. Certainly her appearance wouldn't keep her neck from the noose.

Murmurs rose from the crowd, and Clemency tensed as Judge Sewall marched down the aisle. His clothes were as flamboyant as Moulton's, with the impressive addition of an English judge's full-bottomed wig. He settled himself in the judge's box, and Clemency felt the tiniest glimmer of hope. Despite his regal attire, Judge Sewall possessed a wise, calm face punctuated by sharp hazel eyes. He glanced at her, and she attempted a smile. He frowned severely, and she lowered her lashes. So much for charm.

The town house doors swung shut. "Be seated!" Sheriff Moulton bawled.

Clemency swallowed a lurch of nausea and darted another glance around the room. Mistress Moulton had escorted her to court a half hour ago, and Jamie hadn't appeared. She had endured countless hisses and malicious glares as the crowd shuffled in, and still Jamie hadn't appeared. Judge Sewall rapped his gavel, and she forced herself to take slow, deep breaths. Oh, Holy Mother, where on earth was Jamie?

Judge Sewall clamped a pince-nez on his thin nose and rifled through the papers in front of him. "Magistrate Dixon, since yours is the most pressing case before us this morning, I will allow you to proceed. Read the charges if you please, sir."

Dixon stood and unrolled a document. "Clemency Alexandra Cameron, thou art accused of the following charges, sworn to by warrant and here so presented.

"Firstly, that thou hast maliciously taken the life of a babe through the foul art of magick, and in league with Satan didst deprive this infant of life by wantonly sucking out its breath in full view of witnesses, to wit: the child's own family, in attendance.

"Secondly, that thou hast profaned the orderly workings of our Lord, and endeavored to injure the God-fearing community of Sturgeon's Creek by seeking to insinuate the brazen and harmful trick of smallpox inoculation into its midst; and that thou didst perform this ungodly and dangerous act on a number of children.

"Thirdly, that thou dost cohabit with an unbaptized savage, by name one Mollyocket, who is a known witch; and that thou hast conspired with this witch to injure and harm the God-fearing citizenry of the County of York.

"Lastly, that thou hast flouted God's holy ordinance and the statutes of the community of Sturgeon's Creek by proudly and willfully refusing to renounce thy Papist faith and embrace the true Church, attending it with humble piety and steadfastness.

"In view of such actions, thine accusers come now before this court and do declare that thou hast committed murder, that thou art in league with Satan, and that thou art a witch!"

With a triumphant flourish, Dixon rolled up the parchment document. He pinned Clemency with a malignant glare. Behind her the audience murmured and rustled. A shrill voice cried, "She's evil! Punish the witch!"

Judge Sewall banged his gavel. "Order. Magistrate Dixon, are this woman's accusers now present?"

"Yes, my lord." Dixon nodded, and Matthew Everett stood, blushing and fumbling with a moth-eaten tricorne clutched in his hamlike hands.

"And you are?" Sewall prompted.

"Matthew Everett, m'lord. Tavern keeper in Sturgeon's Creek. My daughter Prudence and me swore out the warrant." He jutted his chin toward Clemency. "She kilt my grandchild!"

A hot blush crept up Clemency's neck. Surely Mr. Everett didn't believe that! He had always been so kind to her. He had even slipped her the latest newspapers from Boston and England before others had pawed them over. She offered him a pleading smile, but he avoided her eyes.

"Were you present at the death, Mr. Everett?" Judge Sewall asked.

"No, m'lord, but Pru, she done told me what happened."

Sewell pursed his lips and looked pained. "Then, I am afraid your testimony is hearsay. You may sit. Mistress Everett?"

Prudence shot up like a scared rabbit. Lank brown hair clung to her smudged face, and her dress was woefully in need of washing. As Judge Sewall questioned her, she mumbled a weepy, incoherent version of the baby's death. Her tears and contradictions, coupled with frequent outbursts from the crowd, slowed her testimony considerably.

The morning sun crept across the courtroom floor, and Clemency's mind began to wander. Jamie must have regretted his gallant impulse. Cut and run, the blasted Scottish rogue. The minutes ticked by, and her spirits sank lower. Oh, why had she thought he might care for her? Why had she jumped at his forced proposal? Of course he hadn't wanted to marry her, but with Hugh breathing down his neck, he had no choice.

She shifted from foot to foot, trying to ease her aching muscles. She wouldn't put it past Jamie to disappear, but where on earth was Hugh? She was sure the gillie loved her like the father she had never known, just as she was sure he had once loved her mother. He would never abandon her to the gallows. Sweat sprang out on her forehead, and she clenched her fists. They couldn't hang her. She just had to be brave. *Faint heart never won the field.*

"Mistress Cameron?" Judge Sewell glared over his pince-nez, looking singularly displeased.

"Yes, my lord?"

"You have been charged with the most heinous crimes

of murder and witchcraft. Both crimes are felonies punishable by death. What say you to these charges?''

"I am innocent, of course. My lord." She hastily added his title.

"I fear there is no 'of course' about it, madam. Now, given the gravity of the charge of murder, I am inclined to overlook the other, lesser charges." The crowd hissed and booed, but Sewall blandly ignored them. "Madam, the death of this child is most serious. How explain you it?''

Clemency wiped her damp palms on her skirt. As she stepped forward, she noticed Lydia sitting in the crowd, a smug look of triumph on her face. Clemency mentally kicked herself. She should have known Prudence never could have engineered this scheme on her own. Judge Sewall cleared his throat.

"I beg your pardon, my lord," she said, bobbing a quick curtsy. "As you know, I serve as healer and midwife in Sturgeon's Creek. Many of the ladies distrust the doctor in York . . ." She halted and cleared her throat. Oh, dear. That comment wouldn't endear her to the court. "Er, at any rate, my lord, my custom in the town has grown rapidly.''

"And as to the charge of murder?''

"Yes, my lord, I'm getting to that. You see, my grandmother was a midwife—''

"Your grandmother was a witch!'' A feminine shriek tore through the courtroom. Judge Sewall pounded his gavel.

"No, she wasn't, my lord," Clemency blurted. "She was a physician.''

"A physician? My dear girl, there are no female physicians.''

"Perhaps not officially, my lord, but nonetheless she was. She was trained in France by an Italian doctor of considerable fame and repute. Dr. Molinari taught her that in some cases respiration may be restored if one breathes into the patient's lungs—''

Angry shouts drowned her words. Sewall impatiently gestured for silence. "Indeed? And does it work?"

"Oh, yes, my lord. I've done it often. Once, a man drowned back in Devon—"

"My lord, this is preposterous!" Reverend Rogers leaped to his feet, jowls quivering with righteous fury. "This is the work of the devil. Only God bestows life, and to say otherwise is to blaspheme—"

Sewall held up a hand. "You are right, to be sure, but is man not God's instrument on earth? Are not healers an extension of our good Lord when they seek to succor?"

"But this woman did not succor. She evilly, wantonly, maliciously took the life of that innocent babe, as commanded by her true master, Satan himself!" Reverend Rogers brandished his Bible, and the crowd stomped their approval.

Sewall pointedly turned his attention to Clemency. "Go on, Mistress Cameron."

"Well, the poor babe was, ah . . . positioned incorrectly." Clemency didn't want to offend the court with graphic terms. "After an extremely difficult travail and with God's help"— this brought a hail of hisses—"I was able to right the child and deliver him. But the cord was around the babe's neck. He wasn't breathing. I . . . I did breathe into the child. I acted as I had been trained. I tried to save his life, to *save* it, my lord, not take it."

Catcalls rocked the room. "She's a witch!" Elihu Staples shouted. "Every time she walks by the forge my fire smolders and I can't hammer a thing. My son's seen her dancing by the lake at night, under a full moon, with a man in a tall black hat!"

His son jumped up. "And I seen her swimmin'. Everyone knows the innocent sink. Only witches float!"

Sewall banged his gavel, and another townsman stood, glowering. "She bewitched my daughter. Since the Everett

babe died, my Judith drops down in a fit whenever she hears
the witch's name spoke!''

"There's been shooting stars every night this week,''
screeched an old lady. "That's the Lord's sign. He's awar-
nin' us of evil in our midst!''

"And the hail storm!'' Elihu Staples shook his fist. "The
witch hadn't been in our midst two days when hail the size
of stones broke every window in the meeting house. That
hail wasn't natural. It was Satan's grapeshot!''

The shouts blurred into a cacophony of hate that went on
and on, biting into Clemency's brain. She covered her ears,
and still the sound buzzed around her. This couldn't be
happening. They were going to find her guilty, and she
would hang!

The crowd's bitter taunts faded slowly from her ears,
drowned out by the horror of her thoughts. She experienced
the oddest sensation, as if time had slowed to a crawl. Her
accusers seemed to swirl before her in a single amorphous
mass. She closed her eyes, and Jamie's handsome, beloved
face suddenly appeared in her mind. Oh, Jamie! She would
never see him again, never have the chance to win his
love. . . .

Sewall hammered his gavel until the crowd subsided.
Witness after witness came forward like the implacable roll
of the sea. Some spoke in her favor—Hepzibah Bryant
testified that the baby had been born dead—but most heaped
virulent condemnation on her head. Despair engulfed Clemency. Why did they hate her so? What had she done but try
to heal the sick?

Judge Sewall rapped his gavel on his desk one last time.
From the position of the sun on the town house floor, she
guessed it must be high noon. Sewall avoided her eyes and
held a whispered conference with the jury of York selectmen.
Then, with a resigned sigh, he scrawled on the sheet of
parchment. He handed the document to Sheriff Moulton.

Clemency sensed the crowd's breathless anticipation. Then Sewall's sharp eyes met hers.

"Mistress Cameron, the jury and I believe you when you say you attempted to save the Everett babe. I have read of such things, and testimony here today supports your claim that the child was born dead. However, due to the preponderance of evidence against you, I have no choice but to find you guilty of the charge of witchcraft."

Clemency's bowels turned to water, and she pressed a hand to her mouth. Biting her lip until she tasted blood, she clenched her eyes shut and began to pray. *Holy Mary, Mother of God, be with us now. . . .*

"Sheriff, read the sentence," Sewall commanded.

Moulton cleared his throat. The courtroom fell silent, and his voice rang through the stillness. "Clemency Alexandra Cameron, having been found guilty of witchcraft, a felony in the Colony of Massachusetts, it is hereby ordered that you be returned to the place from whence you came, and thence be conveyed to a place of execution, where you shall be hanged by the neck until dead—"

The town house doors burst open. Sheriff Moulton's strident voice stumbled to a halt. The crowd gasped.

"I crave forgiveness for the lateness of our arrival, Judge Sewall, but I am sure ye'll want to hear my testimony." The words bore the impeccable, exquisitely educated tone of a British gentleman, with just the slightest tinge of Highland burr. Clemency whirled.

Jamie stood in the doorway. His indigo eyes met hers, and it was as if a lifeline had been thrown across a sea of black despair. She caught it, and his strength flowed into her heart—powerful, warm and sure. Only then did she take in his appearance. Her jaw dropped. If she lived to be a hundred, she would never see a man more stunning than James Ian Alasdair Maclean in full Highland regalia.

He strode forward, and his blue-and-green Maclean tartan kilt swung gracefully about his knees. It was belted to his narrow hips by a black leather strap, and a badger-fur sporran brushed his powerful thighs. The jeweled hilt of his *sgian dhu* glittered from the top of one white stocking, and his high-heeled black shoes were buckled with silver. A full plaid, pinned at the shoulder with a circular silver brooch, crossed his broad chest and fell in loose pleats to his knees. His wide shoulders strained under a black velvet jacket, and a lace jabot accentuated the courtly effect of his snowy linen shirt. With braids at his temples and a dirk in his belt, Jamie was the image of a powerful Scottish laird.

He stood beside her and offered Sewell an elegant bow. "James Ian Alasdair Maclean of Kittery and Sturgeon's Creek, at your service, my lord. I believe you know my companion, Sir Andrew Pepperrell."

Sewall choked out a greeting, and Clemency craned her neck around Jamie's chiseled shoulders. Sir Andrew was a short man with pale skin and clear gray eyes. His azure velvet coat, black riding boots and fine linen cravat bespoke a man of considerable wealth—and style, for he wore his real hair tied back in a ribbon in the latest London fashion.

"Demme, Sewall, I could hardly believe my ears when Maclean apprised me of this outrage." Sir Andrew glanced around the courtroom, distaste in every line of his expression. "Are we to revert back to the notorious idiocies of Salem? 'Tis shocking, sir. Most dreadfully shocking."

Sewall offered him a sickly smile. "You honor us with your presence, Sir Andrew. I appreciate your sensibilities, but I assure you that a proper warrant—"

"Lud! Spare me the dull details." Sir Andrew waved a dismissive hand and languidly sat beside Magistrate Dixon. He flipped open a blue-and-white china snuff box, took a pinch of the powdered tobacco on the back of his hand and inhaled sharply. "Now, do be a fine fellow and get on with it." He caught Clemency's eye and winked. She bit back a wild urge to giggle.

Judge Sewall turned to Jamie. "May I assume, sir, that you have a valid reason for interrupting these proceedings?"

"Aye, my lord." Jamie's eyes glinted, and a smile lurked at the corners of his mouth. "Ye're trying the wrong woman, or a least trying her by the wrong name. She's not Mistress Cameron, she's Mistress Maclean, my wife."

A gasp rent the courtroom. "No!" Lydia leaped up. "'Tis a trick, he's lying!"

Jamie shot her a wintry smile. "I am not the liar here today," he remarked, voice cool and smooth as velvet. Any one else would have retreated before that tone, but Lydia forged on.

"My lord, you can't believe him. 'Tis more of the witch's tricks. She's bewitched him, I tell you!"

Jamie broke into a grin, then winked at Sewall and ran a possessive finger down Clemency's cheek. "Aye—and what red-blooded man wouldna be bewitched by such a beauty?" There was a moment's stunned silence, broken by Sir Andrew's guffaw.

"Lud, Maclean, too right, too right. And a demmed shame you beat me to her!" He doubled over and smacked his fawn-breeched thigh.

Judge Sewall eyed Jamie skeptically. "If she is your wife, sir, what proof do you offer?"

"My lord, I beg you, put an end to this nonsense at once." Reverend Rogers stood, his pious face pained. "These two are not married. The woman is an unrepentant Catholic. As such, I would never consent to marry them."

Jamie's massive shoulders tensed. "My lord, we were married by the ancient Highland custom of handfasting."

The crowd broke into curious, eager murmurs, and Reverend Rogers rolled his eyes heavenward. "Handfasting! 'Tis a barbaric custom, my lord, and carries no legal weight here. In truth, 'tis no more than blatant carnality masquerading as wedlock."

Jamie swept the judge another graceful bow. "My lord,

you are an educated, well-traveled man. As such, surely you are acquainted with the Quaker marriage ceremony? 'Tis the same as handfasting and deemed legal in the Colonies. And rest assured, the moment my wife and I encounter a Catholic priest, we will be properly wed.''

Clemency shot Jamie a startled glance. Did he mean that? His handsome face was impassive, but she noted the wry quirk of his lips. No, definitely not. They were as likely to encounter a three-headed unicorn as a priest in the Colony of Massachusetts.

Sewall pondered Jamie's words. ''Indeed, you are correct as to the legality of the Quaker ceremony, and I am inclined to let it go at that. But as to the charges of witchcraft against Mistress Cameron, er . . . Mistress Maclean, what say you?''

Jamie turned with a flourish so the crowd could see his face. ''My lord, I believe you're a married man, as are most of the good men here. And we all ken how our women folk behave when we're not there to mind them.'' His Scots accent thickened and took on a rakish tone. ''In truth, my lord, my dear wife is no more a witch than ye. She's no' but a wee lass gone and stirred things up when her husband's off to Kittery.'' He shot the judge a knowing wink. ''No doubt to pay me back for my shenanigans in the tavern!''

Laughter rippled through the audience, and several men poked each other in the ribs. ''She wouldn't be the first!'' someone shouted.

Sewall pounded his gavel. ''Mr. Maclean, all of this is fascinating, but quite immaterial. Your wife has already been convicted.''

''Sewall, do correct me if I'm wrong.'' Sir Andrew stood, a distinct glint of mischief in his gray eyes. ''Mistress Maclean seems a healthy young woman.'' He held a gold monocle to one eye and ogled Clemency's waist, then arched his sandy brows and fixed his gaze on Jamie's powerful thighs. ''And, lud! My dear friend Maclean is nothing if not virile. Is it the usual practice of this court to hang a woman who may be carrying?''

The crowd muttered, and Sewall flushed scarlet. "Certainly not, sirrah! I am appalled that you even suggest such a barbarity.'' He appraised Clemency, and she thought she saw relief flicker in his weary eyes. He pinned Jamie with a stern glare. "Mr. Maclean, to the best of your knowledge, is your wife carrying?''

Clemency dug her nails into her palms and breathlessly waited for Jamie's answer. The closest they had come to consummating their marriage was the one dizzying kiss after their vows last night. And she knew Jamie's sense of honor. He would never lie.

Jamie shot her the tiniest of quick winks. "Weel now, a man hates to have what goes on in his bed aired in public.'' He cast the crowd a look of elaborate—and suggestive— chagrin. Chuckles rippled around the room. "And I never was verra good at counting, ye ken. So I suppose I'd have to say there's always the chance a man's wife could be carrying.'' He grinned and winked broadly, and the crowd convulsed with ribald laughter.

"Atta boy, Scotty,'' one man chortled. "Slip her one for me!''

Lydia screeched, "If they are truly married, when did this ceremony take place?''

Jamie held out his hand, and Clemency clasped it, heart bounding with pride. "Weel, let's just say this. At summer's end next year, Mistress Maclean and I better find a priest, or I'll be out on me arse!''

The crowd roared approval, and Judge Sewall pounded his gavel. Clemency looked up into Jamie's dancing eyes. "You are a rogue, sir,'' she whispered, dimpling. "Remind me to think of a suitable punishment for you when we're alone.''

His handsome face broke into a delighted grin. "Promise?'' he murmured. Then he turned her hand palm up and kissed it. His tongue flicked against her skin, and his languid gaze seared across her breasts.

Moments later, dizzy with excitement and confusion, Clemency found herself in Judge Sewall's cramped private chamber. Jamie and Sir Andrew stood beside her. Sewall stripped off his wig, and she smothered a giggle at the sight of his shaved head.

"Sir Andrew, what do you suggest I do with this mess?" Sewall asked. "I've already convicted the wench . . . er, the lady," he added as Jamie's jaw tightened. He flopped into a chair and wiped his sweaty brow.

"Demme, Sewall, I took you for a sharper blade than this." Sir Andrew fluffed out the lace on his cuffs. "If you have convicted Mistress Maclean, then so be it." Clemency gasped, and Jamie cupped a steadying hand under her elbow. "The sentence is the thing, man. Might I suggest banishment instead of hanging?"

Sewall blinked. "Banishment, eh? 'Tis a thought, but I don't see—"

Sir Andrew snatched up the judge's wig and twirled it around one finger. "Sewall, a gentleman never mentions old debts, but in this instance, sir, you compel me." His voice had lost all foppish pretense, and his gray eyes gleamed like gunmetal. Clemency realized a keen mind lurked under his dandified clothes and drawling accent.

Sewall rose and bowed stiffly. "As you wish. Now, let's settle this mess."

Jamie escorted Clemency back into the courtroom, and the crowd leaned forward, tense and expectant. "Be upstanding!" Sheriff Moulton bawled.

Sewall climbed the steps to his box, then sat and sighed heavily. "Mistress James Maclean, this court has found you guilty of witchcraft, and that conviction stands. In light of the peculiar circumstances of this case, however, I commute the sentence of hanging. Instead, I order the following.

"Your property, formerly the farm belonging to Mr. Robert MacKinnon, is hereby confiscated by the County of York to be sold at public auction. You and your husband, Mr. James Maclean, are hereby banished from the County of York for a period of one year. If you break this banishment, Mistress Maclean, you will once again be subject to hanging. Sheriff Moulton will see that you depart this jurisdiction in forty-eight hours.''

There was a muffled thud. Behind them, Lydia sprawled on the floor in a dead faint.

Chapter Seventeen

A solid sheet of rain fell straight down, gushing from the eaves of Jamie's cabin. The air smelled cold and earthy, and the pungent tang of fallen leaves hinted at winter's approach. Clemency leaned against the cabin doorway and imagined she was standing in a cave under a dark waterfall. The constant rush was soothing, and she closed her eyes, wishing the rain could wash away her anxiety.

At dusk, Jamie, Hugh and she had arrived at her cabin across the fields, exhausted by the strain of the trial and the long ride from York. Clemency's brows contracted as she remembered Judge Sewall's order. Her cabin no longer, blast the man! How could he confiscate property like that? It wasn't fair. She rolled her neck from side to side, trying to ease the iron bands of tension that gripped her shoulders.

Mollyocket and Elizabeth had greeted them with hugs and cries of joy. A tiny smile curved Clemency's lips as she recalled Jamie's affectionate reunion with his daughter.

Whatever her new husband's faults, lack of fatherly devotion was not one of them.

Her new husband. Oh, my. She wrapped her arms around her ribs and squeezed, half expecting the pressure to contain her excitement, and her nervousness.

After a hasty supper, Jamie and Hugh had whispered on the porch, darting her oblique glances now and then. Thunder had rumbled in the distance as Jamie had strode up to her at last. His expression was a mask of bland politeness, but there was no mistaking the mischievous glint in his eyes.

"Will ye be all right walking up to the cabin in the dark, *mo druidh?* I want to explain a few things to Elizabeth before I join ye."

She froze like a deer at the end of a long-hunter's rifle. Jamie arched a rakish brow, then leaned down and whispered in her ear. " 'Tis our wedding night, Mistress Maclean. We dinna want to spend it with an audience, aye?"

Clemency's jaw sagged, and a hot blush washed over her skin. Jamie chuckled and opened the cabin door. She blurted a hasty good night, then darted out. The rain had started halfway to Jamie's cabin, soaking her to the skin. After reaching the shelter of his house, she had made several futile attempts at starting a fire with flint and steel. She had then retreated to the porch, too ill at ease to stay inside with Jamie's books, clothes, *bed.*

Icy air seeped through her calico bodice, and she shivered. Holy Mother, what was she going to do? She loved Jamie, and her flesh burned each time she relived the rich passion of his kisses. But her only intimate experience was the one terrifying, degrading, blindingly painful night when a man— a man she had trusted—had brutally raped her. She inhaled slowly and tried to calm her lurching stomach. She wanted Jamie, but she was afraid. What if she didn't please him? Or worse, what if he didn't want her?

The thud of running feet pounded through the dark. With one long stride Jamie burst through the curtain of water and plowed into her. She staggered back, and he grasped her shoulders.

"St. Columba, ye scared the tar out of me!" Water ran in rivulets down his lean cheeks and dripped from the chiseled tip of his elegant nose. His sodden hair shone dark and sleek as sealskin. "Why aren't ye inside?"

"I couldn't get a fire started, and it didn't seem right to be in there without you."

She caught the glint of perfect white teeth as he smiled. " 'Tis your cabin now, *mo druidh.* Didna I say 'with all my worldly goods I thee endow?' " He flung open the door and ushered her inside.

"I . . . I don't remember."

He chuckled and strolled to the hearth. "Weel, that's verra flattering. Is it usual to forget the words to your own wedding?" He struck a spark with flint and steel, and the birch bark kindling began to smoke.

"I don't know. I've never been married."

Jamie shook his head like a wet dog, flinging droplets everywhere. "Aye, so ye haven't." His voice was uncharacteristically neutral.

She peered through the shadows and tried to read his expression. As the fire caught, light flickered across his face and illuminated an expression of deep sorrow. Her hands began to tremble. So that was the way of it. He was still in love with Rebekah.

Clemency must have made some sound, for Jamie's distressed expression vanished. "Och, here I am teasing ye, and ye're wet to the bone." He snatched a coarse linen towel from a peg and lifted it to dry her hair.

"No." She pressed her hands to her damp cheeks and stepped back. Surprise rippled across his face; then he peered down at her, indigo eyes sharp and assessing. "I . . . I mean, you're wetter than I am," she stammered. "You dry off first."

She spun away, then knelt before the fire and cautiously

added larger sticks to the flames. She would not let him read her thoughts, would not let him see her need. No matter how much she yearned for his love, he would have to offer his own first.

He rustled about behind her—bolting the door, lighting a candle, filling the tea kettle with water. Then he hooked the kettle on the hearth's iron rod and swung it above the flames. She felt his eyes on her and averted her face.

"I ken ye're frightened, *mo cridhe.*" His fingers clasped her chin; then he knelt and turned her toward him. "In truth, so am I. We havena spoken of what happened to ye before ye sailed to America, and I think that's for the best." His eyes burned into hers, and his fingers gripped her chin. "I dinna want to dig up the past. 'Tis over and done, aye?"

"Is it?" She jerked away. "If you want my past to be dead and buried, then I'll bend to your wishes, m'lord. But can you offer me the same? Can you honestly say your past is dead and buried?"

His eyes widened, and his face grew tense, pained. Instantly, she regretted her harsh words, regretted her clumsy stab at his heart. "I'm sorry," she blurted. "I didn't mean to be so peevish. I'm just cold and dirty and tired—"

"Hush, *mo cridhe.*" He caught her chin, then languidly dragged his thumb across her lower lip. He leaned close. Quick desire pooled in her belly, but he merely brushed a kiss across her forehead, the way one might kiss a child. He stood, then poured steaming water from the kettle into a washbasin, then grabbed a cloth and turned to her. "Let me bathe ye."

"What?"

Amusement crinkled the tanned skin around his eyes. "Ye heard me, woman. Ye said ye're cold and dirty. Who better to remedy that than your husband?" He pulled her to her feet and set the basin on the table, then undid the laces down the back of her bodice.

"Jamie, please, I—"

He hooked one strong arm around her waist and pulled her back against his hips. The wetness of his coat and plaid seeped through her linen shift, cooling her heated skin. "I said hush," he whispered, lips warm against her ear. The sibilance of the sound vibrated to her toes. Gooseflesh rose on her arms, and her nipples hardened instantly, puckering into sensitive nubs that ached for his touch.

"Mmmmmm." Jamie cupped her breast and rolled one stiff little point between thumb and forefinger. Chuckling wickedly, he grazed his teeth across the warm curve of her throat. "Are ye cold now, *mo cridhe?*"

"N . . . no," she gasped, pressing back against him. His muscular thighs were like iron, and she felt the unmistakable stirring of his manhood against her buttocks. Her skin tingled as he pulled her bodice away and dropped it to the floor.

"Ye're blushing." His apple-scented breath warmed her cheek. "Are ye embarrassed to stand naked before your husband?"

"No," she squeaked as his hands deftly untied the drawstring of her skirt. It fell in a puddle around her ankles, leaving her in nothing but her shift.

Jamie clasped her hips in both hands, then slowly, firmly ran his palms down over her belly and thighs, urging her back against his hardness. He sighed, then stepped away so quickly she almost fell. "Sit down," he commanded, nodding toward the bed. He picked up the washbasin, and she meekly obeyed.

He knelt before her and slipped off her muddy shoes. His fingers trailed up her legs, then stripped away her stockings. Glancing up with languid eyes, he dipped the rough cloth in the hot water, then slowly caressed it up her bare skin. A shaft of pure sensation shot through her. She closed her eyes and bit back a moan.

He coaxed her forward until her buttocks perched on the edge of the bedstead. He murmured something in Gaelic, and his sure hands roamed higher, gently stroking her skin until she thought she would melt and dissolve like the steam rising around them. A tiny part of her mind whispered that she should feel embarrassed, ashamed, but she didn't.

Jamie tucked her chemise around her lap and nudged her knees apart. The damp waves of his hair silked against her skin; then the hot, wet velvet of his tongue traced along her inner thigh. She gasped as he nibbled her sensitive flesh, and her legs spasmed together, catching his head.

He chuckled. Peeping up from between her thighs, he cast her an impish glance. "Did I hurt ye, *mo cridhe?*" As he spoke, his fingernails raked the curve of her bottom, sending her into a near swoon of ecstasy.

"No," she whimpered, blushing wildly. Holy Mother, this was torture! A hot, yearning wetness blossomed between her thighs, and a pulse thudded heavily there, as if her heart had migrated much lower.

"Aye? Weel, I'll take that as encouragement." His aristocratic nose brushed the crisp black curls between her thighs, and she jumped like a scalded cat. His strong hands steadied her hips, his breath caressed her skin, then he leaned forward and kissed her.

Her mind reeled, and she longed to squirm away. This was too intimate, too mortifying.

Slowly, tantalizingly, he ran his tongue along her secret inner folds, up and down, up and down, again and again. An incredible shimmer of sensation shuddered through her, and she lay back, shyly offering herself to his mouth. He rhythmically licked her, and she lifted her hips to meet him, rocking in an ancient dance. She felt mindless, weightless, swirling in a maelstrom of rising pleasure. Then his long finger pressed into her, easing the shock of the entrance to come, erasing the horror of her memories. He probed, circled, slid in and out. She cried with quick, helpless little pleas: "Jamie. Oh, yes—Please . . . I want you."

He grasped her hips with both hands and slanted his mouth to her yearning flesh. His relentless tongue thrust into her again and again, and all her senses sharpened, tightened, focused, taking her to the verge of pleasure so intense it was almost pain. She grasped his head, bucked against his mouth, caught her breath, then exploded in a groaning convulsion of wild, shattering ecstasy.

After a long moment, she wriggled away from him and lay panting on the pillows, too limp to speak. Holy Mother, had she truly ... oh, she didn't even know what to call it, but to do that with Jamie's *mouth*. ... Too embarrassed to meet his burning eyes, her gaze drifted lower, and landed on the formidable bulge straining for freedom under his kilt.

Jamie sat beside her on the bed, his brows knit in a deep frown. "I hope I didna upset ye, *mo cridhe*. I forget that ye ... weel, that ye may not care for a man after what happened to ye."

"Jamie, no, I'm just ..." Her voice dropped low, and she straightened her shift. "Embarrassed. I ... I was frightened, but mostly I was afraid I wouldn't please you." She sat up and pressed against him, reveling in the hardness of his shoulder, longing for him to ease the ache that throbbed once more between her legs. "Please, Jamie. I want to be your wife. Lie with me."

She heard his sharp intake of breath, but pulled away before he could fold her in his arms. Kneeling before him, black hair curtaining her face, she pulled off his shoes and stockings, then carefully laid his *sgian dhu* on the bedside table. She stood and unpinned his silver clan brooch, then lifted the damp wool from his chest. He sat like a statue, muscles tensed. She realized he was holding his breath.

She eased the black coat down over his massive shoulders, then untied his ruffled cravat and unlaced his linen shirt. He raised his arms obediently, and she slipped the garment over his head. The firelight danced across his sculpted muscles, and a rush of desire dizzied her. He was so beautiful, so perfectly male. She longed to kiss and lick her way down his taut stomach, down the tantalizing, red-gold trail of hair that disappeared into his kilt. Her fingers fumbled with the silver buckle of his belt, and his strong hand guided her until the clasp sprang open.

She knelt once more and ran her gaze down his body. Long, tousled waves of hair rippled over his shoulders, and she itched to run her fingers through the dusting of curls on his chest. With a little spurt of shock, she saw that his nipples stood erect.

Looking away in confusion, she grabbed the washcloth and ran it slowly up his long, hard legs. A tiny sigh escaped his lips. Dimpling, she dropped the cloth and dipped her fingers in the steaming water, then danced them up the curves and planes of his muscles until they slipped beneath his kilt. He shuddered under her touch like an unbroken stallion, and she reveled in her power over him. Suddenly she longed to mount him, to clasp her thighs around this narrow hips, to make him beg and writhe beneath her, to ride him until his essence erupted in a primal burst of ecstasy.

Her nails raked his inner thigh. "Good Christ, dinna stop," he panted, neck corded, head thrown back. She knew that any self-respecting Scotsman wore nothing beneath his kilt, but still she started in surprise as her hand brushed the jutting heat of his manhood. Swallowing hard, she pushed his kilt up, then dropped the soft wool with a gasp. "Holy Mother, you're as big as a Percheron!"

Clemency clapped a hand over her mouth and blushed furiously. Jamie roared with laughter. He clasped her hot little hand around the straining upward curve of his erection, then showed her the rhythm he liked. Her fingers teased him, hardening him to marble and driving him mad. Lust roared through him.

"Och, St. Columba," he moaned, "what are ye doing to me?"

To his enormous surprise, she actually giggled. "Well, sir, if you don't know, who's to teach me?"

Somehow he couldn't get control of his breathing; his

heart thundered as if he had sprinted twenty miles. He lay
back and pulled her against him, then gently eased her shift
from her shoulders and exposed the heavy sweetness of her
breasts.

"Och, ye're so beautiful, so beautiful," he husked, cup-
ping and squeezing her lush flesh, dragging his tongue across
her shivering skin. His lips closed over her ripe nipple, and
she arched her back. Groaning deep in his throat, he suckled
firmly, rhythmically, and each suck sent a maddening vibra-
tion straight to his straining cock.

She writhed against him, slick with sweat. "Jamie, *please.*"
She knotted her fingers in his hair, then raked her nails down
his back.

The slight pain spurred his passion, and his control vanished. Rearing up, he stripped off his kilt and straddled her
thighs, then ran his hands over the velvety softness of her
quivering belly. Her green eyes, heavy-lidded with desire,
glinted in the firelight, and her breasts heaved under his
touch.

Suddenly a spasm of fury shot through him. He would
never have the joy and honor of taking Clemency's maidenhead. But she was his wife now—his *wife!* He would mark
her, possess her, make her his.

He clenched his eyes shut and ordered himself to be gentle,
patient, tender. He lay down beside her and took possession
of her mouth, his tongue thrusting deeply, preparing her for
his entrance. With a tiny cry, she pressed against him, and
he inhaled the rich, intoxicating scent of her desire. Then she
reached down and gripped his manhood with firm, feverish
fingers. His heart stalled.

Suddenly she pulled back and stroked his cheek. *"Mo
cridhe,"* she whispered, pronouncing the Gaelic perfectly.
"I know what you're thinking. I can read that handsome
face of yours like a crystal ball. But you are the first, because
you're my husband and my love. Lie with me, Jamie." Her
honeyed breath caressed his lips, and he felt himself sinking

into mindless lust. She nibbled his lower lip, taunting him with tiny nips. Her nails raked down his back, and she grasped his buttocks, urging him closer.

His hand gripped the softness of her thigh, then trailed higher until his fingers touched the wet heat of her womanhood. He stroked her nub until she moaned and rocked against him; then he eased his finger inside.

She gasped, "Oh, Jamie, please don't stop."

He rolled and mounted her in one fluid motion. Gritting his teeth to keep control, he eased the crown of his manhood into her molten heat. Och, he loved this, loved the tight, slick clasp, the delicious resistance as his burning flesh pressed forward. He inhaled sharply and plunged home.

"Och, good Christ," he cried. He clenched his buttocks and arched his back as he thrust into her. She moaned beneath him, not with pain but with lust, with welcome, as if he had been born in her, grown in her and had returned to her at last.

He captured her lips, his tongue swirling and plunging, matching his body's rhythm. He bit her throat and served her with intense concentration, his movements measured thrusts of barely restrained power. She bucked her hips, riding the hardness of his shaft, and he ground deeper.

Suddenly she froze. He stopped instantly, holding his breath to keep from groaning aloud. "What is it, *mo cridhe?*" he gasped. "Have I hurt ye?"

"No, but what if . . . what if we make a child?"

"Och, my darling, darling heart." His smiled down at her, down into those loch green eyes. "Do ye think I'd abandon ye?"

"We only married for a year and a day—"

The muscles of his arms bulged as he lowered himself and kissed her. Her inner muscles gripped his manhood, and he throbbed deep inside her. "Hush now," he murmured. "I promised to protect ye, aye?" Slowly, tantalizingly, he rotated his hips. She whimpered and squirmed against him.

"I'll make ye another promise, my darling witch." He smiled wickedly and rolled his *r*s like a breaking sea. He gave another tiny thrust, then pulled back, all amusement wiped from his face. "Our child will have my name and will be loved and protected as long as I draw breath."

Tears glistened in her eyes. She wrapped her legs around him and pulled him deeper. Gasping, he lowered his head and drove home, home, home.

"I love you," she whispered, so low he barely heard her. Then her body convulsed beneath him. She bucked, writhed, cried out, "Oh, Jamie!"

Instantly, his climax swept over him, its intensity taking him utterly by surprise, leaving him helpless, dashed open, washed clean. And for the first time in his life, amazingly, perfectly alive.

Chapter Eighteen

London, 1763

Lord Francis Bury irritably tapped a hand against his satin-clad leg and stared out over the Thames toward the great dome of St. Paul's. A morning rain shower had cleared the worst of the coal smoke from London's air, and the cathedral glowed golden and mellow in the late afternoon sun. Bury strolled the length of his terrace, waiting, waiting. Then he stopped and looked at the cathedral once more. No matter how often he gazed at it, St. Paul's never failed to fill him with pride.

He turned his back on the river traffic bustling beyond the terrace and surveyed his library. Shining mahogany bookcases rose to the ceiling on all four walls, broken only by the long line of French doors overlooking the terrace. Thick Turkey carpets covered the floor, and a fire crackled in the fireplace, easing the chill from the October air. He walked to the fireplace, his long legs covering the distance in three easy strides. He held his hands toward the flames and shivered. Lately, no matter what he did, he couldn't seem to get warm.

A fit of coughing wracked his thin frame, and he groped for a handkerchief in the pocket of his lavender satin waistcoat. His fingers closed over the intricately carved frame of the miniature portrait, and apprehension shot through him. He shut his eyes and clutched the tiny painting. Would she come back? *She must.*

A discreet knock sounded on the door, and his butler, Madison, entered. "Mr. Thayer, my lord."

Bury bit back a sharp remark as his portly, white-haired solicitor bustled in. There was no use alienating the man. Thayer's personal shortcomings—especially his tendency to tardiness—were more than offset by his skill at managing Bury's estate.

"My lord, I beg your pardon for the lateness of my arrival," Thayer said, bowing low. "The Thames is thronged with traffic today, positively thronged. No doubt our city's fine inhabitants wish to enjoy our perverse and changeable sun while it lasts, but it does make for a crush on the river. My bargeman—"

Bury waved the solicitor toward a chair. "That will do, Thayer. I am quite accustomed to your somewhat lackadaisical sense of time. But as I stated in my message, time is the one thing I do not have. I am sailing on the morning tide, and I must resolve this issue before I depart."

He gazed out the French doors, and a tiny pang invaded his breast, quickly stifled. Would he ever come back to Bury House?

He was inordinately proud of the place. Designed to his specifications and built adjacent to the Duke of Richmond's home, it was the most fashionable address in London. Indeed, in the ten years since the house's completion, Londoners had made it a point to ferry their country cousins along the Thames embankment so they could marvel at the mansion's Georgian splendor.

But what would all this splendor matter in a few months? He wouldn't be around to appreciate it. Irritation surged through him, and he choked back a fit of coughing.

"My lord?"

"Hmmmm?" Bury paced around the room, too agitated to sit.

"I said, my lord, are you entirely set on this course of action? This is the worst possible time to undertake an ocean journey. The storms in the Atlantic can be most fearsome in autumn, and in your condition—"

"Blast my condition to hell and shove it down Satan's throat," Bury thundered. "My condition is none of your concern. Now, is the document ready?"

Thayer's face crumpled like a molded *blanc mange* left too long in the sun. "Yes, my lord. But as your man of business I cannot in good conscience encourage this endeavor, or its potential results. My friends in Parliament tell me the Colonies are positively awash in rebellion since His Majesty's government announced the Stamp Act." Thayer tugged at his cravat and hurried on, flustered by Bury's forbidding frown. "Although the Act won't go into effect for many months, already there has been a deep-throated roar of defiance. Rioting—"

"I am well aware of the situation, Thayer. My health may have compelled me to temporarily vacate my seat in the House of Lords, but it has not addled my wits." Bury's lips thinned into a chill smile. "As usual, our hoydenish brethren across the sea are reacting like savages." Turning away, he clasped his hands behind his back, then paced the room. Once, public duty had been his lifeblood. He had spent his entire career in service to the monarchy, but that was over now. "King George's government must raise revenue," he continued. "The French wars have devastated the Exchequer, and like it or not, the Colonies must accept the price of citizenship.''

"But the colonials are protesting that 'tis a matter of rights—''

"Rights? That may be what they believe, but I assure you, my dear Thayer, money rests at the bottom of it, as it does in all disputes.'' Bury sighed. Damn it to hell, he couldn't even walk the library without becoming winded. He pressed a blue-veined hand against his lips and stifled another cough. "When it comes to matters of rights versus revenues, the government will sacrifice rights every time. And that's as it should be,'' he added, flashing a wolfish smile.

He strolled past a gilded pier glass and halted, shocked. He didn't hear Thayer's response, but stood staring at his reflection. His once-handsome face was cadaverous, a death's head of sickly white skin stretched over perfect, patrician bones. His blond hair hadn't whitened, but rather faded to a noncolor. Only his Wedgewood-blue eyes were recognizable. They were still the eyes of a daring soldier, a ruthless politician, a trusted royal advisor. Once, he had been all those things.

He suppressed a shudder and held up a hand, interrupting his solicitor in mid-sentence. "The day is advancing, Thayer. I would sign the papers so I may complete preparations for my journey.''

Thayer looked pained. "My lord, I appreciate the sentiment behind this sudden whim, but—''

Bury whirled. "Whim? You make it sound like the impulsive folly of a schoolboy. Perhaps if I had been a bit more foolish in the past, I wouldn't be suffering my present agony.'' His hand clutched the miniature in his pocket. "I should have made this change years ago, but I listened to my head, to my advisors, to small-minded men like you. And what has it brought me?'' He sneered at a massive gilt-framed portrait over the library mantel. His dead wife simpered down from it, looking as shallow and vapid as she had in life. "I have no wife, I have no heirs, I have nothing."

"But, my lord, you have your nephew. Lord Geoffrey—"

Bury snorted and collapsed in a chair. "My wastrel nephew is a disgrace. For years I have paid his debts, covered up his scandals, endured his unsavory company, all to keep the estate and the noble title of Bury from crumbling to dust." He pulled out his handkerchief and wiped perspiration from his brow. "As you have so astutely pointed out, I have no choice as to the disposition of the title. It must pass to the next legitimate male heir in the Bury family, and unfortunately that is Geoffrey." He waved his hand, encompassing in one gesture the elegant room and all its treasures. "But everything else is mine. I will dispose of it where I see fit."

A vicious fit of coughing assailed him, and he doubled over, pressing his cambric handkerchief to his lips. Thayer struggled to his feet, face as pink as a boiled ham.

"My lord! Are you all right, my lord? Should I call Madison?" He snatched up a crystal decanter of sherry, dropping the heavy stopper and spilling a few drops on the thick carpet. "Or a drink perhaps?"

Bury waved Thayer away and continued to hack. God's bones, would this disease never give him a moment's rest? Even now he could feel the icy hands of death trailing over his clammy forehead, choking his weakened respiration. Always the taunting talons withdrew, but he knew his time was short.

With enormous effort of will, he straightened up and shoved the handkerchief into his pocket. "Now, Thayer, I will sign the new will now. And I will thank you to keep your opinions to yourself."

Thayer looked aggrieved. "As you wish, my lord. As to witnesses—"

"Call Madison and the housekeeper, Mrs. Dodge. They have been with me for years." Bury pinned Thayer with a sharp glare. "You must be certain this new will stands up in court. There can be no doubt whatsoever of its legality. As you so accurately point out, I may not live to return to London. If that unfortunate circumstance comes to pass, you must act on my behalf to prevent any difficulties. My vile nephew will try to overturn it, but this will must stand. Do I make myself clear?"

"Yes, my lord." Thayer meekly drew several documents from his satchel, then waddled to the door.

Madison and Mrs. Dodge entered the hushed library. Minutes later they withdrew, having signed as witnesses to Lord Bury's signature. Thayer blotted the papers with fine sand, then puffed out his chest.

"My lord, it has been the pinnacle of my career to have served you these past years. As you may recall, I have been in your service since you left His Majesty's army. Always, in every endeavor, I have had your best interests at heart." He folded his pudgy hands over the bulging front on his rust wool waistcoat, as if to underscore the sincerity of his sentiments. "I cannot tell you how it grieves me to consider the course of action on which you are poised to embark. I beg you to reconsider this ill-advised journey. You have no guarantee of a felicitous outcome, and the probable hazards far outweigh the potential gain."

Bury leaned back in his chair, closed his eyes and held up a hand. "My dear Thayer, I have never questioned your devotion or the wisdom of your counsel. But I will not be dissuaded."

Thayer stood in silence a long moment. When Lord Bury did not open his eyes, he bowed deeply. "Then, my lord, I will take my leave. You have my word of honor that your wishes will be obeyed to the letter. Since it grieves me to consider the possible permanent severance of the ties between us, I will not say good-bye, but wish you *adieu.*"

"Thank you, Thayer," Bury whispered. He didn't stir or

open his eyes. After an awkward pause, the solicitor crept out.

Bury swallowed the unaccustomed tightness in his throat. It must be the illness that made him so emotional. Here he was, choking up like a schoolgirl over a pompous farewell from his solicitor! He attempted a sardonic smile, but it died on his lips.

A sudden gust of wind blew open one French door, and the sprightly sounds of river traffic drifted to his ears. Children squealed, women laughed, oars thunked and splashed. Then, silvering down like bells from heaven, the chimes of St. Paul's rang across the water. Bury smiled. Enchanting, magical sound. She had loved it. It had become her habit during their brief time together to sit with him in the library, drinking a glass of sherry as the day drew to a close and the pure, mellow tones of St. Paul's welcomed the dusk.

Hot tears overflowed. He welcomed them. He didn't bother with the handkerchief. It was sullied now, covered with blood. When was the last time he had cried? Foolish question. He new the answer much too well.

His fingers curled around the miniature in his pocket. He wasn't a religious man. He had always embraced the tenets of reason, science, human endeavor. He had scorned the soldiers under his command who made battlefield conversions, but he could no longer afford scorn. He drew the tiny painting from his pocket and pressed it to his lips. Would she forgive him? Would this last, desperate act pay his debt and secure his soul?

Cool blue twilight stole across the river, and evening spread its dark wings over London. Lord Bury sat alone in his library, in the shadows.

Chapter Nineteen

Fort Western, Province of Maine, 1763

October 17. Clear and chill. I am at Home. Mr. Maclean chopping wood. Esquire Howard much troubled in his Mind as to his son's health. Brought me a barrel of Smoked Herring as a present. Also one gallon white Rhum and 2 lb. Sugar as payment for my attendance on his son Noah.

Clemency's quill frayed, spattering ink across the page of her journal. "Blast," she muttered. She snatched Jamie's penknife from the groove in the slanted wood desk, then laboriously cut a fresh point, holding her tongue just so. Mollyocket looked up from the high-backed pine settle by the hearth and slanted Clemency a knowing smile, then returned to the leather-bound copy book in her lap.

In truth, Clemency didn't want to be sitting inside on such a glorious afternoon, but she had promised to help Mollyocket with her penmanship. She sighed and glanced out the graceful bow window overlooking the Kennebec River. She longed to be out-of-doors, reveling in October's beauty. The brazen New England autumn was aflame with golden sun, azure sky and scarlet leaves, and she had never seen anything so marvelous.

Sighing, she forced her gaze from the window and bent over her journal.

The Canker rash has taken poor Noah Howard hard. Throat Ulcers pain him piteously and Rash shocking to behold. Dosed him with Hyssop tea and decoction of vinegar and onions. Resting easy now. Praise God, dear Elizabeth continues well.

Praise God, indeed. The terror of canker rash aside, Clemency had feared that Elizabeth would reject Jamie's remarriage, but the child had been overjoyed that Clemency was her new mama. She had treated the sail from Kittery as a delightful adventure and had deviled the crew on Sir Andrew's sloop to distraction. Clemency grinned, recalling Jamie's high spirits and practical jokes as they had sailed the forty-six miles up the Kennebec from the Atlantic. Elizabeth came by her naughtiness honestly.

Her smile faded. Poor, dear Jamie. He had reassured her again and again that he didn't regret their banishment from York County. In truth, he seemed strangely relieved. The punishment hadn't turned out to be as terrible as she had imagined. Thanks to Sir Andrew's generous friendship, Jamie now possessed two thousand acres of fertile land stretching north from Fort Western into vast, timber-rich wilderness. The land included an ideal location for a sawmill, and Jamie fancied the idea of becoming a timber baron.

A frown wrinkled her brow. Sir Andrew had deeded Jamie the property in exchange for his services as surveyor and agent. Unfortunately, surveying required long trips into Maine's uncharted frontier, and today was the first day Jamie had been home in two weeks.

She tapped her foot and dipped her pen in the inkwell.

*Called from Home to Mrs. Richards of Hallowell last eve.
Her Travail was well advanced and I tarried all night. I
delivered her of a Daughter at eight o'clock this Morning.
They are resting easy.*

Clemency traced the goose quill down her nose. Another
reason to praise God: her notoriety had not followed them
from Sturgeon's Creek. On the contrary, the few settlers in
and around Fort Western had welcomed the Macleans and
Hugh Rankin with warm hospitality. Even strange, mute
Mollyocket had received the kindest treatment, especially
after Clemency had dropped a few hints about the Indian's
skill with medicinal herbs. It seemed the community had
languished some time without a healer, and the goodwives
eagerly embraced young Mrs. Maclean and her native servant.

Indeed, God seemed determined to bless them. Even
Clemency's fears about suitable housing had vanished the
moment they set foot on Fort Western's sturdy dock. Jamie
had roared with laughter as she gaped up the riverbank to
their new home, a stunned expression on her face. Instead
of the wilderness hovel of her imagination, they were to
share the substantial Georgian frame house known as The
Fort. The long building sheltered Esquire James Howard
and his family on the north end, and the Macleans, Hugh
and Mollyocket had gratefully settled into the south end.

She stood and snapped her journal shut. " 'Tis no use,
Mollyocket," she said, trying to sound apologetic. "I can't
concentrate." Not with half-naked Jamie chopping wood
behind the house. Mollyocket waved her away without looking up.

Clemency slipped out onto the granite back doorstep,
feeling like a naughty schoolgirl sneaking away from her
lessons. She settled herself in a patch of sunlight and gazed
longingly at Jamie's bulging biceps as he expertly swung
the axe and cleaved a junk of solid oak. His lithe, powerful

body gleamed in the sun, and sweat trickled over the whitish web of scars on his broad back.

Sudden irritation pricked her spine. Even though she and Jamie were now man and wife, and even though he made love to her with swoon-inducing passion at every opportunity, he still refused to tell her about the whipping or share the horrors of his past. She knew there was some secret there, something of terrible import, but he wouldn't reveal it. She had failed miserably at her attempts to worm her way into his stubborn Scottish heart. He was as much a stranger now as he had been on the day they met.

Jamie turned, and his catlike grace took her breath. He flashed her a rakish smile, then sank the axe into the chopping block with a solid *thunk*. He wiped perspiration from his brow and sauntered toward her, his skintight breeches framing long, muscular legs.

"Ye startled me, *mo druidh*. I didna here ye creep up. More of your witch's tricks, aye?"

She stuck out her tongue and tried to quell her dimples. "Mr. Maclean, you may find it funny that I was almost hanged for witchcraft, but I most assuredly do not."

He sat on the doorstep, and his tanned arm encircled her shoulder. His lips brushed the sensitive corner where her neck met her jaw.

"I missed ye when I got home last night," he murmured. " 'Twas cold, sleeping all alone, but I guess that's the price of marrying a midwife." He nuzzled her ear and trailed his warm finger down her cleavage. A spark of pure lust flared along her veins, and her nipples hardened to aching points.

"Babies won't wait, Mr. Maclean." She twined her fingers in the red-gold waves of his hair and pulled his mouth closer. "But supper will. Perhaps you'd care to join me upstairs?"

"Da, look!" Elizabeth's voice shrilled across the yard.

"Ignore her," Jamie whispered, closing his eyes and lowering his mouth to hers. She dissolved against him, and he crushed her to his chest. His tongue thrust deep into her mouth, twining and dancing, darting in and out like a rapier of velvet. She pressed closer and luxuriated in the drag of rough bodice against swollen nipples.

"Look at me!" Elizabeth's strident tones drew closer.

Jamie chuckled against Clemency's lips. She tried to break free, but he eased her back against the side of the house. He nibbled his way down her throat, then slipped his hand under her skirt and slid it between her thighs. A hot, yearning ache pulsed between her legs, and she gasped as she felt the probing warmth of his fingers.

"Look what I've got!" Elizabeth stamped her foot, and Jamie raised his head.

"Good Christ!" he bellowed, starting back like a spooked stallion.

Elizabeth thrust a huge coiled snake in her father's face. "See, Da? I found him on the woodpile."

"By Saint Columba, ye wee toe-rag! Ye scared me half to death!"

Clemency gaped from her husband's stark-white face to the enormous, writhing snake in Elizabeth's tiny hand. "Good heavens, Jamie, 'tis just an old blacksnake."

Elizabeth frowned. "Here, Da, don't you wanna hold him?"

"Get that thing out of here." Jamie swallowed, hard.

This was too much. Clemency clutched her sides and shook with laughter. "Oh, Jamie, you should see your face . . ."

Elizabeth began giggling wildly. She danced in a circle, waving the poor blacksnake. "The snake wants a kiss. The snake wants a kiss."

Jamie glared down his severe nose with the outrage of a trapped falcon. Clemency crumpled into another fit of laughter. "Oh, you look just like Reverend Rogers. All you need is a Bible."

"I'll thank ye to show some respect, ye saucy wench."

A rueful smile quirked the corners of Jamie's mouth, and he shook his head. "Och, I never thought ye'd discover my weakness so fast. A man hopes to keep his pride for a few months after his wedding, at least."

Elizabeth stopped twirling and stared up at her father. Her jaw sagged. "You're scared of a wee snake?"

Clemency nearly strangled with suppressed laughter. Steeling her face into seriousness, she plucked the snake from the child's hand. "Of course not, Elizabeth. Nothing afrights a Highland warrior. Your da's just teasing. You know what a court jester he can be."

Snake held nonchalantly in one hand, she slanted Jamie a mischievous glance and brushed within inches of his chest. His solemn blue eyes met hers, and her heart contracted. Holy Mother, she loved this man. Every minute of every day brought pure, stunning joy as she discovered each delightful aspect of his mind and body.

Smiling, she strode toward the woods, the snake's long body trailing from her hand. Jamie was a finicky eater, she had learned, and blueberry grunt was his favorite dessert. His thunderous sneezes all but shook the roof, but he never, ever snored. He loved to take long, hot baths while sipping imported Scots whisky, and he only sat still when he was reading or playing his guitar. This, perhaps, had been the biggest surprise of all: her wild Highland warrior was an accomplished musician.

He was also an accomplished lover.

A hot flush swept over her skin, and she felt a familiar wet ache in her womanhood. In the long, dark hours of the night, Jamie explored every inch of her body, kissing, licking and caressing until she thought she would drown in their passion. He deviled her until she admitted that his teeth on her throat drove her mad. He tickled her until she confessed that she liked being taken from behind. He teased her with deft tongue, lips and fingers until she begged him to ravish her.

Caught up in erotic daydreams, she didn't hear Jamie's shout. She reached the edge of the woods, hauled her skirts up and waded barefoot through a tangle of undergrowth. She plopped the traumatized snake under a tree. The poor creature lay stunned for a moment, then slithered away, relief evident in every curve of its body.

"Och, *mo druidh*, didn't ye hear me warning ye?" Jamie stood a few paces behind her, hands on hips, amusement battling with concern in his indigo eyes.

"Warning me? About what? You don't mean that pitiful snake—"

"Nay, not the blethering snake." Amusement won, and his shoulders shook with laughter. "Ye're standing barefoot in a mess of poison ivy."

Two nights later Clemency lay on her stomach in bed, clad only in her shift. Firelight danced on the bed's patchwork quilt and reflected off the steeply eaved, whitewashed walls of the chamber. It flickered across Jamie's lean face, illuminating the elegant slope of his nose and the enthralling slant of his cheekbones.

She gritted her teeth and groaned, and his eyes crinkled with laughter. She glared at him, and he smothered a grin.

"How does it feel, *mo druidh*, being the patient and not the healer?" He picked up the wooden mortar filled with crushed jewelweed and sat beside her on the bed.

"Ha, ha."

"Did I ever tell ye about the priests who educated me?" His eyes danced, and his *r*s rolled like a Highland waterfall. "One of them told me about an Eastern belief called karma. The East Indians believe every good deed is rewarded and every bad deed is punished. So perhaps next time ye get the urge to tease me about a wee snake—"

"James Maclean, shut up!" Oh, Holy Mother, this itch

was driving her out of her mind! "Why on earth didn't you tell me about that blasted poison ivy?"

"I did—"

"You just let me walk through it, barefoot. You were laughing all the while."

"I didn't—"

"You deserve to be horsewhipped!"

He lifted her ankle and chuckled. "Promise?"

"Ohhh!" She writhed against the quilt, nearly mad from the poison ivy's relentless, maddening itch. "How can you joke when I'm lying here in agony?"

He dabbed jewelweed on the angry pink pustules covering her feet, ankles and lower calves. "Too bad ye're so miserable, for ye look mighty bonny from where I sit." He pushed her shift up to her waist, and the fire's warmth licked her naked buttocks.

"Enjoy the view while you can," she snapped. " 'Tis the last time you'll see it." She wriggled her hips, trying to regain some modesty. Jamie caught his breath.

"Och, *mo druidh,* do that again."

"Arrrgh! Stop teasing and slap on that poultice. Are you sure it will work?"

"Mollyocket said—"

"Why didn't you get the rash, anyway? You stomped right through it to pick me up and carry me out. Do you have a pact with the Devil or something?"

Another chuckle. "Should someone with your recent history be referring to the Devil in such a familiar fashion?"

She snatched up a pillow and fired it at his head. A knock sounded on the door.

Laughing, Jamie said, "Cover yourself, witch. 'Tis likely Hugh. Ye dinna want to give the poor man heart failure." She twitched a quilt over her buttocks, and Jamie opened the door.

"I'm sorry to disturb ye, but I'm afraid I've got bad

news." Hugh hovered in the doorway. At the sight of Clemency's dishabille, he stared at the ceiling and blushed.

"Aye?" Jamie's brows drew together.

" 'Tis wee Noah Howard. His *athair* just came by with the news. He's dead."

"That's impossible," Jamie said. "Clemency left him resting easy four hours ago."

Clemency dropped her head onto the pillow. Poor little Noah. He had been so sick, but she had been sure he would pull through. Oh, why on earth hadn't she tried harder? If she had taken greater care, he might be alive now. Her throat constricted, and she bit the pillow to keep from crying. Once again, her foolish, headstrong pride had steered her wrong. She had been so confident in her abilities as a healer that she had ignored the warning signs. Now it was too late.

Hugh left the chamber, and Jamie sat beside her. " 'Tis not your fault, *mo cridhe*. James Howard bears ye no grudge. He's lost bairns before. 'Tis the way of it in the wilderness." He stroked her hair. "There's nothing ye could have done."

She turned her head away. Back in England, she had never lost a patient. Now, in two months' time, two innocent children had died under her care. Pain gnawed at her heart, and she clenched her eyes tight.

For a long time Jamie stroked her back and murmured tender reassurance. At last he rose and crossed the bedchamber, his steps light and graceful on the wooden floor. "Would ye like me to play for ye, *mo cridhe?*" The hearthside rocking chair squeaked as he sat and picked up his guitar.

When she didn't reply, he tuned the instrument to a modal key. For several minutes he strummed random chords, as if searching for the sound that would bring her comfort. At last his fingers found the notes he sought, and he plucked the strings as lightly and smoothly as burn water over stones. His mellow voice filled the room with a ballad of haunting beauty.

My lady, may I have this dance?
Forgive a knight who knows no shame.
My lady, may I have this dance?
And lady, may I know your name?

You danced upon a soldier's arm
and I felt the blade of love so keen.
And when you smiled you did me harm,
and I was drawn to you, my queen.

Now these boots may take me where they will,
though they may never shine like his.
There is no knight I would not kill
to have my lady's hand to kiss.

Yes, and they did take me from the hall
to leave me not one breath from you.
Yes, and they fell silent, one and all,
and you could see my heart was true.

Then I did lead you from the hall
and we did ride upon the hill
away beyond the city wall.
And sure you are my lady still.

A night in summer, long ago.
Stars were falling from the sky.
And still, my heart, I have to know:
Why do you love me, lady, why?

His voice was husky, intimate, and its throaty catch slipped into her heart and enthralled her as surely as any magic spell. The firelight burnished his hair to gleaming amber and darkened his eyes to midnight blue. Still he played, while the flames leaped and gyred and cast spectral shadows on his brooding face. She caught her breath. Together, the fire and the music had transformed her charming husband into a brutal Highland warrior sprung from the mists of time.

The last notes faded, and she crept from the bed, suddenly afraid. Jamie's eyes had grown icy, his generous mouth grim. "That was beautiful," she whispered. "I've never heard that song before. Did you write it?" A sickening thought hit her. What if Jamie had written the song for his dead wife?

He sat frozen, staring into the fire, his nostrils pinched with the harshness of his respiration. At last he met her gaze. His eyes burned with the fierce blue that lies at the heart of the flame.

"Nay. Me uncle wrote it for the great love of his life, just days before he was murdered."

Chapter Twenty

Clemency shivered and tucked her numb fingers under her armpits as she trudged home from delivering a neighbor's baby. It was late November, icy cold, and sere fields rolled away before her in forlorn shades of dun and drab. Lowering gunmetal clouds stretched to the horizon, and the wizened fingers of gnarled black trees raked the sky's gray underbelly.

Panting, she gained the summit of Burnt Hill and silently gloried in the stark beauty around her. Desolate it was, but its austerity suited her bleak mood. It was as if Nature reflected her very heart, for Jamie had been gone for weeks on a surveying trip, and she missed him dreadfully.

Suddenly she halted, startled. "Elizabeth? What's wrong, Pumpkin?"

The child crouched under a barren maple tree just over the brow of the hill. She stared sadly at the distant pewter Kennebec.

"Are you sick?" Clemency asked, kneeling beside her in the dead grass.

Elizabeth heaved a long sigh, drew her legs up and wrapped her arms around them in a gesture exactly like her father's. Mud caked her leather boots, and hairy brown burdocks clung to her woolen skirt. "No," she whispered. She rested her white chin on her knees, and her long red curls slid down her thin shoulders, curtaining her face.

With a wan smile, Clemency reached out and stroked Elizabeth's fiery curls. "Well, if you're not sick, can you tell me what *is* wrong?" She kept her voice low and soothing, the way Jamie always did.

Elizabeth sniffed and huddled deeper into herself. "I'm lonely," she whimpered. "I'm always by myself . . . and I'm l-lonely."

Clemency blinked. For one awful instant, she saw her own five-year-old self curled under a Devon oak, sobbing with loneliness and heartbreak. Anguish seared her heart, and once more she choked down the bitter ashes of a childhood shorn of love.

Then she gathered Elizabeth into her arms and wrapped the folds of her red wool cloak about her. "Oh, my poor, poor darling," she murmured, pressing her lips against the child's silky curls. "I'm so sorry. I know how much you miss your da. I miss him, too, and I'm truly sorry I've been so busy lately. I've neglected you, and I've been a horrible mother. Can you forgive me?"

The little girl sobbed and clung to Clemency's neck. "You're not hor'ble," she gasped, burrowing her head against Clemency's bosom. "I wanted a mama so long. Then you came. I love you."

Hot tears blurred Clemency's vision. Oh, what had she done? All this time she had been obsessed with trying to make Jamie love her, and all along his daughter was starving for attention. She deserved to be thrown in the pillory for neglecting Elizabeth.

"Hush, now, Pumpkin," she murmured, rocking the child. "Your mama's here. Everything will be all right."

Since the day Clemency had married Jamie, she had feared that Elizabeth wouldn't love her. In truth, she had resented that Elizabeth was not her child, but the child Jamie had sired on Rebekah. Although Clemency petted the little girl and enjoyed playing mother, secretly she shuddered whenever she beheld the product of Jamie and Rebekah's love. But that was over now.

"I love you, my darling," Clemency whispered. "And your da will be home tonight. He promised."

Clemency paced the bedchamber floor. Her skirts snagged around her ankles, and her breath came in sharp little huffs. Where on earth was Jamie? It was nearly midnight, and he should have been home hours ago, blast his stubborn Scottish hide! He had promised he would be back today, and so far he had never broken his word.

She snatched up the poker and prodded the fire, sending a shower of sparks onto the hearth's bearskin rug. The rug's hair smoldered in several places and sent pungent curls of smoke into the room. She stifled a sneeze, set her jaw and stamped out the sparks. Jamie had told her a bearskin rug made an excellent smoke detector. As always, the blasted smug Highlander was right.

She coughed and flounced down in the rocking chair. Wait 'til she got her hands on that wretched rogue, she would knock him right into the middle of next week! It was bad enough that he had been gone for a fortnight in freezing weather, off God knew where in the wilderness. It was even worse that he had left his daughter crying with loneliness. But now he had to go and worry his wife to death!

She jumped up and strode to the tiny window under the eaves. Peering out, she contemplated the dim light shining from the houses in the settlement. What if something horrible had happened? There were still Indians in the backcountry—fierce Penobscots and bloodthirsty Micmacs who would kill for Jamie's glorious red scalp. She tucked her icy hands under her armpits. Mollyocket had once told her that the remnants of Maine's Indians didn't scalp Europeans—they just shot them outright.

She closed her eyes and tried to slow her breathing. Holy Mother, what if Jamie didn't *want* to come back?

That poisonous thought grew in her mind like a noxious weed. She had seen this night coming all autumn, as implacably as the advancing cold. Jamie had been distant at first, preoccupied and inattentive. She had assumed he was worried about spending the winter in such a remote locale, but thanks to his hard work and Sir Andrew's generosity, they were provisioned for months to come.

Then Jamie's surveying trips had lengthened, and she had begun to fear something worse. He grew thin and haggard, as if haunted by some awful apparition. He growled at Hugh, ignored Elizabeth and avoided Clemency. After their first glorious weeks together in October, he had jumped at any chance to get away from Fort Western—and from her. Worst of all, they hadn't made love in weeks.

She pressed a hand to her forehead and tried to smooth the hard vertical line between her brows. Jamie had never wanted to marry her in the first place. Now the reality of the situation must be torturing him. Holy Mother, what could she do? She had tried everything to win his love, but he just drifted farther away.

The fire cracked, and she started. She caught a glimpse of her wan face in the wavy window glass and frowned. This was ridiculous; she was behaving like a ninny. What would Granny Amais say if she saw her sitting around, sulking over a man? She stuck out her tongue at her reflection. Clemency Cameron owned no faint heart. If Jamie Maclean wanted to treat her like an annoying puppy, then so be it. But she wasn't going to take it lying down, and she would be darned if she would let him neglect Elizabeth.

She unlaced her bodice, fingers trembling with aggravation. She had waited long enough. If Jamie deigned to come home tonight, he wouldn't find her awake to greet him.

A footfall sounded outside the bedchamber door. She whirled, and her bodice dropped to the floor. The door swung open, and Jamie stood before her.

"Oh, you scared me," she gasped.

A week's growth of russet stubble covered his gaunt cheeks, and lines of exhaustion creased the corners of his eyes. His clothes were filthy and reeked of wood smoke and another more pungent scent. Swaying slightly, he stepped forward and sketched a shaky bow. "Good evening, Mistress Maclean." His eyes fastened on her breasts, and he grinned wolfishly.

Clemency wrinkled her nose. The pungent smell clinging to his clothes was rotgut whisky. "I'm glad to see a Highland laird still keeps his promises, even when he's drunk," she snapped. Her glance flicked to the bedside table, where her granny's rare, three-handed pocket watch lay. " 'Tis almost midnight. You made it home with minutes to spare. Oh, but I forgot, the tavern closed an hour ago. I guess that made it easier to keep your word."

Jamie's brows arched. "I'm no' drunk, if that's what ye mean. Ye're no' drunk if ye can find your arse with two hands." He chuckled and swayed toward her. "And is that the greeting I get after spending weeks in the woods with nothing but bears for company?"

Clemency turned her back and untied her skirts, then let them drop to her ankles. Jamie moved closer and kissed her neck. Whisky fumes hit her, and she whirled.

"You're lucky to get a greeting at all, after keeping me awake for hours, worrying. How dare you stop at Jefferd's and get drunk while your daughter is home crying?"

Jamie stretched to his full six feet, four inches and glared down his nose—the very image of the imperious aristocrat. " 'Liz'beth was abed hours ago.''

"So she was, but not before I found her miles from here, crouched under a tree, sobbing with loneliness." Clemency shot a scathing glance at Jamie's muddy boots and stained buckskin jacket. "I told her you'd be home tonight, that you had promised. But where were you? Drinking in the tavern.''

He looked stricken, but she forged on, intent on venting her anger. "What's wrong with you, Jamie? I've never seen you like this—''

"Like what, madam?" His voice was low and velvet-soft. A tiny part of her mind whispered a warning, but she couldn't stop.

"You're so . . . so cold. You've shut Elizabeth out, just like you've shut me out.''

"Is this wee fankle about Elizabeth or about ye?''

"About Elizabeth. Of course," she added lamely. "She needs you. She loves you, and she misses you when you're gone. Even when you're here, you're so distant and worried lately." Her voice shrilled as he grabbed her arm. " 'Tis upsetting her.''

He lowered his face until their lips were a finger's breadth away. She smelled the whisky on his breath, felt the manly heat of his body, heard the icy anger in his voice. "Since when are ye so worried about Elizabeth? If ye're so fashed about her, why do ye no' stay home, instead of traipsing about physicking the countryside?''

She twisted her arm free. "You know how important my work is. I'm needed here. There's no one else. Don't you dare shove your guilty conscience onto me." She stepped back, frightened by the intensity of his indigo gaze. "If you can't love me, at least love your daughter.''

"Aye, *my* daughter. Mine, not yours. I'll thank ye to remember that." He turned on his heel and snatched open the door.

Panic swamped her. Oh, Holy Mother, he couldn't leave, not like this. He might never come back, and she couldn't stand to be left alone.... "Jamie, don't leave me!" Hot tears burst from her eyes, and she lunged forward. She tripped on the hem of her shift. There was a tearing sound, and her long black hair tumbled from its pins.

Jamie caught her shoulders. "Do ye think I want to leave ye?" His whisper burned like acid, scalding her ears, her brain, her heart. "Do ye think I disappear for days because of ye? Do ye think I crawl like a dog to the tavern and drink 'til my head's swimming to forget ye? Do ye think I neglect my own child because of ye?" His eyes flashed, and he shook her, hard. He inhaled sharply and grasped her face between his hands.

"If that's what ye think, then ye're right. Lydia told me once that ye'd bewitched me. She was right, too. Ye haunt me every waking moment. Ye torture my dreams. I never want to leave ye, and I canna wait to flee from ye."

His feverish fingers crawled across her cheekbones, then pressed hard, harder, as if he meant to crush her skull. Clemency squirmed, heart thundering with panic. "No ye don't," he murmured, lowering his lips to hers. "I'll let ye go when it strikes my fancy." He kissed her, grinding his mouth against hers until she tasted blood.

She squealed and staggered back, hand pressed against her bleeding lip. "What's wrong with you? Are you mad?"

A mask of bland politeness slipped over his features, but his eyes still blazed. "Aye, mad I am, witch. And only getting worse as the months drag by."

He rummaged in his bedroll and drew out a bottle of whisky, then uncorked it with his teeth and took a swig. Arching an inquiring eyebrow, he held the bottle toward her and eased into the rocking chair.

She made a sound of disgust and raked the hair from her eyes. She had enough experience with sick men and cornered animals to know never to show fear. She stood before him and thrust out a hand. "Give me the whisky, Jamie. You've had enough."

He grinned and dangled the bottle in front of her. "Not until ye come here and greet your husband properly."

"I'll greet my husband properly when I get a proper husband."

He clutched a hand to his chest and rocked back. "Och, ye wound me, witch." He tilted his head and scrutinized her heaving bosom. "All right, I'll cut ye a deal. I'll give ye the whisky if ye answer me a question."

"Deal. But one question only."

He grinned with elaborate innocence. "I see ye dinna trust me. Och, weel." His teasing expression vanished, and he leaned forward, eyes deadly serious. "Why are ye so upset by the thought of me leaving?"

She felt the color drain from her cheeks. How had he managed to turn the tables? She tried to step back, but his arm snaked out and grasped her around the waist. "We made a deal, *mo cridhe*," he murmured. He pulled her onto his knee.

Mo cridhe. My heart. Her eyes devoured his handsome face, so wild looking with that rough beard. How should she answer him? His fingers stroked her thigh, and she raised her chin. Why should she bare her soul when he refused to give her even the tiniest glimpse into his?

"Let's expand this deal," she said. "I'll answer your question, and you give me the whisky. Then you must answer a question."

"Aye? And what do I get in return?" He uncrossed his legs, and through his breeches she felt hard—Holy Mother, rock hard!—evidence of just how much he had missed her.

"What do you want?" She wriggled into a more comfortable position and relished his quick intake of breath. A low chuckle rumbled in his chest, and he nibbled her ear, sending waves of gooseflesh over her arms and throat.

"Isna that obvious?"

"Yes . . . well." She pursed her lips, gathered her courage and spoke. "I didn't want you to leave because I've been left too often in the past." Oh, Holy Mother, should she tell him? Would he understand, or would he turn from her in disgust? She drew a quavering breath. "My parents neglected me when I was a child. I was alone constantly, and I can't stand it when people I care about leave me."

She twisted a thin lawn fold of her shift and waited for Jamie's response. To her surprise, he set the whisky bottle on the floor, then wrapped his arms around her and pressed her head against his cheek.

"Och, me poor wee lassie," he murmured. "Is that why ye fashed so over Elizabeth?"

"I didn't mean to yell like a fishwife, but seeing her so sad—"

"Hush now, I ken." He crooned in Gaelic and rocked her as if she were his child. She inhaled the muskiness of his beard and the smoky, cold tang of evergreens clinging to his jacket. After a long pause he said, "Are ye going to ask me a question?"

His tone was so hopeful she almost giggled. She caught his stubbly chin in her hand, then looked into his eyes. "What did you mean when you said I haunt you? And what's been bothering you so badly lately?"

His lips quirked. "That's two questions, *mo druidh.* Can't ye count?" His eyes actually twinkled. "Two questions, two rewards, aye?"

"You're a rogue, sir." She pinched his chin. "I'll agree to your terms, but you must tell me the truth."

His beguiling expression vanished. He shifted her off his lap and stood, back to her, staring down into the fire. "I canna answer either question, *mo cridhe,* not if ye want the truth."

"Why, you cad! Here I am, baring my soul—"

"Dinna!" He whirled, cheeks flushed, eyes blazing. "Dinna throw your honesty in my face. Dinna ye ken it sticks in my craw and sickens me? I want to match your honest heart, but I canna. I've told ye before, I'm not the man ye think. I'll bring ye nothing but grief and shame. I never should have married ye."

She stood as if frozen, paralyzed by his vehemence. He snatched up the whisky bottle and brandished it under her nose. "Ye think words will heal everything, but they willna, no' this time. That's why I'm drinking in the ordinary instead of bedding ye."

"Jamie, I—"

He ground a fist into his eye socket. "Dinna stare at me with those green eyes! Ye'll drive me out of my skull. Dinna ye ken how I burn for ye, how I long to open my heart? Why must ye ask what I canna give!" His voice rose in a bellow, and he hurled the whisky bottle into the fireplace. It shattered, and flames *whump*ed up, startling them both.

With one long stride, he crossed the room and crushed her to him. The burning curve of his erection ground against her belly, and she felt the rage pulsing through him, sensed the savagery that fueled his lust and hardened his cock. To her astonishment, her own anger vanished, drowned by a riptide of desire. It swept away everything but the need to couple, to mate, to drain Jamie's fury even as she drained his seed.

He bent her back. His fingers spiraled over her breast, and he pinched her erect nipple between thumb and forefinger. Pain shot through her, and a low moan escaped her lips, a husky, primitive cry of want. He bit her lip and thrust his tongue in her mouth again and again, a prelude to his ravishment. He fondled her buttocks; then his hands roamed low between their cleft, seeking the wet heat of her womanhood.

"Ye drive me mad," he murmured, raking his teeth over her earlobe. "One moment I want to cherish ye like a new babe. The next I want to take ye and use ye like a whore.

I want to drain myself in your mouth, make ye beg for my cock . . .''

He ripped the chemise from her shoulder and dragged the roughness of his beard across her tender skin. Her knees sagged, her nipples ached and a frenzied pulse throbbed between her legs. He snatched her off her feet, then lowered her to the bed. The wooden bedstead bit into her buttocks, and her feet dragged the floor. He fell to his knees and ripped open his breeches. A button zinged across the room. His enormous penis jutted out, hot and thick and erect. He closed her fingers around his flesh and gripped, hard.

"Stroke me," he commanded. She squeezed and rubbed, glorying in his manhood. He was like an iron bar sheathed in velvet. His head fell back, his hips pumped and he groaned, "Dinna stop, witch."

Wild need overwhelmed her. She wrapped her legs around his narrow waist, then guided his shaft between her thighs. The silky, slick crown of him rubbed against her wet folds, and she groaned, urging him on. He reached down and deftly stroked her nub until she begged him for release. Then he set his jaw and plunged into her. With a wrenching cry, he clamped his hands on her hips and thrust forward again and again.

"Ride me, use me," he groaned, surging into her with furious power.

Clemency's nipples burned, and she shuddered, moaned, writhed against him. He sucked her lower lip between his teeth, then bit until she cried out. His fingers tangled in her hair, and he held her down, pressing her into the feather mattress as he thrust faster.

"Come with me, witch," he ordered. Spasms of ecstasy shot through her, and she ground against him, crying out.

"You're mine," he said. "Mine!" He arched his back and groaned long and low, pulsing into her, riding the shuddering waves of his climax.

* * *

"Ye vanquish me, *mo cridhe.*" Jamie turned his head and glanced a kiss on Clemency's silky hair. It was fragrant with the scent of lavender and gleamed like a thousand midnight skies in the dying firelight. They lay snuggled deep in the featherbed, the patchwork quilt tucked around them. Her head rested against his shoulder, and her delicate fingers stroked his chest, sending little thrills of pleasure through his tired body.

A fierce wind buffeted the eaves, and the winter's first snow crystals ticked against the chamber window. Jamie suppressed a shiver. He could be out in that storm, alone, lonely and freezing.

Clemency pressed against him, her breasts damp with sweat from their lovemaking. "You shivered." She nuzzled his cheek, voice husky. "Are you cold?"

All at once his eyes smarted. He drew a long, quavering breath, half amused, half amazed. By St. Columba, she was a witch. He hadn't so much as twitched, yet somehow she had sensed his mood. He closed his eyes and caressed the luscious curve of her breast. Could he risk opening up to her?

Since that nightmarish night four years ago when his darling Rebekah had died, he had sealed off his heart, the way one seals a corpse in a tomb. He had interred every emotion except for his fatherly love for Elizabeth. Oh, many women had tried to resurrect him, Lydia most of all. He stirred, and his mouth stretched in a mirthless smile. But no one had succeeded. He was beyond hope. He hadn't wanted to be revived. Until now.

Clemency sat up. Pouting enticingly, she straddled his hips and stared down at him. Her eyes glittered, smoky and green as the peaty depths of Loch Linnhe. Her waist-length black hair slid forward until it brushed his shoulders and tented around them. He reached up and caressed her cheek, marveling at the alabaster perfection of her skin. He traced his finger over her lips. Surely the good Lord had fashioned them to drive a man wild, for their seductive curves promised a deep and lavish sensuality.

She kissed his hand. "Jamie, what's wrong?"

Her voice was soothing, understanding. Her *dotair's* voice. He tried to laugh off the sudden surge of tenderness that choked his throat, but for once humor failed him.

"You asked me why I got so upset when you tried to leave," she said. "What I told you was the truth, but there's more." Her eyes held his, and he longed to drown in their celadon depths. "I love you, Jamie, and I cannot bear the thought of you leaving me. I know you don't feel the same way, but a lass can hope, can't she?" She gave him a crooked little smile, and his heart contracted. "I also know something is bothering you. Can't you tell me what's wrong? Please?"

He wanted to slide from under her, to slip away and run, but her eyes—those green, magic witch's eyes—held him fast. For a moment he fancied he could see straight into her heart, into her very soul. What he saw left him shaken and humbled.

"Is it the past?" She leaned closer, voice barely audible. "Can't you let it go? I know how much you loved Rebekah, but—"

He laid a finger against her velvet lips and eased her off his body. Och, he wanted to pour out the truth, but she would never understand. *Never*.

She sat on the edge of the bed, crossed her long, elegant legs Indian-style and wrapped the quilt around her luscious nakedness. In the faint firelight with her black hair hanging down, she looked like an Indian, a beautiful savage who had captured his heart. After several long minutes, she spoke again. "Jamie, you can't run from whatever's bothering you. You can't run from your own thoughts."

Her voice was remote and professional, definitely the doctor's tone now. He had heard her speak just this way to an old man who refused to let her pull a tooth. Jamie groaned and shrugged.

"Ye're irresistible, witch. Heaven help the man who ever tries to stand up to ye." One corner of his mouth twitched into a smile. "You want the truth, aye? Well, I willna lie, but there's some things I canna tell." She started to protest, and he arched a stern brow. "Take it or leave it, *mo druidh.*"

"All right, what can you tell me?"

For one dizzying moment, he considered bolting from the room. A blizzard was less daunting than her level gaze. Then another icy gust of wind rattled the windows, and he reconsidered. He reached up and pulled her down beside him. Stroking her hair the way one might stroke a cat, he began his tale.

Chapter Twenty-one

"I ken how much ye love a story, *mo druidh,* so I'll tell ye of the Battle of Culloden. It has all the elements of those Defoe novels ye love—treason, betrayal, honor, revenge—and murder. My tale's not the bonniest to arise from the Forty-five, nor the most famous. 'Tis but one of hundreds, nay, thousands that have gone untold, until now.

"As your mother Margaret will have told ye, the Macleans and the MacKinnons supported Charles Edward Stuart, our own Bonnie Prince Charlie, in his fight to regain the throne. Bonnie he was, I vow, but not terribly bright. His early victories over the English at Falkirk and Prestonpans had gone to his head, ye ken, and he wouldna listen to his advisors. Of course, they weren't perfect, but they did care for the Highlanders. I didna see it then, but I've come to realize we were just pawns for Charlie."

Jamie shook his head and chuckled ruefully. "Och, what a great gawking lad I was then. Stronger in body than in judgement, and itching to fight the bloody Sassenachs. But me oldest brother, Lachlan, woulda hear of it. Lachlan became laird after my *athair* died, ye ken, when I was but seven. 'Twas the pox that took Da. I wish we'd had your inoculation then, *mo druidh*. Anyway, Da left behind three strapping sons—Lachlan, Diarmid and me, the baby of the family.''

Jamie pulled the quilt tighter around them. ''Lachlan and I weren't close, and at the first opportunity, he sent me to France to study for the priesthood.''

Clemency snorted with laughter. ''You're joking! You— a priest?''

Jamie tickled her ribs, delighting in the feel of her body squirming against his. ''Aye, witch, dinna look so shocked. But ye're right—by the time I was thirteen, 'twas clear my body wasna made for chastity.'' She jabbed him in the ribs. ''Ooof, watch it, woman. Do ye want me to paddle your arse? Aye, I can see ye do. Later I will, but for now, shall I tell this story or no'?''

She cast him a contrite look, belied by her dimples. A thrill of tenderness shimmered through him, and his manhood hardened. Och, what was she doing to him? Here he was, baring his soul, and his body just wanted to mount her and rut.

''When I returned from Calais, I lived with my uncle, Alexander Robert Bruce Maclean. He was my *athair's* brother. In truth, he was more a father to me than Da or Lachlan ever were. I was even named for him—Alasdair is the Gaelic for Alexander.

''Ye never saw such a man as Alexander Maclean. Handsome enough to make the lassies swoon, yet the fiercest warrior in the Isles. He had no bairns of his own, and when his wife died, he made me his heir.'' Jamie paused and swallowed, unsure of his voice. ''Och, how can I tell ye how I loved the man? He was my hero.'' He trembled, and for a moment he was afraid Clemency would laugh, but she just squeezed his arm.

"When he and me brother Diarmid marched off with Sir Hector Maclean—the clan chieftain—to fight for Bonnie Prince Charlie, I thought I'd burst with rage. My head was crammed full of the glories of war. All I longed to do was to fight, to heap glory on the clan, and on myself most of all." He snorted and shook his head. "Muckle-headed idiot, I was. But Lachlan wouldna allow me to fight. Someone had to help him with Taigh Samhraidh—"

"What's *Taigh Samhraidh?*" She stumbled over the strange words.

"My family's estate. It means 'summer home' in Gaelic and 'twas the clan chieftain's retreat on the sea loch of Linnhe, before my ancestors were granted it as reward for fealty. Since I was heir to both Lachlan and Alexander, I had to stay and protect our lands and people."

Clemency tilted her head. "Why didn't Lachlan fight?"

Jamie bit back a sudden surge of rage. Och, why was he mucking around in the past? After a long moment he spat, "Lachlan's wife was half English, with the other half Campbell—cursed Sassenach vassals, all. Her brother fought for the English, and Lachlan felt he couldna battle his own wife's kin." He avoided Clemency's questioning gaze. Nay, he wouldn't tell *that* story tonight—or ever. That door to the past had been slammed and locked forever.

He took a great breath and resumed. " 'Twas early April, 1746, when Hugh arrived at Taigh Samhraidh with news. He had fought with Alexander since Falkirk and the prince's early victories, but now everything had changed. The English army under the Duke of Cumberland was chasing Prince Charlie back to Inverness. The Prince's Highlanders were exhausted, starving, disillusioned. 'Twas spring, and many had deserted to tend their land and plant a crop before their bairns starved. The situation was so bloody awful that

Diarmid and Alexander relented. Against Lachlan's wishes I went to fight.

"Diarmid and I joined up with the Highlanders as they marched into Inverness. I was dizzy with excitement. At last I had my chance at glory. Ha! One look at my fellow soldiers smashed that idea. The men were ragged, bare-footed, starveling wraiths, but their courage still survived. And och, when I finally saw the prince! He truly was hand-some, and with rare personal charm. The Stuart royals were all blessed with that charisma, ye ken. No wonder thousands followed Charlie to their deaths."

He stopped, feeling the old ice clamp over his heart. Why was he dredging all this up, after burying it so deeply for sixteen years?

Clemency rolled up on her elbow. "I know it must be torture to speak of it." She smiled with such love that he thought his heart would break. "But you trained to be a priest. Confession is good for the soul, aye?" She mimicked his Scottish accent so perfectly he had to chuckle.

"If ye say so, *dotair.*" He inhaled sharply, nostrils pinch-ing. " 'Twas the Duke of Cumberland's birthday—April fifteenth—the night I joined the army. Word reached us that Prince Charlie was planning a surprise night attack, no doubt assuming that the Sassenachs would be drunk from celebrat-ing their leader's birth. So the prince's officers rounded us up, and we marched in utter silence out over the dark moors, sleet drenching us to the skin.

"I marched behind Diarmid and Alexander, and they whispered the while. I was too cold and hungry to care for their talk. My exotic dreams of the glory of war were freezing as fast as my ballocks. Just as I stepped up to ask what they were planning, an officer ordered us to retreat. We were to march back to Inverness and face the duke in the morning.

"Ye never heard such griping. The Highlanders were bold, courageous warriors, but they kent the value of a surprise attack. They also kent that the duke's troops outnumbered us four to one. Facing the Sassenachs on an open battlefield in the light of day would be suicide. So as we trudged back to Inverness, bit by bit, in pairs and small groups, many of the Highlanders slipped away.''

Jamie scrubbed a hand over his face. ''Och, 'twas all so foolhardy. The next mornin' we were down to bare bones, literally. More Highlanders left in search of food, but there was none to be found. Even the prince went hungry. I saw an officer hand him a bannock and a dram of whisky, but Charlie said, 'If my men cannot eat, neither shall I,' and he dashed the food to the dirt.'' Jamie quirked his mouth to one side. ''I had to admire his style, though it would have been wiser to give it to one of the soldiers.

''Weel, they lined us up like cattle for the slaughter, and slaughter it was. I almost pissed meself when I saw an ocean of Sassenachs roll toward us over Drumossie Moor. They were hale and dressed in bold scarlet uniforms, with the cavalry mounted on fine horseflesh. And the weapons! Och, *mo druidh*, ye never saw the like. Scores of cannon and shining new muskets with wicked bayonets. I still shudder to think of it.''

He ground to a halt, hands trembling. He forgot Clemency and the fire and the cozy featherbed. Suddenly he was back there, facing death.

Jamie's hands shook so hard he could barely hold his claymore. He couldn't see through the billowing black smoke. The Sassenach cannon exploded again, shaking the earth, thundering in his ear. A ball shrieked past his head. He plunged to the ground and rolled through the icy mud, trying to escape the hail of lead. A piercing, inhuman scream knifed through the driving sleet. He struggled to his feet.

Och Christ! The bloody Sassenachs had hit the prince's horse! The poor creature squealed and plunged, its white flanks streaked with foam and blood. He started forward.

Suddenly Alexander appeared out of the sleet, his face smoke-blackened, his eyes blazing pits of hell.

"Dinna be a fool!" he snapped, dragging Jamie back. "They're trying to hit the prince. Go near him and ye're a dead man!"

Grapeshot whined to their left, and three Highlanders fell, their blood gouting up in bright scarlet streams, pumping in time to their cries. Another cannon thundered. Jamie and Alexander dove to the ground, and Jamie scrabbled back until he hit something. He turned and met the ravaged gaze of a corpse. One side of its skull was blown away, and its gray brains oozed out, mingling with the blood on the muddy ground. Jamie clenched his teeth, swallowed. He couldn't puke in front of Alex.

A hoarse Gaelic roar tore the air, and the MacIntosh clan broke and ran, racing straight into the English cannon. The Highlanders were charging! Plaids swirled, claymores glinted, dirks flashed, pistols cracked. Jamie lunged to his feet, there was another *boom* and all went black.

Jamie woke to find a man on top of him. Warm blood trickled down Jamie's cheek, and he tasted it, slick and coppery, in his mouth. Was it the man's or his own? He grunted and tried to shift his fallen comrade's body. His nostrils flared. St. Columba, what was the horrible smell? With a groan, he sat up and pushed the corpse away. His stomach heaved. The cannon had ripped the man in two, splattering blood and entrails across Jamie's face and arms.

"Jamie lad, follow me." Alex yanked him to his feet, and they tore across the moor, Diarmid close behind. The battlefield was a nightmare of mindless screams, biting sleet, and choking smoke. A riderless horse bucked across their path, squealing madly. Still they ran—straight into the English line.

A knot of Sassenachs broke and let them through. A beefy guard grabbed Jamie, then jabbed a bayonet at his throat.

"We've information!" Alex bellowed. "News of the Young Pretender's battle plan. I'm to report to the duke."

Jamie froze. Had the cannon deafened him? Alex couldn't be a spy!

"Bloody 'ighland savages. Slinkin' over to our side like sailors after a whore." A Sassenach infantryman snickered and half turned, then whirled and punched Alexander with all his strength. Jamie reached for his dirk. The guard's bayonet pierced his skin, and he felt a hot trickle of blood.

"I've no time for the likes a you," the infantryman snarled. "If you got somethin' to report, the duke's over there." He jerked his chin toward an elegant officer on a sleek charger.

Alex pushed the bayonet from Jamie's throat, and they ran. The moment they were out of the soldiers' earshot, Jamie stopped. "I'll have no part of this—"

Alex halted. His mud-caked plaid, held in place only by the silver Maclean clan brooch, slipped down over his shoulder. "Look, lad—"

Jamie stabbed his finger at Alex's brooch. "Virtue Mine Honor—that's the Maclean motto. I'll not sully—"

"Och, *mo cridhe,* I forget I hadna told ye. I'm not a spy." Alex gestured toward the Sassenach officer on the magnificent horse. "This is the only way, lad. The prince's only hope is for us to assassinate Cumberland." English cannon exploded to their left, and acrid white smoke singed Jamie's nose. His ears rang, and he could hardly hear Alex shout, "Charlie canna win—"

Grapeshot rained around them. A Sassenach soldier staggered past, blood geysering from the shredded flesh that had been his throat. A bone-shattering concussion knocked Jamie to the ground. Ragged screams rose around him, followed by another explosion and a shower of hot lead. Killing pain lanced his ears, stabbed his brain, shredded his reason. Hands pressed to his skull, he screamed and staggered to his knees. What he saw stopped his heart.

Alex ran toward the English officer, then grabbed the charger's bridle. The Sassenach leaned down, an expression of supreme disdain on his aristocratic face. Alex's hand flew up. There was a flash of cannon fuse, a glint of *sgain dhu* blade. The Sassenach saw it. He drew his pistol and grabbed Alex's wrist. There was a dull explosion, a spurt of flame, a cloud of smoke.

Alex dropped to his knees, his beloved face blown clean away.

Jamie's stomach roiled, and a scalding tear squeezed under his lid. He clenched his jaw and ordered himself to forget, *forget!* This was a mistake. He never should have allowed himself to remember, to feel. Clemency cradled his head on her bare breasts and stroked his wet cheeks. Sobs wracked his body, and he buried his face in her soft, warm flesh. Och, how could he let her see him like this?

"I know what you're thinking, my heart." Her voice quavered, and she kissed his hair. "But you've been through hell, and you've kept it buried for sixteen years. You'd be inhuman if you didn't cry."

He sniffed and looked up at her. He had married a witch. How could she read his mind so accurately?

She kissed his dripping nose, then looked around. She glanced at her naked breasts and smiled. "I don't appear to have a handkerchief. Will the quilt do?"

"Aye." He leaned back against the pillow and accepted the proffered corner of quilt. He mopped his face and closed his eyes, too embarrassed to meet her gaze. He hadn't cried since . . . when? Since the night Rebekah had died.

On the hearth the fire had burned to glowing embers, but it still warmed the room. He shivered again. What was warmth to those buried in the frozen ground?

"Do you still love her?" Clemency asked.

Hair prickled along the back of his neck. He dropped the

quilt and swiveled to face her. "How do you know what I'm thinking?"

"It just came to me. I just know."

His brows shot up. "Does this happen often?"

"Sometimes. Especially when we ... when we lie together."

He chuckled and pulled her against his chest. She had grown so precious to him, and he owed her the truth, at least what truth he could give. "Aye, I will always love Rebekah; but I've mourned her deeply, and I know 'tis time to move on. She saved me, ye ken, she and Andrew Pepperrell. They took a grieving Highland lad and gave him something to live for. Och, neither could give me back Taigh Samhraidh, and neither could ever replace my uncle Alex. But Rebekah gave me a reason to live—a reason besides revenge. She gave me laughter and music and my precious Elizabeth."

He stopped and swallowed convulsively. His throat didn't seem to be working right. "Then, when I lost her, grief and revenge were all I had once more."

Clemency lay stiff and silent in his arms. He knew it wasn't the answer she wanted. He shut his eyes and prayed she would understand. Och, he was a fool not to tell her the *whole* truth, but doing so would break her heart and would drive her from him forever. And that would surely kill him.

After a long time, she laid her hand over his heart. "I'm glad you told me. And ..., and I'm glad you had Rebekah's love. She must have been a fine woman." She quavered to a stop, and her tears scalded his chest.

He gathered her close and kissed them away.

Hours later, Jamie awoke to find the bed beside him empty and cold. He sat up, heart pounding.

Clemency was curled in the rocker by the hearth, her red wool cloak wrapped around her. Sometime during the night she had hauled her enormous trunk into the middle of the chamber where it lay open, books and clothes strewn everywhere. He pulled the quilt around his naked body and padded over to her.

"Mo cridhe? Are ye ill?"

Her vacant gaze slid across his face; then she stared into the ashes on the hearth. "Jamie, could you please tell me what happened to your uncle Alexander?" Her voice was so hoarse and low he could barely hear her.

Surprise flickered through him. Then he clenched his fists and spat, "I told ye. He died on the battlefield, killed by that vicious Sassenach dog."

"But what happened to his body?"

He flung off the quilt and stalked to his pile of clothes at the foot of the bed. He couldn't believe she was asking this. What right had she to rip open his wounds? "I dinna ken," he snapped. "The battle worsened. Diarmid and I were both wounded, and then the Sassenachs captured us." He snatched up his sark and felt the muscle twitch in his cheek. "They kent we weren't spies after we attacked the wrong officer—"

"You were never able to bury him?"

He jerked the sark lacing tight. Why this ghoulish fascination with his uncle Alex? "Nay, he was buried in a mass grave on the battlefield. I've never even seen it." Curse the bloody Sassenachs to hell for destroying everything he had loved. But someday he would have his revenge. Honor demanded it.

"Do you have no keepsake from him?" Clemency's voice sounded dead, and a trickle of worry slipped down his spine.

"Nay. Hugh was in the battle as well. He recovered Alex's clan brooch after . . . after Alex fell. He gave it to Alex's betrothed." Jamie's lips twisted in a mirthless smile. "Old Hugh's a muckle-headed romantic. I think he loved the lass. She was reputed to be a verra great beauty."

"You never met her?" Clemency's cheeks were ashen.

"Nay." He pulled up his breeks and strode toward her. "Is something wrong? Ye look a wee bit peaked."

Like a statue come to life, she held out a clenched hand, then opened it to reveal a silver clan badge. The gray dawn light slanted off the circular brooch and illuminated the engraved lettering: Virtue Mine Honor. Jamie stopped breathing. He had seen this badge a thousand times. Alex—

He snatched the brooch from her hand. "Where did you get this?"

Clemency flinched. "From my mother, Margaret Dierdre MacKinnon." She rushed on, voice thin with mounting hysteria. "My mother spoke often of her Highland lover in the weeks before she died, but she always called him Alasdair. I . . . I never made the connection, not 'til you told your tale—"

He sank onto the bed and raked a hand through his hair. This was impossible! Alex was buried in a mass grave on Drumossie Moor. Jamie had never been able to trace Alex's betrothed.

Then, one by one, memories clicked into place. Jamie realized it was the truth. Alex had told him of his betrothal just days before Culloden. He had referred to his lover merely as Margaret, not as Margaret Dierdre MacKinnon, daughter of Chief Iain Dubh MacKinnon, The MacKinnon himself. Jamie clutched Alex's badge until it bit into his skin.

Clemency's mother had been that great love of Alex's life.

All at once, a great roaring wave of emotion surged through him. He longed to cry, to laugh, to shout, to crush Clemency to his heart. He felt as if he were being swept along on a current that suddenly, strangely, wonderfully made sense. He sprang up and reached out—

Clemency raised her hand as if to ward him off. "Jamie, who killed your uncle at Culloden?"

He rocked back as if she had slapped him. What was this

obsession with Alex? He had told her enough. Why did she persist with these morbid questions?

With sheer force of will, he tried to block the horrible battlefield vision from his mind, but again and again, like searing bolts of lightning, he saw his uncle's face explode in a mass of blackened blood.

He whirled and snatched up his buckskin overcoat. How dare Clemency resurrect the vision that had tortured him every single day for sixteen years?

"He was one of Cumberland's finest officers," Jamie snapped. "He ordered the murder of hundreds of innocent Scots and slaughtered the wounded left on Drumossie Moor." He flinched as the coat's soft material settled over his back. "Och, and since ye're so curious, he was also the man who flogged me. Forty lashes I got, for trying to secure an extra half cup of weevily oats for my fellow prisoners."

He shoved his feet into his brogues, then towered over her. She looked as though she was about to faint, and he felt a twinge in the region of his heart. Och, he shouldn't be so harsh. The past wasn't her fault—she had only asked a simple question—but he had to punish anything, *anyone* who reminded him of his uncle's murder.

"For sixteen years I've sworn to kill the bastard," he hissed. "I will avenge the honor of my clan." He leaned close, then bowed with a flourish. "His name, madam, is Lord Francis Bury."

Chapter Twenty-two

"I declare, 'tis all too, too mysterious!" Abigail Frost waved her ivory-boned fan in time with her tongue and made sure of her audience's attention. "Is it not delicious to have a real British peer of the realm right here in Kittery?"

Lydia tapped her foot and tried to quell the urge to snatch the fan from Abigail's fingers. The Frosts were one of the finest families in the area, but Lydia couldn't abide the fact that Abigail had already met Lord Francis Bury. This gave Abigail the social high ground, and all evening long she had exploited her advantage by gossiping with a maddening air of authority about their enigmatic host.

Abigail rapped her fan across Lydia's knee. "Of course, you must forgive Lord Bury for not receiving you properly. He suffers dreadfully from the cold and became indisposed just before you arrived. No doubt Bury House—that's his London mansion, you know—isn't half as drafty as this hired place."

Lydia's avid gaze assessed the elegant double parlor. Faith, Lord Bury must have spent a fortune furnishing his new home! Everywhere she looked there were magnificent gilded pier glasses, jewel-bright Turkey carpets and graceful Chippendale tables and chairs. Real, imported Chippendale, Lydia noted with a pang, not colonial copies done by inferior local craftsmen. Her father had never been able to afford such finery. Why, the azure silk window hangings alone were worth half a ship's cargo of rum.

At the far end of the parlor Lord Bury's guests milled about, illuminated by the flickering glow from hundreds of honey-scented beeswax candles in shining silver candelabra. The golden light seemed almost magical, shimmering on the damask upholstery and gleaming mahogany tables. Lydia suppressed a little shiver of excitement. This was what she wanted—this elegance, wealth, *power*. She could have had it, fool that she was, if only she hadn't married Samuel, if only she had waited for Jamie! She knew Jamie was strong enough to become as rich as Lord Bury. Indeed, he had been, before his fatal alliance with Bonnie Prince Charlie.

"Here you are, m'dear." Her father handed her a sterling punch cup brimming with syllabub. "Deuced fine 'freshments this Bury offers, I'll say that for 'im." Patrick Stevenson slurred his words, and his bleary eyes teared up. His sour breath hit her cheek, and her gorge rose.

"You look jus' like Rebekah sitting there," he wheezed. "It plum startled me out o' my wits. Big with child like that, you're a regular Madonna, jus' like she was—" He stumbled to a halt, and his face crumpled. "Oh, I miss your sister so much!" His voice rose in a wail, and the Frosts stared, mouths agape. "She was my angel, my darlin'—"

"Why, Papa, look there." Lydia dug her nails into his velvet-clad arm and nodded across the room. "Mr. Westbrook is trying to catch your attention. Do go and say hello."

Patrick Stevenson rose, then swayed across the parlor, still mumbling and shaking his head, punch cup clutched to his chest. Lydia steeled herself to smile after him. Damn his maudlin, rum-soaked ramblings. How dare he carry on about Rebekah in public!

Kittery society had always known that Rebekah was Patrick Stevenson's favorite child. They didn't need reminding. Rebekah had been the beautiful angel, the adored daughter, the kindly saint. Lydia had been nothing but her gawky little sister—pretty enough, but without that *glow*. Lydia had heard the cruel comments a thousand times, whispered behind her back by catty goodwives and thrown in her face by her own father.

She forced herself to swallow a creamy mouthful of syllabub. Well, Rebekah was dead, and she—gawky, cold Lydia—would show them who was truly superior. All she needed was Jamie. With his intelligence and talent under her direction, she would at last take her rightful place among the gentry. She didn't care one whit that he had been her dead sister's husband. Faith, that merely added to his attraction. His marriage to Clemency had been a serious setback, but Lydia had one final trump card to play. Smiling slyly, she straightened her spine and folded her hands over the hard curve of her belly. There was no way that English whore was going to beat her.

"This is all so pagan, is it not?" Abigail Frost asked.

"Celebrating Christmas is a respectable custom in England," Lydia said, airily waving her hand. " 'Tis merely our Puritan roots that keep us from burning the Yule log or singing carols. Faith, there's no harm in it."

Abigail's gray eyes widened, and her thin lips twitched into a shocked smile. She hitched her chair closer. "Say you so?" Her gaze swiveled to the mistletoe hanging in the doorway between the two parlors, and her foot tapped to the fiddler's sprightly rendition of "The Holly and the Ivy."

" 'Struth, I half expected the church elders to censure Lord Bury. After all, a *Christmas* party! But I declare, Deacon Walker stands over there conversing with the Lord of Misrule." Abigail tilted her head toward a tall gentleman dressed in black and a wiry young fellow clad in a gaudy jester's costume.

When Lydia and her father had arrived earlier in the evening, the Lord of Misrule and a ragtag band of musicians dressed as mummers had just entered the parlor. The musicians danced, piped and fiddled their way around the candlelit rooms, heralding the appearance of the Yule log—a junk of wood gaily decorated with holly, ivy and mistletoe. With great ceremony and many bawdy jests, the Lord of Misrule had placed the log in the fireplace and lit it to welcome the Christmas season. Kittery had never seen the like.

"Lud, it is daring of his lordship," Abigail's husband drawled. He sniffed and adjusted his meticulously curled black wig. "But we know nothing of the man. I ask you, if he is as rich and powerful as Pepperrell claims, why should he risk the Atlantic gales to spend the winter on our dreary shores?"

A small ring of guests crowded around Lydia and the Frosts. "I heard he plans to buy a vast tract of land on the Maine frontier," said an elderly gentleman. "He intends to start a lumbering empire."

"Nay, 'tis Pepperrell's scheme you speak of," Frost replied. " 'Tis more likely that his lordship is here to assess the fitness of Governor Hutchinson."

"Perhaps the man's a spy," said a thin young fop. "Imagine—he's been sent to gather intelligence against those opposing the Stamp Act."

The elderly gentleman chuckled. "Then, he would have to report us all—"

" 'Struth, if you would listen for a moment," Abigail interrupted, cracking her fan across her husband's knee. "I said Bury's arrival was mysterious. I didn't say no one knows the truth about him." She smirked and ran a bright gaze around her audience. "Because I do!"

Lydia rolled her eyes. What a ninny Abigail looked in her baby-pink silk and snowy-Alp wig. It was inconceivable that intelligent people should pay attention to her at all. But since she was the only person in their little group who had met Lord Bury, the guests hung on her every word.

"Faith, do tell," Lydia snapped.

Abigail fanned herself with quick little flicks. "Well, I had it from Sir Andrew Pepperrell, in strictest confidence." She lowered her voice, and they all huddled closer. "His lordship is dying. He's come here searching for someone."

"For whom?" the elderly gentleman demanded.

"That's the mystery. I don't know. Sir Andrew refused to tell me. It was most ungallant of him." Abigail widened her eyes and glanced over each shoulder. "But it must be someone very dear to Lord Bury. After all, he risked death on the ocean to find them, whomever they are."

Her husband snorted and fluffed out his lace cuffs. "Madam, you are an incorrigible romantic. Perhaps he's come here to settle an old vendetta—or to kill someone."

A thrill shot like chain lightning through the guests. At that exact moment, Lydia looked up and saw a tall, aristocratic man standing in the parlor doorway.

"That's him!" Abigail hissed.

Lord Bury bowed with an air both courtly and cold, then strolled into the crowded chamber. One by one he kissed each lady's hand and inclined his head ever so slightly to the gentlemen.

Lydia's pomp-starved heart pounded, and her dazzled eyes devoured his cream silk coat and gold-embroidered waistcoat. His gold-and-sapphire signet ring carved with the Bury family crest flashed and gleamed in the candlelight. Lydia sighed. She had lived through many a miserable winter on dreams of unassailable wealth and power, and to her, Bury seemed like a god descended from Mount Olympus.

Suddenly he stood before her. She held out her hand, and

he took it in his long, icy fingers. Abigail Frost blushed and simpered. "My lord, may I present Mistress MacKinnon?"

A startled expression flashed through Bury's eyes, but Lydia was so taken with their unusual aquamarine color that she didn't bother to analyze it. "Your servant, madam," he murmured, bowing. He cast her a remote smile and released her hand. "Your husband is Scottish, Mistress MacKinnon?"

"Yes, my lord." Lydia dropped her gaze, suddenly embarrassed by her huge girth and unflattering sacque gown. It was scandalous for a woman so far gone in pregnancy to appear in public, but she hadn't been able to resist the chance to meet an English lord.

"And he is indisposed this evening?"

Lydia set her jaw and met Bury's eyes. He couldn't possibly know the real reason Samuel wasn't with her. "No, my lord. His duties keep him on our property in Sturgeon's Creek."

Bury smiled and held out his arm. "Unfortunately, madam, my health is precarious. My physician—tiresome toady that he is—requires that I avoid drafts. I believe my library is a trifle more snug than this mausoleum of a parlor. Perhaps you will honor me with your charming company there?"

"Thank you, my lord. The honor would be mine." Lydia rose with as much grace as her condition would allow. From the corner of her eye, she saw Abigail's jaw drop. Ha! Let the ninny stew. Bury had recognized a true lady when he saw one, even if no one else did. Lydia smiled demurely and tucked her hand in the crook of his elbow.

They sailed through the crowd, and Lydia heard the susurrus of genteel whispering in their wake. The guests would be gossiping about her in earnest tomorrow, but what did she care? If her plans were to succeed, she must accustom herself to gossip.

They entered the library, and Bury settled her on a low divan covered in gleaming sapphire silk. It sat precariously close to the roaring fire, and perspiration beaded between her breasts. Bury poured sherry into petite crystal goblets and handed her one. With a bland smile, he sat and crossed his long legs. He wore no wig, and she noticed that his silver-blond hair was unpowdered.

He raised his goblet and inclined his head. *"Slainte mhor."*

She smiled uncertainly. "Pardon me?"

"Slainte mhor. The Gaelic for 'good health.'"

She eyed him over the rim of her goblet. He was unnervingly handsome, if gaunt cheeks and hollow eyes didn't put one off. "Yes, I know," she said. "It merely surprised me on the lips of an Englishman, my lord."

He smiled, and she was surprised to see hard, masculine dimples bracket his finely shaped mouth. "I see you adhere to the colonial custom of plain speaking, Mistress MacKinnon. May I be equally plain?" He arched a dark, peaked brow, and she realized he was flirting.

She set the goblet on a graceful gilt side table. "Of course, my lord. You may do as you wish."

His brow arched higher, and she had a bad moment. Faith, perhaps she had misread him. He eyed her coolly, then stood and leaned against the marble mantel. Suddenly a terrible fit of coughing wracked his broad shoulders, and he doubled over. Lydia struggled to her feet.

"My lord, should I call your servant? May I get you some water?"

He waved her away, then pressed his handkerchief to his mouth. "You see, Mistress MacKinnon, the rumors about me are true," he said. "Oh, I know the local gossip has me at death's doorstep. Sir Andrew Pepperrell is astoundingly adroit at relating the juiciest tales. He's been most helpful that way." He smiled in response to Lydia's puzzled frown. "But in one area he remains stubbornly unhelpful. That, Mistress MacKinnon, is why I need you."

"Me?"

"Yes. You are married to a farmer named Samuel Mac-Kinnon, are you not?"

Lydia wiped perspiration from her brow. "He's not a farmer, my lord, he's a landowner. But I don't see—"

"His brother was Robert MacKinnon, now deceased?"

Lydia nodded, unsettled by Bury's intent gaze. She feared he had a fever, for his aquamarine eyes positively glittered.

He sat and leaned his head back against the divan. His profile was perfect, and she decided his image could grace any coin in the realm. He sighed and drew a thin hand across his eyes. "I've waited so long, traveled so far," he murmured, as if she were no longer present. "Only to be thwarted by this deuced illness and hundreds of miles of impenetrable Maine wilderness—and that ridiculous marriage of hers!"

He lunged to his feet and hurled his handkerchief into the fire. "How could she? I tried to stop her the first time, but she was adamant. Then when I heard the man had died, I scarcely dared hope. After what she suffered, it was insane to believe she would return, but still, I had to try." He whirled and pinned Lydia with a glittering gaze. "Then to arrive and find her gone, married—"

Lydia held up a hand. "My lord, of whom do you speak?"

He halted. Then a slow smile warmed his aquiline features. "Why, my dear Clemency, of course. Mistress Cameron. Ah!" he exclaimed as if in pain, "Mistress Maclean, now." He stepped close and caught Lydia's hand. His breath smelled of expensive sherry laced with the coppery tang of blood.

"And, my dear Mistress MacKinnon, I will make it very worth your while if you help me get her back."

Chapter Twenty-three

Clemency shivered and huddled close to the crackling fire, then tucked her blue wool skirt out of harm's reach. Last week, her neighbor, Mistress Fones, had suffered terrible burns to her legs when her skirt brushed the fireplace coals and burst into flames. Clemency had tended the poor woman's blistered skin with garlic, goldenseal and willow bark, then vowed to be more careful around the hearth.

Outside The Fort's graceful bow window a glorious winter day beckoned. A blinding blue sky stretched to infinity, and the frozen February sun glittered like diamonds on the endless white drifts of snow. Last night another blizzard had encased the wizened tree limbs in sparkling crystal shells, and long, daggerlike icicles dripped from the house's steep eaves.

The kitchen door swung open, and Jamie stomped in, accompanied by an icy blast of wind. Clemency wrapped her shawl around her shoulders. "Holy Mother, close the door!" she cried. She tried to cast him a severe look, but his blue eyes danced so mischievously she couldn't manage it. She dimpled instead. "Were you raised in a barn?"

Jamie tracked snow across her scrubbed-pine floor, then pressed his frigid cheek to hers. She squealed and he chuckled. "Weel, as I recall, ye told me once I was hung like a Percheron, so perhaps I was." He rolled his *r*s like a Highland waterfall, and his mittened hand attempted to unknot her shawl. She smacked it.

"Get those paws off me, Scottish rogue." She stood and pushed him down onto the hearthside settle. "You must be freezing. Your cheeks are solid blocks of ice." She cupped his lean face in her hands and kissed his frosty hair. "And where's the hat I knit you?"

"Weel, let's just say ye should stick to physicking, *mo cridhe.*"

She stuck out her tongue. "Ingrate. After I slaved—"

He pulled her onto his knee, then bent her back and kissed her soundly. His lips were icy, and the air's frosty tang clung to his clothes. His hot tongue thrust into her mouth, and she gasped, then melted against him. His raised his head and winked.

"I'm not ungrateful, witch, just fashion conscious." He reached into his buckskin jacket, ignoring her attempts to squirm free. "Jack Chason just came upriver from the coast. He brought a fresh load of supplies, and this." He drew out a crumpled letter. " 'Tis addressed to ye."

She snatched the letter and jumped up. "Who on earth would write to me?" She studied the unfamiliar handwriting. They were so isolated here in Fort Western, so bereft of any social contact now that winter held them in its grip. A letter was a thrilling treat, indeed.

"Weel, open it and see." Jamie's tone was sharp, and she eyed him with surprise.

"Is something wrong?"

His bland expression didn't quite reach his stormy eyes.

"Nay. I'm just fashed about getting my load of beaver skins to market, but Chason says the river will stay frozen another month or two. He'll take them down on his sledge tomorrow." He sauntered to the oak sideboard and reached for a skillet of fresh corn bread. "Weel, are ye going to read your letter or no'?"

Clemency slid a finger under the sealed flap and opened the heavy parchment. " 'Tis from Lydia!"

Jamie dropped the corn bread back into the skillet. For a long moment he met her gaze, a look of utter desperation in his eyes. Then his mouth thinned into a harsh line, and his skin paled. Her heart lurched.

"Jamie, what on earth is the matter? Are you sick?"

He closed his eyes and drew a long, quavering breath. Then his shoulders sagged, and his hands clenched into fists. She stood on tiptoe, held her palm to his brow and checked for fever. He shrugged her away and turned to gaze out the bow window.

"Ye better read it," he whispered. His voice was strained and hoarse.

Clemency swallowed convulsively. Something must be terribly wrong, something Jamie was afraid to tell her. But that was impossible. Jamie was the most courageous man she had ever known. He feared nothing. She lowered her eyes to the letter.

January 7, 1764

My dear Clemency,

 I collect that this Letter must come to you as a Shock. Our parting, when you were so grievously Banish'd, from York County, was a Burden to us both. However, it is my Hope as your distant Kinswoman by Marriage, that you will see fit to forgive any Harshness on my part as the actions of a Mother afeared for her Babes. It is that Fear that compels me now to Write. I tremble, I quake as my Pen recounts the Danger in which my children lie.

There is Smallpox in Kittery, where I have pass'd the Winter at the house of my Father, Patrick Stevenson, Esquire. There are only a few Cases now, but such is the vile Habit of the Pox to spread with alarming Speed. By the instant this plea reaches you, a Plague could be rampant among us.

I beg you, my dear Clemency, to show Mercy. Forgive my hard Heart and make haste to Kittery. I beg you to prick my dear Sons against the Pox—to perform that dread Inoculation that has so weighed on my Conscience. For if my vainglorious Pride had not stopp'd me from allowing it in the Past, my dear Babes would now be safe from the depredations of the Angel of Death.

Only you can save them. I beg you, I implore you, follow your Conscience, follow your Heart. Let not stubborn Pride prevent you from succoring the Anguish of this town—and of my beloved Sons. Make haste before All is Lost.

I remain, in vigilant Hope of your Forgiveness and Mercy,

Your cousin, Lydia MacKinnon

Post Scriptum—
I apprehend that your Husband may oppose your flying to our aid. Please do not listen. His Heart is harden'd against me. I can but count on your Calling as Healer to save us from our Plight.

"Jamie, there's pox in Kittery!" Clemency scanned the letter's date, and her pulse raced. "Holy Mother, this was written over two weeks ago." She flung the letter down and tore off her heavy pinner. "Was Jack Chason walking all the way from Kittery? Why, in three weeks time half the town could be dead!"

She stopped, suddenly realizing that Jamie stood with his back to her. "James Maclean, listen to me! Your nephews are in danger, if they're not dead already. Lydia is asking— no, begging—me to come inoculate them."

He shook his head, then turned and lumbered toward her like a bear waking from hibernation. He loomed over her, and her jaw dropped. Having lived with Jamie for months, she sometimes forgot what a giant he was. He grabbed her shoulders and scanned her face, his indigo eyes wild. Startled, she stepped back. He blinked owlishly, then snatched up the letter and scanned it. The despairing look left his eyes, replaced instantly by wariness.

He crumpled the paper into a ball and tossed it into the fireplace. "Ye canna be taking this seriously. 'Tis another of Lydia's tricks."

"Tricks? Are you out of your bloody Scottish mind? If there's pox—"

"*If*, that's the question. I wouldna put it beyond Lydia to lie."

Clemency shoved past him and strode toward the sideboard, suddenly furious with his dismissive attitude. He never respected her healer's skill, unless it benefited him, of course. Simply because she was a woman, he believed he could dictate to her. She squatted down and hauled her medical box out from under the sideboard.

"Why would Lydia lie?" she snapped. "You know she can't abide me. She would never want me back unless her sons truly were in danger."

She threw back the box's lid and rapidly checked the contents. Her supply of herbs was low, but she could replenish them in Kittery. What mattered was the green glass vial containing the powdered pox scabs she had taken from Elizabeth. With God's help, inoculation with this weak variety of pox could save Jamie's nephews and a few other poor souls besides.

Jamie's shadow blocked the pale sunlight. "Clemency, listen to me. Ye canna go. If there is an epidemic, it would be raging now. There's nothing ye could do—"

"How can you say that?" She leaped up and glared at his handsome face. His expression was remote, his eyes cold. "Even if Lydia's sons are dead, I have to go! I'm a healer, 'tis my gift, 'tis what I was trained for. Why can't you see that? Why must you always treat me like a child?"

He arched a sardonic brow and glared down his knife-straight nose. "Weel, if the shoe fits."

"Oh!"

"Listen to yourself, *mo cridhe*. Just the other day ye were grinding your teeth over Lydia's many sins against ye. And now ye're chomping at the bit to play angel of mercy—"

"Play! Is that how you see what I do?" Oh, she wanted to slap that patronizing expression right off his face. "Was I playing when I saved Elizabeth's life? Have you forgotten how you thanked me for saving the one thing on earth you loved? The one thing besides yourself, that is."

A pained expression flashed across his face. She ground her teeth. "Don't you dare give me that hurt-puppy look, Jamie Maclean! You started this."

He caught her wrist and drew her to him. "Dinna fash so, *mo druidh*. I didna mean to belittle your skill. Ye're a brave, canny healer and I'm proud of ye—aye, proud." His voice grew warm, cajoling. "I'm just trying to protect ye. That's a husband's job, aye? Ye could get in serious trouble if the magistrate learns ye're back in York County, and I dinna want ye risking your neck for we dinna ken what. Lydia's prone to exaggeration. There may have been a wee bit of sickness—"

"Lydia saw Robert die of smallpox. She would know if there's a real threat or not. Jamie, the pox is deadly! You know there aren't enough doctors in Kittery, and with new people coming in on ships every day, why, the disease could spread like wildfire."

She bit her lip and jerked her arm away. Here was her chance to make up for the deaths of the Everett baby and young Noah Howard. Jamie had to let her go.

Jamie set his jaw and pinned her with a piercing blue gaze. "Clemency, I ken we married under verra strange circumstances, but for a year and a day at least, ye're my wife. I willna have ye traipsing off through a snowbound wilderness in the dead of winter."

"Oh, you won't, eh? And just how do you plan to stop me?"

A slow red tide washed across his high cheekbones. If she hadn't been so furious, she would have laughed, for Jamie was the image of a stubborn Scottish bull, head lowered, ready to charge. "Dinna push me," he growled. "I tan Elizabeth's bottom when she misbehaves, and I'm not above turning ye over my knee."

"You'd enjoy that, I'm sure," she retorted. This argument was going nowhere. Well, if faint heart never won the field, then it was time to act. She darted around him. "You can stand there and bellow all you want, but I'm packing. In the morning, I'm leaving for Kittery with Jack Chason."

Jamie caught her shoulders in an iron grip. His eyes blazed like blue flame. "I'm not fooling, woman. Ye're not going!"

She froze, startled by his fury. She had never seen him so angry. This couldn't be her Jamie. Her Jamie was a lighthearted tease, a tender lover, a protective father. *He's also the man who has sworn revenge against another for sixteen years,* her memory whispered. The hair rose on the back of her neck.

Her shock must have shown in her face, for as quickly as he had grabbed her, he let her go. He slumped down onto the settle and stared into the fire. Its flickering light revealed the pain in his eyes. The sun had lowered while they argued, and the glowing red fingers of sunset stretched across the room and burnished his hair to cinnamon, russet and amber. He leaned forward, elbows on knees, and buried his face in his hands.

She crept up and knelt before him. "Jamie, please hear me out. I didn't mean to upset you. But you must understand, I have to go. 'Tis my duty, my calling. I wouldn't be who I am if I couldn't heal those in need. I understand your concern, truly I do. What I don't understand is your anger. Why are you so upset?"

He dropped his hands and stared into the fire. The writhing flames cast demonic shadows on the planes and angles of his face, and she felt a shiver of unease. She gathered her courage and touched his knee.

"This isn't like you," she whispered. "You're the kindest, gentlest man I've ever known. I know how much you love your nephews. You can't mean to leave them to a possible death sentence. You love them too much. You couldn't bear to lose them."

After what seemed like hours, he turned and met her gaze. Tears glistened in his indigo eyes, and he sighed, a long, low, quavering sound. He caressed her hair, then bent and kissed the top of her head.

"Nay, *mo cridhe*. You're the one I couldna bear to lose."

Chapter Twenty-four

"I'm telling ye, *mo druidh,* there is no pox!"

Jamie shot Clemency a cross glance, then rapped on the roof of the hired carriage. As the vehicle clattered to a halt in the cobbled street outside Patrick Stevenson's waterfront house, Clemency noted the stubborn thrust of her husband's jaw. Now was not a good time to argue. In truth, what little they had seen of the town so far indicated that Jamie was right.

They had landed at the Kittery docks less than an hour ago. While Jamie hired a carriage and supervised the loading of their sparse baggage, Clemency had stood in the frigid wind gusting off the iron gray harbor. Her toes were half frozen from the knifing cold, and she had stamped her feet to regain feeling. She had said a quick prayer for guidance and thanked the Holy Mother that Elizabeth was safe and warm in Fort Western with Hugh and Mollyocket.

A bedraggled urchin had approached her. "Give us a

penny, marm?'' He wiped a filthy hand across his runny nose. "I ain't had no victuals in a fortnight."

Clemency eyed the healthy pink skin under the boy's artful grime and seriously doubted his claim. She dug a coin from her muskrat muff and held it out. "Tell me, lad, is there smallpox in the town?''

The boy gaped at her as if she had two heads. "No, milady. Leastways none I heard of, and I keeps up with the grapevine, I do." He snatched the coin and raced off.

With their baggage stowed, Jamie and Clemency had jounced down a bustling warren of streets toward the Stevenson home. No black mourning wreaths hung on front doors, no death carts heaped with pox-riddled corpses trundled by, and no fires smoldered in an attempt to purify the diseased air.

Clemency bit her lip and glanced out the frosty carriage window at the Stevenson house. Surely Lydia wouldn't have lied about something so serious as a smallpox epidemic. Jamie helped her from the vehicle, and she offered him a placating smile. With a stern blue glare, he grasped her elbow and hustled her up the front steps. He raised his hand to the brass knocker just as Lydia opened the door.

"Jamie! Oh, thank heaven you've come. I scarcely dared hope." Lydia swept across the threshold and threw herself into Jamie's arms. He stiffened, then untwined her clinging arms from his neck. His face was utterly expressionless.

"Lydia," he said, voice as icy as the wind. His wintry gaze swept over her figure, and Clemency's jaw dropped. Lydia's tentlike black gown couldn't conceal the fact that she was heavy with child.

Lydia's thin lips curled in a complacent smile. "Yes, Jamie, 'tis true. The baby will be here in a matter of days, and now that you've arrived, everything will be perfect." Her eyes flicked to Clemency and grew opaque. "Thank you for bringing him. I knew I could count on you."

Clemency glanced from Lydia to Jamie. If any emotion

seethed beneath the chill blue surface of his eyes, he wasn't revealing it. She swallowed. Holy Mother, this was like stumbling into a play in which she had no part. "Are the boys all right?" she asked. "I saw no signs of pox on the way from the harbor—"

"Faith, I guess the cat's out of the bag now." Lydia shrugged her shoulders and motioned them in out of the cold. They stepped into the foyer, and Clemency caught a quick impression of *faux* gray marble walls and a polished walnut floor.

Jamie ignored the hand Lydia held out for his tricorne and cloak. The muscle twitched in his cheek, and his complexion had paled to the color of dead ashes. "Let's dispense with the formalities." His voice cracked like breaking ice. "If ye've something to say, Lydia, say it now."

"Don't be vexed with me," Lydia said. "I know I shouldn't have fibbed—"

"Fibbed? Then there is no smallpox." Clemency's hands clenched inside her sealskin muff. Was it a sin to slap a pregnant woman?

Lydia flashed her a brittle smile. "It was the only way I could think of getting you here. I know how devoted you are to the healing arts, and I do so hate all the Kittery doctors. When Rachel Hammond raved about your wondrous skill with midwifery, well, I decided I wanted you to attend me in my travail."

"You mean we risked frostbite and drowning—and worried all the way down the Kennebec that your sons were dying—because you want me to deliver your baby?" Clemency heard the shrill of hysteria in her voice.

Lydia's brows knit together. "Yes, but there's more. I've felt so guilty about what happened to you, and I wanted to apologize. I must confess I doubted you once, but now I know you truly are my husband's kin. I thought if I could get you back here, we could mend the rift in the family. We could start over. Samuel and the boys miss you dreadfully, and they want you back.'' She widened her eyes and touched Clemency's arm. ''Please stay and let us be a family again.''

Clemency fidgeted with her gloves. Instinct screamed that she shouldn't trust Lydia, that she should turn and run into the street, but guilt at tearing Jamie from his home and family held her in place. Perhaps she owed Lydia one last chance. ''Well . . .'' She glanced uncertainly at Jamie.

He stared at Lydia as if she were a coiled viper. Clemency touched his arm, and he started. ''Is that all ye have to say?'' he asked Lydia. His voice was velvet-smooth, and Clemency shivered. She knew that tone. Jamie appeared calm, but he was about to snap.

Lydia smiled, and her eyes warmed. ''Oh, Jamie, I know I owe you an apology, too.'' She glided close and reached up to unbuckle the clasp on his cloak. ''Can't we forget our past disagreements and begin again?''

Quick as a striking eagle, Jamie caught her wrist. ''I have begun again,'' he hissed. He released her and stepped back, then sketched a mocking bow. ''Now, if you will excuse us, my *wife*''—he bit emphasis into the word—''and I will bid you good evening.''

He grasped Clemency's elbow and spun her around. His black wool cloak swung wide, blocking Lydia's face from view.

''Thank you, madam. It has been my pleasure serving you.'' The hatchet-faced little apothecary bowed low, and his nose almost scraped his spotless counter.

Clemency nodded politely and swept out of the herb-scented shop, accompanied by the sound of jangling door bells. She lifted her skirts from the mud and quelled the urge to dimple. Holy Mother, arriving in Sir Andrew's expensive new carriage emblazoned with the Pepperrell crest certainly made shopping easier. All morning, clerks had scurried to do her bidding, offering their finest wares and extending endless credit. Unfortunately, since she didn't possess Sir Andrew's fortune, she had confined her purchases to the bare necessities: medicinal herbs.

"Demme, Mistress Maclean!" Sir Andrew waved away his footman and helped Clemency into the carriage. "Shall I send a dray for the balance of your purchases? You appear to have procured everything Apothecary Baines has to offer."

They lurched off, and Clemency arranged her skirts on the carriage's quilted red-silk seat. Suddenly, Sir Andrew's thin nose began to twitch, and a nauseated expression crept across his face. Clemency stifled a giggle.

"Oh, dear, I forgot." She rummaged among her brown-paper-wrapped parcels. "I bought some *asafoetida*. It smells wretched, I know. Most people believe it drives out illness, but I use it to keep people away from my patients, so they won't catch things." She held out the reeking packet. "Perhaps it should ride up front with the coachman."

"Indubitably." Sir Andrew clutched a cambric handkerchief to his nose and leaned out the window to hail the coachman. Clemency glanced at the passing street scene. With a start, she realized they were in front of the Stevenson residence. Jamie came hurrying down the steps, a frown of deep concentration on his handsome face. Sir Andrew spied him and opened his mouth to call a greeting.

"Don't!" Clemency grabbed the edge of Sir Andrew's black velvet cloak and yanked him back with all her strength.

"Lud, Mistress Maclean, we just passed your good husband. Do you not desire his charming presence?" Sir Andrew appraised her through his monocle, gray eyes glittering. "Judging by the haste with which the pair of you retired to your bedchamber last night, I would have hazarded that you were still on your honeymoon. Surely you can't wish to avoid him *this* early in marriage."

She pressed her hands to her cheeks. She could feel their

heat through her thin kid gloves. Her stomach lurched, and for one horrible moment she thought she might vomit on Sir Andrew's silver-buckled shoes.

"Mistress Maclean, are you ill?" Sir Andrew's languid drawl had vanished. He snatched up her limp hands, then stripped off her gloves and chafed her chilled skin.

Clemency closed her eyes and willed herself not to be sick. Why on earth had Jamie been at Lydia's house?

After arriving at Sir Andrew's mansion last evening, she and Jamie had struggled through a strained supper under their friend's watchful gaze. The moment politeness allowed, they had slipped off to their bedchamber, then plunged into a bitter argument. Jamie was furious that Lydia had tricked them, and had insisted that they return to Fort Western in the morning.

Somehow Clemency had found herself defending Lydia. She had told Jamie that if delivering Lydia's child would bring them all together again, then she would do it. Besides, as a healer, she couldn't refuse a request for aid.

Jamie had dug in his stubborn Scottish heels and declared that they would return to Fort Western as soon as he could arrange transportation. Until then, they were both to steer clear of Lydia. Now, less than ten hours later, Jamie was leaving Lydia's house. Clemency leaned back against the seat. Not only had Jamie broken their agreement to avoid Lydia, but he had lied about it.

This morning at breakfast a messenger had arrived with a letter. Jamie had read it, then hurled it into the fireplace, where it curled and blackened on the coals. When she had questioned him, he stated icily that business required that he spend the day on the docks arranging for the sale of his beaver pelts. She doubted Lydia had any use for beaver pelts.

"Mistress Maclean, are you quite all right?" Sir Andrew asked again.

"Yes. 'Tis just a fit of the vapors."

* * *

A soft knock sounded on the bedchamber door. "Madam, there's a gentleman to see you in the front parlor," Sir Andrew's housekeeper called.

Clemency stood and hastily smoothed her hair, then straightened her rumpled skirts. She had spent the afternoon on the comfortable little chaise lounge by the fireplace, where she had attempted to rest. Unfortunately, her mind had whirled with nameless worries and unanswered questions, and she had succeeded only in tiring herself further.

She hurried down the curving staircase. Who on earth could have come to call? She stepped into the parlor doorway and stopped dead.

"Ah! My dear Clemency." Lord Francis Bury swept her a deep bow. He crossed the room in three long strides, then grasped her shoulders and bent to kiss her cheek.

Shimmering blackness descended, the room began to spin, and Clemency slipped from his embrace to the floor.

"My dear, wake up!" Bury cried. She opened her eyes and stared muzzily into his face. Two hectic red spots glowed on his ashen cheekbones, and his aquamarine eyes were wide. "My darling girl, if I had known this would be such a shock—"

"Holy Mary, Mother of God! What on *earth* are you doing here?"

Bury threw back his head and laughed. "My dear, how it invigorates my heart to hear that charming Catholic outrage of yours." He helped her to a chair. "You are a rare tonic— five seconds in your company is better than five thousand pounds' worth of quacks' remedies." He turned her hand palm up and kissed it. His eyes met hers, and his aristocratic accent wavered. "You're so like your mother—"

"Stop it!" Clemency wrenched free and scrambled up. "Stop, stop, stop! What are you doing here? You're supposed to be in London." She raked a hand through her tumbled hair and stormed across the parlor, skirts swirling around her ankles.

Bury chuckled and sank onto a yellow-silk settee. "My dear, your utter lack of felicity at seeing me is most humbling, indeed."

"You have no idea!"

A gilt clock on the mantelpiece chimed five o'clock, and Clemency's heart lurched. She sped to the window and looked out, then darted back to Bury. "You must leave at once! My husband will be home any moment—oh, Holy Mother, he might be home already. I was resting upstairs. I don't know if he's here or not."

Bury stood and smiled indulgently. "My dear, we must speak. 'Tis a matter of urgency. I've traveled all the way from London to make you a proposition—"

"Hush! Listen to me. Where are you staying?"

"I've let a house on Bay Street, but—"

"I'll call on you when I can, but you must leave, *now*. Please, I beg you."

Bury's smile faded. He picked up his walking stick and bowed stiffly. "Considering what lies between us, my dear, I cannot say I blame you for this less-than-rapturous welcome. I will await your visit with ardent anticipation." He fixed her with an intense aquamarine gaze, then strode out.

Holy Mother, would this day never end?

Clemency flipped the hood of her scarlet wool cloak over her head, then stepped out into the night. Instantly, fierce cold slapped her face and stole her breath. Crunchy little snowflakes skittered through the darkness around her, illumined by the flickering golden glow from the carriage lanterns. At the end of the cobbled drive, beyond the frosty lawn, the black Atlantic whispered on unseen ledges.

"My dear, are you quite set on this course?" Sir Andrew

helped her into the carriage, then tucked a mink lap robe over her green-silk skirts.

"Yes." She dimpled and shot him a wry glance. "If you think Jamie is stubborn, you've never dealt with me." She leaned forward and called to the coachman, "The Blue Whale, please." Sir Andrew nodded and stepped back. The vehicle lurched off.

She snuggled down under the soft fur and settled her feet on the heated brick that served as a foot warmer. The carriage swayed most soothingly, but doubts nibbled at her mind. Should she be flying off like this? After all, it was practically the middle of the night. Then she jerked her chin and sat up straight. Jamie was her husband, and something was terribly wrong. She owed it to him, and to herself, to find out what.

"The Blue Whale, indeed," she muttered.

Earlier in the evening, she and Sir Andrew had waited for Jamie for hours before sitting down to a cold dinner. As they dawdled over dessert, a messenger had arrived with a note for Clemency. *Do not expect me tonight,* it read. It was signed with an elegant, slanted *J.* Beneath the signature, obviously added in haste, Jamie had penned, *I'm sorry.*

She had dropped the note on the table and squeaked in dismay. Sir Andrew called back the messenger, and a moment's questioning revealed that a tall, redheaded gentleman had sent it. The gentleman had been well into his cups at a popular tavern called The Blue Whale.

The carriage jolted to a halt, and after a moment the coachman opened the door. "We're here, marm. Do ye want I should go in after the gentleman?"

Clemency peered out on a narrow alley. Yellow light from the carriage lamps glimmered off the greasy cobblestones and cast a wavering glow on the tavern's carved sign. Since most sailors couldn't read, the sign bore an excellent rendering of a spouting whale, painted blue. Snow swirled around it, and it creaked back and forth in the rising wind, adding an eerie descant to the mournful reel that drifted from the tavern. The tune was one of Jamie's favorites.

"Yes," she said. "I'm almost positive he's in there playing the fiddle. Please ask him to step outside. Tell him a lady wishes to see him, but don't say my name."

The coachman bowed, then hurried into the tavern. The minutes ticked by, and she tapped her foot in time to the melancholy music. Holy Mother, what was taking them so long? Surely Jamie hadn't ignored his request. He had impeccable manners.

A gust of wind hit the carriage, and her temper snapped. This was ridiculous! If that blasted coachman couldn't do the job, she would. She flung open the carriage door and jumped down just as a group of sailors erupted from the tavern. They spotted her scarlet wool cloak.

"Oy mates, we're in luck! Not all the bawds are huddled up out o' the snow." A wiry sailor with teeth sharpened to points swayed forward and caught her around the waist. "What's yer price, luv? Group rate, that is." His companions roared.

"Get off me!" Clemency snapped. "I'm no streetwalker. I'm waiting for my husband." She tried to wrench free, but the sailor held her fast. He reeked of rotgut rum and putrid flesh. For the second time that day she battled the urge to vomit.

The gang surrounded her. "Lookit that there carriage," hissed a one-eyed Portugee. "She's a lady, a'right."

Someone slapped the horse's rump. The animal leaped forward, and the carriage wheels spun, catching the hem of Clemency's cloak and jerking her back. She gasped and frantically ripped open the garment's clasp as the heavy fabric tangled in the spokes.

"What luck," gloated the man with pointed teeth. "Now we got us a choice piece of arse and a fine rig." He ripped away Clemency's lace fichu and thrust an icy hand down her bodice. His filthy fingernails raked her breast, and she shrieked.

"Untie the 'orse," the sailor ordered. He shoved Clemency up the carriage steps. "Let's get 'fore the watch hears."

She fell back against the seat, and the sailor lunged on top of her, pulling the door shut behind him. He groped at his buttoned fly, and his fetid breath seared her nostrils. She couldn't breathe; he was too heavy, too putrid. Holy Mother, his hands were down her bodice, up her skirt—

Suddenly she heard a horrible cry and the thud of pounding fists. The horse reared, the carriage swayed and the sailor sprawled to the floor. He cursed and struggled up. Clemency dove, grabbed the heated brick foot warmer and slammed it between his legs. He doubled over, moaning and clutching at his crotch.

The carriage door crashed open, and Jamie bounded in. With a ferocious growl, he grabbed the sailor's throat and pinned him against the red-silk wall. Lamplight flashed on his dirk blade, and the sailor yelped.

Clemency cried, "For God's sake, don't kill him! He's not worth it!"

Jamie's eyes glittered. Blood seeped from his battered knuckles, and his massive shoulders heaved. "Aye, I dinna doubt ye provoked him, witch." He reared back, dragged the man from the carriage and threw him to the icy cobblestones, where the other sailors lay crumpled in a groaning heap. "Back to Sir Andrew's!" he yelled at the coachman. Then he vaulted into the carriage and slammed the door.

He rounded on her. His hair had flown loose from its black-silk ribbon and waved about his face like russet flames. Blood trickled from a gash on one wide cheekbone, and his lower lip was beginning to swell.

"Good Christ, Clemency, what in bloody hell are ye doing here? This part of town's not fit for any woman, least of all my wife." He grabbed her arm and dragged her against him. His eyes blazed like blue flame, and whisky fumes enveloped her.

"I . . . I'm sorry," she stammered. "I know it was dangerous, but I was so worried and angry when I got your note. I had to come find you. I had to know what's wrong."

He glowered at her. Then his lips curled into the devil's own taunting smile. He wrapped his arms around her and dragged her breasts across the damp, rough wool of his coat. "Must I always be rescuing ye, witch?"

He lowered his mouth and flicked his tongue across her lips. His knowing fingers found the curve of her breast, and his eyes darkened. With the powerful grace of a mountain cat, he slid down the length of her body until he knelt on the carriage floor. He rucked up her skirt and petticoats, then spread her legs. He gave a low, possessive growl.

She gasped, suddenly limp with helpless desire. "Jamie—"

"Hush, witch. Ye're mine, and dinna ever forget it." His Scottish accent thickened and slurred, and she realized he was drunk.

He closed his hand around the back of her head and thrust his tongue into her mouth. She tasted expensive Scotch whisky mingled with salty blood. He grasped her hips and yanked her to the edge of the seat. His eyes seared into hers, glittering demon eyes, fire eyes—the eyes of an attacking wolf. Instantly, she caught his frenzy, his primal urge to mate. Lust knifed through her, and she wrapped her legs around his narrow waist.

Jamie plunged his icy hands into her bodice and freed her aching breasts. He nipped her neck, then clamped his mouth around her ripe nipple, delivering a sensation so wild and potent she cried out. The carriage jolted through the silent streets, and he suckled in time to its sway. His lips were rough and insistent; his teeth on her flesh drove her to madness, forced soft, pleading whimpers from her throat while her body quivered with need.

Suddenly he pulled back, and her slick nipple popped

from his swollen mouth. "Och, I'm glad ye came after me," he murmured, "but perhaps ye need a bit of punishment for being so headstrong, aye?" He eased her lengthwise across the seat; then his fingers trailed tauntingly through the damp curls between her thighs. Her body jumped with shock, with pleasure. Her swollen nub ached, throbbed, yearned. One expert touch of his finger on her inflamed flesh would make her explode, but he didn't provide that touch.

"Oh, Jamie, don't tease," she sighed. He chuckled wickedly and nipped her neck until gooseflesh rippled across her skin. She tilted her hips to afford him access, then grasped his hand and urged him on. His finger slipped into her, and she groaned against his shoulder. He chuckled again, a low, wolfish sound, and eased a second long finger into her slick flesh. She writhed against him, desperate for release.

With one hand he yanked open the buttons on his tight breeches. The hot, heavy bar of his manhood jutted free. She gripped him, and he jerked and pulsed under her stroking fingers. "Now who's teasin'?" he murmured in her ear. He slid his throbbing erection between her thighs, gritted his teeth and thrust home.

Clemency gasped. The coachman cracked his whip, and the carriage sped forward. Jamie bent his head and drove into her. She clasped his taut, round buttocks and bucked against him with intense concentration, working herself on his enormous shaft, oblivious to everything but his hardness. The relentless head of his manhood pushed against a spot deep inside her and she cried out—a hoarse, mindless sound of pure lust.

"Ye like that, aye?" he whispered. His eyes gleamed devilishly in the guttering lamplight. Again and again he stroked there, teasing her, driving her mad with pleasure, splitting her apart with agony, forcing her toward a shattering climax. She was almost there, almost there. She whimpered, cried out, "Jamie . . . I can't—please . . . finish me—"

"Ye can and ye will," he husked. He sheathed himself

to the hilt, hard against the aroused spot, then reached
between their bodies and stroked her inflamed center. She
exploded. A ragged shriek ripped from her throat, and she
ground against him again and again, riding the crashing
waves of ecstasy, clutching him with her inner muscles as
shudder after shudder of pleasure and release surged through
her.

"Och, Christ!" He arched his back and froze, his head
thrown back in a silent cry. His seed pulsed inside her, and
he groaned again, reveling in the raw power of his climax.
After a long moment, he collapsed against her. Nearly stifled
by his weight, she slid sideways and curled around him on
the narrow seat.

Their breathing slowed, and Clemency shivered in the icy
air. She groped for the mink lap robe and tucked it around
Jamie's powerful shoulders. He opened one dark blue eye
and smiled like a little boy, then cupped his hand around
her breast—a simple gesture of trust, of possession, of
belonging. The carriage slowed, and he drew a long, ragged
sigh

"Mo cridhe, there's something I must tell ye."

Outside the carriage, a muffled cry cut through the night.
The vehicle clattered to a halt; then a moment later the door
flew open. Malcolm Stevenson's panicked face appeared in
the flickering lamplight.

"Thank God I found you!" he cried. "Mistress Maclean,
you must come. My daughter Lydia has gone into labor."

Chapter Twenty-five

Clemency stood with her cheek pressed to the frigid windowpane and stared out over the silent night streets. The snow had retreated, but had left behind a light dusting of white, as if the roofs, doorsteps and windowsills of Kittery were coated with sparkling powdered sugar. A crescent moon dipped low in the sky, and an eerie silver-blue sheen limned the sleeping landscape. For an instant Clemency recalled the stark beauty of Fort Western. She missed its endless miles of black evergreens and the glittering snow that rolled away into silence, lovely, dark and deep. She wished she were there, or in Sturgeon's Creek or even back on Devon's moors. Anywhere but Lydia's bedchamber.

"Arrrrgh!" Lydia writhed on the great walnut bedstead, her pale face a rictus of pain. The black servant girl hurried forward with a bowl of cool, herb-infused water. Clemency shot the girl a distracted smile, dipped a cloth in the infusion and placed it on Lydia's brow.

"Shhhh, breathe now. In through the nose, out through the mouth. It helps with the pain." Clemency barely recognized her own voice. Surely that calm, soothing tone couldn't be hers. She rolled her shoulders back and forth and tried to ease the iron bands of tension gripping her neck. Holy Mother, if only the baby would hurry! Then she wouldn't have to listen to Lydia's endless whining.

"Where's Jamie?" Lydia gasped.

"I told you, he's waiting downstairs with your father." Clemency turned away, unable to trust her expression. This was the second time Lydia had asked after Jamie. She hadn't asked after her husband Samuel at all.

"Oh, thank God, the pain's easing," Lydia sighed. "Give me some water."

Clemency picked up a pewter cup and held it to Lydia's lips. "Just a sip. More could make you sick."

Lydia gulped noisily, then collapsed back onto the pillows. "Talk to me. It takes my mind off the pain."

"We've talked for hours. You need to rest and save your strength."

"No." Lydia reached up and grabbed Clemency's wrist. "Tell me about you and Jamie."

"I beg your pardon?"

Lydia's ice-blue eyes grew mocking. "I always wondered why he was so quick to marry you. Jamie's the soul of honor, but to marry you after he swore he would never marry again—"

"Lydia, you shouldn't—"

"Does he love you?"

Clemency's cheeks flamed with fury and humiliation. She pulled her wrist free and scrambled up. Lydia was not going to use that catty tone with her.

"Well, does he?" Lydia demanded.

Clemency bit her lip and stalked to the window, then leaned her forehead against the chill windowpane. Did Jamie love her? That was the question, indeed. After six months of marriage, he treated her with the utmost kindness and respect. He petted and teased, he admired her skill as a healer, he protected her with his very life, but he never, *ever* had said he loved her.

"He doesn't, does he?" Lydia nearly crowed with triumph. "Faith, I knew it! He married you out of duty and pity, nothing more."

Clemency whirled. "I don't see 'tis any business of yours."

A spasm of pain shot across Lydia's pinched features. "Oh, 'tis my business, all right. Ahhh!" She knotted her hands in the towels Clemency had tied to the bedposts, then arched her body against the agony of childbirth.

Clemency spread Lydia's thighs and performed a quick examination. Then she glanced down at the precious three-handed watch Granny Amais had given her. "Lydia, stay with me now. The pains are coming fast. It won't be long."

"Oh, God!" Lydia panted. "What do you know about pain? Ooooh." She bent double and gave a low wail. After several torturous minutes, the pain seemed to ease. Clemency dabbed the sweat from Lydia's brow.

Lydia swiped the cloth away and aimed a scathing gaze at Clemency's tiny waist. "You've been married six months. You should be pregnant by now."

Clemency's eyes fluttered shut, and a familiar, hungry ache gnawed at her breast. Her distress must have shown on her face, for Lydia sniggered. "I knew it. He hasn't made love to you, has he?"

"That's enough!" Clemency leaped to her feet and paced across the bedchamber. "What goes on between my husband and me is none of your business." She stooped and grabbed up a log, then threw it into the fireplace. Sparks showered up around her as if mimicking her fury. "But for your information, we are lovers, very much so."

Oh, how could she have gotten herself into this situation? She should have listened to Jamie. She never should have agreed to deliver the baby, never should have trusted Lydia.

She planted trembling fists on her hips and stalked forward. "Since you're so interested, my husband and I had just made love when your father found us."

"Oh! You . . . you . . ." Another pain crashed over Lydia. She clawed at the sheets and writhed in agony. "The baby's coming, I can feel it."

Clemency hurried to the bed and gestured to the black servant. "Help me get her up." They eased Lydia into a sitting position, then piled pillows behind her back. "Lydia, listen to me. When I tell you, push."

"Oh, God! Jamie—where's Jamie?" Lydia shrieked. "I want him, I *need* him! You don't deserve him; you'll never make him happy." She whipped her head from side to side, crazed with pain.

"Hush, listen to me. You need to push."

Lydia panted like a mad beast, eyes clenched, teeth grinding, face scarlet. "You don't understand him," she gasped. "You don't even know who you married. Arrrrgh!"

Clemency held her tongue between her teeth and concentrated on delivering the baby. Granny Amais's voice whispered in her mind: *Remember, girlie, you're a healer.* No matter what her patient said or did, she must ignore it; she must do her duty. It was the pain making Lydia rave so vindictively. Nothing more.

"You bewitched him!" Lydia shrieked. "I could tell. You should have been hanged as a witch!"

"Stop it, Lydia. You're raving. Now push." Blood gushed over Clemency's hands, and Lydia's privates bulged alarmingly. "I can see the baby's head. Push!"

Lydia held her breath and went rigid as granite. "Oooooh!" She expelled the breath in a rush. "Get Jamie—*get him!*" She glared at Clemency, eyes nearly popping from their sockets. "He's mine. He would have married me if it hadn't been for you!"

Inky black fury billowed through Clemency's brain, blotting out compassion, reason, duty. She inhaled deeply and willed herself to stay calm. Lydia was hysterical, mad. There was nothing to her ravings. Nothing. "Shut up," Clemency snapped. "Jamie is my husband and I love him. Now the baby's head is coming. Push."

Lydia keened in agony. Blood and fluid gushed over Clemency's trembling fingers, and the baby slithered into her hands. It was smeared with blood and a waxy, grayish substance.

Lydia's chest heaved. "Love him?" She clawed matted blond strands from her sweaty face and laughed, a maniacal sound that froze Clemency's blood. "Will you love him now that I have borne his child?"

Clemency gasped and rocked back, the slippery, squalling baby still clutched in her hands. For a split second the room seemed to tilt. She couldn't hear, couldn't move, couldn't think. Then blinding agony swept over her. Oh, Holy Mother, this was what Jamie had been hiding. This was the secret that had tortured him all these months. She bent over the squirming baby, her mind reeling from pain and shock. She wanted to shriek to the heavens, slap Lydia's face, dash the baby to the floor.

The baby. Holy Mary, Mother of God. She held the slimy creature up and giddily wiped blood and mucous from its mottled body and face. It was a little girl—tiny, perfect, beautiful—with whorls of Jamie's red-gold hair on her precious head.

Lydia held out her arms. "Give her to me. She's mine— mine and Jamie's." Her voice was weak and raspy, but there was no mistaking its malice. "Jamie and I were lovers. I was going to divorce Samuel. We would have married if you hadn't cast your wicked spell. But he'll be mine now." She struggled up on her elbows, and her opaque eyes gleamed in triumph. "He's always wanted another child. He'll come back to me—"

"Stop it!" Clemency gasped. She dredged up a self-control she didn't know she had and cut the cord that bound

the baby to Lydia. Her fingers shook as she tied it off. Then
she stood and handed the baby to the servant. "Take the
child." Swiftly, she washed her hands. Oh, if only she could
wash away this pain! "Can you deliver the afterbirth?"

"Yas'm."

"Good." Without another glance at Lydia, she snatched
up her cloak and strode from the room.

Halfway down the stairs she saw Jamie standing in the
foyer. The chandelier's flickering candles burnished his long,
tousled hair to amber. His face was ashen, his eyes hollow
and lilac-shadowed. Something in her frozen expression
must have told him she knew the truth, for the harsh lines
of his face deepened. He held out a hand and whispered,
"Please—"

The sound jolted her to life. She gathered up her skirts
and plunged down the curving staircase. He moved as if to
stop her, but she brushed past. Then she was outside, racing
down the silent street, sobbing like a mad woman. The frigid
air froze her tears to her cheeks until she thought her flesh
would shatter. Nearly blind with grief and rage and shock,
she staggered forward and slipped on the icy cobblestones.
Her feet grew numb, and her fingers ached; but she welcomed the cold. She longed for it to freeze the agony searing
her soul. She stripped off her scarlet wool cloak, then ran
on.

She rounded the corner of a brick warehouse and skidded
to a halt. Somehow she had reached the docks. Although it
was nearly daybreak, all was silent. No doubt the good folk
of Kittery were home in their beds, warm and secure. No
one was around to see her, no one to notice or care if she
slipped into the cold, gray harbor and disappeared.

She crept forward, shivering uncontrollably. Frost
squeaked and crunched underfoot as she edged onto the
dock's weathered planking. She skirted around a barnacle-
crusted anchor. Below her, the tide sloshed against the pil-
ings, a hollow, mournful sound that brought on a fresh spurt

of tears. She sank down on a frozen coil of rope and pounded her fist against her thigh.

"Oh, Jamie, how could you?" she wailed.

How could such an honorable man have lied to her? Again and again over their months together she had begged him to tell her what was tormenting him. Always he had evaded her, fobbing her off with jokes and excuses. Only once had he revealed his heart: the night he had told her about Culloden and his vow to avenge his uncle's murder.

She ground her fists into her eye sockets. How could she have been such a fool? She had honestly believed that she could make Jamie love her, that if she were strong enough she could win his heart. She dug her numbed fingers into the prickly, frozen rope. Ha! That miserable Scottish bastard had no heart. Oh, he had tried to warn her; she would give him that much. But no warning could make up for the depth of his betrayal.

The frigid air pinched her lungs, and her ears ached from the cold. She stood and staggered to the edge of the dock, then stared through a thicket of ice-rimmed masts toward the gray glass sea. Oh, she was a fool to believe she could win the love she craved, a fool to believe she could escape the shame and loneliness of her past. She swiped the back of her shaking hand across her runny nose.

But she had found love: She loved Jamie. She loved him even though his every kiss was a lie. She loved him even though he loved another woman. God help her, she loved him even though that woman had borne his child!

She squatted down on the edge of the dock and stared at the slushy water. Oh, Holy Mother, she had wanted Jamie's baby so badly, had longed to give their child the love she had never known. Then perhaps she would have someone who loved her. She pressed a fist to her mouth, then bit the knuckle, reveling in the throbbing pain. She had to face the truth: Jamie would abandon her the moment their handfast marriage reached its end.

"Clemency."

She froze, her toes in their thin slippers curled over the dock's splintery edge. There was no mistaking that low, velvety voice, that heathery Scottish burr. His sure steps moved toward her, crunching in the light snow. She jumped up, heart thundering. Holy Mother, she couldn't meet his eyes; she couldn't look at the handsome, beloved man who had betrayed her utterly.

"Clemency, *mo cridhe,* come away from the edge. Ye'll fall—"

"Shut up!" Her shriek echoed off the ice-crusted ships. "How dare you call me 'my heart?' You wouldn't know a heart if it walked up and slapped you in the face!"

Pain and shame flickered across his features, but he kept walking toward her. "I'm so sorry, *mo cridhe.* Please, take me hand—"

"Get away from me!" She edged sideways and prepared to dart around him. "How could you do it? Lydia is a monster, a cruel, vicious monster! How could you make love to her? How could you father a child—" Agony pierced her heart, and she bit her lip until she tasted blood. "I loved you! I wanted your baby. And all along you were lying and rogering that bitch—"

"That's enough." In one smooth rush, Jamie shot forward, grabbed her waist and swept her up into his arms. She kicked and flailed furiously, skirt and petticoats flying.

"Put me down, you stubborn Scottish sonofa—"

"And let ye drown yourself in a fit of temper? Not bloody likely." He turned and strode toward Sir Andrew's carriage, which, in her misery, she hadn't heard approach.

"I wasn't going to drown myself," she spat. "You're not worth it, you vile, lying, bog-trotting bastard!"

They reached the carriage. As he leaned down to open the door, she freed her arm, drew it back and slapped him with all her strength. He inhaled sharply and dumped her onto the seat. She scrambled into a sitting position. He vaulted in beside her and pounded on the carriage roof, then glared at her down that knife-straight nose. They lurched forward.

Jamie watched her, his eyes as wintry as the frost-gray harbor. "I'm not a man who begs, *mo cridhe,* but I'm begging ye to forgive me."

"Forgive you?" Clemency's teeth chattered, and shivers wracked her body. "After you c-committed adultery with your d-dead wife's sister? Are you insane? I loved you, and all you've done is lie to me!"

He snatched up the mink lap robe and tucked it around her. His shoulders were rigid with tension, and white slashes bracketed his grim mouth. "I ken I lied, and it's been tearing my soul apart. Do ye no' think I have a conscience—"

"Conscience? Ha! Any man who would roger his dead wife's sister is beyond conscience." She cuffed his hands away, then tore off the lap robe and hurled it at him.

"It wasna like that!" He kicked the robe to the floor. "I never wanted it—"

"Oh, and I suppose she raped you." Clemency dashed her tumbled hair from her eyes and shot him a venomous glare. Christ, she wanted to kill the lying bastard!

With an expression both bereft and pleading, he reached for her. "Please listen—"

She lunged for the carriage door. "Don't you dare touch me. I hate you! I'm leaving you—"

"No ye're not!" he thundered. He grabbed her shoulders and pulled her against his powerful chest. "Ye're still my wife, at least 'til summer's end. Leave me if ye must, but if ye go, ye'll go with the truth in your ears."

Chapter Twenty-six

With the toe of his shoe, Jamie lifted the crumpled lap robe from the carriage floor, then grabbed it with one hand. Clemency felt like a frozen granite statue in his arms—if a statue's shoulders could heave with fury. He tucked the mink robe around her. He had to get her warm before she caught her death.

He slowed his breathing and willed his anger away. The sight of her teetering on the edge of the dock had nearly scared him witless, and as always, he nearly had responded by losing his cursed Scottish temper. He knew he shouldn't have manhandled her, but his only thought had been to save her from falling, or jumping, into that bletherin' harbor.

That awful thought upset him all over again. He hugged her closer, and the lush curve of her breast pressed into his arm. He caught his breath. She squirmed like an eel against him, and her icy black hair brushed his jaw. He ached to kiss her brow, her lips, her poor wee frozen hands, but he dared not.

"*Mo cridhe* ..." Shame clawed at his heart, and he flinched. Och, she had every right to hate him, to despise the very sound of his name. But couldn't she see that he was terribly, bitterly sorry?

And couldn't she see that he loved her?

All at once, a glorious shimmer of warmth surged through him, and he pressed his lips against her hair. St. Columba, why hadn't he told her that he was in love with her? He had known it since the moment she had slipped his uncle's clan badge into his hand, but he hadn't been able to bring himself to speak. His damned, stubborn Scottish pride had stopped him. That, and the dreadful secret that Lydia was carrying his child. He ground his teeth, silently cursing his bad judgement. He had been sure if he told Clemency the truth, he would lose her forever. So he had lied and lived in constant fear.

Clemency dug her elbow into his ribs, and he released her. "Listen to me, *mo cridhe,*" he murmured, trapping her trembling hand between his. "For I mean to tell ye the truth of what happened, as God is my witness, and whether ye want to hear it or no'.

" 'Twas May the twentieth, nearly a full month before ye arrived in the Colonies. My wife had died on May the twentieth." He closed his eyes and swallowed. How could it still hurt after all this time? "Och, for nearly five long years that date has haunted me. I couldna stand to be alone then, for all the pain of my loss to torture. Samuel and Lydia kent my grief, so they invited me to supper.

"Ye've seen for yourself how they both can drink, and on that night, I was more than eager to drown my sorrows." He gave a contemptuous snort. "I always say ye're no' drunk if ye can find your arse with both hands. Weel, that night, I couldna. After Samuel had passed out, Lydia insisted I sleep in the barn. She said she was afraid I'd get lost in the woods and be eaten by bears. So I staggered to the barn and fell asleep in the haymow.''

He was dreaming. He knew he was dreaming, but he didn't care. He clenched his eyes tighter, willing himself not to wake, for Rebekah—his darling, beloved Rebekah— lay in his arms. Her scent—sunshine and fresh lemons— drifted to his nostrils, and he inhaled, long and slow. His hands glided down her naked body, and his heart leaped in his chest, delirious with joy. Instantly he grew hard, his manhood straining, aching. It had been so long! Christ, how he wanted her—his darling, his love, his life.

She whispered, "Jamie," soft and low. He mounted her, and his blood roiled with desire. She moved beneath him, eagerly, urgently, and his hand found her wetness. He was hers once more. Och, the joy to lie between her thighs, to offer up his love! He thrust home. And the dream vanished.

"Even now I canna believe I did it. But Lydia truly is near to Rebekah's twin—ye've heard it said yourself. And she was wearing Rebekah's lemon toilet water.'' Jamie shook his head. ''I suppose I just longed for it to be Rebekah. There's no excuse, I ken, but my body was already bent to the task. It had been four long years since I'd lain with my wife. I'd never so much as kissed a lass since, and, well . . . my manhood would have its release.'' He dragged his hands down over his face, longing to erase the memory of his shame. ''My brain was screaming that it was wrong, that I must stop, but I couldna.''

He shuddered to a halt, breath rasping between clenched teeth. Clemency's beautiful face was ashen in the gray dawn light. She pressed back into the corner, into the shadows, and he couldn't read her expression. Nearly shaking with a fear he couldn't understand, he lifted his hand and traced her cheek with the searching fingers of a blind man.

"Stop it!" she wailed, slapping his hand away. "I don't want to hear another word!"

The muscle in his cheek leaped and twitched, and he bent forward, too ashamed to meet her stricken eyes. "I canna bear to hurt ye, but I must confess, aye?" He swallowed and plunged on.

"The moment I was finished, I staggered up, eaten to my verra soul with self-disgust. Lydia must have seen the horror in my eyes, for she started crying. She told me she loved me. She was going to divorce Samuel so we could marry. All I wanted was to run, to wash myself and drown myself in whisky until my brain was blank. I told her 'twas a dreadful mistake, that it would never happen again."

He leaned down and caught the silken hem of Clemency's skirt. Och, please God—she must forgive him! He bowed his head and pressed it to his lips. "And it never did. I swear it on my daughter's life."

"Which daughter?"

Clemency's ice-green gaze pierced his heart. A chill froze through his veins. His pulse slowed to the dull, leaden thud of a heart on the brink of death. The carriage rattled to a stop, and some still-functioning part of his brain realized that they must be back at Sir Andrew's. Clemency edged forward, and her white fingers gripped the door handle.

"How long have you known Lydia was with child?" Her voice was a mere croak.

"Since the night of the husking bee."

"Do you love her?"

"Nay." He reached for her, hesitated, reached again. "I told Lydia I could never love anyone but Rebekah—"

As the words—the foolish, ill-chosen words—flew from his mouth, Clemency slipped through his fingers. She swirled out the carriage door and vanished like a fleeting dream on a cloud of green-silk skirts.

Clemency huddled under the eiderdown coverlet and watched the flaming sun slip behind the bare branches and dark rooftops of Kittery. Lassitude weighted her limbs, and she idly wondered why sunsets were always so spectacular in the dead of winter. Was God seeking to make up for the wretched cold? Listlessly, she turned her gaze to the elaborate crewel-work hangings on the canopy bed. The jewel-toned embroidery depicted a fanciful Garden of Eden and an enticing Tree of Life. There was a motto in Latin, embroidered onto the cream-colored wool with garnet silk. She translated it roughly as *Yield Not to Temptation*. How ironic. She closed her eyes and bit back a groan.

A fire crackled on the hearth, but she still shivered violently. How could she be so chilled? It had been hours since she had left Jamie sitting in the carriage in Sir Andrew's snowy drive. She should be warm by now. She swallowed back tears and burrowed deeper under the eiderdown, feet skittering away from the sheet's icy spots. She would not think about Jamie. She couldn't bear the memory of his bereft expression as she had fled from his arms.

With a tiny sigh, she rolled onto her side and winced. All day long her muscles had ached, and nausea swept over her every time she tried to get out of bed. She longed to fall asleep, but she couldn't still her thoughts. They whirled and raced through her mind as if stimulated by some devilish herb.

A soft knock sounded on the bedchamber door. She sat up and drew the eiderdown around her shoulders. "Come in."

Lord Francis Bury sauntered through the door. He carried two goblets and a crystal decanter of amber liquid. "So, my dear, you're awake at last. I was beginning to worry about you.''

Clemency smiled wanly and propped the goose-down pillows behind her. "I must thank you for allowing me to descend on you like this." She lay back with a sigh. "And I suppose I owe you an explanation."

"I must confess, it was rather startling when you showed up on my doorstep, bag and baggage.'' He arched an elegantly peaked brow at her threadbare satchel, which rested on the hearth-side wing chair. "Although I use the term 'baggage' loosely. I must say, rusticating in the wilds of America has done nothing to advance your position in life.''

A flush swept over her cheeks. "I'll thank you to keep a civil tongue in your head, my lord. My position in life is none of your concern." She flicked her long black braid over her shoulder. Oh, no. Lord Bury had sacrificed any claim on her long ago. "Any man who has behaved the way you have—''

"Tut, tut, my dear." Bury perched on the edge of the bed and set the decanter and goblets on a tilt-top side table. "I am merely concerned for your welfare. You know how precious you are to me—''

Clemency snorted. "You should have thought of that before you ruined my life.''

A pained expression flashed across Bury's patrician face, and he lowered his aquamarine gaze. *"Touché.* As always, my dear, you have me at a disadvantage." He reached for the brandy, and his thin hand trembled slightly. He poured the amber liquid into a goblet, then held it out to her. "But perhaps we can declare a truce in our ongoing war. Why don't you tell me what has driven you into the arms of the enemy.''

Clemency snatched up the goblet. "Well, as the colonists say, I suppose I shouldn't look a gift horse in the mouth."

Bury chuckled. "What a quaint expression. Whatever does

it mean?'' Suddenly he began to cough with great, hacking spasms.

''Not to be ungrateful.'' Clemency slammed her goblet on the bedside table and scrambled to her knees. ''My lord, what's wrong?'' He pressed a handkerchief to his bluish lips as she touched his heaving shoulder. His bones were as thin and brittle as a baby bird's. All at once, realization dawned. She snatched the fine cambric handkerchief from his hand. Tiny spots of scarlet blood were spattered across it. ''Holy Mother, 'tis consumption, isn't it?''

The coughing subsided, and Bury groped for the blood-stained square of cloth. ''Yes. That is why I followed you here. I couldn't die until I had made my peace with you. I wronged you so terribly—''

''Shhhhh.'' Clemency pressed a finger to his cold lips. Two hectic red spots floated on his high cheekbones, and his skin was the pale blue-white of a walking corpse. Her heart lurched. Oh, Holy Mother, he couldn't be dying.

For years she had despised Lord Francis Bury and chafed under the shameful burden of his power over her life. Then, after her mother's death, financial destitution had forced her to depend on him as never before. Slowly, his kind attentions had earned her trust, and bit by bit, they had begun to craft a fragile bond of affection. Clemency reached behind her and groped for the brandy goblet. Could that happy time truly have been only twelve months ago? For a few glorious weeks, she had thought she had found the love she craved. But it had been smashed—destroyed by rape and betrayal.

Her lips twisted bitterly. Bury had betrayed her, just as Jamie had. Was there something about her that attracted such mistreatment? She thrust the brandy at Bury. ''Here, drink this.''

He took the goblet and set it down. ''My dear girl, I've come here to make reparation, and to make a proposal. You know how much I love you.'' He raised her hand to his lips and kissed it tenderly. ''I beg you, please return with me to

England. I'm not long for this world, and I yearn to spend my final days making you happy—making up for lost time."

She tried to pull free, but he held her fast. "Listen to me," he said. "I've had my solicitor draw up a new will. After what happened . . . well, let's just say I should have done it long ago." He raised his tapered hand and stroked her cheek. "You're the beneficiary, my dear. My entire estate will be yours, but you must come home with me. You must take my name."

Clemency caught her breath. "But I'm married."

Bury snatched up the brandy and tossed it back. "Forgive me if I am mistaken, my dear, but I collect that your marriage is not entirely . . . shall we say, satisfactory?"

Clemency sloshed brandy into the second goblet and gulped it down. It burned her throat and warmed her stomach. "You're right. That . . . that's why I'm here." She fished her robe from the foot of the bed and pulled it on, shivering with an odd sensation of hot and cold. "I . . . I just found out that my husband fathered a child on another woman."

"I beg your pardon?" Bury pivoted, his expression autocratic, his gaunt frame imperious.

All at once she had a vision of him commanding King George II's troops in the field. *And slaughtering innocent Highland women and children on the streets of Inverness,* a tiny voice hissed through her brain. She gave herself a mental shake. What Jamie had told her couldn't be accurate. After all, hadn't he just proven himself a liar?

" 'Tis true," she murmured. "Oh, I counted the months. Lydia was pregnant before I even met Jamie, but—"

"Lydia? Do you mean Mistress MacKinnon?"

"Yes, my lord." She made another grab for the brandy decanter. "I knew something was wrong, but Jamie wouldn't tell me what. He just kept lying and lying . . ." Her voice rose in a little wail, and she halted, embarrassed to show such weakness.

After several long minutes, she glanced up. Bury's face wore an expression of cool appraisal, oddly mingled with an air of deep affection. He caught her eye and positioned his long fingers like a church steeple. "Do you love him?" he asked.

Chapter Twenty-seven

The question hung between them as if suspended in mid-air. "Yes," Clemency whispered. "More than life itself."

Bury's eyes fluttered shut, and a tiny sigh escaped his lips. Then his glittering aquamarine gaze pierced through the shadows. "My dear, far be it from me to defend a man I have not met—although every report I have heard of Maclean has been extremely complimentary." He shook his head and looked baffled. "So complimentary that I can hardly fathom that the man is a Highland Scot—and a damned Jacobite."

Clemency's head shot up. "You know Jamie was a Jacobite?"

"Of course. The moment I arrived in Kittery I did everything in my power to ascertain if you had contracted an unfortunate alliance. Imagine my chagrin at learning that your husband had been a bond servant, banished for Jacobite treason." Mild disdain flickered across his thin features, and he fluffed out his lace cuffs. "As I said, far be it from me to defend a man who has hurt you, my dear, but if you love this man as much as you say, perhaps you should entertain forgiving him.''

''Why should I forgive that stubborn Scottish . . .'' She clutched the goblet until her fingers turned white. ''All he did was lie—''

''My dear, any man would have done the same in his place, no matter how honorable he is.'' Bury grinned ruefully, shrugged his shoulders and turned his hands palm up in a charming gesture more French than English. ''Do you not realize that all men are scoundrels when it comes to such matters?''

Suddenly his smile vanished. ''My dear, there's something else you may not know.'' He took her hand and arched a sardonic brow. ''Adultery is a capital crime in Massachusetts Colony. Your husband and Mistress MacKinnon could both be hanged if news of this . . . ah, indiscretion ever reached the ears of the magistrates.''

Clemency's jaw dropped. ''You're joking!''

''My dear girl, you seem to forget that this is not England. You now live among God-fearing Puritans.'' Bury pronounced the word with distaste and began to untie his immaculate linen cravat. ''Lud, these are the people whose ancestors beheaded Charles the First. They take their sin most seriously.''

Clemency collapsed back against the pillows. The room tilted, and nausea sloshed through her in sickening waves. ''Holy Mother, no wonder he lied.'' She swallowed the bile at the back of her throat and pressed a hand over her eyes. Bury rustled out of his coat, and her ears twitched at the clink of crystal.

He sloshed brandy into the goblet and held it to her lips. ''Drink this, my dear. You look dreadfully peaked.''

Her eyes flew open. ''Arrgh, get that away. The fumes— I think I'm going to be sick.'' She clapped her hand to her mouth and held her breath. Sweat broke out on her skin, and for long, horrible moments she felt as if she were burning alive. Finally the sensation passed.

She gave Bury a wan look. He cocked a speculative brow, and his gaze swept over her figure. "My dear girl, are you carrying?"

"What?"

Both brows arched up. "Lud, you are married, my dear. Don't look so appalled. If Maclean got a child on another woman, he certainly is capable of getting one on you." He lowered his gaze to her breasts and cleared his throat. "Forgive my frankness, but as I recall, you were never so . . . ah . . . voluptuous when we lived together in England."

Clemency twitched the coverlet up to her chin. Could it be true? She had been so frenzied with worry since receiving Lydia's letter about smallpox that she hadn't bothered to keep track of her womanly cycle. Her cheeks burned, and she frantically counted days. Holy Mother, she was three weeks late. She was carrying Jamie's child!

Her heart gave a great, exultant bound of joy, and she thrilled with a sudden wild impulse to dance, to sing, to shout from the rooftops. Jamie's child! Giddy with happiness, she pressed both hands against her hot cheeks as if to keep herself from exploding.

Bury's sunken eyes sparkled. "Then my observation is correct." He grasped her hand and lifted it to his lips. "Oh, my darling girl, I'm overjoyed. I scarcely can believe it." He sat back, a stunned expression on his face. "To think you're going to make me a grandfather."

A timid knock sounded on the door. "My lord?" the chambermaid called. "There's a gentleman here to see Mistress Maclean. He says he's her husband, and he's powerful upset."

Clemency struggled into a sitting position. "My lord—"

Bury was already on his feet. "Why, this is marvelous.

At last I shall have the pleasure of meeting my grandchild's father.''

''Listen to me—''

''My dear girl, if you truly love this man, you must forgive him.'' He bent over and caught her shoulders. ''Remember, you're carrying his child.'' He embraced her gently, then kissed her forehead.

Clemency's heart hammered against her rib cage. Oh, Holy Mother, if Jamie saw Lord Bury, he might well try to kill him. For sixteen years, he had vowed revenge against his uncle's murderer. Now his prey lay within his grasp.

She flung the bedclothes aside. ''But you don't understand. There's a terrible problem—''

Bury straightened the ribbon that held back his silvery hair, then sauntered toward the door. ''Nonsense, my dear. I am fully cognizant that your husband is a damned Jacobite. But lud, that unpleasant business was over nigh on seventeen years ago. Surely civility and family feeling will allow us to overcome any little differences between us.''

He opened the bedchamber door and flicked a hand at the maid. ''Tell Mr. Maclean to wait in the drawing room. Mistress Maclean is indisposed, but I will be down to greet him directly.'' The scrawny girl bobbed a curtsy and scurried away.

Clemency struggled to her feet. Dizziness spiraled through her, and she clung to the bedpost. ''My lord, please listen to me—''

Heavy footsteps pounded up the staircase, and a familiar Scottish accent reached her ears: ''I ken she's indisposed, but I will see my wife.''

Bury stepped forward, a welcoming smile on his patrician face. Clemency gave a little cry and swayed toward him. Then the world began to spin, her knees turned to butter and she crumpled into her father's arms. Jamie strode into the room and stopped dead, a look of utter shock on his handsome face.

After a moment of stunned silence, his indigo eyes blazed into hers, and his lips thinned into a grim line. "What the devil is the meaning of this?" His voice was deadly soft.

Clemency reached out. "Jamie, please—" Bury's arms tightened around her sagging body.

Jamie's eyes never left hers. The muscle in his cheek began to twitch. "Sir Andrew told me ye were staying with an old friend from London. I imagined your friend would be a lady." His tone dripped with acid sarcasm. "I should have kent ye'd land on your feet—witch."

Suddenly he swept off his tricorne and dropped into a mocking bow. His black wool cloak swirled around him. "I beg you to forgive my shocking breach of manners, but it is not every day that I find my wife in the arms of another man." His Scottish accent had vanished, replaced by the clipped, cultured tones of the British aristocracy. "Tell me, madam, have I the honor of addressing your lover? Is this the scoundrel who deprived you of your maidenhead?" His jaw hardened, and his gaze grew impenetrable. "Although from the looks of things, rape was not necessary."

"Jamie—"

"That will be enough, Maclean." Bury eased Clemency into the wing chair, then advanced toward Jamie's towering form.

For the first time since entering the bedchamber, Jamie's gaze flicked to his rival. He blanched and grew utterly still. Then a slow wave of livid red washed across his high cheekbones. His shoulders went rigid, and his gaze burned into Bury's face.

"I know this must look demmed peculiar," Bury said, "but there is no need for theatrics. Your wife was taken ill by the stresses of the day and the shock of your sudden arrival. I merely prevented her from falling into a faint." He sketched an elegant bow. "Perhaps if I introduce myself, we can clear up any misunderstanding—"

"I ken who ye are," Jamie rasped, voice thick once more

with Highland burr. "For years ye've haunted me night-mares. Your name is branded on me brain. I willna hear it spoken again 'til 'tis read at your funeral."

Bury froze in mid-bow. His Adam's apple bobbed convulsively. "Lud, Maclean, are you mad?"

Firelight licked the hard planes and angles of Jamie's face, bathing his sharp cheekbones and severe nose in flickering shadows of black and gold. Clemency struggled to her feet and prayed not to faint. She had to stop him before he throttled her father. Holy Mother, why must Jamie cling to his role of bloodthirsty Highland warrior?

"Nay," Jamie whispered. His hand shot to the dirk in his belt. "I'm sane for the first time since Culloden, for tonight I avenge the honor of the Macleans." He grabbed the front of Bury's shirt and yanked him off his feet. The cloth ripped. Bury gasped.

"No!" Clemency cried.

"I see by the look in your cursed eyes that ye dinna recognize me." Jamie's nostrils flared, and he pressed the razor-sharp dirk against the Englishman's pale neck.

"No," Bury gulped, "I—"

Clemency clutched her husband's arm. "Jamie, listen to me—"

"Stay out of this." His gaze never left Bury's. Sweat beaded his brow, and his knuckles were white. " 'Tis too late to protect your lover."

He tightened his grip on Bury's shirt and shook him like a rat. "Listen close, English dog, and take this thought to your grave. I'm one of the thousands of men ye and your bloody Sassenachs mowed down on Drumossie Moor. But I didna die, I lived—only to rot in a Sassenach jail and see my clan and hundreds of innocent Scots destroyed around me." His breath came in harsh, ragged gasps, and he lowered his face until it was inches from Bury's. "I was flogged until I prayed to die. I was starved and tortured, but that was not the worst of it."

"For God's sake, man, I was a soldier," Bury croaked. "I followed orders, I did my duty, nothing more."

"Was it your duty to murder my uncle?" Jamie thundered. "To shoot him down like an animal?" He slid the dirk's blade along the throbbing pulse in Bury's throat. A bright thread of blood beaded there.

"Stop it!" Clemency shrieked. She locked both hands around Jamie's wrist and struggled to break his iron grip. "Don't you dare hurt him. He's my father!"

All at once, Jamie went deathly still, like a ship becalmed in the eye of a hurricane. For an agonizing moment the only sound was the fire's crack and Bury's labored breathing. Jamie's gaze remained riveted on the Englishman's face; then slowly, oh so slowly, he turned his head and looked at Clemency. He appeared stunned. His indigo eyes were blank, his expression faintly bewildered. She stared up at him, too frightened to breathe. His brow wrinkled and his lips parted, but no sound came out.

" 'Tis true," she whispered. She released his wrist, but her gaze still held his, pleading, imploring. "Jamie, if I mean anything to you, anything at all, *please* let him go."

Jamie expelled his breath as if it had been knocked from him by a savage blow. He dropped his hands to his sides. Then he sheathed his dirk and turned sharply away.

Bury staggered back and collapsed in the wing chair, hand clutched to his throat. Clemency stood frozen between the two men. Then with a tiny whimper, she reached out her hands and swayed toward Jamie's broad back, pleading, supplicating. She had lost him now, lost him forever. . . .

At that precise moment, Lord Bury doubled over into a violent coughing fit. His ragged, blood-choked hacking echoed through the room. She cast one final, despairing gaze at her husband's back, then turned and knelt by her father.

For several endless minutes Jamie paced back and forth in the shadows, pounding his fist into his thigh with each long stride. Finally he stopped. His shoulders sagged, his head slumped forward and his hands hung limp at his sides. Suddenly, a tremor shuddered down the entire rigid length of his tall frame. With a strangled cry of rage, he shot forward and smashed his fist into the wall. Then he whirled and was gone.

Clemency clutched her arms about her waist and collapsed to the floor. Her bitter sobs muffled the sound of his quick footsteps retreating down the stairs.

Chapter Twenty-eight

Jamie lay sprawled across the canopied bed in Sir Andrew Pepperrell's finest guest chamber, shirt rucked up under his armpits. He awoke, sniffed and grimaced. St. Columba, he smelled as if he had spent the last three days in a dockside gutter, doused with rotgut rum. He cracked open an eye and instantly regretted the impulse. The tall damask draperies were closed, but brilliant sunlight lanced in through the gaps and stabbed at his brain. He groaned and heaved himself into a sitting position, then muzzily gazed around. Och, the bedchamber looked as if he had hosted a Roman orgy! His cloak, stockings, shoes and tricorne hat lay among a truly dizzying array of whisky, rum and brandy bottles. The icy, stale air stank of spirits and musky male flesh.

Shivering, he bent down to retrieve a stocking. His stomach roiled, and he bit his lip, determined not to be sick. He must be getting old. Any self-respecting Scot could handle his liquor better than this, although from the looks of things, he had quaffed enough grog to fell an ox.

He wrapped the soft woolen folds of his cloak around his chilled body and shambled to the window, then twitched back the expensive drape and squinted out. The snow had melted, and Sir Andrew's cobbled drive gleamed like wet pewter in the lemony sunlight. It must be about midday. Sighing heavily, he let the drape fall back, then collapsed in a fragile Chippendale chair.

He slumped down and dangled his hands off the chair's arms. How long had he shut himself away in here? He tried to concentrate on the distorted images that fled through his mind: the chambermaid scuttling away from his enraged bellow, the butler carrying a tray of whisky. Suddenly one clear, horrible memory crystallized in his brain. He shook his head, oblivious to the pounding ache in his skull. Surely his wits were paralyzed, for he could not process the thought. How could Clemency, his beautiful, courageous, loving wife, be Lord Bury's child?

Bury. God curse the Sassenach to hell!

Rage shot through him, and he dug his fingers into the chair's arms. When the cat-o'-nine-tails had flayed his back, he had vowed to smite Bury for destroying the Highlands. Chained in the foul, vermin-ridden hold of a brutal prison ship, he had promised to hunt his uncle's murderer to the ends of the earth. Through the long, lonely years since Rebekah's death, he had sworn to kill Bury like the vicious swine he was.

He lunged to his feet and paced across the elegant bedchamber, kicking viciously at empty bottles with every long stride. Christ, how he had ached to slit that bastard's throat! Even now his blood thundered in his ears at the thought of Bury's pale skin beneath his blade. He gritted his teeth, then spat a stream of furious oaths and smashed his fist into the bedpost. Clemency's stunning revelation had nearly stopped his heart, and it had taken all his strength to keep from dropping to his knees like a wounded animal. For a moment, he had been sure that he couldn't have heard her right, but the pleading, frightened expression in her loch-green eyes had screamed the truth.

The truth. His lips twisted, and he almost laughed at the perverse irony of the situation. Why, just hours before her staggering disclosure, Clemency had been screaming at him for hiding the truth.

"Maclean, open the door." Sir Andrew's voice was crisp. "You've wallowed in there for three days, sir, and I will allow it not another minute."

Three days? Jamie felt a ripple of chagrin, followed by a jab of worry. Anything could have happened in three days. He turned the key and yanked open the door.

Sir Andrew bustled in. His foot struck a brandy bottle, and his brows arched. "Demme, Maclean, 'tis like a tavern after a brawl in here. I always knew you were a gentleman of sizeable appetites, but isn't this a bit overboard, even for you?" Despite his bantering tone, Sir Andrew's gray eyes were shadowed. He clapped a hand on Jamie's shoulder. "All you quite all right?"

Jamie snorted bitterly. "Aye, unless ye count my splitting head and heaving gut."

Sir Andrew turned and spoke to the hovering chamber-maid: "Send up my valet with the hip bath, and have Cook boil water. Mr. Maclean wishes to dress. When we are finished in here, you may clean the chamber." He closed the door and crossed to the hearth, where he bent and stirred up the fire. "Demme, 'tis like a tomb in here. You'll be down with a fever at this rate." He straightened and shot his friend a shrewd glance. "Shall I send for Mistress Maclean, in the event you require nursing?"

With iron control, Jamie smoothed his baleful expression into an impenetrable mask. "Is she still staying with Bury?" He almost bit his tongue choking out the galling name.

"Yes." Sir Andrew's cultured voice grew soothing. "Jamie,

we've been friends a long time. I knew when Mistress Maclean left here that she had gone to stay with Lord Bury, but I didn't know until yesterday that he was her father. She said—''

"Dinna speak of it! Did she also tell ye who Lord Bury is?" Jamie jabbed his forefinger into Sir Andrew's thin chest. "Did she tell ye what he did to me?" Another jab. "Did she tell ye that bletherin' bastard wiped out my clan and murdered my uncle?"

Sir Andrew grabbed Jamie's finger. "Yes, she did. And if you poke me one more time, sir, I shall be forced to call you out."

Jamie stared as if he had been addressed by a mouse; then one corner of his mouth twitched. "Och, dinna do that. I ken ye're fierce with a sword."

"Jamie, she's been ill."

His head shot up.

" 'Tis not serious," Sir Andrew added. "Merely too much worry."

Jamie closed his eyes and pinched the bridge of his nose between thumb and forefinger. Relief washed over him, and he felt weak as a wee kitten. Thank God Clemency wasn't seriously ill. And thank God she hadn't run off with that Sassenach bastard she called a father. He braced both hands on the marble mantel and leaned forward, slumping his head between his arms, too overcome to speak.

"I think you should go to her," Sir Andrew said.

Jamie raked a hand through his hair, then cursed as his fingers caught in a snarl. "Go to her? Are ye mad? She's living with my worst enemy!"

Sir Andrew sniffed and flicked a particle of dust from his immaculate blue-velvet sleeve. "From what I understand, her removal to that household was not altogether unprovoked."

"Unprovoked? Of course it was unprovoked! I explained what happened with Lydia. I begged Clemency to forgive me. And did she?'' Jamie jerked his chin and clawed at his shirt lacing as if it were strangling him. ''Nay, she pitched a fit and flew off to be with that bloody murdering Sassenach!''

Sir Andrew looked unperturbed. ''Be that as it may, allow me to remind you that she is your wife, at least temporarily.'' He tilted his head to one side and tapped a finger against his chin. ''Quaint custom, that handfasting of yours. But demme, Maclean, what happened before she was born is not her fault.''

''Not her fault?'' Jamie thundered. ''She kent I was sworn to avenge my uncle's death. Honor requires it—''

''And your pride demands it?''

He ignored Sir Andrew's jibe. ''She kent better than anyone what I must do. But she stopped me, God help the scheming witch. She stopped me!''

His heart roared in his ears, and he felt as if his veins would burst. He stormed across the room, breath ragged through clenched teeth. The bedchamber door swung open just as his foot struck a bottle. Swift as lightning, he snatched it up and hurled it against the wall. It exploded in a shower of green glass, inches from the tartan-swathed figure on the threshold.

''By St. Ninian! If that's the way ye're goin' to greet me, lad, I'll hie me back to the woods.'' Hugh Rankin scowled and stumped into the room.

Goody Lewis sailed in from the kitchen yard, an enormous split-oak basket of potatoes, carrots and turnips over her plump arm. ''Gorry!'' she sang at the top of her lungs, ''did ye ever see such a bonny afternoon?''

Clemency winced, then managed a slight smile. Goody Lewis was Lord Bury's nurse. She was also an excellent cook who had spent the last three days conjuring up wholesome broths and succulent puddings to tempt her employer's and Clemency's failing appetite. Unfortunately, Clemency's bouts of morning sickness seemed to last all day, and she hadn't managed to keep down so much as a bite of the old woman's delicious fare.

"Och, ye should be out gettin' some fresh air, lass." Goody Lewis plopped the basket on the trestle table and pinched Clemency's cheek. "Yer as pale as milk, mere skin and bone, but just ye wait. I've a new receipt from Goody Clay. 'Twill get the curves back on ye in no time."

Clemency's throat ached. Like Jamie, Goody Lewis was a Highland Scot, and her accent alone could reduce Clemency to tears. Suddenly the old woman let out a shriek. Clemency whirled. Mollyocket stood in the kitchen doorway, an enigmatic smile on her mahogany face.

"Begone, ye beggin' savage," Goody Lewis ordered, waving her cleaver. "Ye scared me half to pieces, standin' there grinnin'."

Clemency hurtled forward and threw her arms around the Indian. "Oh, Molly, I'm so happy to see you! What on earth are you doing here?"

Goody Lewis rounded on Clemency, mouth agape. "Do ye mean to say ye ken this savage?"

Clemency drew Mollyocket into the kitchen. "Of course I do. She's a dear friend come all the way down the Kennebec River to see me."

Goody Lewis stripped off her voluminous calico apron. "I don't hold with savages in me kitchen. I'll step next door and visit with Goody Clay." She snatched her cloak from a peg on the kitchen wall and glowered at Clemency. "Keep an eye on me knives, and remember Lord Bury needs his tea." She jerked up her chin and swept out.

Clemency smiled wanly and waved Mollyocket onto the settle by the kitchen fireplace. The Indian wore a gray wool bodice over a wide, quilted skirt of rust-colored onasburg. A brown wool cloak covered her shoulders, and a kidskin reticule dangled from her hand. Despite her stylish attire, she still wore her black hair in two long braids, and an amulet of beads and feathers encircled her neck.

"Goody has a kind heart despite her manners," Clemency said apologetically. "You must forgive her rudeness." She sat beside the Indian, nervousness shimmering through her veins like minnows through a mountain stream. Her hand trembled as she touched her friend's forearm. "Is Hugh here with you, and . . . and Elizabeth?" Oh, Holy Mother, it hurt to say the little girl's name. What if Jamie never allowed her to see his daughter again?

Molly nodded and gestured toward the north.

"They're staying with Sir Andrew Pepperrell?" Clemency asked. She was used to one-sided conversations with the mute Indian and had grown adept at interpreting Mollyocket's gestures and expressions. Sir Andrew's concerned gray eyes floated through Clemency's mind, and a thought struck her. "Did Sir Andrew send for you?"

Mollyocket nodded. Clemency sighed and leaned against the settle's high back. "In that case, I'm sure you know why I'm here. Sir Andrew has many fine qualities, but the ability to ignore gossip is not one of them." She fidgeted with her muslin pinner. "Did . . . did you see Jamie?"

The Indian nodded, and her black eyes grew soft with sorrow.

"I . . . I take it he doesn't want to see me, then." Clemency swallowed. "When Sir Andrew came by yesterday, I asked him to tell Jamie how sick my father is. I thought Jamie might give up his wretched vow of revenge. You see, my father is dying."

She jumped up and paced in front of the hearth. She was too numb and exhausted to cry, yet aching grief strangled her heart. Oh, why couldn't Jamie understand? Through the dark, endless hours of nursing, as her father lay coughing his life away in great, glistening clots of blood, he had explained Alexander Maclean's death. Her father had been a soldier under orders, defending his life on the battlefield.

It had not been cold-blooded murder. As to Jamie's other terrible accusations ... well, some things could not be excused; they could only be forgiven.

She sat and cast Mollyocket a pleading look. "You understand, don't you? I'm a healer. I can't just leave Lord Bury."

The Indian patted her hand. Tears choked Clemency's throat, and she bit her lip. She wouldn't cry in front of Mollyocket, who had suffered far worse than she. "Oh, Molly, 'tis so terrible." Tears slid down her cheeks in defiance of her resolve. "It has been a nightmare. The worst part is, I knew Bury was Jamie's enemy, but I couldn't tell him. I love Jamie. I was afraid if he knew the truth, he'd leave me forever." She swiped at her runny nose and gave an ironic laugh. "Now I've lost him anyway."

Mollyocket grunted. She pointed at Clemency, patted her hand over her heart and shook her head.

"I don't understand," Clemency said.

Exasperation flashed across Mollyocket's lean face. She pointed at Clemency and pounded her hand over her heart. Then she set her jaw, clenched her fist and drew it in toward her body.

Clemency rolled her eyes. "Write it down, Molly. I don't understand what you mean."

Mollyocket pursed her lips and rolled her eyes right back. Then she drew her leather-bound copybook and a stub of pencil from her reticule. She rose, graceful and straight-backed as a queen, then glided to the trestle table.

As the Indian began to write, Clemency gazed into the fireplace. The weather was unseasonably warm and sunny for late February, so she had let the fire burn down to a few winking coals. She grabbed the poker and prodded the embers until they broke apart, revealing their glowing hearts.

Mollyocket stood and thrust the smudged copybook at Clemency. The Indian's penmanship was shaky.

You say you love your man. But you love a Dream, not the Truth. The brave Heart loves through the dark night, the bad storm. You have the brave Heart. Beneath this, underlined three times, Molly had written, *You must forgive.*

"How can you say that?" Clemency slapped the copybook down on the settle. "Jamie slept with Lydia! He sired a child on her, for heaven's sake, and he lied about it for months. How on earth do you expect me to forgive that?"

Mollyocket stared at her, face distressed, black eyes desperate. Then she snatched up the copybook and began scribbling furiously. She finished with a flourish and waved the book under Clemency's nose.

I lov'd Robert even when he vow'd to marry you. I forgave even that.

Clemency dropped the book on the settle. A slow flush burned across her cheeks, and she avoided Mollyocket's piercing gaze. Somehow she had always known that Molly and Robert were lovers, but she had avoided admitting it, even to herself. For whatever reason—duty, respectability, the desire for an heir—Robert had decided to marry her instead of Mollyocket. That was all Clemency had wanted to know.

She stood and swung the tea kettle over the coals, then added a handful of kindling to the fire. Moving as if in a trance, she set a silver tray on the shiny Welsh dresser and began placing the tea things on it. Why on earth had Robert offered her marriage when he loved Mollyocket? In truth, she probably would never know, for men were a mystery beyond even Granny Amais's powers.

But how had Mollyocket been able to forgive Robert's choice? Had her love truly been so strong that she could nurse him until his dying breath, all the while knowing he was betrothed to another woman?

She reached for a teacup, acutely aware of Mollyocket's gaze on her back. Suddenly an enormous sense of shame rippled through her. The teacup slipped from her hand and shattered on the brick floor. All her life she had been desperate for love. She had viewed love as a charm, a perfect cure that would heal her lonely heart. But her selfish little emotion was a charlatan's hoax compared to the power and magic of Mollyocket's love.

As Clemency swept up the broken china, a voice whispered through her mind. She couldn't tell if it belonged to Granny Amais or to Mollyocket, or perhaps it was her own: *The brave Heart finds love within.*

Chapter Twenty-nine

It was dark by the time Clemency slipped out the front door and hurried down the cobbled street. Thank heaven Lord Bury had finally drifted into a fitful doze, assisted by her strongest infusion of valerian and skullcap. Three days of intense nursing had eased his crisis, and she now dared hope he would survive, at least long enough to sail to England.

Her cloak snagged on a black iron fence picket, and she jerked it free. All afternoon Lord Bury had badgered her about returning to England with him. She would be rich, he said, a very great lady. By next summer her bizarre marriage would be over, and she could have her pick of England's most powerful peers.

She cut through the neighbor's back garden, a ghostly expanse of bare stalks and dry shrubs lit by the radiant moon. Turning north, she hurried across two narrow lanes, then entered the town's cemetery. Here the silvery light slanted off a haphazard array of granite headstones. Many of the thin slabs were carved with a spectral, winged death's head that proved Lord Bury right: The God-fearing Puritans took their sin seriously. Even in death, they wished to remind their neighbors of the judgement to come. She glanced over her shoulder and began to run. If there was ever a place a suspected witch didn't want to be caught, this cemetery was it.

Her heart hammered against her tight stays, and her breath came in painful gasps. She stopped and pressed a hand to the stitch in her side. What on earth had possessed her to think she could walk all the way to Sir Andrew's? But ordering Lord Bury's carriage would have entailed an explanation of where she wished to go, and she hadn't wanted to tell her father about her decision.

She strode forward, heart racing, skirts swirling about her ankles. She wasn't returning to England, and she would never be looking for another husband. She knew what she had to do, and by the Holy Mother, she was going to do it!

"Faint heart never won the field," she whispered. Then she snatched up her skirts and ran. No matter what Jamie had done, no matter what lies and problems and misunderstandings stood between them, she loved him. All she had to do was tell him, and he would forgive her. They could start again, a real marriage this time.

One worry kept buzzing through her mind, stinging at her hopes like a venomous insect: Jamie had never said he loved her. Perhaps he didn't want her back. She batted the thought away and dashed forward, lured on by the faint sound of the Atlantic breaking on Kittery Point. She was almost to Sir Andrew's. There was no time for second thoughts or lost courage.

She straggled through a small wood of balsam and maple, then broke out onto Sir Andrew's cobble drive. The white clapboard Pepperrell mansion loomed ahead of her, beautiful and serene in the moonlight. An owl called once, twice, nearly startling her from her skin. She caught her breath and angled to her right, toward the ocean and the front of the house. Through the fringe of bare branches she could see the moon's shimmering path reflecting off the black glass sea. She rounded the corner of the house and stopped.

A carriage stood in the drive, its single horse tied to the granite hitching post. Her heart lurched into her throat, and for an instant she thought she might faint. The carriage belonged to Malcolm Stevenson.

For a long time she stood in the moonlight, listening to the rhythmic wash and drag of waves on the ledges below the house. Her heartbeat returned to its normal rate, and her awful, sinking nausea lessened. Yellow rectangles of light spilled from Sir Andrew's front windows onto the drive and the frozen, snow-patched lawn beyond. Should she march up and ring the bell? Surely Jamie was there, but somehow she had never imagined he would have visitors.

Visitors, ha! Who could have arrived in the Stevenson carriage but Lydia?

Clemency took several bracing gulps of icy air, pressed the back of her fist to her upper lip and crept halfway across the lawn. Brittle grass crunched under her boots, and she clung to the shadows. If Jamie caught her skulking out here, she would never be able to explain herself.

She turned and peered into the parlor window. At first she could see only the glowing whale oil lamp and the fringe on Sir Andrew's prize red-damask draperies. She edged to the right, until she was less than a foot from the Stevensons' carriage. The horse jerked its head and whickered. Clemency jumped. ''Shhhhh,'' she whispered in what she hoped was a soothing tone. Then she looked back to the window.

Jamie stood near the lamp, tall and aristocratic and powerful. He was dressed in snug fawn breeches and an unbleached muslin shirt which lay open at the throat. His hair waved loose to his shoulders, gleaming russet, gold and amber in the lamp's warm glow. Cradled in his powerful arms, wrapped in endless yards of snow-white swaddling, lay his new baby girl. He tenderly rocked the child as a smile of bedazzled enchantment lit his handsome face.

For what seemed like a chill black eternity, Clemency stood, feet frozen in the snow. Her eyes traced his strong chin—oh, how she had loved to kiss its devilish cleft! Her gaze devoured his generous mouth and lean, tanned cheeks, dimpled now with his beguiling smile. With deepest love and boundless yearning, she memorized his high, slanted cheekbones and peaked dark brows; his wide-set indigo eyes which crinkled at the corners when he laughed; and his nose—that long, elegant, knife-straight nose. Oh, Holy Mother, how she had loved his mock-stern glares down that severe nose!

Suddenly Lydia appeared at Jamie's elbow. She looked tired and ill, and gazed up at him with unconcealed adoration. Jamie glanced down at her, then raised their baby high overhead in an ancient gesture of pride and triumph. Then he lowered his tiny daughter and kissed her cheek.

Clemency turned and fled down the drive.

Jamie handed the baby to Lydia, then bowed—an action that proved astonishingly painful. Perhaps the tension gripping his neck and shoulders had brought on his headache, or perhaps it was the last gasp of his hangover. His lips crooked in a rueful smile. Served him right for being a bloody fool.

He turned and bowed to Samuel. "Thank ye for bringing the bairn to see me. She's a bonny lass."

Samuel rose from a delicate gilt chair in the corner and walked into the lamplight. He acknowledged Jamie's bow with a nod, then turned to his wife. "Lydia, please tell Sir Andrew and Hugh that we are departing. I would speak to Jamie alone."

Lydia opened her mouth to protest, but Samuel held up

his hand. Jamie arched his brows at the steely glint in his old friend's pale eyes. Surprisingly, Lydia subsided.

"I hope we'll see you again," she told Jamie. Samuel grasped her elbow and ushered her toward the door. "Your banishment will be over in September. Perhaps you'll come home then?" she called eagerly over her shoulder.

Jamie bowed again, but remained silent. The polished mahogany door clicked shut behind her.

For several long moments, Lydia stood in the chill foyer, not quite daring to press her ear to the closed parlor doors. Faith, she would give anything to know what her miserable scrap of a husband was saying to Jamie.

The baby stirred in her arms, then subsided into sleep. Lydia glanced down at the little girl's dear, pink face, then tilted her head back, eyes clenched, teeth gritted. A bitter wail of despair clawed at her throat, but she battled it back. She would not, could not give up!

"Madam?" She whirled and gaped at Sir Andrew's butler. No doubt the wretch had been lurking in the shadows, spying on her. "May I assist you in some way?" The man's face was impassive, but she thought his eyes held a faint glint of disapproval.

"Yes." She swept across the foyer into the library, settled the baby on a divan, then snatched up a quill pen. "I want you to send a footman to York with this message." She scrawled a few lines on a scrap of paper, sanded it, then sealed it with Sir Andrew's red sealing wax.

"But, madam—"

She drew herself up and haughtily thrust the note at the butler. "Do as I say, man, and not a word to Sir Andrew, or by God, you'll answer to the magistrate."

As Lydia left the room, Jamie all but collapsed onto Sir Andrew's best Hepplewhite divan. He slouched down, narrowed his eyes into slits and stared into the parlor fire.

Och, he longed to break into his friend's crystal decanter of Scotch, but he had sworn off. As Hugh had so bitingly reminded him this afternoon, whisky never solved anything. Fine words, those, from a Highlander. Jamie wiped a hand over his mouth to hide his sudden, affectionate smile. Hugh was turning into a right old biddie.

He glanced down at the expensive Turkey carpet and caught sight of Samuel's worn boots. They shifted awkwardly back and forth as the silence in the room lengthened. At last Samuel spoke.

"Jamie, there ... there's some things I need to say." Samuel's voice was high and reedy, but resolve underpinned his halting words. "We've known each other all our lives. I've always looked up to you, admired you. Och, I'll speak the truth—you're the best man I've ever known."

Samuel slumped down on a dainty side chair, and a livid blush swept across his thin face. His storklike knees jutted nearly to his ears, and his bony hands dangled almost to the floor. "Lydia is a hard woman, but I love her. Perhaps if I'd been more of a husband, she ... well, she wouldn't have done the things she did."

Jamie winced and held up a hand. "Look, perhaps we shouldna—"

"Listen to me." Samuel jumped up and snatched his tricorne from a rosewood table. "I ken Lydia tricked you; but she's my wife, and she'll remain so as long as I draw breath. I don't want her hung, nor whipped, nor fined. Nor do I want to lose your friendship." He fidgeted his hat end over end, then gaped down at it as if amazed to find it in his hands.

"Here's the deal I offer you," he said, dropping the hat back onto the table. "You know you can never acknowledge the bairn, so I'll raise her as mine—" Jamie lunged to his feet, but Samuel rushed on. "She'll have the best home I can offer, and there'll be no more drinking or chasing after wenches, I promise you."

Jamie paced across Sir Andrew's fancy rug and snatched up the whisky decanter. Och, Samuel was right. No matter how much he longed to, he could never claim the wee lass as his own. To do so would bring ruin on the whole family. But neither could he leave his flesh and blood to Lydia, who had no more maternal instinct than a snake. He slammed the decanter down on the table.

"Nay, I canna do it. The bairn needs a mother who loves her—"

"But Lydia does love the lass, for she's yours. 'Tis my bairns she doesn't love."

For a long moment, Jamie stared at his old friend. A slight sheen of sweat covered Samuel's pock-marked face; but his rabbity chin was thrust out, and his narrow shoulders were squared. Jamie expelled his breath in a harsh sigh.

"Ye're a good man, Samuel." He hesitated, then reached for his dirk. "I'll let ye raise *mo nighean,* but ye must swear she'll never come to harm." Och, his voice wasn't working properly; he sounded as weak as a bairn himself. "And . . . and will ye name her Alexandra, after my uncle?" His heart gave a wild flutter, and he swallowed, hard. Alexandra was Clemency's middle name.

"Aye," Samuel said.

Jamie clasped his dirk in his left hand, then made a quick, hard slash across his right wrist. Blood welled from the wound, and Samuel gasped. Jamie thrust out his cut arm, blood glistening ruby in the firelight. "A blood oath," he rasped. "Will ye do it?"

Samuel held out his wrist.

Jamie inhaled a great lungful of salt air and plunged down the embankment toward Kittery's bustling docks. The weather had continued its springlike whim of azure skies and dazzling sun, and the Atlantic stretched to the horizon like a plane of brilliant sapphire. Seagulls swooped and mewed overhead, and a brisk morning southerly sprang up, snapping and singing through the ships' rigging.

Jamie sidestepped an enormous chest of tea being lowered by block and tackle from a British East Indiaman, then scanned the quay for Jack Chason. He had arranged to meet the French trader to complete the sale of his beaver pelts, but as usual, Chason was late. Jamie's lips twitched into a smile, and he looked around for a secluded place to wait. No doubt Chason was bidding a languid Gallic farewell to whatever light o' love had entertained him through the night.

He sat on a sun-drenched coil of rope and stretched his long legs. Despite the noise and activity eddying around him, he felt a measure of peace for the first time since Hugh and Mollyocket had materialized with Elizabeth three days earlier. Together, the old gillie and Sir Andrew had badgered him with the single-minded relentlessness of a pit bull with a chicken in its jaws. They wanted him to reconcile with Clemency.

Jamie scowled and folded his arms over his chest. Reconciliation be hanged. Clemency had left him. She was the one who had run off to live with that bloody Sassenach cad. Let his friends preach to her about reconciliation, the stubborn witch.

He ground his teeth and shifted on the lumpy coil of rope, his muscles suddenly constricting. Och, who was he fooling? No matter what Clemency had done, he missed her terribly. He missed her low, throaty voice and the way she flicked her braid over her shoulder when she was vexed. He missed the saucy tilt of her head when she teased him, and the emerald flash in her eyes when he took her in his arms. Most of all, he missed her in his bed. His flesh burned at the memory of her rose-tipped breasts, succulent and quivering under his lips . . . .

He flushed and crossed his legs, suddenly aware of the uncomfortable bulge in his breeks. Och, curse his feelings to hell! No matter how he missed her, he would not surrender in this battle of wills, not as long as she remained under Bury's roof.

"Maclean, I look for you everywhere, and where do I find you, eh? Basking in the sun like the lion—the Scottish lion, no?" Jack Chason whipped off his black knitted cap and bowed low, an impish grin on his whiskered face. Jamie stood and smiled down at the little Frenchman.

"Me, I think not to see the Scottish lion wearing the smile," Chason said. His black eyes, sunken into a sun-burned web of laugh lines, flashed with an odd combination of humor and wariness. "*Non,* after what I hear, I expect to find the claws bared, eh?"

Jamie turned and shouldered his way toward Chason's boat. "What are ye bletherin' about, mon?"

Chason plucked at Jamie's coat sleeve. "*Alors,* then you have not heard? Mistress Maclean, she has not told you?"

Jamie halted and tried to shake off a pang of uneasiness. "Heard what?"

Chason's eyes bulged at Jamie's sharp tone. He scuttled back a few paces. "Me, I do not like to be the bearer of the bad news. You will not kill the messenger, eh?" His bright gaze darted to Jamie's dirk.

"Out with it."

"Not an hour ago I saw *la belle* Madame Maclean."

"Here on the quay?" Jamie realized his face felt stiff, as if his flesh had petrified.

"*Oui.* She was with *le sieur* Bury, an English nobleman."

"I ken the man," Jamie snapped. The muscle leaped in his cheek. "What did my wife tell ye?"

"That she is sailing for England, *mon ami,* on the ship *Golden Eagle.* And that she is not returning."

Chapter Thirty

Sunlight flashed like liquid diamonds on the Atlantic's cobalt swells, nearly blinding Jamie with its brilliance. With an expert flick of the sloop's tiller, he came about, then dropped the jib and mainsail. He snagged the floating mooring with the gaff hook and secured the vessel with a neat bowline knot, then hopped into the tiny dory and rowed toward Appledore. Below him, the shallow water was as clear as air.

All afternoon he had sailed the frigid waves around the Isles of Shoals, hoping that salt spray and biting breeze and the glory of the sea would ease his tortured mind. It hadn't. He beached the dory with a vicious pull of the oars, then vaulted onto the shell-strewn sand. Och, what a fool he was, what a mooning, calf-eyed lackwit. To think that he had been on the verge of forgiving Clemency! Good Christ!

He shipped the oars and dragged the little boat above the high-water mark. This deserted cove in Appledore's lee—

a wee curve of sand, granite boulders and rockweed crowned
with a few scrubby balsams—was just the place to sit and
think. His lips thinned into a cruel smile. To think, *not* to
lick his wounds. He selected a long, bare rock in a pool of
golden sun, arranged his hips and shoulders in the rock's
warm hollows and closed his eyes.

Jack Chason's revelation had stunned him so badly that
he hadn't thought to ask when Clemency planned to sail for
England. Not that it mattered, for the lying witch would go
without a single word of farewell from him! Their handfast
marriage would be over by September, so there would be
no trouble on that score, and indeed, he doubted an English
court of law would consider Clemency a married woman
once she arrived in London as Lord Bury's protege.

His muscles tensed as a tempest of emotion stormed
through him. St. Columba, he should have killed that murdering Sassenach cur when he had the chance. Then at least
he would have vengeance as comfort—cold comfort, aye,
but comfort nonetheless. He ground his teeth, and his fingers
spasmed into fists. He was a bletherin' fool to have trusted
Clemency—och, God help him—to have loved her, damn
her to hell! He had sacrificed a blood oath at her plea for
mercy!

Clemency. Aye, mercy was the meaning of her name, but
she had showed him no mercy. His lips twisted bitterly. She
had batted him aside like a housewife swats a fly, leaving
him with nothing, not even revenge.

Suddenly he heard the unmistakable thunk and splash of
oars. He sat up. "Good Christ!" he yelled, vaulting to his
feet and striding down the beach. "What in bloody hell are
ye doing here?"

Hugh placidly beached his dory and clambered out.
"Comin' after ye, ye muckle-headed booby. I ran into Chason on the quay. He said ye'd lit off like a horse with a
firecracker up his arse and stolen his boat."

"I didna steal it, I borrowed it." Jamie glared down at

the old gillie, unsure whether to lift him bodily into the dory and push him back out to sea, or to drown him outright. "Why in hell are ye chasing after me? Canna a man get a moment's peace?" He turned and stalked back to the rock. "Och, ye're worse than a broody old biddy hen."

Hugh stomped after him. "I'm followin' ye 'cause someone needs to do yer thinkin' for ye. What in bloody hell are ye doin' out here when yer wife's plannin' to board a ship for England?"

Jamie slumped on the rock and ran a trembling hand down over his face. Hugh was his oldest friend, but right now he longed to smash his fist in the gillie's pugnacious jaw.

"Look," Jamie said, "I ken ye love Clemency like she was your own, but face facts. She's leaving 'cause she canna stand to be married to me. She canna forgive me for lying with Lydia and getting her with child." He reached down and peevishly popped the air bladders on a rubbery brown strip of rockweed. "She canna forgive me for lying to her."

Suddenly he pounded his fist on his thigh. "She's a fine one to speak of lying, after she lied night and day about her real father!" He kicked at a purplish mussel shell and sent it skittering down the sand. "Och, how can she live with such a devil? She's nothing but a little cat-whore like her mother—landing on her feet with a rich, powerful lord, not caring that he's a murderer—"

Hugh's gnarled hand shot forward and grabbed Jamie's throat. "That's enough! I'll no' hear ye speak so of Clemency, nor of her mother." Jamie cuffed his hand away, and the two men froze, shoulders heaving, red faces inches apart.

"Yer uncle Alex gave me the care o' ye, lad, and I'll no' see ye throw yer life away," Hugh muttered. He drew back and seemed to be battling some inner dilemma. "Ye'll hear what I have to tell ye," he said at last, "then the good Lord help ye if ye canna make the right choice."

Hugh sat on the packed sand, drew his knees under his chin and stared off toward the horizon. "Margaret Mac-

Kinnon was the bonniest lass I e'er clapped eyes on,'' he began, voice soft and meditative. "Och, she was all but a legend in the Highlands, and Clemency fair resembles her in face and body. But in spirit . . . weel.'' He grinned and rolled his eyes. ''Margaret couldna ha' been more different. Dreamy, she was, and fey, and folk whispered she had the second sight.

"Margaret's father was Iain Dubh, chief of Clan MacKinnon. Ye ken he was a powerful laird, with estates at Kilmory and Strathaird on the east coast Skye. He pampered his only daughter somethin' wicked. She was a meek, sweet lass. Only once in her life did she show raw courage, and that's the tale I tell ye now.

"Margaret was but seventeen when The MacKinnon, his sons, and his nephews marched off with Bonnie Prince Charlie. Margaret and yer uncle Alex had been betrothed in secret before the Risin', and on the eve of Culloden she was quartered in Inverness, not far from Drumossie Moor, hopin' to see him.

"When the battle commenced she near died o' fear. All day she cowered in her room, head under a pillow to drown the sound o' the cannon. When the ragtag remnants of Charlie's army began to limp into Inverness, Margaret ventured into the street, askin' every mon she met if they had news of her betrothed, Alexander Maclean of Duart. At last a wee lad told her that he kent Alex well, and that he was dead.

"Margaret was heartbroken and near mad with grief, but she gathered the tatters of her courage, walked to the bloodsoaked battlefield and searched for Alex's body. A Sassenach officer tried to drive her away, but she begged him to help her find her kin. The officer didna ken where Clan MacKinnon had fought; but her great beauty touched his cruel heart, and he took her to his commander, Lord Francis Bury.

" 'Twas Bury who told Margaret that her brothers were dead, and that he held her cousins and The MacKinnon in a makeshift prison in one o' the Inverness kirks. Margaret decided then and there that she must do somethin' to save her kin, no matter how her honor keened in protest.

"There was no mistakin' the admirin' hunger in Bury's eyes, so she made him an offer: he could have whatever he wanted in exchange for the lives of the men she chose. Bury agreed to banish her kin to the Colonies if she would swear to remain his mistress for as long as he desired. Margaret swore, and Bury deflowered her." Hugh swiped at his leathery cheek, and Jamie thought he saw a tear glimmering there.

"The next morn, Margaret questioned one o' the Sassenach guards and learned I was alive. She had me brought to Bury's quarters, where she fell to her knees and wept to break me heart. She explained that she had been dishonored and begged me to tell her family that she had been killed. At first I protested; but Margaret had conquered me heart long ago, and I could deny her nothin'.

"She swore me to secrecy—made me vow never to reveal the true nature o' things, and 'til now, I've kept me promise. Then Lord Bury strode in, and she called the names o' the men whose lives he was to spare." Hugh paused and looked straight into Jamie's eyes. "Those names were Chief Iain Dubh MacKinnon, Robert and Samuel MacKinnon, Hugh Rankin, Diarmid Maclean, and James Ian Alasdair Maclean."

Jamie's brows flew up. Hugh shot him a disgusted look. "Aye, ye best look surprised, ye great stubborn booby. Ye draw breath and walk this earth today because o' Margaret MacKinnon's brave heart."

A sharp northeasterly sprang up, and Jamie blinked back the sting of sudden tears. "I had no idea."

"Aye, weel, now ye ken," Hugh snapped.

"Why did Clemency never tell me?"

"Most likely Margaret made her swear to keep it a secret, as she did with me." Hugh slanted Jamie a canny glance. "Besides, ye ken how independent and headstrong Clemency is. Perhaps she didna want ye to feel beholdin' to her mother. She wanted ye to love her free, no' shackled."

Like a bird trapped against a window, Jamie's heart fluttered wildly in his throat. Nay, Hugh's tale couldn't be true! Margaret MacKinnon had been a whore, a light-skirt who had saved her neck by sleeping with the enemy. And if Margaret had been so devoid of honor, then Clemency must be even worse.

Jamie stood and paced the narrow beach, never raising his eyes from the damp gray sand. Och, God help him! Hugh's words had the ring of truth. Margaret hadn't been a whore; she had sacrificed everything—even honor—for the sake of love.

The sun lowered, and the air grew icy. At last he wheeled and faced Hugh, jaw hard, arms folded over his chest. "Bury killed Alex—"

Hugh clapped his hand on Jamie's shoulder. "For all the evil Bury did, lad, Margaret more than made up for it."

Jamie shrugged him off, then squinted across the shimmering water toward Portsmouth Harbor. A frigate-built ship knifed through the swells between the Isles and the mainland, and he could just make out the antlike sailors swarming her rigging and setting her sails. All at once the frigid northeasterly gusted across the tiny cove. It bent the scrubby trees and whipped the water into whitecaps.

He shivered and closed his eyes. "But Clemency chose to leave me. For all her talk, she doesna love me enough to try again—"

Hugh's fist smashed into Jamie's shoulder, knocking him sideways. "By St. Ninian!" he bellowed. "Ye're the stubbornest Gael I've ever been cursed to ken. Why do ye think I was on the quay lookin' for ye?" He grabbed the front of Jamie's shirt and shook him. "It wasna for the pleasure o' yer company, I'll tell ye that. I was comin' to warn ye. The sheriff's after Clemency for breakin' her banishment and returnin' to York County. It seems someone tittle-tattled to the magistrate—me guess would be Lydia.''

Ice shot through Jamie's veins. "But Chason never said—''

"Chason's a bletherin' frog who couldna hold two thoughts in his mind at once. If ye'd stayed to listen instead of chargin' off like a bull, he'd ha' told ye. She's runnin' from the sheriff, mon! They can hang her for floutin' her banishment!'' Hugh planted his hands on his hips and thrust out his jaw. "Now, me fine laird, what do ye plan to do about it?''

Slowly, Jamie's knees buckled, and he sank to the pebble-strewn sand. Dampness seeped through his breeks, but he hardly noticed. Hugh's words whirled through his brain like sea foam in an autumn gale. Clemency hadn't wanted to leave . . . Margaret had saved his life. . . .

A seagull shrieked, and he looked up. The flaming sun had almost slipped below the western horizon, and the ship was closer now. A strange trick of the waning light colored the glassy swells a thousand shades of green, from emerald on to celadon. Emerald, like Clemency's eyes. Och, St. Columba! His trembling fingers closed around a smooth, flat stone, and he hurled it into the water with all his strength.

He could not survive if she left him, for she had enchanted his heart.

For a moment he sat absolutely still; then he threw back his head and roared with laughter. Lydia had been right all along, damn her hide! Clemency *had* bewitched him. She had charmed him, healed him, given him back his life, his heart—och, good God in heaven, his very soul!

An enormous wave of love surged through him, and he wiped tears, tears hot as blood, from his frozen cheeks. He felt weak, broken open, washed clean. He might have been Lazarus, raised from the dead. Clemency's love had saved him. He knew that now. And he would gladly sacrifice his newfound soul if he could only get her back.

He struggled to his feet. "Hugh—''

At that instant, his eyes fell on the ship plunging down the five-mile stretch between the Isles and the mainland. His eyesight was as sharp as a falcon's from years at sea, and he could clearly make out the figurehead thrusting from her prow: squat and bearded, its somber clothing ticked out in glossy black paint, the carved wooden image bore an excellent resemblance to the ship's captain, Abiel Reed.

Jamie's heart stopped. The ship was the *Golden Eagle*.

The *Golden Eagle*'s pristine deck pitched and rolled to larboard. Whitecaps smashed against the hull, and salt spray leaped up to sting Clemency's face. Her stomach lurched, and she grabbed the oak rail. Above her, miles of canvas billowed and caught the wind, and the westering light stained the creamy expanse to rose and gold. The rays of the setting sun slanted low across the water, and gleamed peach and lavender against the jade waves. Aloft in the rigging, sailors played out the hemp halyards and set the sails to catch the wind—the wind that would take her away from Jamie forever.

Although her lips trembled, she raised her chin and turned her back on the receding dark bulk of the Colonies. Seagulls mewed and cried mournfully overhead as if bidding her farewell; then they, too, were gone. Tears slipped from her eyes, and she dashed them away. She must be strong now, stronger than she had ever been. Jamie had made his choice and she had made hers, and there was no hope in looking back.

Lord Bury slipped up and stood beside her. For a long moment neither spoke. She still gripped the polished rail, and he laid his gloved hand over hers. Off the bow, low and barren against the horizon, a group of islands dotted the water.

"The captain tells me they're the Isles of Shoals," Bury

said, his voice much too tender for such trivial information. "They're the last point of land in the Colonies."

Her tears were flowing in earnest now, frigid and salty as the ocean waves. They froze against her skin until she thought her face would crack. She couldn't stop them, couldn't control her agonizing grief.

"My dear," Lord Bury murmured. He lifted her hand and held it to his lips. "Will you be quite all right?"

She pressed her free hand to her belly. Jamie was dead to her now, but his child, blood of his blood, bone of his bone, lived within her. When the coming summer had ended and autumn's chill gilded Devon's moors, she would have this precious part of him to love and to cherish, always. She would give this child the love she had never known.

She slanted Bury a wobbly smile, then turned to face the eastern horizon. "As Granny Amais used to say, 'Faint heart never won the field.' And I own no faint heart."

"Bloody hell. Mr. Thornton, are ye sure?" With dazzling precision, Captain Abiel Reed spat a stream of chewing tobacco into a bolted-down brass spittoon, then glowered at his first mate.

"Aye, Captain. 'Tis a vessel in distress, right enough. Your orders, sir?"

"But what the bloody hell's the problem? The weather's clear as a preacher's conscience—"

Lord Bury sharply cleared his throat, and Captain Reed halted, then blushed to the roots of his greasy black hair. He inclined his head toward Clemency. "Your pardon, m'lady. Me years on the sea oftimes drown me manners. Now, if ye'll excuse me, I best see what's what. Help yourself to me sherry." Reed bustled out of his quarters, leaving Clemency and Lord Bury sitting amidst a jumble of navigational instruments, charts, playing cards and brandy bottles.

Lord Bury arched an eyebrow toward the sherry. "Finest

Spanish amontillado, my dear. Just the thing to settle your stomach.''

Clemency held out a green glass goblet—as green as her cheeks, no doubt. ''Holy Mother, how am I ever going to survive this crossing? I was never seasick before.''

Lord Bury smiled and poured the sherry. The sea air had pinked his pale skin, and he hadn't coughed for days. ''You weren't carrying before—lud!''

At that instant the ship yawed and heeled violently to larboard. Chronometer, sextant, bottles and charts careened across Captain Reed's shining mahogany table, and sherry sloshed over Clemency's hand. She and Lord Bury exchanged startled glances as Captain Reed's shout drifted down the companionway.

''Brace the sails, then heave to! We're takin' her aback.''

Clemency jumped up. ''We must be stopping to help.'' She set down her half-full glass of sherry and tugged at Bury's arms. ''Come, my lord, let's go above. Mayhap this will be the only excitement we have 'til we reach London.''

Moments later they gained the upper deck. The sun had set in a long orange band over the western horizon, and the sky to the east was a deep, tranquil blue. Directly overhead, soft lavender-gray clouds glowed with the last fading light, and the sea was an endless expanse of darkness.

The deck seethed with activity. The *Golden Eagle* wallowed through the waves, heading westerly across the wind as sailors scrambled aloft the rigging and frantically trimmed the sails. Captain Reed spun the great gleaming wheel, and once more the ship heeled madly to larboard. Clemency staggered into Lord Bury, and they both gasped as the wind bellied smack into the sails. The heavy canvas snapped back against the masts, and all forward motion stopped.

''Lud, I've never seen the like,'' Bury said, straightening his cravat. He eyed the stubby, soberly dressed little captain with new respect.

Captain Reed gave the wheel to his first mate. ''As soon

as they're safe aboard, lie to larboard, then come about and brace the sails." He strode aft to the chattering knot of sailors on the larboard stern. "Throw down the rope ladder, ye witless curs!"

Clemency and Lord Bury followed him to the rail. A small open boat drifted toward them across the black water, then hit the *Golden Eagle*'s massive hull with a dull thunk. The boat's single mast was down, and the sails dragged like wet laundry over the gunwales. Clemency caught an indistinct glimpse of two men aboard the stricken craft; then Captain Reed caught her elbow.

"Careful, m'lady. Don't want ye overboard in all the confusion." He turned and thundered to the second mate, "Throw down a line! Time is money and time's awasting."

There was another spurt of activity, and somehow Clemency found herself amidships. Her teeth began to chatter. She wanted to watch the excitement; but the sea air was freezing, and she longed for her cloak. A shout went up by the taffrail, and she darted toward the lower-deck companionway. If she ran, she could snatch her cloak from her cabin before the men shinnied up the ladder. A shiver of despair trickled down her spine. Perhaps they had a dramatic tale about their mishap. She would listen to anything right now, anything at all, as long as it took her mind off Jamie.

Blast, one man was already clambering over the rail. She had to hurry!

She hopped backward onto the narrow ladder to the lower deck. She would slide down without using the steps, as she had seen the sailors do. Closing her eyes, she gripped the polished handrails and jumped. As her feet left the ladder, her long wool skirt snagged on a cleat. Her hair tumbled loose, her hands slipped from the rails, then she was falling backward. Her nails scrabbled against the steps, desperately trying to break her fall. She had to protect the baby—

A hand grabbed her flailing wrist, a hand strong and unerringly sure. Her arm nearly wrenched from its socket.

She banged hard against the ladder, then staggered back, safe on the lower deck.

"Ow!" She gripped her shrieking shoulder and tried to claw the tangled hair from her eyes. "Holy Mother, you practically broke my arm—"

"Is this how ye thank me, *mo druidh?* And this the fifth time I've rescued ye, at the verra least."

Clemency gave a great gasp, as if the wind had been knocked from her lungs. Holy Mary, Mother of God, there was no mistaking that teasing Scottish burr. Blast it all, she couldn't see a thing! She bent forward at the waist, flung her hair back, and—

"Jamie—"

And there he stood. He planted his hands on his narrow hips and stared down that elegant nose, amusement and affection mingled in his indigo eyes. A shocked cry choked her throat. The passageway was cramped and narrow, his muscular height overpowering. She reached out, hand trembling, to touch him, to convince herself he was real. Oh, Holy Mother, it couldn't be. . . .

She gave a tiny squeak of joy; then all went black.

Moments later she awoke in his arms. He was crouched on a bunk in a cramped, fetid cabin lit by a flickering whale oil lantern. He murmured in Gaelic and chafed her hands. Then his eyes met hers. The corners of his mouth quirked, and he flashed her a dazzling smile. She blinked, almost blinded. It was like gazing on the face of the sun, for his eyes shone with love.

"What . . . what are you doing here?" she croaked. Somehow she found herself raising a quivering hand and stroking his lean cheek. He winked and slanted a kiss on her palm.

"Weel now, let me see. First I had to break the mast on Jack Chason's boat—"

"That was you?"

His lips curved in an impish grin. "Aye. I didna think Captain Reed would stop just to pass the time of day."

She squirmed into a sitting position. This couldn't be happening—she must be mad, delirious, dreaming. "But why? A man doesn't just flag down a merchant ship under full sail, then hop aboard to say hello!"

A sudden horrible thought struck her, and she struggled to her feet, panic clawing at her heart. "Who . . . who was that with you? It wasn't the sheriff—"

Jamie's brows drew together. "The sheriff? Och, lass, is that what you think of me?" He yanked her back onto his knee, then rolled his eyes heavenward, as if praying for patience. "Woman, I've just about had enough of this. 'Twas no easy feat overtaking this ship, ye ken. 'Twas Hugh with me—"

She started to speak, but he laid a long finger against her lips. "Nay, *mo cridhe*. For once ye'll listen to me. Ye're still me wife. Do ye think for one single moment I'd let ye turn tail and run back to England?" She opened her mouth again, and he clapped his hand over it. "I said nay, woman. I've sworn to protect ye, aye? How can I do that if ye're half a world away?" He dropped his hand and arched an eloquent brow toward the companionway. "And from the looks of things, ye still need protecting."

She straightened her spine, folded her hands in her lap and demurely lowered her lashes. One side of his mouth twitched. "Aye?"

"Permission to speak, sir."

"Granted."

She looked him straight in the eye. "You still haven't told me why you're here."

He groaned and gripped her shoulders. "Isna that obvious?"

"Not to me."

Almost unconsciously, she laid a hand over her womb. Did she dare tell him she was carrying his child? There had been too much evasion between them already, but what was the use of honesty if it only brought pain? Jamie had two children—would he want this one as well? Oh, he had promised to care for any child born of their handfast marriage, but she would not use a child as bait. She could not sink to Lydia's tactics.

She raised her chin and flattened her palms against her thighs. "So, James Ian Alasdair Maclean, tell me why you're here." He cast her a look of such blue-eyed innocence that she dimpled in spite of herself. " 'Tis not like you were in the neighborhood."

He gave a great shout of laughter and crushed her to his chest. He was hard and warm and smelled of musk and cinnamon and sea salt. She burrowed her head against his throat, and a silent prayer of thanks pealed from the very depths of her soul. Even if he could never love her, even if they went their separate ways, at least she had known one true love—and a man like no other in heaven or hell or in a woman's wildest dreams.

"Och, *mo cridhe,* ye'll be the death of me." Jamie wiped tears from his eyes, then bent forward and kissed her forehead, as tenderly as one might kiss a child. "I broke every rule of maritime protocol, wrecked a boat and made a damn fool of myself just to tell ye this." He lowered his lips to hers, and his kiss was no longer tender. His tongue thrust deep into her mouth, and he claimed her, marked her, made her his once more.

At last he raised his head, and his hand closed over her breast. "I love ye, witch. I have for months—nay, I have since the night I married ye." His deep voice quavered and grew hoarse, betraying the depth of his emotion. "Och, Christ, I have since the verra day we met. I was just too stubborn and full of pride to admit it." He trailed hot kisses down her neck. "Ye're me life, *mo cridhe,* and I canna live without ye." Tantalizingly, he rolled her nipple between thumb and forefinger, and his tongue traced the sensitive curves of her ear. "Say you'll marry me all over again. And this time, 'twill be 'til death do us part."

Clemency threw her arms around his neck, and her heart

gave a great exultant bound of joy. Oh, she loved this man, she loved him! She wanted to be part of him, one flesh for all eternity. In utter surrender she raised her mouth to his, and their souls mingled in a kiss of blessing and absolution.

Suddenly the ship began to move, and her stomach lurched. She broke away and laid a finger across his lips. "I'll marry you again, under two conditions. First, I need to tell you the truth about my mother. I ... I'm illegitimate—"

"Hush, *mo cridhe*. I ken, and I love ye, no matter what."

She lowered her head until her hair curtained her face. "And I need to tell you about the ... the rape. You thought it was Lord Bury. It wasn't—it was his nephew, Geoffrey. Bury defended him at first—"

She felt his thigh stiffen against hers; then he gently brushed the hair from her eyes. "I told ye once, the past is dead and buried, and this time I mean it—including what lies between your father and me. 'Tis over.'' His strong fingers caught her chin, firmly demanding that she raise her head and meet his eyes. "Now then, any more conditions?"

"Yes. I'll marry you"—she took a deep breath and pressed his warm hand to her belly—"only if you want the both of us."

Jamie's brows shot up, his lips parted, his breath caught and his eyes went completely blank. Then he grinned—that rakish, beguiling, elfin grin that had stolen her heart.

"Good *Christ!*" he bellowed. He scooped her into his arms and squeezed her until she thought her ribs would break. "Och, me darlin', darlin' heart, I've never been so happy in all me life!" He bent her back and kissed her, and at last she found in his embrace all the joy and love and promise a brave heart could give.

He released her, and his eyes sparkled with devilry. "Ye're looking a wee bit peaked, *mo cridhe*. Overcome by lust, are ye?"

"No—nausea. We're under way again."

"Weel then, since we're six miles out to sea, Captain Reed can marry us this verra minute." He stood and flourished his arm in a bow of stunning masculine power and elegance, the very essence of the man she loved. "Shall we, Mistress Maclean?"

Epilogue

The Kennebec's waters caught the golden October sun and transformed it into a thousand glimmering flashes. Brilliant orange leaves danced and swirled in the water's ripples, then floated across the deep azure pool, drifting away from the splash and roar of the Maclean's Mill waterwheel.

Jamie stood on the millpond bank, smoke-tinged air cool on his cheeks. He skipped a flat stone across the water. After three meager hops, the stone sank.

"Da! Do it again." Elizabeth hopped up and down beside him, long curls bright and brazen as the autumn woods around them.

Jamie halfheartedly stooped for another rock. Distracting Elizabeth was difficult at the best of times, but now it was maddening, for his mind, heart and soul were across the field in the front bedchamber of The Fort, where Clemency was laboring to bear their child. All morning he had hovered at her bedside, brow wrinkled in helpless worry, until

Clemency and Goody Lewis had turned as one and ordered him out.

"Da. Throw it!"

Jamie drew back his arm.

"Jamie lad, come quick!" Hugh ran toward them across the field, flapping his arms like a wizened goose.

Jamie flung down the rock, spun on his heel and raced toward the house. Och, St. Columba, why had he ever let Clemency out of his sight, even for an instant! She was bearing their child, she might be dying—

He hurtled past the little gillie, stormed into the house and raced upstairs. "Clemency! Och, *mo cridhe*—" He barreled into the sunny room and skidded to a halt.

Clemency was crouched on the bed, her face a rigid mask of pain. Mollyocket wiped sweat from her brow. Goody Lewis hunched before Clemency's spread thighs and murmured encouraging words. Jamie caught a horrible glimpse of blood—blood everywhere. Clemency's shriek tore through his soul. . . .

Clemency opened her mouth to shriek just as Jamie vaulted into the room. His indigo eyes blazed, and his hair waved around his face like russet flames. Their eyes locked, and once again he threw a lifeline at her worst moment of need. She grasped it, and his strength flowed into her, strong and warm and sure. She clenched her teeth. Holy Mother, she loved him. Now that he was here she could bear the pain. She would give him a son. . . .

Jamie skidded to a halt. He opened his mouth, but no sound came out. The color drained from his face, his eyelids fluttered, then his eyes rolled back and his towering frame crashed to the floor.

Goody Lewis spat out a Gaelic curse, then stepped nimbly over Jamie's inert form to guide the baby's head. Despite a wave of killing pain, Clemency began to chuckle, and another Maclean came into the world to the sound of joyous, loving laughter.

Jamie woke, spluttering and choking on the whisky Hugh had dashed in his face.

"Up, lad!" Hugh roared, grabbing Jamie's arm and dragging him to his feet. "Come greet the newest Maclean laird."

"Laird?" Jamie shook his head, dazed and more than a little embarrassed. "Clemency—"

"Here I am, my brave Highland warrior." Her voice was weak, and more than a wee bit teasing. He turned toward the bed, and his heart nearly burst with love.

Clemency lay back among the pillows, hair brushed long and loose like midnight silk around her shoulders. A white bundle wriggled in her arms.

Elizabeth leaned against Clemency, eyes intent on the bundle's contents. "He's so pink!" she cried. "And he's got red hair."

"Away wi' ye, ye wee toe-rag," Hugh grumbled affectionately. "Let yer *athair* see his son."

Elizabeth gave Clemency a kiss, scrambled to the floor and followed Goody Lewis, Hugh and Mollyocket out the door. As it closed, the little girl's voice drifted down the hall: "Uncle Hugh, when are you and Molly gonna have a baby?"

Jamie bit back a grin. Mollyocket and the old gillie had married on Midsummer's Day. He knew the pair had found happiness at last.

Feeling strangely diffident, he perched on the bed and leaned over his wife and child. Clemency drew back a corner of the soft white blanket, and he gazed down on the tiny, wrinkled, perfect face of his son.

"Well, Highland rogue," Clemency murmured, resting her head against his cheek. "Will this wee lad be a good start for Clan Maclean in America?"

"Aye." Jamie's voice quavered. "Och, my darlin', darlin' heart. Will ye ever ken how much I love ye?" He pulled her close and pressed desperate kisses on her brow, her eyes, her lips. "How can I tell ye? How can I show ye?"

Clemency lightly stroked their son's downy cheek. "He's so handsome—just like his da." She snuggled against Jamie's chest, then yawned. "I never knew having a baby was so hard. Holy Mother, 'tis much easier when you're the midwife." She dimpled, and her green eyes drifted shut. "I swear I'll never go through it again. Although I did rather fancy a daughter—"

Jamie gave a delighted shout of laughter, kicked off his shoes, flung back the quilt and crawled in beside his wife and son. "A daughter, aye?" He grinned down at her, enchanted by her beauty, her love, her power over his heart. "Another wee, green-eyed witch, ye mean. Och, a man would be daft to live with two of ye!"

She raised her lips for a kiss. His mouth closed over hers, and he slipped wholeheartedly into the joyous magic of her spell.

If you liked SUMMER'S END, be sure to look for Lynne Hayworth's next release in the Clan Maclean series, AUTUMN'S FLAME, available wherever books are sold April 2001.

To inherit the tobacco plantation where he worked as overseer, Diarmid Maclean had to take a wife—immediately. In desperation, he bought a British bond slave as his temporary bride—a wild gypsy of a girl he planned to polish into a lady, then free once his inheritance was assured. But spirited Lucy Graves soon made Diarmid forget he meant to keep the marriage chaste. . . .

COMING IN FEBRUARY 2001 FROM
ZEBRA BALLAD ROMANCES

__MORE THAN A DREAM: Angels of Mercy #1

by Martha Schroeder   0-8217-6864-6 $5.50US/$7.50CAN

Catherine Stanhope dreams of life as a healer—And it is while nursing the wounded in the army hospital that she meets Dr. Michael Soames, who seems determined to test her mettle—and tempt her into desiring a love she never thought she wanted . . .

__LOVING LILY: Daughters of Liberty #1

by Corinne Everett   0-8217-7012-8 $5.50US/$7.50CAN

Lily Walters is an ardent Patriot. But when she discovers that her brother has taken up with a group called the Sons of Liberty, she can't help but worry. Her concern only deepens when she meets their new leader. Now this shadowy stranger's raging passion could steal her heart.

__ONCE A REBEL: Jewels of the Sea #2

by Tammy Hilz   0-8217-6779-8 $5.50US/$7.50CAN

A hatred for the aristocracy leads Joanna Fisk into the heart of London, where she meets Nathan Alcott, who represents everything she despises about the nobility. When Jo is launched into a dangerous adventure with Nathan, she soon falls in love with the very man she's supposed to hate.

__CARRIED AWAY: Happily Ever After Co. #2

by Kate Donovan   0-8217-6780-1 $5.50US/$7.50CAN

When Erica Lane's fiance proves inattentive, she decides to teach him a lesson by accepting a match made by the Happily Ever After Co. But when Erica sets sail fully expecting her fiance to follow, she gets the surprise of her life . . . the chance at true love with Captain Daniel McCullum.

Call toll free **1-888-345-BOOK** to order by phone or use this coupon to order by mail. ALL BOOKS AVAILABLE FEBRUARY 1, 2001.

Name _____

Address _____

City _____ State _____ Zip _____

Please send me the books I have checked above.

I am enclosing	$ _____
Plus postage and handling*	$ _____
Sales tax (+ in NY and TN)	$ _____
Total amount enclosed	$ _____

*Add $2.50 for the first book and $.50 for each additional book.

Send check or money order (no cash or CODS) to:

Kensington Publishing Corp., Dept. C.O., 850 Third Avenue, New York, NY 10022

Prices and numbers subject to change without notice. Valid only in the U.S. All orders subject to availabilty. **NO ADVANCE ORDERS.**

Visit our website at **www.kensingtonbooks.com.**

Put a Little Romance in Your Life With
Betina Krahn